Splintered

SPLINTERED

LAURA J HARRIS

authorHOUSE®

AuthorHouse™
1663 Liberty Drive
Bloomington, IN 47403
www.authorhouse.com
Phone: 1-800-839-8640

Published by AuthorHouse   06/04/2012

ISBN: 978-1-4678-8241-5 (sc)
ISBN: 978-1-4678-8242-2 (e)

DRAMATIS PERSONAE

Jonathan Prior – ex – DI, works as Head of on the
Golden Camus. Security

Marc Davies – security, ex – barman

Kelly Livingstone - artist

Captain Jason Andrews – boat captain

Christine Kane – criminal psychologist

Rona Jacobs – actress

Edmunds – maitre'd

Dr Karen Matthews – chief medical officer / physician

Dr Stuart Winningham – second physician

Adrian Kemp – head nurse

Craig Roberts – boat second in command

Leigh – murderer

Tony Blakely – deputy chief engineer

About the Author

Born and raised in the good old North-West of England, Laura J Harris grew up in Whitby, Ellesmere Port and had a fabulous childhood filled with laughter and fun and butterflies and candyfloss bunnies!!!

She whole-heartedly blames this amazingly fun-filled childhood on her fabulously warm and caring family; particularly her patient and incredibly understanding parents and her wonderfully talented and ever-encouraging sister!

The author attended Ellesmere Port Catholic High School until the age of eighteen where she gained thirteen GCSEs and four A-Levels.

She then went on to study Drama and Writing at Edge Hill University, then wrote and staged her original psychological thriller, Forget Me Not© in 2006 before returning to education to study for a BTEC in Production Arts!

Following this she taught Performing Arts at local college.

Now that she's all grown up, Laura is committed to becoming a full-time Writer, as was always her dream and ambition.

She hopes that SPLINTERED will be the first successful novel of many.

I've certainly had my set-backs in the past and I wouldn't have managed to complete and publish this book without the help and support of some incredibly wonderful and loyal people.

You will all know who you are, but I would like to thank specifically; my Dad for his trust and support and my Mum for much the same as well as her attentive and ever-scrutinising eye!

Very helpful!

I'd like to thank my sister for always being right where I needed her and for truly being the greatest sibling anyone could ever wish to have. I really do know how lucky I am.

Thank you to all those at AuthorHouse that have guided me through this process. Thank you for your encouragement and facilitation.

I also owe a great and monstrous thank you to Mark Billingham, without whose generous time, kind words and gentle encouragement this novel would not have been completed so readily.

Finally, I need to thank my partner, Terasa, for all her support over the years. Not only for her trust and belief in me as a writer, but for the way she has helped me daily for so long and for simply being my best friend.

Along with my partner comes my inherited little boy, who — though he won't be reading anything like this for some time! — reminds me everyday why it is so important to stop and laugh at the world. I love you both.

And very finally . . . thank you. I really appreciate you — yes you! — investing your precious time and money in me and I commend your incredibly wise decision in choosing to purchase this book!

Thank you for your patronage, your faith and — of course — your support.

Prologue

Running, racing. Fast and wild. Just the way he liked them.

He had been watching another; had his eye on another girl for the better part of the night. This scraggy bag of bones wasn't a patch on the other one, but then that was probably why she had been left behind and the other snapped up.

Snapped up by a hunter other than himself.

This one was a real Bambi, taking her first fumbling steps into the world of grown-ups and lies. She shouldn't even have been in that club. But, that was just his good luck.

Sixteen-years-old. Chaste and trusting as the day she was born; poor foolish little fawn.

A wolfish smile licked to his lips as he skipped off in pursuit once more.

The brittle September branches cracked under his colossal strides, sounding ever-more like breaking bone as he imagined pressing himself against her young pelvis. What would his mother say if she knew he had such thoughts? That he had *always* had them?

The repulsed look she wore so often on her good-neighbourly face flashed before his eyes.

She would have disowned him so much sooner had she known even a quarter of the truly vile thoughts, wants, needs and whims that swamped the darker recesses of his overactive mind; that itched beneath the surface just begging to be scratched. Begging.

He loved it when they begged and pleaded, offering to do whatever he wanted and to do it willingly. Promising they wouldn't report it to the police, that they wouldn't scream . . . if he would just let them go afterwards.

But, he liked it when they screamed, or tried to scream at least.

And no one ever heard them. Or, if they did, no one *ever* came to help. No, the majority of the local law-abiding populace would be tucked up in bed by now; locked away, safe and sound inside their cosy little homes.

And they were deep in the cover of the forest now.

He had used this spot before, liked it for its privacy and the way the sound dissipated. The way it simply evaporated. Brilliant.

God! She was quick this one . . . but, there . . . she was beginning to falter.

She went over on her ankle as the uneven, detritus-sodden ground gave way before her.

She gasped in pain as she continued to push herself, stumbling on and on at an incredible pace; the faintest whimper of a stifled sob escaping every time her right foot had to bear her slight weight.

He darted to the left taking the trunk of the fallen tree before him like a practised hurdler and coming up sharp in front of her. She anticipated; leaning into her right and surging through a tangle of nettles and brambles, their spiny fingers clawing at her bare arms and legs, catching and snagging the fine cotton and lace of her baby blue dress.

Oh, baby blue.

Now more a wild horse than Bambi she panted forward, her chest rising and falling under strained breaths. What a way to celebrate your sixteenth birthday!

Crack!

The rock hit the back of her head and she crumpled to the dank forest floor.

His aim was improving.

He rolled her over, hard as the rock he'd thrown and aching for release.

This ugly, little duckling had been a surprising tease, working him as no other had done in a very long time. Maybe for his next catch he would *actively* seek a sprinter. Maybe he would watch her train in the cute, little shorts that hugged the arse nice and firm and moved fluidly with her every movement.

Yeah.

He took the ever-present silver chain from his pocket and looped it around her neck, squeezing just tight enough to rouse her. She clawed his hands urgently, her eyes popping open, large and glistening like a china doll; those near-dead eyes that still bore a facade of life behind them.

She watched him, desperate, her hands falling away from his, away from her neck and the chain tightening around it. Down to the dank, forest floor.

His brother's silver tags glistened in the dark. He was never without that chain, and so he was never alone.

They had always done everything together. *Everything*. Always. Matty was his whole world.

Had been.

He thrust harder and harder inside of her, fighting back tears for the loss of his brother; feeling her muscles clench around him as his grip tightened on the chain, his knuckles white; his head spinning.

'Time to play.' he whispered.

Crack.

Now he was truly inside.

Chapter One

Jonathan Prior paced the slim line of floor space that divided one half of the eight-by-ten-foot security office from the other. Computer monitors, printers, communication relays, heavily pinned notice boards and a mass of folders, logbooks and disassociated papers adorned the surfaces and walls of the poxy, windowless office.

Prior had been informed, on more than one occasion, that it was for 'ease of access and to show an active presence' that Security was located mid-ship near the reception area. That it had absolutely nothing to do with squeezing as many top-notch, celebrity-priced suites and guest amenities into every other square inch of the ship.

Golden Star Cruise Liners had a cheek really, suggesting that six men could work comfortably in such a confined space. But, it seemed his protestations would continue to go unaddressed.

Just like being back in black.

But, it was the *no window* aspect that really got to his back up. He headed a small team that were part of a crew sailing between England and the Caribbean; they worked hard — every day — to ensure the safety and security of the ship, the rest of the crew and the passengers . . . and yet they weren't even entitled to a view for their trouble!

It was a major sore point for the ex-DI as it had ultimately been the lure of the breath-taking views that had convinced him to hang up his shield, up-sticks and join the ranks of the *Ianus* in the first place.

Well, something like that anyway.

A nice view and a quiet life at sea, that's what he had wanted. A world away from drug-raids and mobsters, from murders, paedophiles and gang violence.

Prior had seen his fair share of bodies laid out on a cold, metal gurney. Been present at enough sterile and detached autopsies on innocent victims and cross-fire casualties to last him a lifetime. He dared not try and recount the number of Merseyside and Cheshire doors he'd knocked on to question a suspect or a victim, or to simply deliver the unfortunate news that no family — no matter who or what they'd spawned — ever wanted to hear.

'Guv'?'

It made him smile that, although he was no longer a DI in official circles, his team treated him with the same respect and trust he'd built up over so many years of hard work and through the many sacrifices he had made in simply being part of the police force. And it didn't hurt that most of them were ex-coppers who knew the drill; an instant extended family. They knew when they could and couldn't push their luck with Prior and he — for the most part — felt equally comfortable with them.

He raised his eyebrows, simultaneously acknowledging and questioning the owner of the voice.

Davies, a young officer — a Scouser with a wave of bleach-blonde hair and big baby-blues that made all the girls fall instantly in love with him — held a phone up in Prior's direction, covering the mouthpiece as he spoke.

'There's a fella on the phone, says he's your dad.' he said, shrugging his shoulders, 'Malcolm?'

Marc Davies had previously enjoyed an active career working as a doorman in both Manchester and Liverpool before his move to cruise-line security. He was hard-working and enthusiastic, buffed and tanned as a well-waxed surf board and twice as preened.

There were times he missed working the doors along Canal Street, checking out all the pretty boys as they checked into Babylon or Cruz. He missed being the centre of their alcohol-fuelled, hyper-sexualised, lavish, week-end attention. *Janus ?*

Life on the *Ianus* was different. A slower pace.

Still, the pay was better than any other job he'd ever had and he didn't have to pay for food or board. And he got to see the world.

It was a fair trade, really.

And it wasn't as though the ship was ever in a deficit of cute boys. Or girls. After all, their passengers needed good entertainment and — as such — there was always a fresh influx of hot, new dancers, actors and performers.

'Yeah, that sounds like my dad.' said Prior, cutting through Davies' train of thought and taking the mobile phone from his hand.

He waited a moment before putting it to his ear. It seemed he was gearing himself up, preparing himself for the inevitable.

Davies stifled a laugh and Prior clipped him lightly around the head.

'Hi dad.'

Though Davies couldn't hear the counterpart of the conversation he could well imagine, from Prior's unenthusiastic responses, the direction it was taking; So, how's the job? When do you put to sea? Have you met anyone nice? Why this? How that? And when the other? Etc. Blah, etc.

Prior's tone was hinged somewhere between plain disinterest and an over-developed sense of duty, all whilst trying to feign some semblance of honest curiosity. It wasn't working.

'So, how is Stella?' he asked.

Davies smiled, raising an eyebrow.

Prior rolled his eyes in return. What else was there to talk about?

Stella was Malcolm Prior's latest wife. And though he knew it shouldn't really affect him anymore — a grown man who'd long since flown the coop — the ex-DI couldn't help but feel a stab of guilty annoyance every time he thought about his father and her together in their lavish Cheshire Estate — complete with heated pool and stables that were Stella's requisite — while his mum still lived in Birkenhead; in a two-up-two-down terrace with her boyfriend.

Boy being the operative word.

This was what annoyed him. Each of his parents was as bad as the other and the more he thought about it, the more it wound him up.

Apparently, both his mum *and* his dad had slammed head-first into the fabled mid-life crisis at a synchronised speed. And while the cliché would have you believe that his father would have invested in a nippy, little sports car (something red and shiny and shaped like a penis), leaving his mum for a younger model, it was to Prior's absolute surprise and confusion that very much the opposite had happened.

Oh, his dad *had* gone out and bought a car. But, that wasn't until two weeks after Terri Goodwin-Prior had left *him* to shack up with Danny-the-prepubescent-prick Macintosh following their secret, six-month affair.

So, three weeks before his fifty-third birthday and four hours after wandering around Audi, BMW and Porsche dealerships, Malcolm Prior had stepped out onto a crumbling garage forecourt and invested five-hundred pounds ... in an R-reg Renault Clio. One of the old ones that you could still tinker with.

Even the then-DI Jonathan Prior could not have predicted that one!

The seemingly ordinary, if not a little dull, but loveable accountant that Prior had always known to be his father was in fact no more than a family-man mask he'd worn for the past twenty-nine years; a persona he'd adopted since the moment Terri had begun flushing her pills down the toilet.

Malcolm Prior was — in fact — a natural mechanic with an amazing mind for machines and engines, pistons and pumps.

He quickly stripped the rusted, old bucket-of-a-car and with some oil and elbow grease (several new parts, a body-kit, sound system, decent paint-job and a lot of TLC) he'd completely overhauled, customised and sold the Clio on at a profit in under three weeks!

And, now that he was no longer required to play the part of the dependable bread-winner he swiftly put his heart and soul (not to mention his personal life savings and his share of the money from the sale of their family home) into his brand new customising business. He bought a yard and lock-up from which to work and began buying in Subaru's, MR2's, MG's and all sorts.

And to his son's surprise — to everyone's complete surprise — it took off!

Four years on and *Prior Custom* was now a multi-million-pound business. Malcolm Prior now owned and managed no less than eighty yards across the UK and had just opened two more in L.A. and Miami.

And in those last four years, he'd been married another two times.

Fortunately — still being sensible old Mal' on some level — he'd had a pre-nup drawn-up and signed by both parties prior to the wedding.

Good job too, when it came to dealing with the divorce of his second wife!

Still, credit where credit was due, Stella — wife number three — had been around for a year and a half now and she seemed to make his dad happy. They had been married for a nearly year, which was already double the length of the time compared to wife number two.

Prior hoped that it really would be *third time lucky*. He didn't think he could take another of his father's weddings.

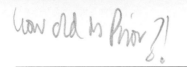
How old is Prior ?!

'Good. I'm glad all's ok.' Prior continued, 'Listen dad, I'm going to have to go. I've got checks to do before we can get underway and ... Yeah, I will ... Speak to you soon. Yeah, bye dad. Bye.'

He hung up the phone and pushed out a great sigh of relief.

No longer able to contain himself, Davies snorted out the laughter he had clawed to hold back for the entire duration of their conversation. He stood and moved past his boss, patting him on the shoulder as he went. 'Well done, mate. Very well done.'

'What?' asked Prior, smiling, 'I'm not good on the phone ... or even in person when it comes to my parents.'

'Say no more. You're preachin' to the choir.'

'Don't get on with yours either?'

Davies sighed, shaking his head. 'Let's just say they don't entirely agree with some of my ... choices.'

'Ah.'

'Yeah.'

Davies grinned, adjusting his uniform and picking up one of the *Ianus* security mobile phones. 'Their loss. They'll come 'round one day.'

Prior nodded as Davies pushed out of the office to begin tending to his duties. He didn't have the heart to air the question he was certain Davies had already contemplated; *And what if they don't?*

Prior plucked the rota and itineraries from the workstation before him and began cross-checking. He liked to know which of his officers were on duty; where and when. He liked to plan ahead.

It wasn't that he anticipated any trouble on this leg, but it was better to be prepared.

It seemed they had a few minor celebrities on board. None of them appeared to be divas; they hadn't made any special requests at least. So far.

Still, he liked to plan ahead.

'Guv'.'

Davies' head appeared in the doorway once more.

'I think you might want to come and take a look at this.'

Waiting.

She hated waiting like this. Not because she was impatient, but because she could feel the eyes of every other passenger waiting to board behind her boring a hole into the back of her skull. And it wasn't even *her* fault. These were the tools of her trade. She hadn't even entertained the thought that she might have to phone ahead and check that she would be *allowed* to bring them on board.

Stupid rules!

Stupid me!

And this trip was supposed to be relaxing. Ha! She hadn't believed that for a moment. No, it had been purely stressful from the first time she'd sat down to try and book the damn thing.

To make things worse, three days before she was due to depart, the Dean of Art and Design — her immediate boss — along (she was informed) with the board of Governors, Contributors and other senior Management had seen fit to place her in the *wonderful* position of contributing to a published work spanning her earliest instalments, designs and other pieces through to her latest collection.

Fucking joy!

If she'd wanted to be a writer she would have pursued a career in journalism or fiction instead of art! But, no. She was an artist!

But, the university had demanded that she actively take part in this publication and, as they did pay the wages that kept her afloat, there were only so many times she could turn them down politely or offer a flat-out 'no fucking way' in reply to the money-making schemes and publicity stunts they consistently thrust into her lap. She was, after all — as she was reminded almost daily in the stream of emails she received from the Dean — *their* artist in residence. A fact they constantly loved to push and to publicise.

'What seems to be the problem?'

A tall, athletic-looking wall of a man stopped short of the mobile conveyer belt and the junior security officer that was sat behind it. Unlike the ginger mop-top that stuttered with apologies before her, it was clear that this man commanded attention and authority wherever he went. His green eyes glistened in the early morning light that stole into the crowded reception-come-security-check-in area; his close-cut dark hair (that didn't quite mask the pencil-thin scare running lengthways over his skull) adding a boyish quality to his handsome, if not slightly weathered face.

'Are you in charge here?'

'I am the Head of Security on board the *Ianus*, yes.' he said, his voice husky and attractive in keeping with his physical appearance.

She smiled, despite herself.

'This lady,' the mop-top piped up, stumbling as soon as he had started, 'she's got a ... erm ... a set of ...'

'I've brought some of my work on holiday with me.' she cut in, saving him further embarrassment.

'Really? And what is it that you do?' The Head of Security smiled pleasantly at her.

'I'm ... an artist and — '

'She has a set of knives.' the junior finished.

'I see.'

He clearly didn't.

Annoyed, her eyes flicked up to the wall-mounted, flat-screen T.V. silently reporting the latest regional news; apparently the Chief Constable of Merseyside Police was retiring following events that had culminated in a botched partnership operation with the Cheshire Police force and the discovery of human remains in Delamere Forest.

Delamere.

It struck a chord and she frowned at the screen.

'You know I'm going to have to confiscate these, Mrs ...'

'Miss.' she said, snapping her attention back to ole green eyes, 'Livingstone. Kelly Livingstone. And you can't confiscate them. I need them.'

'I'm afraid I don't have a choice. These are classed as dangerous weapons,' he said, unrolling the set of beautifully crafted artist knives, 'and as such cannot be carried by any passenger onto this ship. Now, do you have anything else in your bags that you might want to declare? Work-related or not?'

Kelly shook her head a little quicker and a little more emphatically than she'd meant to, instantly rebuking herself. But, she couldn't help it; he'd set her on edge now.

The Security Chief eyed here for a moment before passing her bags back through the x-ray scanner, pausing to take a good look at the contents as they appeared on the screen before him.

'He's done that once.' Kelly objected, nodding towards the mop-top.

The annoyingly handsome security officer simply smiled at her.

'Just routine, Miss Livingstone.'

He handed the bags to the ginger one who gleefully prised open the first and began riffling through her clothes and personal belongings.

'Hey!'

'Everything alright, Mr Prior?' a male voice hollered suddenly from behind her.

'Yes, sir.' answered the man she now knew to be called Prior.

'Then what's the hold up?'

This second man, the one spitting questions at Prior did not have a naturally authoritative voice, but one that was well practiced in giving orders. Kelly turned to see the white uniform along with the stripes signifying the rank of a Captain approaching her.

'This lady, Miss Livingstone, was found to be in possession of a set of knives — '

'Livingstone?' the Captain cut in, eyeing Kelly properly for the first time, 'Kelly Livingstone?'

She nodded, slightly bewildered by the succession of events so far.

'I'm a great admirer of your work. If I might say, I think you're one of the greatest living artists of our time. Your reclaimed pieces are some of my favourites.'

'Thank ... you ...' she said slowly.

'Captain Andrews. Jason Andrews.'

Taking his extended hand, Kelly shook it, smiling; feeling a sudden heat flushing her cheeks as she did. This was exactly what she'd hoped to avoid. Still ...

Andrews broke off the hand shake and turned to Prior. 'Return Miss Livingstone's possessions to her bag. I can personally vouch for her credibility and — '

'With all-due respect, sir, these are not mere possessions. They are classed as potentially deadly weapons that — '

'Do not try and quote the rule book at me Prior.' he said, squaring up to the Security Chief, 'I am exercising my discretion as Captain of this vessel. If you have a problem with that you can submit a complaint — in writing — to *Golden Star*, but until such a time as they reply I suggest that you return Miss Livingstone's things and continue with your duties so that we might depart without further delays relating to a slow security check-in. Else I might be forced to submit a complaint to *Golden Star* myself. Something along to lines of incompetence and insubordination. Do I make myself clear?'

'Crystal. Sir.' Prior muttered through clenched teeth, never taking his eyes from his commander.

Kelly could almost smell the testosterone!

As she quickly moved to collect her bags, the mop-top junior pulled out three, well-sealed eighth-bags of green. Prior looked instantly to Andrews, who in turn looked to Kelly. Kelly dropped her gaze, cursing that she hadn't been quick enough.

'And what about that, *Sir*?' Prior questioned.

In one swift move Andrews took the bags from the mop-top and pocketed them. 'What about *what*, Mr Prior?'

Then, Andrews lifted Kelly's bags from the conveyer belt and with a final determined look at Prior, led her through the reception/security area and into an adjoining lounge.

Prior shook his head, his teeth still clinched. As she followed Andrews, Kelly heard him exhale an obvious — though barely audible — curse and smiled to herself.

'Prick!' he muttered.

When they were out of Prior's view, the young Captain stopped and addressed Kelly once more. 'I'm sorry about that. He's a good man — and an excellent officer — but he can be difficult to work with at times. But then that's coppers for you.'

Kelly nodded, smiling almost dumbly, not quite knowing what to expect next.

'Well,' she said eventually, 'thanks for ... coming to my rescue.'

'It was my pleasure.'

Waving his hand at one of the stewards, Andrews silently called him over and, taking a crisp twenty-pound note from his wallet, tipped the robust, yet compact-looking young man in advance. 'Niko, will you take Miss Livingstone's bags up to the Athena suite please?'

The steward nodded, pocketing the twenty and picking up her bags in one, fluid motion.

Had she just been up-graded?

'Thank you, again, Captain Andrews. But, I thought I was in room ...' she paused, scanning the paper print-out still tucked inside her passport.

'Think of it as compensation ... for the hassle.'

Kelly smiled, genuinely and pleasantly surprised (and even a little awed) by Andrews' generosity. But what were the conditions of his charity?

'I have only one request to make.'

Ah, right on cue.

Andrews extended his hand once more and as Kelly pressed her palm against his she felt something other than flesh. Something plastic.

'That you will join me at the Captain's table for dinner tonight?'

Kelly hated social functions. Particularly when they involved eating.

But, in all reality, how many times would such an offer materialise again? And how many Captains would have gone out of their way to intervene with security issues on behalf of someone like herself? How many would have upgraded her, tipped a bell-boy and returned her confiscated weed so freely?

If a social dinner was all that he was interested in, she was more than happy to oblige.

'How could I refuse?' she said.

His smile was one of unadulterated, child-on-Christmas-morning joy. 'Good. Great. Then, I'll see you this evening.'

He released her hand and moved away from her, striding through the bustling lounge.

Kelly felt the palmed bags with the tips of her fingers quizzically. Opening her hand ever so slightly, she glanced down. Two bags.

Two. Not three.

She looked back up at Andrews, who simply winked as he marched confidently on.

Kelly shook her head, a soft smile spreading across her face.

'Cheeky bastard.'

10:35

Friday 13th May, 2011

Christine Kane sipped at the large glass of merlot, savouring the taste as the world — literally — began to drift away from her.

As she sat out on the balcony that was part and parcel of the luxury aft-port-side suite, she felt as though she was finally beginning to leave the troubles and woes of the past year behind her. Beginning, perhaps. Though there was no guarantee that she would succeed in completing this particular course of treatment. That she ever would — or could — truly leave the past behind her.

Hence the large glass of merlot for breakfast.

She scribbled notes, as ever, in the brown faux-suede journal that was never out of arm's reach for the now-retired criminal psychologist. Profiler. Whatever.

She was done with all of that.

Absently, she stretched out her right leg. A twinge of pain bolted up and down the limb, beginning and ending like arthritic lighting at the knee. Her new prosthetic knee.

Rubbing the joint as if it were still her own, Christine traced the course of the pins and hinges through her loose black trousers. Tentatively, she thumbed the precise rods of metal that held the new mechanism in place; that enabled her to walk again. Even if it was with the aid of a stick.

The doctors had made a good job of rebuilding her leg and she'd made a sizable donation to the hospital upon receiving a generous amount of compensation on top of her early retirement payout. She felt it was the least she could do after they'd managed to save not only her leg, but also her life.

And after they'd tried so hard, also, to save the life of Janet.

But, let's not think about that now. I'm on holiday for a reason.

And, oh how she wished that reason didn't feel so much like running away. How she wished she didn't feel guilty every single, waking moment. Guilty for living; guilty for feeling; for remembering; for forgetting; for drinking to forget.

But she never truly forgot any of it. Who could dare to suggest that she ever would, or should ... or wanted to?

Her latest academic work *Personality and Profiling* had soared to the top of various book charts following the recent events and unwanted media attention. Media interference. And Christine's publicist (along with her own G.P.) had eventually insisted that she take a break; recuperate and escape it all.

Like it was that easy.

Still, it had sounded like a good idea at the time and Christine reluctantly complied. Not something she was particularly renowned for, or in the habit of doing very often at all.

Turning the page of her journal to continue with her train of thought she was halted by a small square of luminous pink paper. She hated being disturbed mid-flow at the best of times ...

She picked up the note in her beautifully soft and slender hand, silently mouthing the words as she read them:

You're at the Captain's Table tonight (13th). Hope you find this in plenty of time. Helena.

Helena Wainholme. Christine's publicist.

Great.

Christine sighed. Clearly Helena wasn't going to allow her to simply disappear into the recesses of her suite and her mini-bar and not emerge until the end of the trip after all.

Damn.

She wasn't great in the face of social gatherings, especially since ... all of that.

Yes, merlot for breakfast had been a very good choice. And apparently a pre-emptively deserved and necessary one!

She sighed and took another sip.

13:20

Friday 13th May, 2011

The raked floor of the proscenium-arched stage had been transformed into an other-worldly forest; dank and ominous as the hazer spilled a light, creeping fog across the scene.

The technical crew had built out from the proscenium creating a sloping thrust stage so that the audience sat on three of the four sides of the action; immersing them in the very physical and technically spectacular adaptation of Shakespeare's lengthy poetic work; *The Rape of Lucrece*.

After months of hard work, everything was finally coming together. The *Dionysus Theatre* had never looked so ... accessible. So realistic. So intrinsically believable.

Shona Jacobs sat in the cushioned stall seats taking it all in, feeling the cool water spill over her warm throat and thirsting tongue as she drank from the plastic bottle in her hand.

The company had started working on this performance — this modern operetta — nearly six months earlier. They had studied the poem together; broken it down, restructured and reinvented it, looking also to Benjamin Britten's chamber opera — *The Rape of Lucretia* — for some inspiration before throwing it out completely and bringing their own composer on board.

And, bam!

Within a week he'd written an entirely new score. A score that included all the usual suspects in terms of orchestral instruments as well as a virtuoso for the electric guitar, a keys and rhythm section and some of the most beautiful and surprising arias Shona had ever heard or had the privilege of performing.

But, after two hours of physical and vocal warm-ups followed by the final rehearsal before the dress, she was feeling more than a little wiped out.

'What's up Lucrece?'

Shona sat up, suddenly aware that she'd relaxed right down into the stall seat, leaning her head against its soft, cushioned side. 'Mike.'

She forced a smile as he sat down next to her.

Mike had landed the male lead of Sextus Tarquinius playing opposite her Lucrece. The villain of the story who's dishonourable deeds leant its name to the performance.

And in some ways it suited him.

Mike was an amazing performer; a great dancer; fantastic voice; he had good, strong features and was compact without being overly muscular. He was even a decent actor.

It was just such a shame that he *knew* it.

He was a nice enough guy ... when he wanted to be. Easy enough to get along with. A good laugh, generous with his money and not too bad in the sack. But, Mike had the unfortunate habit of transforming — at the drop of a hat — into the nastiest and most demanding of divas. Not to mention an out and out bully.

Shona didn't know which was worse. Which one of those two horrid colours she hated most on him.

The two of them had been together for about four weeks just over a year ago. Like everyone before her she'd been lured in by his charm and his confidence. It all seemed like ancient history now, but it was *their* history. And, try as she might to put it aside — to just be fucking professional about it all — it still made Shona very uncomfortable.

Still, he was in a good mood today.

Not in the least because the proverbial barrel had just been well-stocked with a fresh new batch of fish; keen and energetic, stunning and eager-to-please. She had noticed him eyeing the new dancers as they had warmed up together this morning.

These girls weren't involved in *Lucrece*, but no doubt they would all converge and work together at some point. The new twirlies would — in all likelihood — be performing cabaret acts in the various smaller show-rooms that punctuated most of the upper decks of the *Ianus*.

'What's up with you?' he said.

She raised her eyebrows and shook her head. But, it did nothing to appease his curiosity and he waited in silence, watching her.

Becoming slightly uncomfortable, Shona's dark, almond eyes moved from his face to the stage and finally back to him. He was still staring.

'I think I'm just feeling it today.' she said, eventually.

He settled back into the chair next to her, taking the water bottle from her hand and drinking down a great gulp. 'You seemed distracted . . .'

'I could say the same of you!' she said, laughing in spite of herself.

'What d'you mean?'

'Don't try and tell me you didn't notice the hot, little blonde with smouldering eyes and the red top.'

Mike grinned impishly. 'Yeah, don't try and tell me you didn't notice her either! Man, what an arse.'

'At least let her find her feet first, Mike.'

'Her feet won't touch the ground, mate!'

Shona shook her head feeling a strange twinge of guilt in simply knowing his routine; his obvious and unapologetic, appalling sexual habits. Knowing how he'd whisk the girl away in a whirlwind romance before breaking her heart in the cruellest of ways. She'd watched him do it to so many other girls.

Fortunately, she hadn't had to experience it.

As far as she knew she was the only girl — at least the only one the ship — who'd been quick enough to break up with him first.

'So, how's Jemma then?' she asked, already knowing the answer.

'We broke up.'

'Well, there's a surprise.'

Jabbing her playfully in the ribs, Mike handed the bottle back to her. 'How's things with you and Rachel?'

Mike hadn't been the one Shona wanted to first air this with, but since he had asked . . .

'She decided she couldn't handle a long-distance . . . thing.'

'And by thing you mean *relationship*.' He said it as though it were a foreign word and again she found herself laughing with him, even as she slapped his leg. He recoiled, feigning injury.

'Yeah. One of them.' she said, her voice filled with more sadness than she realised she bore towards the issue.

Mike rubbed his thigh, a red mark already pulsing where she'd caught him. 'You back on men then, now? Or you still . . . dabbling?'

'You're a twat, d'you know that?' she said, a grin spreading across her face.

'I have been told as much. Yes.'

Unable to resist the urge to really wind him up, Shona stood, leaning seductively over Mike as she spoke. Her chest rising and falling; her lips only millimetres from his.

'You'd know if I started dated men again.' She said pausing, allowing her words to really sink in and watching his sharp intake of breath as he swallowed hard. She placed her palm flat against his chest, feeling his heart begin to race. God only knows what his other organs were doing! 'You'd know, because I'd send you a copy of the list.'

'The . . . list?' he stuttered.

Yes, actually stuttered!

She was enjoying herself far too much. Enjoying the power that — until that very moment — she'd had no idea she held over him.

'Yes,' she whispered, tracing a slender finger over his vested chest and abs. Feeling every breath he took. 'Yeah, you know, like a wish-list. And your name would be right up there at the top ...'

'Really?'

'Yeah, right at the top of the 'you wish' list!' she said with a giggle, 'Come on, if your name was on any list of mine, it'd have to have a thick black line through it anyway!'

'Line?' he repeated, slowly emerging from his stupor.

'Yeah. What is it you always say?' She smiled, turning her back on him, 'Been there ... done that.'

Mike shook his head, but managed to smile at her.

'Come on, you walking penis,' Shona called back as she made her way towards the doors, 'let's grab some lunch before the dress.'

Yes. The dress rehearsal would start in a couple of hours.

Food. Need food. Maybe a drink too.

A real drink.

Mike was shaking. He could barely catch his breath. Was it excitement or embarrassment? He couldn't tell.

Was it anger?

Slowly, he climbed to his feet and followed Shona out of the theatre.

19:29

Friday 13th May, 2011

Kelly strolled into the *Grande Central* dining hall just before seven-thirty, scanning the lavishly decorated art-deco-esque room for the coveted Captain's Table.

She spotted the unmistakable facade of the man who had both come to her aid and also lightened her baggage load earlier.

Andrews was not an overly tall man, but he seemed taller purely in his attitude and manner; the natural confidence he exuded. He was every inch an officer and filled the room with an energy that was more than authority, it was personality.

He was clearly the bell of the ball!

Clean shaven with almost baby-faced features, he stood near an imitation open-fireplace surrounded with emerald and black tiling, fully engaged in conversation with a flock of doting women and a gaggle of well-dressed men who each nodded in agreement, laughing dutifully.

Kelly stepped forward, drawing in a deep breath as she entered the lion's den.

It was immediately clear that only the senior officers and the most elite of the *Ianus'* passenger manifold dined in here. And she felt it.

Every step she took drew an icy stare from one well-suited old barrister to another and *tut* after *tut* from every one of the horse-faced, fake-tan, peacock-eyelashed creatures she could only assume had once been little girls and women. Before the money had spoiled them.

Still, it was nice to see that the judgemental bias of class discrimination was still alive and well in the twenty-first century!

'Excuse me madam, can I help you?' Kelly heard the man's words, but his tone made it very clear that he — in fact — was keen to do anything *but* help.

Kelly turned to find herself confronted by a moustachioed penguin and had to clamp her lips tight shut to keep from laughing in the man's face.

He was tall and skinny in an unattractive way that didn't suit him. He wore a plastered look of disgust that could only be described in terms of him catching the scent of some foul smelling odour and believing her to be responsible for it. His mouth was twisted in a bitter-lemon pout under his thin, tight moustache.

In short, he was every inch the stereotypical stuck-up and repugnant sort of maitre d' she had expected to encounter in a place like this.

She instantly disliked him. And whilst she'd previously been apprehensive about this evening, wishing — praying — for some reason to cancel, Kelly was suddenly more determined than ever to take her seat at the Captain's Table and mingle with the toffs!

'I'm expected.' she said.

The penguin stepped back, studying her; taking in her dark, slim-fit jeans and the chunky belt that featured a gleaming silver buckle in the shape of a skull and which hung gun-holster-low over one hip. His eyes fell down to the immaculate white trainers that covered her feet before tracing his way slowly back up and over her body; over her tight, blue Ben Sherman shirt, to her silver necklace, her azure eyes as they glistened through smoky colours and fine black lines, right up to the blue-black hair that fell in a side fringe over to the left of her face. He sneered as though the cut of it had actively offended him; clearly it was too severely short and oddly asymmetric for his liking.

She could almost hear his thoughts; they were splashed across his arrogant face. *I mean trainers for heaven's sake! Not in the Grande Central. Not on my watch.*

A prematurely self — satisfied grin pushed his sour-lemon lips from their pout as he clearly anticipated having to have her escorted from the restaurant. 'Expected?' he repeated, 'By who?'

Kelly wanted, so much, to just punch him right in his smug and leering face as it bobbed before her. Tempting her.

She didn't.

'I have an invitation to join Captain Andrews.'

'Of course you do.' he taunted.

'No, really.' She said, fast becoming frustrated, feeling the anger rising with every breath. 'I do.'

'Well then,' he continued in the same self-satisfied tone, motioning to several of the waiting-on staff; calling them over, ready to have her promptly and presently ejected, 'if I can just check your reservation, you'll be free to join Captain Andrews and his guests.'

'Reservation?' She couldn't believe it. 'I don't have a reservation. I met him today during check-in. He helped me out and invited me ... like this ...' she opened and closed her mouth several times pointing at it before continuing, 'he said *would you join me at the Captain's Table for dinner tonight* and I — foolishly — agreed. He didn't give me a piece of ...' she exhaled, biting back the expletive on the tip of her tongue, 'I don't have a *written* invitation.'

Don't rise to the bait, she thought. *He's just itching to throw you out. Come on Kelly, don't let this prick get the better of you.*

'Well, I'm afraid that with no — '

'Edmunds.'

She knew that gruff and husky voice. Again, from this morning. She knew exactly who it belonged to. The Security Chief; Prior.

'The Captain's waiting — '

'Yes sir, Mr Prior, I was just about to have this lady — '

'Miss Livingstone.' Prior cut in, his eyes darting assertively from the Penguin's to hers and back again.

'Er, yes,' Edmunds said, faltering for the first time; his haughty confidence diminishing before her eyes. How could Prior possibly know this woman? 'She ...'

The words failed him.

'She's expected.' Prior continued, 'Miss Livingstone is the final guest that Captain Andrews is waiting on. Waiting to begin the first evening meal of the voyage ... and *you* are holding all of that up.'

'I'm sorry sir, very sorry. I didn't think she ... she had no reservation.' Edmunds stuttered as he continued to deflate.

'She has a personal invite from the man himself.'

'I did try and tell him.' said Kelly.

'I didn't ... believe her, sir.' Edmunds bowed his head by way of apology and in acknowledgement of his error.

Choosing to dismiss him with some of his pride still intact, Prior reassured the Maitre d', 'You were doing your job. There's no harm in that.'

Edmunds gave a small nod, his head still bowed, silently thanking Prior for the way he'd dealt with the situation. For not causing a scene.

Kelly, however, was less satisfied. Clearly Prior was a very chivalrous sort of bloke; intervening on her behalf despite their run-in this morning, before sparing this tight-arsed penguin-suited twat the humiliation he himself would have heaped on Kelly without a second thought. A humiliation he'd been goading her towards since she'd entered the room.

Prior stepped back extending his arm.

As Kelly passed Edmunds she turned, unable to contain herself any longer, 'By the way, it's *whom*.'

'I ... er ...'

'You asked 'by *who*' I was expected. Your grammar is a little lacking there, little waiter.'

Prior shook his head. Only slightly, but it was there.

'My apologies. Again.' Edmunds offered. And all three of them knew that it wasn't for his misuse of semantics.

Kelly Livingstone; one point. Annoying, self-appointed, pretentious bastard; nil.

'Thank you.' she said quietly, as Prior led her across the surprisingly vast dining hall. She found herself falling in step with his measured, almost regimented strides.

'You didn't have to do that,' he returned without looking at her, 'He was already embarrassed. You didn't have to humiliate him like that.'

'I don't see why not. He was trying his best to do the same to me.'

'So, what then? An eye for an eye, is it?'

'I don't know about you, but I was always taught to treat others as I'd like to be treated myself and if that's how he gets-off, trying to publicly belittle people then he deserves some of the same in return.'

Prior stopped, the tiniest of half-smiles sitting on his lips. 'I'd have to say I agree. Which, is why I was in two minds about leaving Edmunds to do his job in throwing you out,' Kelly opened her mouth to protest. Prior continued, unhindered, 'but, I heard Captain Andrews talking, just now, about how his favourite artist would be joining us tonight. He really seems quite taken with you. With your work.'

Kelly was shocked. Noticeably shocked. But, not by the discovery that Andrews was a fan; she knew that much already.

'So he didn't *ask* you to . . .'

'What? You thought Andrews had sent me over to . . . mediate.'

Nodding slowly, Kelly felt her cheeks begin to redden at her mistake.

'I'm afraid not.'

'I'm sorry,' she said, 'I just didn't think . . . especially after this morning . . . that you would, you know . . . willingly . . .'

'Come to your rescue?'

'Intervene.' she said resolutely.

He smiled at her fully for the first time since they had met. It wasn't a joyous smile, or even an overly friendly one. It didn't cause his green eyes to sparkle as she imagined a truly contented smile would, but it was honest.

'Why don't we start again?' he said, extending his hand to her, 'Jonathan Prior.'

Perplexed by this intriguing officer, she accepted his hand.

'Kelly Livingstone. But then, you already knew that.'

As they continued towards the table, she noticed Prior nod to a beautifully uniformed woman of rank. She had large aqua eyes and long red hair that bounced when she walked. She smiled at him, a secret sort of smile and then she was gone.

Prior pulled out Kelly's seat before making his way around to the other side of the table and taking his place in between Andrews — who had also only just sat down — and an attractive lady, who Kelly judged to be a little older than herself. The intriguing woman was currently focused on the task of inspecting the silverware before her.

She wore an expensive classic-cut black trouser suit with a white blouse. Her hair was pulled back and pinned in some sort of a pleat which kept a mass of shining, chocolate curls at a safe and orderly distance from her face. They spilled from her crown like the spiralled paper-strips from a weddings-worth of party poppers and Kelly could only imagine the amount of time and patience it must have taken to harness them.

Suddenly — almost childishly — she felt the overwhelming desire to pluck out the pins. One by one. And let her hair fall free.

Kelly continued to watch as the woman meticulously — yet as discreetly as possible — gave each of the pieces of cutlery that were laid before her a visual once over, adjusting them and aligning them to her personal specifications as she went.

As though feeling her stare, the woman paused in her labour and looked up. Their eyes met and they held one another's gaze for a moment; each feeling they had been caught out by the other.

Obsessing about hair-pins.

Obsessing about cutlery.

They exchanged a brief smile before Kelly found herself being introduced to all those around her.

To her left sat the ship's physician and Chief Medical Officer; Dr Karen Matthews.

Matthews was a stern-looking, blonde-haired woman of about thirty. Her pale blue eyes seemed already tired, though they had not yet been a day at sea and, while she was not unattractive, she had a severity about her that put Kelly in mind of some sort of Swedish dominatrix. She dared not air this view of course; for fear of the punishments she might receive!

Kelly stifled a laugh behind her white linen napkin.

Next to Matthews was the second physician, Dr Stuart Cunningham. Put simply, Cunningham looked like Death. He was grey in every imaginable sense that a person could be grey!

A little older, perhaps, than Dr Matthews, Cunningham looked like he had been destined to become an undertaker; but — Kelly supposed — a doctor was often close enough. His slothly, ashen face nodded in acknowledgment of his name as Captain Andrews quickly did the rounds, introducing everyone.

To Kelly's right was the head nurse, Adrian Kemp.

Kemp was small and broad with wild, brown hair and eyes to match. He was like an electrically-charged ball of barely-harnessed energy just waiting to break free from the protons and neutrons that chained him.

Andrews was sat opposite the Swedish Dominatrix; his second-in-command, Craig Roberts, on his right. Prior sat to his left, opposite Kelly . . . and next to him was the somewhat obsessional and intriguing, chocolate-haired woman.

'Christine Kane.' she interjected with a soft Scottish accent as Andrews reached her.

Kelly smiled.

'*Dr* Christine Kane.' Andrews repeated, stressing her professional title.

Something Christine had clearly neglected for a reason.

'Table of doctors,' Kelly said, 'feel like I'm here for an assessment or something.'

There was a teeter of laughter as their first course arrived at the table.

'You have a doctorate don't you, Miss Livingstone?' It was Prior. And it was the second time this evening that the man had managed to surprise her completely.

'Yes,' she said, sipping tomato and basil soup from a silver spoon, 'but, I'm by no means a medical doctor. Never had the brains . . . or the stomach for anything like that!'

Again, a small wave of subdued laughter.

'Do you suffer a weak stomach?' This time the question came from Andrews.

'Sometimes.'

'That surprises me.' Prior, again.

'Well now, that makes two of us,' she said. Prior raised an inquisitive eyebrow. 'Most of my own work colleagues seem blissfully unaware of or are, at the very least, obstinately unwilling to even acknowledge my academic qualifications.' She paused, smiling, 'But, not you it seems.'

He grinned, expelling a small laugh that bore the slightest hint of resentment. 'Well, the Captain isn't the only one acquainted with your work or your career … Miss Livingstone.'

Strike three.

It was rare that a man — any man — ever truly surprised her even *once* in a given period of time, let alone three times in one evening. But, it would seem that Jonathan Prior was ever proving himself to be the exception to the rule.

'So, you don't like the title of *Doctor?*' Christine asked, slicing through the uneasy atmosphere that seemed to have descended upon the table.

'Not really.'

'And why is that?' barked the Dominatrix.

Kelly knew that her opinion of use of the preamble of *Doctor* as being a socially discriminating, middle-class-versus-working-class tool of elevation and oppression would not be much appreciated at this table. Or — in fact — anywhere in this room.

'I … just … I don't feel I've earned it.' she said, lying through her teeth.

After that, the table broke into smaller groups of chit-chat, the guests talking amongst themselves and enjoying a main course of lamb roast, salmon en-cruet or Mediterranean vegetable lasagne. Kelly had ordered the latter, much to the disbelief and almost open-mouthed horror of the wild-eyed Kemp, who tucked hungrily into the meat on his plate.

For him the term *vegetarian* just didn't compute.

As their dishes were cleared away in anticipation of dessert Kelly felt the heat of a feminine body press against her own. A slender arm appeared to the right of her, taking up her plate and cutlery with a mastered precision and speed.

'Thank you.' she said, looking up into a pair of dark-chocolate, almond-shaped eyes; warm, but understated tones and a slash of liner lending a feline air to the already seductive and devilishly dark, glistening orbs.

'You're welcome.' replied the smiling young woman.

Kelly watched her move off, navigating the obstruction of tables with ease.

The waitress had great poise and — from where Kelly was sitting — she seemed to be blessed in every other conceivable way as well. Long, shapely legs; toned arms; all the right curves in the right places, great . . .

'. . . assets.'

'Sorry?' she said, crashing back down to earth and the dinner table conversation with such a thud it almost hurt.

Apparently the compact carnivore had been talking to her. But, for how long?

And about what?

'To pay off the solicitor's fees and inheritance tax.' He continued as if she'd been paying attention. Which she hadn't. She stared blankly at him, trying — so hard — to think of something relevant to say. 'After my father passed away.' he said finally, still waiting for a response.

Oh, she was going to hell!

'I'm sorry, I'm not feeling too good.' she lied for the second time that evening.

'You did look a bit spaced out for a second.' he said.

Yeah, just a bit!

Had he noticed that she hadn't been listening to him? Or had she somehow managed to get away with it?

'Well, they ripped us off anyway.'

His tone said it all. He was clearly pissed off.

Having watched the events from a little way off and seeing Kelly now sweating under the pressure, Christine joined the conversation.

'I had a similar experience,' she said, 'when we lost my Mother.' This appeared to both content and overwhelm the young — and somewhat emotionally unstable — male nurse, who smiled sweetly at Christine; tears suddenly glazing his eyes.

Breathing a sigh of relief, Kelly mouthed the words *Thank you*, to which Christine smiled a subtle reply as Kemp continued to speak.

'I don't suppose that you get on well with solicitors, full stop.' he said, pulling himself together, 'Especially if their anything like that last one.'

Christine instantly threw up her guard. Shield, walls, castle and moat.

The change in her was physical, absolute and instant. She was an entirely different woman. Closed, locked down and giving nothing away, save a very clear message; *Do not go there.*

But Adrian Kemp was relentless. For a nurse he didn't seem to have a clue about when to stop pushing and Kelly found herself wondering about his bedside manner, which — she couldn't help but think — might be more than a little lacking.

'What was his name?' He raised his voice, opening the conversation up to the rest of the table, 'That guy . . . the solicitor that got Butler off recently?'

'Thomas Butler?' Dr Matthews questioned.

'Oh yes, the Butler case.' chimed Dr Cunningham dryly as he finished a glass of red wine, 'I thought I recognised your face, Dr Kane.'

Matthews moved Cunningham's glass across the table before it could be topped up, silently reprimanding him. He shot her a burning look, before returning his attention to Christine.

She was blushing.

It wasn't the humble blush of someone recognised for their own particular fame, nor was it wholly borne out of embarrassment, but something else. Kelly stared at the strong woman sat across from her, trying to figure her out.

Their eyes met once more. And in that instant she knew.

It was guilt.

It was, unmistakably, guilt that flushed her cheeks and flooded her eyes. Guilt and regret.

Kelly raised her eyebrows, silently questioning her.

Christine gave a small, discreet nod.

'Lomax.' Captain Andrews said, choosing to join in with the conversation that appeared to be awkward for no one other than Christine.

For her it seemed excruciating and Kelly felt it as she watched her dark eyes filling. 'Kevin Lomax.' Andrews continued, 'He's the man every criminal low-life wants to represent him. Makes Cochrane look like an amateur.'

Christine tried her best to smile, but she was on the verge of tears. And no one seemed to care.

'I think I could use some air,' said Kelly suddenly. She wasn't even sure the voice had been hers, but she was on her feet none the less, 'How about you Dr Kane?'

The relief on Christine's face was as clear as a cloudless day; as loud as a holler on the wind. She smiled and fumbled to grasp something besides her, something just out of Kelly's view.

Next to her, Prior stood up. This appeared to be partly out of gentlemanly respect and partly in offer of assistance, which Christine reluctantly accepted. She thanked him as she moved slowly around the table ... leaning heavily onto a polished, dark-wood walking stick.

Kelly waited, allowing Christine to go before her.

The further they walked the more Christine's leg appeared to loosen and by the time they'd reached the open deck, her limp was barely noticeable.

'Thank you.' Christine said, breathing a great sigh as she leant against the railings, watching the waves crash against the hull.

'You did the same for me. With Kemp. Just thought I'd repay the favour.'

Kelly looked around the deck. It was a warm night with a warm breeze, yet there weren't that many people about. Perhaps they were still eating. Or drinking. Maybe both.

'Quiet, isn't it?' Christine said, as if entering her mind.

Kelly nodded.

The pair remained in silence, watching the waves, seeming to enjoy one another other's company without the need to speak about it. Eventually Christine turned, making her way towards a small table with two chairs already set up.

Kelly followed and as she sat, a violent pain — violent like a bolt of jagged lightning — cracked through her skull; her temples suddenly throbbing, her eyes burning. She pressed her hand to her head, wincing and massaging the tender pressure points.

'Are you okay?' Christine said, her voice expressing the true concern that accompanied the worried look in her eyes. Kelly struggled to nod, unable to offer any further answer for several moments more. Taking in breath after deep breath and feeling the bile rising in the back of her throat she desperately fought the urge to vomit. Gradually, very slowly, the pain began to subside.

'Sorry.' she started, 'I suffer with these . . . headaches. Painful fucking headaches. It's usually when there's crappy lighting in a room or something. Atmospheric pressure and stuff like that.'

'Have you ever seen anyone about it?'

Kelly shook her head. 'There's no point. I've always had them. Ever since I can remember. But, fortunately they don't tend to last too long.'

'Still, you shouldn't have to put up with pain like that.'

'I'm fine.' A nervous smile broke across Kelly's face that told Christine she didn't want to talk about it. Not yet. Christine didn't push. 'But, it looks like I can add *travelling at sea* to the list of things that I know set it off. Should make the rest of the journey ... interesting, if nothing else.'

'Do you have some painkillers?'

Kelly nodded, touched by Christine's concern. It was her third white-lie that evening. She did have something to take the edge off the pain, but it certainly wasn't an over the counter remedy.

'I'm fine,' she said, 'Honestly.'

They sat in silence a few minutes more. But, it had now become a strained silence, the kind that begs to be broken.

Christine's move.

'Do you have any plans for the rest of the evening?'

'Actually, I do.' Kelly said, still rubbing just above her eyes, 'I'm never usually this organised, but yeah. I actually have a ticket to see the show tonight; *The Rape of Lucrece*. I know ... sounds like a barrel of laughs, doesn't it.'

Christine chuckled, 'Should certainly be fun with a bad head.'

'I know. Typical. But, I suppose that's what I get for trying to be all cultured and shit.' she said with a smile, pausing for a moment, 'Will you be there?'

'No. It's not really my thing.' Christine said, noting the disappointment that had played — just for an instant — on Kelly's face, 'It's had great pre-show reviews though. So I've heard.'

Kelly laughed, knowing that she'd slipped up; that she'd been caught out. That Christine seemed able to read her like an open book. But, it had been worth it. Just to see that warm smile curl her soft lips again; to see the walls torn down once more.

Yes, it was definitely worth it.

'What?' Christine asked as Kelly continued to chuckle.

'I don't know, I just assumed that someone like you ... I just thought you'd have a ticket that's all.'

Now it was Christine's turn to laugh. 'So, what? Because I'm not going tonight I'm not one of the cultured people after all?'

'I never said that.'

'Sorry to disappoint.'

Kelly shrugged; don't worry about it. 'Why'd you ask, anyway?' she said after a moment. 'About my plans for the evening.'

Christine took her time, considering her answer. 'I might have asked if you wanted to go for a drink.'

Kelly nodded. Involuntarily. There was clearly ... something ... between them.

Exactly what that *something* was she didn't yet know, but then, discovery was often half the fun. 'We could meet up tomorrow.' she said, 'For breakfast or something ... If you wanted to.'

Christine looked at Kelly, tilting her head as though she were trying to solve a puzzle. 'You haven't asked about my leg?'

'None of my business.' Came the reply.

Christine held back, waiting for the inevitable question; *But as you've brought it up . . .*

It never came and she smiled at Kelly, instantly regretting having tested her.

'You can tell me anything you like, whenever you like.' Kelly continued, 'And whatever you don't want to talk about, you keep it to yourself. I'll never push you. I'm just not that type of girl.'

Christine couldn't resist, 'So, what type of girl are you?'

Kelly smiled, sucking her teeth absently. 'One who's not interested in boundaries or labels, or other people's bullshit concepts of right and wrong ... we live in such a fucked up world, anyway.' she paused, looking out across the sea, 'And you only live once. So what's the point in worrying?'

Christine weighed the statement and gave a small nod of acknowledgement and approval, 'That sounds like something we should have toasted.'

'Then, why don't I get us a drink?'

'Do you have the time to?'

'Yeah.' Kelly said, jumping up, 'You should never let a nice evening and good company go to waste. What d'you fancy?'

Christine didn't voice the first answer that sprung to mind, though her reddening cheeks spoke volumes. But then, was that *really* what she wanted? Was she simply becoming swept up in her own conflicting emotions?

Was this just an overwhelming — if not slightly psychotic — response to the first person who had treated her humanely since . . .

Or was she actually attracted to this wild, young artist? This very secure and self-assured, very attractive, witty, funny and very *female* artist?

She'd never even questioned her sexuality before, but there was no doubt about it; she was already developing — no! — she had already developed feelings for this woman; Kelly Livingstone.

Strong, intense, powerful, throbbing, pounding, red-hot feelings!

She swallowed, realising she hadn't yet given an answer, 'I'll have . . . anything. Surprise me.'

Kelly found her way to the nearest bar, which had been cunningly disguised as some sort of Tikki hut. She dug down into her pockets, searching for her cardkey. This trip was all-inclusive, but, it seemed, they liked to keep tabs on just how *inclusive* you were being.

'What can I get you?'

Looking up, Kelly was momentarily dumbfounded to find herself gazing into the same big, brown eyes and dark complexion she'd encountered in the restaurant. The young woman smiled. 'Well, well. We'll have to stop meeting like this. People will start to talk.'

'Best give them something worth talking about then.' said Kelly, returning an equally flirtatious smile.

'What can I get you?'

'I'll have a coke please and . . .' she looked around for inspiration, 'what's . . . nice?'

'Well that depends.' came the confident reply, 'If we're talking drinks ...' Kelly nodded, 'I'm quite partial to a *Mojito* or *Sloe Comfortable Screw*.'

'I'll have to remember that.' Kelly said, swallowing, 'but I think I'd better go for the *Mojito*. For now.'

'For now?'

'Yeah. Play it safe.'

Laughing, the girl behind the bar passed Kelly a pint of coke and began preparing the *Mojito*. 'I'm Shona, by the way. Shona Jacobs.'

'Kelly Livingstone.'

'So, who's this for?' Shona asked as she worked, 'Friend or lover?'

Kelly thought carefully about the question before making her answer. 'We've only just met.'

'Ah, one of those.'

Kelly shrugged. 'Never say never.'

Shona laughed, briefly and huskily. She was wholly attractive and Kelly felt herself begin to melt inside. As pathetic as it sounded, it was true!

And she really hadn't meant to fall for *anyone* on this break, this cruise, this ... working-holiday. And now there were two! Two very different women she'd fallen very hard and very suddenly for in a matter of hours ... and this was only the first day!

Maybe they were pumping pheromones through the venting system or something.

No, don't be stupid. And for God's sake don't say that. She'll think you're crazy. You'll sound like a crazy person!

Kelly listened to the little voice inside her head and chose not to mention anything about the pheromone conspiracy.

She handed over her card, thanking Shona. 'Put one through for yourself. If you like.'

'I tell you what. How about you meet me for dinner tomorrow?'

'You're not waiting-on tomorrow?'

Shona slid the card through the till, tearing the receipt, 'No. I've been covering for someone. I've got a busy night, though. I'm in entertainment.'

I bet you are. Kelly thought, pressing her lips together to stop the crude reply before it escaped. 'You're not in *The Rape of Lucrece* are you?'

'Are you kidding?' Shona replied, her voice suddenly sharp with excitement, 'I *am* Lucrece!' She took a pen and quickly scribbled her number on the back of the receipt.

'In that case,' Kelly said 'I'll see you tonight. Even, if you don't see me.'

'I'll keep an eye out for you, but ...' Shona tucked Kelly's receipt and card back into the breast pocket of her shirt. 'Just in case I *don't* see you later ... call me.'

Kelly couldn't believe her luck.

Finding her way back to Christine, she couldn't help but mull over the events of the evening ... no, the day! She laughed to herself, even as a small, but painful twinge began swirling in her temples once more. She laughed out loud.

What a fucking day!

21:07

Friday 13th May, 2011

Back in her room Kelly could not help but smile as she dried herself with one of the soft and immaculate bath towels embroidered with the intertwining letters G and S.

Golden Star.

Leaving Shona to her duties behind the bar she'd made her way back to Christine, drinks in hand. The evening was still warm and the sky had been surprisingly light as the pair found themselves caught up in conversation after conversation that was so much more than idle chit-chat.

Kelly now knew that Christine was — or had been until recently — a criminal psychologist . . . and, more importantly, she was a published author. Her quiet modesty had pressed her into down-playing this fact until Kelly revealed the seemingly gargantuan task she'd been asked (yeah right, *asked*) to complete by the university. Armed with such an exchange of information, they had quickly come to an agreement that seemed to satisfy the both of them.

Christine would help Kelly with her submission so that she didn't look like a complete nob! And in exchange Kelly would introduce and talk Christine through some of her artistic works; giving her a personal guided tour from her earliest through to her latest pieces.

'Just don't tell Captain Andrews. I don't think I could handle the bitch-fit he'd throw if he thought he was missing out!'

Christine had stifled an explosion of laughter, if only to save Kelly from being covered in *Mojito*.

She seemed to have really enjoyed the drink. Good call, Shona.

Ah, Shona.

Pulling her phone from the jeans she had stepped out of on her way to the shower, Kelly then searched for the receipt — the golden fucking ticket — that Shona had inscribed with her number and slipped inside her shirt pocket earlier.

She unlocked the phone, her fingers gliding over the sleek reflective surface, the touch-screen responding eagerly to her commands as she entered a new number for the second time this evening.

Christine Kane had dictated her number before they had parted ways fifteen or so minutes earlier. She had watched Kelly with interest as she'd added her details and asked her to smile before taking her picture and attaching it to the mobile number, email address and all the rest that she now had stored in what seemed to be her micro-computer.

'I'm so rubbish with phones,' Christine had confessed, overwhelmed by Kelly's apparent skill, 'I must have lost at least four and I know I've definitely broken two on top of that ... maybe three.'

'I don't know what I'd do without mine.' Kelly had said, laughing as they had stood in the rotunda; the central hub that would lead them back to their rooms at opposite ends of the impossibly vast cruise ship. 'It's like having a personal assistant.'

Pulling on a fresh pair of jeans, a plain, slim-fit t-shirt and grey-with-pink v-neck cardigan, Kelly hurried to reapply her eyes.

A master of shading and liner, it all took less than three minutes.

She flitted around the room, distractedly.

Give the fringe a quick straighten. Good old *GHD*! Add a little moulding wax; scruff up the top some.

Scent ... hmm, tricky one. She ran her fingers along the tops of the six au de toilette bottles lined up like soldiers on the dresser before her.

Ralph?

She brought the bottle to her nose, inhaling. Eyes closed. A scent filled with memories; good times. Yes. Ralph it was.

Spraying the perfume and replacing it precisely, she slipped her feet into a pair of converse and headed out of the door ... turning back just before it closed. She ran into the room and grabbed the cardkey.

I'll be needing that later.

Making her way towards the *Dionysus Theatre*, Kelly checked her watch. Nine fifteen. Not bad, not bad at all. A new personal record even.

Rounding the corner, Kelly slammed suddenly into a human wall. She proceeded to filter into the dressed-to-the-nines crowd, falling into step as they pressed through a set of heavy wooden doors before spilling into the wonderfully atmospheric auditorium.

Taking her seat — an aisle stall-seat ten or so rows from the front — Kelly took in the scene around her; the world she found herself suddenly swallowed up inside. It was a living, breathing fairytale nightmare that even the Brothers Grimm would have had trouble contending with. It was fabulous!

As the lights began to dim and the orchestra — under the firm guidance of an eccentric-looking conductor — proceeded to generate the opening phrases of the score, Kelly felt the monstrous headache beginning to claw its way back from behind her eyes, her stomach instantly somersaulting.

No!

She'd hoped a nice shower would sort her out. Apparently not.

Struggling to follow the action as she battled against the pain in her head and the urge to regurgitate her expensive, Captains-table meal, she focused on Shona. And somehow, watching her *own* the stage so completely seemed to make it ... bearable. No, more than that, it made it worth the pain; like travelling through purgatory to gaze upon a saint. Or something shit like that.

Though, she hoped Shona wasn't too much of a saint. Sinners were so much more fun.

Her head continued to spin, throbbing as the male lead pushed Lucrece to the damp forest floor. The timpani exploded into life; the rumbling of kettle drums and percussion; guitars wailing as the Chorus took up an eerie, cursing chant, closing in on Tarquinius even as he forced himself on Shona.

No, not Shona. *Lucrece.*

Kelly struggled to stand. Everything was blurred; merged into one. All that surrounded her was real — she knew it — and yet all was strangely distant. Eyes. Eyes everywhere, watching her.

Stumbling — not too quietly — out of the nearest door, feeling the cold, harsh glaring looks lapping against her as she went, Kelly raced up the three flights of stairs that took her to the open deck. Finding the nearest bin — and not a moment too soon — she launched herself over it, throwing-up . . . again and again; the red heat of shame creeping across her chest and up to her cheeks.

She couldn't stand to meet the eyes of those around her. Staring at her.

Head down, she fled back to her room.

Disgusted with herself.

22:19

Friday 13th May, 2011

He watched the strange young woman stumble from the seat in front of him. Grinning as she struggled to escape the stifling theatre, drawing *tuts* and knife-edged glances from the snobs that pressed against them.

She didn't look well at all.

Shit! If that's what opera did to you, why was it so popular? And so bloody expensive!

He'd watched her rubbing her temples and pressing her thumbs into her eyes for the better part of half an hour and felt a dull pain beginning to claw its way up from the base of his own skull, squeezing the back of his neck. Was that ... what did they call it ... psychosomatic?

Maybe it was just *this* bollocks. Getting to him. Grating on his nerves.

Vince had told him to 'lie low', to do things he wouldn't ordinarily do, go places he'd normally avoid like the plague. So here he was.

For fuck's sake!

They were off again. Warbling and prancing about, making a big song and dance — literally — over some tart getting exactly what she deserved, flooding the performance with morality lectures; diluting *his* idea of a perfectly good night out with notions of right and wrong; of comeuppance, judgement and punishment.

Nah. Bollocks to this.

He couldn't take another minute; the pain in his head was now expanding at a rate of knots, peaking his already-elevated irritability scale to its absolute zenith. He didn't want to end up feeling as rough as that dark-haired dyke had looked as she'd staggered out just now.

Painkillers and stiff drink. That's what he needed.

He could hear his mother's pointless voice somewhere in the back of his mind telling him that a bit of fresh air would do him the world of good. Not bloody likely! Not on this thing.

Stupid woman.

Now, Vince, he was a good man. Well, no, Vince was actually a very, very *bad* man, but he was good at his job; a good mate and — above all — an excellent right-hand. He trusted him in everything; with his very life even. But, arranging for him to hide out on a bloody cruise ship?

Maybe he wasn't such a great mate after all!

Vince was older than him. Old enough to be his brother ... Though he wasn't. Still, they could have been family and for as much as Vince followed his orders to the letter, there were also times that he knew Vince had kept him in check. Reined him in ... for his own good.

But, Vince knew he hated water. That he was fucking petrified of the sea.

Not his fault; he couldn't bloody swim!

He'd watched small animals drowning in a lake near his house when he was younger, seen their bodies bloat as they floated on the surface for days and weeks after. He'd watched other kids struggling in chlorinated pools with those awful plastic arm-bands that pinched at the tender flesh.

Instinctively he rubbed his arms.

He had woken up a little earlier in a fabulous suite with a great, big fucking window and a view of the ocean! They'd clearly had to knock him out to smuggle him onboard. Nice one, Vince!

Still, the police were also aware of his mortal fear of water and so would be unlikely to search for him in such a hellish place.

He could probably come and go unnoticed and undiscovered for the rest of his life were he to invest in a boat of his own. The thought instantly tied his stomach in knots and set his teeth on edge.

Besides, he'd never really been one for a *quiet* life.

His head thumped over and over. He couldn't take this any longer, no chance of holding out for the interval. Pushing out of his seat, he strode quickly towards the double doors. Climbing a flight of stairs and stepping into the nearest *Ianus* mini-market he could find, he made his way directly to the till, his eyes scanning eagerly over the behind-the-counter products.

'Can I help you?' asked the young, Polish girl opposite him.

'Don't you have anything stronger than paracetamol?'

'I'm afraid not.' she said, leaning over the counter and lowering her voice as she spoke in her delightfully clipped accent, 'The company was have trouble with people, you know ... overdose.' she paused, ensuring he'd understood her, 'If you want stronger now you must get from pharmacy. You must see doctor.'

Typical! Fucking toffs and bastard celebrities! Why couldn't they just do that shit at home? Why spoil it for everyone else!

'Okay,' he said, 'I'll take a pouch of whatever mellow tobacco you have and a packet of papers.' He was pretty sure Vince wouldn't have sent him on a trip without any of his favourite recreational drugs. He'd roll a nice fat joint when got back to his room ...

'You know there's no smoking in room.' the Polish cashier piped up as if reading his mind, 'only open deck. They have sensors.'

'Oh for fuck's sake.' he said, 'this is worse than prison!' Producing a note from his pocket he slapped it on the counter, stealing up the papers and tobacco. 'Keep the change.'

He started back towards his room, checking his pocket for the card key. Still there. Good. He'd simply have to face his fear; open the balcony door — the glass, fucking door — just a crack and blow out the smoke. Like a kid sat on his bedroom windowsill, trying not to be caught by his parents. Fucking hell!

His stomach churned at the thought, the pain in his head pounding harder than before.

Shit. He should have bought the paracetamol after all. For all the fucking good it'd do.

Then again, maybe he *should* go speak to the ship's doctor. Might even be able to whizz some sleeping pills from him.

He had a love for trying new pills. It was somewhat of a hobby. The best he'd ever had was a blue one with a yellow dot in the centre that wasn't exactly an E.

It was better!

He'd felt like Katrina and the Fucking Waves for three days! And talk about hard-on, he'd shagged eight or nine girls, and possibly two boys — he couldn't quite remember — before he'd collapsed of exhaustion, sleeping off the twelve-hour come-down. Then he had thrown himself into the shower and taken matters into his own hands as he recounted the explicit memories; the faces, positions, mouths, eyes, terror, delight, flesh, blood. Bodies.

Vince had cleaned up after him. He always did.

Good ole reliable Vince.

Without really thinking about where he was going he found himself stood before the open-planned waiting area of the Medical bay.

The place looked deserted. No receptionist, no nurse . . . no other people. He was about to leave the sterile half-room that smelt of disinfectant and French vanilla, when the greyest, most miserable-looking man he'd ever seen emerged from the room opposite.

Looking like a mortuary assistant in a lab-coat, the man struggled to focus on him.

'Yes?' he said, trying — with little success — to cover the slur in his voice.

'I was looking for a doctor.'

'I'm a doctor.' He announced the fact as though in expectation of a medal or — at the very least — a round of applause. 'What do you want?'

Wow. Nice bedside manner!

'I've ... I'm suffering with these ... like headaches and sickness ... I was told you could prescribe something stronger than — '

'You shouldn't be bothering me with this. There are plenty of nurses stations on this ship ... they can deal with you.'

'Can they prescribe?'

The doctor squinted in defiance. 'Some of them.' He turned his back on him, heading towards the room he'd just come from.

'I tell you what, how about you give me some painkillers and some sleeping pills,' he said, advancing suddenly on the grey man, 'and I won't report you for being drunk on duty.'

'You can't threaten me. There's CCTV here ... and you — '

'Come on, don't try and kid a kidder. You and I both know you've turned those cameras off.' He smiled carnivorously as the doctor hung his head in defeat.

They stepped inside the room which could have been any standard office in any GP surgery across the country; a desk, a large comfy chair, a computer screen, a second chair — not nearly as comfy-looking as the other. On the desk there stood an all-but-empty bottle of red wine. A large single wine-glass next to it.

'Drinking alone?'

The doctor shot him a look, taking a large bunch of keys from his top drawer.

'Surfing the web?' he pressed, nodding towards the doctor's crotch as he fumbled with the keys to open a second door. The grey man ignored him as he laughed to himself.

Following Dr Drunkard, he stayed close to the wall, waiting as the lights blinked slowly into life. This room was much larger than the previous, pokey little office. It was much more open and even more sterile.

The room was littered with stainless steel everything . . . three benches stood in the centre, two desks lined up against the far wall, another computer and another. There was a vast free-standing medicine cabinet, fridges, lab equipment, instrument trolleys and gurneys; masks and paper suits.

'Wow.' he said genuinely, turning to his left as his took in the room. There he spied eight, small, stainless steel hatches that glimmered and gleamed; four across, two deep. The scents of bleach and polish filled his nostrils.

He'd always liked the smell of bleach. Bleach could kill anything. Even AIDS . . . apparently.

He stepped forward, drawn to the metallic fronts. 'Are they . . .'

'Don't touch them!' snapped the drunken doctor, 'Don't touch anything. I cleaned everything down earlier. This is meant to be a sterile room.'

'They're for bodies aren't they?'

A simple nod.

'Dr Matthews can't stand fingerprints on *anything*, obsessional woman!' he slurred, holding up a spray bottle, 'Had to bleach everything. On my own.' he returned the bottle to a cupboard spilling with bleach-based cleaning products.

'Sounds like demeaning work for a Doctor. You must be in her bad books.' He grinned impishly, moving closer, 'Does she know about your . . .' he inhaled, making an obvious retort at the overwhelming smell of alcohol, '. . . habit?'

'Get out!' the grey doctor hissed suddenly. He slammed the painkillers onto the work-top next to a bowl filled with instruments soaking in sterilising fluid.

'What about the sleeping pills?'

The doctor cocked his head, staring with a renewed intensity through his intoxicated haze.

'Don't I ...'

'What?' he demanded.

'Don't I know you?'

Why? Why did he have to do that? Why even say it?

Maybe there was still time to defuse the situation, to convince the inebriated medic that he had been mistaken.

'No, I don't think so.' he said, reaching for the painkillers. He felt his hand beaten back, swotted like a fly, as the doctor pulled them from him. 'Don't do this.' he warned.

'No, I do know you ... I know your face ...' He was clearly intent on doing this. Shit. 'You're that — '

With surprising speed he plucked a scalpel from the bowl, planting it soundly — and somewhat satisfyingly — in the doctor's drunken head.

Watching the doc' slump to the floor, limbs twitching and sprawling as a bubble of dark and sticky blood crept over the bridge of his nose drew a wry smile from his assailant. His heart fluttered; his breaths light and shallow. It had been so long since he had taken a life with his own hand.

'I did try and warn you.'

Still, he couldn't have been in a better place to deal with this unexpected little distraction. And, in all fairness, it wasn't as if he hadn't enjoyed sticking the blade square in the plastered physician's stupid, dreary face. And at least it was nice and clean!

The other doctor — Matthews — should appreciate that particular facet when she found him ... eventually.

He hauled the body over to the freezer units, feeling a heat of excitement in his stomach. And his trousers. Opening the hatch and sliding out the tray, he tucked the doctor in for the long sleep before returning the tray and shutting the door.

Now to clean up. Good job they were well stocked.

He hummed a merry tune as he set about his task.

Killing ... death, blood, murder ... slaughter. His head swam with a world of possibilities.

It was at this point that Vince usually stepped in, taking over; calming him down. Talking sense and reason.

Think logically ... don't let it get the better of you.

But, Vince wasn't here.

He'd forgotten just how much he enjoyed it all.

How much more he could do? How far could he go? How *creative* could he be now that he was alone? Now that no one could throw restraint upon him.

Ah, Murder. It was the most dangerous and seductive of all his favourite drugs; it was the quiet stranger he had missed for so long. And taking this man's life — this pathetic puke of a medical man — was like the welcoming home of an old friend.

A friend who'd been subdued for far too long.

Chapter Two

'Throw down your weapons!'

Jonathan Prior shouted over the clamour of bullets that ricocheted off the metal beams and breezeblock surrounding him. The deafening *boom* of discharged shotguns and semi-automatics was accompanied by the distinctive, ringing *pop* of at least twelve pistols being fired and reloaded in rapid succession.

But all this noise did nothing to distract him from the one sound he'd never — ever — be able to shake for the rest of his days. A sound that would haunt his dreams for years to come.

The sound of grown men crying.

Good officers and scum sobbing alike as the life seeped from their bodies in ribbons of red. Lying at his feet, Prior's partner clutched the open-wound that used to be his stomach, coughing up blood with every tortured breath.

'Hold on, Yates.' he whispered.

Ducking down behind the crates and junk of the warehouse he removed the empty clip from his gun, slipped in a new magazine and was picking off two more enemies in under thirty seconds. The men were pacified — each shot in the right shoulder — but not dead. Nor were they likely to die from their injuries. Unlike Yates.

His team were bound by rules and red-tape to do their best to protect these low-lives, to bring them down in one piece. One piece that could be questioned afterwards. The last thing the department needed was more bad press; more accusations of police brutality. But what about a botched-up raid? An out-and-out blood bathed shoot 'em up? These scum-bags didn't aim to pacify; they shot to kill.

It pissed Prior off that they'd been sent in so ill-prepared. After months of surveillance, of tailing, under-cover operations and evidence-gathering; after building such a strong case against Simmons and his cronies. But senior management had pushed. And pushed.

Elections were coming up. And the city council wanted to remind the people of Merseyside exactly why *they* were in power and why they should remain there. And it didn't matter if a few uniforms were lost along the way.

It didn't matter that a good DI with a string of appraisals, an unblemished history of service, a wife and three young daughters was bleeding to death at this very moment. What did matter was that the council appeared tough on organised crime and to hell with the lives of his officers and their families.

Fucking politicians. Fucking bureaucratic bastards!

'Fuck this!' he thought.

He needed to clear a path if he had any chance of saving Yates, of calling for extra units. Or paramedics. He'd get Yates to the hospital himself; blues-and-twos it down the M53. There would be no hope in trying to make it back across the water from Birkenhead at this time, but he could get to Arrowe Park Hospital in around five minutes if he floored it. Radio ahead, get Yates seen quickly.

Maybe there was a chance.

But, if he didn't pick off someone important — and quick — they'd sit here shooting at him and his few remaining men like tin-ducks at a fairground stall until they ran out of ammo.

He peered through a gap between a stack of metal barrels to find Keating – Simmons' right-hand man — taking a knife to a young cadet. Prior didn't know the boy personally, but that wouldn't make it any easier when it came to offering condolences to his family. Knowing they would want to be told that his death had been quick and painless.

The boy was screaming, sobbing, begging for his life as Keating sliced at his face, tearing his young flesh and discarding it onto the metal mesh of the upper floor. His hands were tied and he wriggled and squirmed as the knife was suddenly thrust into his thigh and twisted. The boy yelped in agony and pleaded to deaf ears.

Keating's nick-name was *The Scalpel*.

The reasoning behind that name was fast becoming more and more vividly apparent. He was certainly skilled with a blade; a self-professed sick fuck who prided himself on keeping his victims alive and suffering for as long as possible.

As long as *he* liked.

And yet sicker still, laughing and taunting even as the young cadet spat blood and pleaded with them to stop, was the twisted face and head of this mismatched criminal family; the reason they'd all come together in the first place. Jacob Matthew Simmons.

And to think, his mother had given him such a biblical name. The only kind of righteousness Simmons knew was self-righteousness; he was a swindling crook, a thug, a pimp and a general, all-round bastard.

Prior knew he had no other choice. Knew they'd torture the boy for fun, keep him hanging on for hours — or days — if they could.

He had no clear shot at either Keating or Simmons and, cursing under his breath, raised his gun to put a single bullet in the lad's head.

His body slumped to the deck.

He shouldn't have even been here.

Keating turned, pissed that someone had dared to interfere with his *happy-time*, while Simmons, who had just been giggling like a twisted, sadistic schoolboy, was momentarily stunned into silence.

Then suddenly the heavy-looking fire-door behind the pair was thrown open and Simmons moved towards it with such a speed that it caught Prior almost completely off guard.

But, he wasn't about to let them get away so easily.

He moved from his hiding place under heavy fire from Simmons' minions as he darted forward to get a clear shot. Red-hot metal tore through the flesh of his arm, another bored into his thigh as he threw himself painfully against a length of pipes.

But now *The Scalpel* had him in his sights.

Time seemed to slow as events collided in a surge of blood and bullets.

'I told you to stay outside!'

The voice belonged to Simmons. He blocked the fire-escape and the slight figure that stood beyond. A tiny figure, nothing more than a silhouette. A girlfriend, maybe? Who could tell?

One thing was certain, he wasn't getting away this time.

Prior took aim, steadying himself against the wall. He pumped off two rounds.

They found their target. The first severing Simmons' spinal cord at the neck and the second splitting his head wide open, splattering the minute figure that stood before him with brain matter, shattered bone and blood.

In the next moment Prior was thrown forward — *pressed* forward — by a vent of scalding hot air that surged suddenly from the pipe behind him.

It seemed that *The Scalpel* was not only good with a knife, but also incredibly accurate with a gun.

Prior heard a something which sounded totally inhuman. It was somewhere between a scream and a low, rasping moan. He felt the flesh on his back began to bubble and burst. And only in his final moments of consciousness, before the falling crates and barrels pinned him in agony to the dusty cement floor — before he split his head so wide that it would later require sixteen stitches — only then did he realise that the terrible, painful sound had been born in him.

That it had issued from his lungs. And passed his lips.

Prior jumped.

He sat bolt upright in a bed cold and wet with his sweat; a thin, clammy film covering his body. A film that sheathed his lean torso and solid abs. His scarred back.

A perfect bead rolled down between his eyes and over his strong nose as he panted, trying desperately to regulate his breathing. To regain control.

It was just a dream. Just a dream.

A nightmare.

A memory.

He pressed his palms into the mattress, trying to steady himself, pushing back the bile that torched its way up from his stomach. *Come on, Jon. Get a grip!*

He looked at the digital clock on his bedside table. **08:05.**

Shit!

Why hadn't his alarm gone off? Maybe it had. Maybe he'd hit the snooze button in his sleep again. That was happening more and more lately.

And it wasn't just the getting-up he was having trouble with, but actually getting to sleep in the first place.

He swung his legs off the mattress and, wiping his face — massaging the sleepy skin — he forced himself to his feet.

Quick shower today.

Then again, it usually was.

As he passed the bathroom mirror he caught a glance of the scarring that crept across his back and his right shoulder; a mass of thick, white webs spun across torched-red flesh that still looked tender fifteen years on. Scarred tissue creeping over his collar bone like a long, bony finger; the hand of Death reminding him just how close he'd come to never leaving that warehouse.

He'd stopped trying to hide the pencil-mark scar that cut back from his hairline a long time ago. It was visible, but not all that noticeable.

Unless you were looking for it.

Prior exhaled a sigh. It was the breath of an apology. The same apology he'd made silently to his team all those years ago; that he had made with every breath he had taken in and exhaled ever since that day. That awful day when he had been the only one to survive.

One of eighteen.

He supposed that made him lucky. But that didn't stop him feeling guilty. It only made things worse.

Come on, you self-pitying dick.

He reprimanded himself, turning on the shower. Checking the temperature was only degrees above luke-warm, the ex-DI stepped inside the awful, cream, plastic cubicle.

The bile rose in his throat once more.

09:40

Saturday 14th May, 2011

He stirred. Groggily. Head still thumping.

Where the hell . . .

Ah. It came back to him. The sea; the nausea; the opera; the headache; the Polish girl; the nausea; the doctor . . . the doctor!

A self-satisfied, satanic grin spread across his face as he rubbed his eyes. Sitting up, he took stock of the lavish room that Vince had clearly spared no expense in booking. Good. At least he'd be travelling in style, even if he did feel sick as a dog!

Painkillers!

He searched the bed frantically. Picking up his trousers, he went through his pockets. He found his cardkey, four pound twenty-six in change, a pre-rolled joint, a lighter . . . but no painkillers.

He hadn't . . . Oh, he fucking had! He'd left them in the Medical bay!

Fuck! After all that!

Still, at least he had the joint.

He crawled on his stomach towards the glass doors. They opened inwardly and would lead anyone who'd actually be crazy enough to want to go out there onto a dark-wood decked balcony.

He pulled the left door open. Just a crack. There was a wrought-iron and glass patio table with a parasol and two matching chairs bolted to the deck outside.

Not that he'd be sitting in either of the chairs!

Lighting up, he rolled onto his back, inhaling deeply. The sweet, sweet green calming him; numbing him with every drag. Working its way across his brain; snaking towards his pain receptors.

He lay this way for several minutes, contented. Drifting.

Ah, yes. That was so much better.

Dragging his last hit down to the roach he held onto the smoke, tossing the butt outside and slowly exhaling through his nose. He turned over and lay on his stomach for several minutes more. Eyes closed. Breathing in the salty air.

Maybe this wasn't so bad after all. Being at sea.

He could feel the soft motions of the ship on the water; he was even *acknowledging* the fact he was actually on water instead of trying to convince himself otherwise. The air was fresh and nice and full of potential. The potential to sit outside and enjoy himself, to bask in that morning sun that was already delightfully warm.

He opened his eyes just as a stray wave splashed up, spraying the decking. Spraying his face.

Fuck that!

Throwing the door shut, he turned and rolled — army-style — towards the centre of the room before hauling himself on his elbows across the lush, cream carpet towards the bathroom. Once inside, he pulled down the toilet lid and sat there, head in hands, breathing deeply.

Though the joint had numbed the pain in his head greatly, it was still present. Nagging behind his eyes, drumming his temples from the inside, squeezing at the base of his skull like a ferret clamping onto his spinal cord! Gnawing. Gnawing.

He looked up and out across the room. It was fairly neat! But then it was early days yet.

Suddenly, and with great delight, his pale blue eyes fell upon the untouched mini-bar.

Thank you, God!

How had he missed that before now?

Snatching the cardkey from the bed, he swiped it through reader on the side of the fridge and opened the door. Oh, well-stocked heaven of alcoholic beverages!

Taking two vodka miniatures and a blue-canned energy drink from the top shelf he scooted back to the bathroom, careful not to notice the watery view in his periphery as he went.

He burst the packaging on one of the non-descript plastic tumblers that were always provided in hotel bathrooms then emptied one tiny bottle of vodka into the tumbler before opening and pouring in half a can of the honey-coloured fizzy drink. While it settled he opened the second vodka bottle, swigging half of it in one shot.

He grimaced and shook his head, pouring the remainder into the tumbler.

Sitting on the toilet once more, drink in hand, he leaned back against the cool tiles, sipping at the drink and feeling his brain begin to spark as he recalled the events of the previous night.

He sat there, smiling. Contemplating death.

Not his own. No, God no, that would be morbid!

He thought of death; the act.

Of physically holding the life of another in his hands ... and slowly ... slowly squeezing. The pure, unadulterated pleasure of it burst like the golden bubbles on his tongue.

A vibrant thrill tickled inside his stomach. It stirred at his groin.

Yes, the sea air *was* full of potential. Just not the sort he'd first imagined.

There was the potential here — miles away from land and coppers — to get really creative with death. Unbridled and free from Vince — for all his good intentions — he could finally make his mark.

So ... where to begin?

10:15

Saturday 14th May, 2011

Christine Kane sat in the conservatory beyond the *Grande Central* restaurant. She had been relieved to find the doors open, though it was still incredibly humid inside.

Her polished cane was leant against the soft-cushioned chair next to her and — as was her usual routine for this time — she was busy updating her journal with her thoughts, her views and her feelings concerning the events of the previous night. Though she had already managed to fill two pages on that particular subject upon returning to her room after leaving Kelly that evening!

Sleep had been nowhere in sight and simply could not be tempted near. Even after a shower and a glass of red as she slipped under the crisp, new duvet of the luxurious double bed; even as she ate up the latest chapters of her favourite author. She was simply nowhere near tired enough to drift off and sleep.

No matter which way she had tried to occupy her brain, her thoughts would return to settle around the idea that this big, comfy bed would be an awful lot comfier and somewhat more exciting if a certain someone were sharing it with her.

Stop it!

She was feeling giddy again; butterflies in the pit of her stomach. It was stupid. She was acting like a doe-eyed school girl, lusting after ... after ... the successful and confident young woman she'd met only the night before. The virtual stranger to whom she had even given her number!

She *never* did that!

She knew she was falling for the raven-haired artist with the amazing blue eyes.

Who was she kidding? She had *already* fallen for her.

This woman who was fifteen minutes late for their breakfast date. No, not a date. A meeting. Or was it a date? No, it should definitely — for the time being at least — be a friendly breakfast meeting between two people interested in getting to know one another. But then, wasn't that a date?

Oh, damn it!

Not that it mattered if she didn't bother to show up.

Then she'd be glad it hadn't been a date after all. She had never been stood up by a woman before and didn't plan to be on her first ever date with one.

Not that this was a date!

'Would you like to order breakfast now, Dr Kane?'

The friendly, young waitress had been twice since she'd seated her; once to refill her coffee and once to asked that same question. But, that had been over thirty minutes ago. And Christine was beginning to feel the waking growl of the hunger that had been slumbering inside her stomach.

She smiled at the blonde-haired girl who waited patiently.

'I'm waiting for someone.' she said.

The waitress returned her smile with a small nod and shifted her weight to continue serving other guests.

'Actually,' Christine conceded, 'Can I have the full English without mushrooms or black pudding, please?'

'Sure.' The waitress laughed, scribbling her order, 'D'you want toast with that?'

'Please.'

'White or brown?'

'Brown.'

'Marg or butter?'

'Oh, butter.' Christine smiled, 'Definitely butter.'

'Coming right up.'

Christine returned her attention to her journal, spelling out KELLY LIVINGSTONE for the umpteenth time.

God, she had it bad!

But, there was still no sign of Kelly.

Good job it wasn't a real date.

10:15

Saturday 14th May, 2011

Up on deck.

He felt pretty pleased with himself; with his accomplishments so far. He didn't dare walk too near to the edge, just kept to the centre of the top deck, already crowded with couples, laughing and sunbathing. And children — too many children — running around without a care.

How could they do that? How could they run around like that? Without fear or hesitation! He apparently needed a strong smoke and a double vodka before he could even brave the idea of the open air. It would take a lot more to get him running around!

He shuddered.

Congregations of older people hovered on the upper terrace, or reclined on the sun-loungers well away from the pool below with its noise and its water slides and hordes of yet more spoilt children being shooed from their disinterested parents as they longed to be simply left alone. *They* were on holiday too, after all!

He made his way towards a little Tikki-hut bar, cardkey in hand. As he moved past a crowd of Geordie lads he caught a glimpse of a dark-haired girl in the centre of their midst. Seeming to feel his gaze she looked up, locked eyes and smiled.

Her smile was warm and inviting and — even as she continued her conversation with the excitable boys — her amazingly dark eyes remained on him until, despite himself, she had coaxed from him a genuine smile in return.

He queued at the bar, still eyeing the latte beauty who he now recognised as the main character from the god-awful opera that he had been unfortunate enough to witness the night before. She was even finer in real life than she had looked on the stage. Curvaceous and confident with the tightest, most delicious-looking arse he had ever seen; barely covered in a tiny pair of cut-off denim shorts.

A torn white t-shirt with some colourful image on the front hugged her perfect breasts — and he didn't use the word *perfect* often, but, fuck, they were perfect — revealing the soft flesh of her mid-riff; her toned, flat stomach and neat, little bejewelled bellybutton, that sparkled with a sapphire stone.

He wondered whether and — more importantly — *where* she might have any other piercings.

Oh, just the sight of her made him ache. And he couldn't help but contemplate what kind of sounds she would make. Yet, strangely, he had no real desire to cut her or hurt her. To place his hands around her throat and squeeze . . .

No. He couldn't understand it.

Well, maybe a little squeeze of that tender neck after all. But, he liked the way she looked now. He liked this one *alive*. He didn't want to change her, which was a new kind of feeling for him.

But, perhaps a smack or two . . . to get things going. Yeah. Take a nice handful of that lush, dark hair and wind it tightly around. Pull it. She'd be on all fours . . . and that arse . . .

'What can I get you?'

The voice was rough, but not too gruff. A young man trying to sound older than his true age; clearly insecure about something!

He stared at the barman.

'D'you wanna drink, or wha'?'

'Pint of lager.'

The insolent boy questioned him belligerently as to *which* lager he would like. He pointed his reply and threw his cardkey onto the bar, never taking his eyes off the young actress. His mind already playing out the movie he'd like to make with her.

His pint arrived along with the returned card and he drank a delightfully cold mouthful down before approaching the brown-sugar beauty and her dispersing crowd.

'They bothering you?' he asked as the last of the lads drifted away; smitten, gormless and loudly proclaiming his intentions to the rest of the gaggle as he went.

'Were you coming to my rescue?' she laughed.

'Something like that.'

She smiled that warm, friendly smile again and he felt suddenly as gormless as the Geordie who'd just left. 'You were good last night.'

'I don't think we've had that pleasure yet.' she flirted. And again, he couldn't help but smile, his thoughts returning to those he had been so immersed in only moments before.

He raised his eyebrow as he spoke, 'I meant on the stage.'

'Oh,' she pretended, 'So you enjoyed it then?'

'Yeah.' he lied, 'It was great.'

Silence.

'So, what did they want?' he asked.

Why did he care?

'Stag do. They wondered if I'd dance at a private party tonight.'

'And would you?' he asked.

She considered the question for a moment. Considered her answer; her eyes never leaving his. 'If the price was right.'

'And was it?'

She smiled. 'Not yet, but they have the rest of the day to think it over.'

He raised his glass.

'Good girl.'

She beamed at him as if they'd shared some great secret. The kind that was plain for all to see, but which no one picked up on. He downed the pint and returned the glass to the bar. Her smile disappeared.

'Thirsty?'

There was a strange ring to her voice. And that look in her eye.

Surely she wasn't one of those *teetotal* types. He really didn't see the point in that; you had to live a little. And he liked to live *a lot.* He wouldn't apologise for drinking. To anyone.

No matter how cute an arse they had.

'I don't suppose you've got anything to kill a really bad headache?' he said, choosing to ignore her previous comment.

'Is that what you're trying to do?'

He nodded.

She made her way over to the bar, her hips swinging naturally, enticing him. *Follow me . . . follow me. Come and play.* He didn't. Though he wanted to. Desperately.

Bit of self control!

He watched as she spoke to the prick that had served him; stared as she leaned across the bar. That arse again. Mmmm.

And he could only imagine the eyeful Mr Pre-Pubes was enjoying. And yet, with her, it seemed that imagination alone was enough to stir his nether brain into a waking state.

He really couldn't take his eyes off her.

He felt like such a dick!

Clearly he'd gone far too long without shagging something . . . anything. He'd have to put that right. This was just ridiculous! Captivated — no — absolutely, boyishly smitten with some whore of an actress; some latte-skinned female Lothario.

But, still, that fucking arse . . .

'Here.'

She pressed her body against his, slipping her slender fingers inside his trouser pocket. Finding her way. Or so it seemed.

She kept her hand right where it was.

Was she . . . surely she wasn't going to . . . not up here with everyone standing around watching. Not with Grandma Drool less than two metres away, baking in the early-morning sun; that glazed expression on her wrinkled-parchment face. Not with little Johnny Destructive and his friends racing rings around them, dam-busters style!

Surely not.

He struggled to swallow as her short, manicured nails scratched at the thin lining of his pocket, grazing his inner thigh in the most seductive manner. His heart was racing; his downstairs brain throbbing and aching just as violently as the one that rattled around his skull.

She smiled impishly at him. 'See you later.'

With those three departing words she made her way down the steps to the lower deck and back indoors, turning at the last moment to throw a tantalising wink and a wave in his direction.

He closed his mouth.

Yes, apparently he *had* been following her movements all slacked-jawed and bewildered. What a nob!

He thrust his hand deep into his pocket, feeling the corners of something brittle and plastic. He pulled it out.

A blister strip of Ibuprofen.

He shook his head, smiling. 'Fuckin' tease.'

10:15

Saturday 14th May, 2011

Prior's legs ached. His heart pounded furiously as though it were trying its best to burst through his sweat-drenched chest.

But he couldn't give up. Not now. Not when he was so close. He was coming up to the ten kilometre mark on the sleek, GymTech treadmill that whirred and clunked incessantly under his rhythmic footfall. He wiped the sweat from his sopping brow and pushed out another long breath . . . as he sped towards his invisible finish line.

There you go!

He smacked the 'Cool Down' button, exhausted at the thought of another two minutes on his now nicely jellied legs. But he knew the importance of correct cool-down procedure. And the last thing he needed was an excess of adrenaline sitting in his muscle tissue, aching and cramping up while he tried to do his job.

Thirty-nine minutes wasn't bad for a 10K run. It wasn't as impressive as twenty-eight minutes; his average time only two years ago. But then he *was* two years older now. He had always known the day would come when he would have to start listening to his body a little more keenly.

He was nearly forty-three, after all. Yeah, thirty-nine minutes for a 10K run was still quite impressive. Even if it had nearly killed him!

'Hey, Jon-boy!'

He knew that voice. Cringing inwardly, he slowed the treadmill down to a walking speed for the last thirty seconds and smiled as the squat form of Adrian Kemp made his way towards him.

The man never ceased to amaze Prior in his ability to look absolutely dishevelled and bedraggled no matter what he wore. You could dress him in an Armani suit with the finest Italian shoes and still he would resemble a shaggy, great ape more than a human being. Or, at the very least, put you in mind of a freshly washed and starched hobbit.

Prior didn't like to think of himself as capricious or mean-spirited, but, even in his designer gym-wear Kemp struck him as vivid, modern Tolkienian nightmare.

It wasn't just his height — or lack thereof — or his compact stature, or even the chaos of hair that refused to be managed no matter how he tried to style it. It was the wild look in his eye. Prior had seen it before, in others; distant, but untamed. Almost feral.

Unhinged? Maybe.

Still, he seemed to be a pretty decent guy. Even if he did insist on calling him *Jon-boy*. What was that all about? And yet, oddly enough, Adrian Kemp was one of the only people on the *Ianus* that Jonathan Prior was on first-name terms with.

Go figure.

'Adrian.' Prior sighed, stepping off the treadmill.

Other crew members tended to shy away from him socially; matters were always kept very formal whenever Prior was involved. Perhaps it was the job; the title. But then, maybe he liked it that way. Maybe he created and instilled that unease in his colleagues and co-workers as a first-line of defence. Maybe he didn't want to get too close to anyone.

Again.

So why was it different with Frodo?

Prior shook his head, mental slapping himself — one — for getting caught up in psychoanalysing his own thoughts and actions and — two — for being so damn mean!

'Another ten this morning?' Kemp asked.

He handed Prior a fresh hand towel and waited for him to wipe his face and neck, looking briefly at his watch. 'You're a little behind today.'

No way!

Adrian Kemp knew his routine. And not only his routine, but also how long he generally took in that routine.

It was quite simply the creepiest thing Prior had ever experienced and he felt a chill run down his spine.

'Been keeping an eye on me?' Prior asked, taking a swig from his juice bottle.

'Come on, you're like clockwork! You get in here for a quarter past eight, do a few warm-ups, then cardiovascular, the muscle groups and finish with a 10K before hitting the pool. And what is it in there? Twenty-four laps?'

Prior pushed the towel back into Kemp's hands, forcing a smile though he felt strangely violated. 'What are you? My number one fan?'

'No, I just ... I have to do things in a certain way too. Everything has a place and an order and so if something's out of place or out of time ... I just notice.'

Kemp shifted his weight, trying — hopelessly — to fill the silence.

Prior found himself wondering just where about on the autistic scale this male nurse would actually sit. Come to think about it, where would *he* sit? Since he too was clearly entrenched in such an obvious and rigid routine and also suffered a compulsion for numbers in sets and laps!

'I was a bit late getting up this morning.'

'Oh.' said Kemp. 'Not Like you.'

Prior stifled a cringe. 'No.'

There was that silence again.

This time it was Kemp who broke it. 'I know what you how feel. I had to cover for Dr Cunningham this morning. Been rushed off my feet ... which I don't mind, but, it was just unexpected. I had to alter my routine and — '

'Why did you have to cover?' Prior cut in.

'He didn't show up this morning. Dr Mathews has been going mental, snapping at everyone.'

'The woman's a nightmare ... Professionally speaking.'

Kemp smiled. 'She reckons he's back on the booze again.'

'We're only one day in!'

'I know, but he's had trouble ... in the past — '

'I remember.'

'And there's rumours that him and his Mrs have been — '

'Rumours Adrian?' Prior shook his head. Kemp was the Perez Hilton of *Golden Star*. He couldn't help it, he just loved to talk.

To gossip.

It was like verbal diarrhoea when you got him going. And was apparently incurable.

'I know. I know.' he said, holding up his hands. 'But he did polish off a fair amount of wine last night.'

Prior had to give him that. He had seen it for himself.

But, if the man had a problem that he couldn't control he really shouldn't have been cleared for a return to work. It wasn't as though they had an abundance of Doctors on board.

'He's probably just sleeping off the hangover.' Kemp continued, 'I'm sure he'll claw his way into Medical later. Probably just couldn't stand the fury of the Dragon while he's got a bad head.'

'She'll have you for that, if she hears you.' Still, Prior couldn't help but laugh as the image of it nestled itself into his visual cortex; a head-sore Dr Cunningham in full Knight-garb attempting to ward-off a three-headed and scaly Dr Matthews.

'Don't tell her, will you?' Kemp pleaded playfully, 'She'll have me cleaning surfaces for a month! D'you know, sometimes I think about creeping back into the medical bay after everyone's left and simply dragging a great, big smeary hand-print across the front of all that bloody stainless steel.'

'You're a truly scary person, do you know that?'

Kemp smiled. 'The best part is that she wouldn't be able to prove it was me. Even with the prints. I mean, it's not like we have any decent crime scene equipment.'

'Don't I know it. And it's not for lack of trying, I can tell you. But, the *Powers That Be* just don't seem interested. I told them how much time, money and manpower it could save in the long run. But they just see the initial pay out.'

'It's bollocks isn't it.'

Prior nodded absently, 'I'm not happy with Cunningham though. He knows procedure. Even if he is hung-over, he needs to log in with security so that we know he's safe. And he hasn't done that, or at least he hadn't when I stopped in at the office earlier.'

'Sorry.' Kemp said honestly, 'Have I made more work for your now?'

'Keeps me out of trouble.'

Prior threw a pleasant, half-smile at Kemp and made his way out of the gym. He wasn't going to let Cunningham's incompetence disrupt his routine. Twenty-four lengths of the pool before he showered — again — and began his rounds.

Twenty-four lengths.

Just as Kemp had noted.

Prior suppressed another shiver.

11:35

Saturday 14th May, 2011

He followed her. Quietly, cautiously. Always six or seven paces behind her. Now and again he'd let her round the corner, put some distance between them. Just in case. He didn't want to alarm her.

Not right now, anyway.

Up on deck she'd made such a fool of him. Been giving him the come-on and talking about all kinds of shite.

And he'd listened! He'd actually listened to her drivelling on . . . he'd even actively engaged with her. Offered advice on the various, pointless, inconsequential problems she'd droned on and on and on about.

He'd bought her a drink. Well, he'd *cardkeyed* her a drink. But, still.

Stacey Atkins.

Bride-to-be. Degree in Art and Design, just completed a PGCE and gained QTS. Couldn't wait to start teaching in Surrey after the big white wedding to Michael, who — incidentally — was a mortgage advisor or something and . . . blah, blah, blah. He really didn't care.

But, she was having doubts.

Was it too soon? Was she too young? Was this going to be it . . . for the rest of her life? Apparently his family could be quite intense. There had been so many things she had wanted to do, places she had wanted to visit. Which was one of the reasons why Michael had surprised her — and her friends — with this all-inclusive hen-party cruise.

What a guy.

She had pondered aloud on the subject of his family's wealth. They certainly weren't strapped for cash. But was that, in fact, the real reason for her accepting his proposal? Was that the reason! Had she been blinded by the money? Just seen the secure future and . . . agreed?

He didn't care. Really. Didn't. Care.

But, she was good to look at. And the more she moved that big mouth of hers, rolling her tongue around and around, the further his mind wandered towards the idea that he could be putting that particular talent and energy to far better use.

Her blonde hair had bounced about her shoulders, softly framing her animated face as she had continued to bend his ear. Chewing it off more like. And all over nothing!

He'd never understood how — or why — people could get so caught up in these strained relationships. These strangled, tortured things that rendered both parties miserable and alienated.

'Why don't you just leave him?' he'd asked, cutting her off mid-ramble.

'I couldn't do that.'

'Why not?'

'Well … Because.'

As if that was a valid answer.

'Because why?'

She'd finished her drink, replacing the empty glass on the bar. She'd turned to him, staring at him … into him. But, she'd made no attempt at an answer.

'So you love this fella, then?' he had prodded.

'Of course I love him.'

'No you don't.'

'How dare you!'

'If you did you would have said so before. But, you didn't. You said only *because*.'

'I don't have to justify myself to you.'

He'd smiled capriciously. This spoilt, little rich girl wasn't used to being pressed and opposed. She was flustered and he knew it. He felt it.

'Have you ever cheated on him?'

Immediately her gaze dropped.

What was it they said? About the eyes being the windows to the soul? The unspoken truth was like a ten-ton weight anchored to her soul, dragging down her gaze until her head hung so low that it would have been pointless to try and deny it.

She was quiet then. Like a chided child. 'You have. Haven't you?'

'They were mistakes.'

'Mistakes?' he had said with a grin, 'Plural?'

'Only twice. But, two different guys.'

He couldn't help but laugh then and — to his surprise — the faintest of smiles had even curled the corners of Little Miss Not-So-Angelic's lips. 'Well, three's the charm.' he had said, 'Wanna see if I can convince you that there's other options out there?'

This is what he'd struck up the conversation for. It had taken the better part of an hour to get to this point, listening to the bollocks she'd whined on about; turning it all into such a fucking drama!

He hadn't wanted any of that!

And just why she'd felt the need to open up and start divulging ... to him ... he had no idea.

'I beg your pardon?' she had said. Seeming genuinely surprised.

'You heard me. We can go to your room if you want ... or my suite.' He reached out, taking her by the chin, holding her gaze. 'See if we can't broaden your horizons.'

It was all downhill from there.

'Don't take this the wrong way.' she'd said, 'but you're not my type.'

The wrong way! Was there a *right way* to take a statement like that?

'You little slut!' He'd hissed, feeling the slap of her words as if they had been her palm across his cheek. 'It's girls like you that get a fella in trouble. Lead him on until he can't control himself, then say *No, I've changed my mind* and have the cheek to whinge about the consequences.'

'What are you talking — '

'Don't say another word to me.'

Then he had stormed off. Angry, dejected. And horny as hell. But, there were too many people about on the open deck. Too many spectators to remember his face.

He couldn't afford to cause a scene in the open.

But, he knew that eventually she'd leave the safety of the herd and return to her room. So he'd waited. Patiently.

Fairly patiently.

It wasn't one of his better qualities, but still, he had waited.

He hung back again as Stacey rounded another corner. They were now well within the bowels of the ship and, as the day was turning out to be deliciously warm and dry, there was hardly another soul in sight.

Excellent.

Listening as she swiped her cardkey and waiting for the telltale *click* as the lock disengaged, he chose his moment perfectly, bolting quietly from his hiding place to Stacey's room and jamming his foot in the door before it could close.

Stacey swung round curiously. Just in time to see him burst into the room.

The flat of his palm connected with her nose, breaking it instantly. She fell to the floor, clutching her face as he calmly closed the door behind him.

11:50

Saturday 14th May, 2011

Prior pulled himself out of the Olympic-sized swimming pool after only fourteen laps.

He was annoyed with himself for not finishing his usual set and irritated with Dr Cunningham for being so totally irresponsible that he now had to go and check up on him and possibly have to file a written warning against him.

Being Head of Security he got all the best jobs!

He didn't want to have to issue Cunningham with a warning. He understood that people had problems. Sides of themselves they didn't want to share with the rest of the world. Hell, he knew it all too well.

But, when it started to bleed into their professional life, when it started to affect their day to day performance ... well, there were only so many times you could look the other way.

It was a shame too. Captain Andrews had never liked Cunningham. Perhaps he'd spotted the drink problem before the rest of them. Whatever the reason, a written warning — along with the other, smaller misdemeanours in his file — would give Andrews the ammunition he needed to build a strong case against Cunningham. To have him removed and replaced.

Prior didn't want an atmosphere on the ship in the meantime. It was too restricted a space; too contained. Even for the enormous size of it.

He showered and dressed quickly, before making his way to the office.

To the Tin!

Davies smiled absently as Prior pushed in through the sliding glass doors. He didn't return the smile.

'Morning Guv'.' Davies said, pouring a cupful of boiling water from a small plastic kettle. 'D'you want one?' he asked. Turning to look at his superior he saw the thunder in his face. 'Is everything ok?'

Prior shook his head, checking through the day's logs and rotas, looking for any messages. He picked up his security mobile phone — number eight — and checked the battery.

'Have you heard anything from Dr Cunningham?'

Davies shook his head.

Prior sighed, dialling the number — followed by his code — to pick up any voice messages from crew reporting in sick that day. One message. His heart seemed to pause in anticipation as he waited.

It wasn't Cunningham.

A lighting technician had injured her hand whilst rigging in the *Delphic* theatre space and would be out of action for the rest of the week.

Well, at least he knew that the messaging service was working. But that didn't help in locating Cunningham.

'He didn't turn up this morning.' Prior continued, hanging up the call and tucking the phone into the deep, knee-pocket of his black combat trousers. He liked trousers with plenty of pockets. Lots of room for ... stuff.

'D'you want me to go check his quarters?'

Prior flashed a brief smile at Davies. 'You've just made yourself a brew. And I need to go and speak to Dr Matthews anyway, so I'll check in on him on my way.'

'What've you got to go see Dr Dildo for?'

Prior couldn't help but smile. 'You shouldn't call her that. She'll find out, you know.'

'I'll tell her that Kemp came up with it.'

Prior shook his head, laughing. Davies could be a right little shit at times, but he was a shit you could have a laugh with and — as odd as it seemed — Prior felt a sort of paternal duty towards the lad.

'Why Dr ... Why that name, anyway?'

'Cos, she's artificial! There's just no feeling there.' Davies said with grin, 'She does the job all right, but she's not quite the real deal, you know?'

Prior shook his head again, stifling a laugh, 'She's a perfectly ... adequate doctor.'

'Yeah, and a dildo is a perfectly adequate substitute. But, it isn't real. It's numb.' Davies laughed out loud and watched Prior for a moment, knowing that the Security Chief understood him perfectly and maybe even agreed with him. A little. 'So, come on then. What is it?' he pushed, 'You're not out of Viagra already are you?'

'Cheeky bastard! Like I ever get the chance.'

'I don't know, Guv'. There's a few people on board with a bit of a thing for you.' Davies paused, 'I don't see it personally, but, there's no official check on individual taste is there. Although, you think they'd pick something up on the mental stability assessments!'

'D'you know, it's a good job I like you.' Prior said, 'Anyway. Right. I'll be back shortly.' He made his way through the small office, pausing as he reached the door and turning back to Davies. 'And anyway, Viagra? Just, how old do you think I am?'

'It's not just about age, Guv'.' Davies grinned, pulling a packet of rich tea biscuits out of the metal cabinet draw, 'there's all sorts that can affect your, er ... performance, you know. At least that's what they're saying on the telly.'

'Well, there's nothing affecting me apart from a lack of opportunity.'

'Denial doesn't help either, you know.'

'You're going the right way for a slap, you lad.'

Davies chuckled and dunked the biscuit into his cup, throwing a wink at Prior as he pushed out of the room with a small grin on his face.

Making his way through the ship, he soon found himself stood before Dr Cunningham's door.

Knocking. Waiting. Knocking a second ... third, fourth time.

No answer.

Shit.

Now he was officially AWOL. Now there would be no way of avoiding a written warning.

'Cunningham.' Prior said to no one but himself, 'You daft bastard.'

12:40

Saturday 14th May, 2011

Kelly pressed into the *Grande Central* conservatory, grappling with the heavy glass door as she struggled not to spill her black coffee all over the battered portfolio tucked under her arm.

Christine was sat in the far corner. Near an open door. Thank the gods for a breeze!

Thank them too that she was still here at all.

Pleasantly surprised, Kelly made her way towards her new-found friend knowing that she herself would never have waited *this* long for some random girl she'd only just met. Especially when it was looking more and more likely that she was going to be stood up.

But, Christine was still here. What a diamond.

Did that mean she was interested? As in *interested* interested. Or maybe it was just one of those 'comes with age' things; a greater sense of patience. Either way, she was more than pleased to see Christine who — seeming to sense her presence — looked up and beamed a full-toothed, glimmering brown-eyed smile as she approached the table.

'I was worried I might have missed you.' she said taking the seat opposite Christine and hauling the portfolio onto the chair besides her.

'I was beginning to think you might have changed your mind.' she said, in soft accented tones. And though she strived to keep a lightness to it, there was an unmistakable break, a twinge of something like sadness in Christine's voice.

Kelly felt instantly, horribly guilty. Which — she noted — was unusual for her.

While Christine did not seem embarrassed by the emotion which had just betrayed her, she did appear more than a little bit eager to move the conversation along. 'But, here you are, so . . . . have you eaten?'

'No. I just grabbed this on the way. Help me wake up.'

'You just woke up?'

'Not long ago, yeah.' said Kelly, stifling a grin at the mock-reprimand as she sipped her coffee.

'At least I know you weren't just messing me around then. You know, contemplating whether or not to come and meet me at all .... Should I stay? Should I go? Should I forget the whole thing or simply play hard to get.'

'Wow ... you've been thinking about this a lot.'

'I've had the time to.'

'Ouch.'

'Besides, I'm a psychologist.' Christine continued as Kelly feigned a wounded look, 'It's kind of what I do. When you spend as much time as I do trying to get inside other people's heads, trying to understand why they do the things they do; how and why they make those decisions ... well, it's a hard habit to break. You can't just ... switch off.'

'So I guess that means you're always turned on.' Kelly said, cheekily, 'Lucky lady.'

Christine flicked her eyebrow, 'You're incorrigible, Kelly Livingstone. I'll give you that.'

'Ooh, I like it when you say my name.'

Kelly took another sip of coffee, her eyes locked on Christine who chuckled, shaking her head. She watched her parted lips as she laughed, spying a small chip in the left front-tooth of Christine's otherwise pristine pearly-whites.

'So ... all this head stuff,' Kelly said, 'does it help?'

'Well, it's enabled me to help the police solve a fair few cases in the past.'

'Yeah? Like through profiling killers and stuff?'

'Amongst other things.' Christine said with a nod.

'And what did the Coppers make of you, then?'

Christine's half-smile was a stifled mirroring of Kelly's wide, impish grin as she contemplated her answer. 'They ... warmed to me. Eventually.'

'I bet.' Kelly said, finishing her coffee. She leaned forward, sliding the mug across the table, out of the way. 'So, who gets to analyse you?'

'Oh no. No, No one should ever have to suffer *that* particular ordeal.'

Kelly cocked her head. Waiting.

Silence.

She really wasn't budging.

'Is that why you carry this around?' she ventured, nodding towards Christine's journal.

For the briefest of moments Kelly watched as the brown-eyed beauty before her flushed a deep crimson; purple flecks suddenly mottling the curve of her cheeks.

'I suppose I do self-analyse more than enough to make up for anyone else having to do the job.' she said, resigned.

'Well, if you ever need to air anything ... out loud, I mean ... sometimes a problem shared is a problem halved. That's what they say, isn't it?' Kelly paused, thinking for a moment as that small, curling smile returned to Christine's lips, 'Although in my case it's usually "a problem shared is equal to the hypotenuse of a right-angled pain-in-the-arse divided by the amount of time invested in any given circumstance and multiplied by the enjoyment of that particular engagement"!'

Christine laughed out loud, trying not to spill the last of the tea in her cup. 'You're insane!'

'Is that your *professional* opinion, Dr Kane?'

'It may be the basis of a good, solid preliminary diagnosis, yes. Dr Livingstone.'

'Oh, don't.' Kelly shuddered, 'At least you deserve your title, you worked for it . . .'

'And I'm sure you worked for yours too.'

'Maybe. I suppose. But, mainly I just did it to shut my Gran up!'

'Oh?'

'She's, well . . . she's a formidable woman. And by that I mean scary as shit!' Kelly said, nodding emphatically, 'I was practically drafted into doing my Phd!'

Another silence descended, heavy and thick. Kelly took in a deep breath and exhaled slowly, her eyes falling away from Christine entirely, 'My mum and dad had been putting money away for me since I was born . . . they had wanted me to go to university and do well for myself.'

'They must be very proud of you.'

Kelly smiled sadly, 'I know what you're doing.'

Christine held up her hands. 'How old were you when it happened?'

'Five. This police officer and — I think — a social worker picked me up from school. I'd been waiting ages. They took me to . . . I don't know . . . a foster house. I only stayed the one night.'

'What happened?'

'D'you mean did I run away?'

'No.' Christine paused, then reconsidered. 'Did you?'

Kelly shook her head. 'They took me to my Gran's the next day. She'd been at the Bingo hall the day before. Always tryin' her luck that woman . . . and to be fair, she usually did quite well. Rarely came home empty-handed, even if she only won a tenner.'

'Lucky lady.'

'Oh, she was.' Kelly shifted in her chair and shuddered, clearing her throat. And Christine knew that was the end of *that* conversation. For now.

'So, are you going to allow me the opportunity to take a look at your work?' she asked evenly.

'I don't know. Would you let me read your journal?'

Christine eyed Kelly. This one *was* a test. 'One day . . . I might allow you to suffer that unfortunate pleasure.'

Kelly smiled, 'Then I'll look forward to that day with a spring in my step and a song in my heart!'

Christine laughed out loud once more. 'You really are a crazy, crazy lady, Kelly Livingstone. And that *is* my professional opinion.'

'Well good. 'Cause you know what they say, Doc . . . Two's company.'

13:00

Saturday 14th May, 2011

Prior rounded the corridor and entered the Medical Bay with such an intense speed that the duty nurse physically jumped, spilling a tray of freshly sterilised instruments across the non-slip vinyl floor.

'Natalia!' Dr Matthews hissed as she flitted from one surface to the next, then to the pc, the cabinet, another surface and back again. Prior had no idea what she was doing.

Looking busy. He thought.

The nurse stuttered an inaudible apology while the look on her face conveyed her hopes of being swallowed up by the ground she was now kneeling on.

'Now they will all need to be sterilised again. As if there isn't enough to be done!' she said, turning on Prior like a predator. 'And what do you want?'

'Excuse me?'

'I'm sorry, Prior. I'm a little stressed at the moment.'

'Cunningham still hasn't shown up then?'

'How did you know?' she asked, an odd expression pinched across her tight face.

'Because, I've spent a good chunk of my morning looking for the daft ...' Prior stopped himself. He wasn't with Davies or Kemp, or any of the other lads now. It hadn't been a great morning, but that was no excuse to forget himself. 'I've just come from his quarters. There was no response there and no one's seen him since last night.'

'Did you see him at dinner ...' she said, before mouthing; *With the wine?*

'I think everyone saw it.' he said. *And I don't think you helped matters much.* 'He was supposed to be on duty last night, right?'

He knew the answer, but still.

'Yes.' Dr Matthews nodded furiously, her head bobbing about like a nodding Churchill on the parcel shelf of a car.

'Do we know if he turned up at all? Did he swipe in?'

'Yes.' Dr Matthews said as she led Prior to a small card reader near the freezers. Swiping her own card through, she swiftly keyed in several dozen numbers to access the main menu and from there scrolled down to *recent activity*. 'That's odd.'

'What?'

'Dr Cunningham swiped in, but he didn't swipe out.'

'Has he ever forgotten to do it before?' Prior asked.

Dr Matthews hesitated. 'No. Never.'

Sensing that there was more to this than she was giving voice, Prior pressed her.

'What is it? Doctor, we are literally minutes away from me having to file a Missing Person's here. And there's only so many places you can go missing on a ship. D'you know what that means?' Prior paused, 'All-stop. Ship's engines turned off, which is a nightmare in itself. And then I have to send my men in the waters to try and recover what I can only hope won't be a bloated body ... so please, if you know something, *now* is the time to tell me.'

'Natalia, wait outside.' Dr Matthews barked. She sighed, long and heavy, as the petite, chestnut-haired nurse left the room. 'I shouldn't be protecting him anyway. It's his problem ...'

'Look, I know about his drinking — '

'Of course. Everyone knows about the drinking!' she said, her stern expression softening ever so slightly, 'Stuart had problems. But, then we all have problems. I was trying to help him ... thought if he was working he wouldn't dwell on ... other things.'

Prior thought about asking her what exactly she meant by *other things*, but time was against him now. 'How,' he said, 'How did you help him?'

'I ... I forged his medical examination documents.'

'You did what?' Prior exclaimed.

'I'm telling you this because I'm worried about him, but it can go no further. Do you know what could happen to me? And it was only something simple. Tiny. Easy to overlook.'

'I think you'd better let me be the judge of that.' Prior said, folding his arms across his chest.

'All I did was give him a clean bill of health.' Matthews paused. Prior raised his eyebrow. 'I said that he'd stopped smoking.'

'That's it?'

'That's it? Yes, that's it!' Dr Matthews said, annoyed. 'What were you expecting? That he was snorting ketamine? Injecting Diacetylmorphine when my back was turned? No. He smoked. He *still* smoked. Even though he was supposed to have stopped ... Captain's regulations for Medical staff ...'

'I didn't think he had the authority to ...'

'Apparently so.' Matthews cut in, 'I wanted to help Stuart. So I said that there was no nicotine present in his system; that he'd been at least six months without a cigarette. I did this for him. So that Captain Andrews would agree to have him back on board. Which, he did. Reluctantly.'

Prior nodded, remembering some of the mistakes Cunningham had made last season.

'But he hadn't given up. And I know he used to slip out the back there,' she pointed beyond the freezers and medical cabinets to a discreet exit, tucked away, 'it leads out onto a bit of balcony. Not very big. But, he'd go out three or four times a night for a smoke, which was fine really. It wasn't harming anyone else ... and it seemed to help him cope.' she paused, 'Only … when I opened up this morning there was a near-empty bottle of red wine in the office. One glass.'

'Jesus! He could have gone out there for a smoke and fallen overboard!' Prior said in horror and disbelief, 'Why didn't you say something earlier?'

'Because I didn't think of it like that … I hadn't … I just didn't think. I was angry before. Annoyed with Stuart. I thought he was just sleeping off a stupid hangover and leaving me to deal with everything on my own. Cleaning up after him as usual. But, now … well, what if that *is* what happened?'

Prior shook his head angrily. 'I need to speak to Captain Andrews.'

'You can't say — '

He didn't wait to hear her protests. Striding across the Medical Bay, he left Dr Matthews to her wondering; to her suppositions and her guilt.

16:40

Saturday 14th May, 2011

He puffed on a menthol cigarette. One of Stacey's cigarettes. He had never tried them before — he'd certainly never buy them himself! — but, she wasn't going to need them now.

He lay back on a recliner, staring at the cloudless sky. This whole *being at sea* thing really wasn't so bad if he just concentrated on the sky and tried not to think about the open ocean beneath him.

His stomach lurched.

He lifted his head, raising the shades that covered his blue eyes and blinking in the bright sunlight. Silently, he summoned a wandering member of the ever-present bar-staff and gestured to his empty pint glass. The young-looking lad nodded, taking up the empty along with his cardkey and returning swiftly with a fresh glass of cold, amber-coloured nectar; a small head of bubbles glistening in the sunlight.

'Thanks.'

It was one of the few words he'd uttered since leaving Stacey — or what was left of Stacey — in her room.

Despite her best efforts she had been unable to please him. To do anything for him!

He had imagined shooting his mounting load into the mouth of that foxy little bride-to-be; he thought he'd smile as he watched her drinking down his own frothy liquor, reeling in delight as he relaxed back into the shiny white tub that stood inside her pokey little bathroom.

But, no.

There'd been nothing. No sign of life down there at all.

And it wasn't for a lack of trying on her part. No, Stacey had given all she that she could ... given her life even, which went some way towards making up for the rudeness of her dismissive comments earlier.

this was upsetting and served no purpose

Not my type! Ha!

She had sucked and licked, nibbled and teased, but all to no avail. She had even kept her promise not to scream or shout and he had liked that ... that small sense of cooperation. Of acceptance.

And then, eventually, he had lost his patience.

He couldn't quite remember when it happened, when it all changed. When *he* had changed.

He remembered taking a fistful of her thick, yellow hair and lifting Stacey's tear-stricken face; looking into those cloudy, hazel eyes one last time with a twisted, lop-sided grin.

The perfect imitation of undiluted evil.

Then — suddenly the picture of calm — he had proceeded to smash her face against the side of the bath. Once. Twice. Three times. More.

Her cheek had splintered under the soothing, balanced, rhythmic process that seemed to bring both peace and excitement to every inch of him simultaneously.

It quelled some deep, dark desire that he couldn't explain or even locate in its fullest sense. And yet it had spurned in him a new desire; to delve deeper into that darkness.

Like the feeling of extinguishing a flame in a dark wood with the knowledge that it is your only light; that point when fear and excitement tingle every sense and touch every nerve. When the mind screams out to light the flame anew, but that sensation ... oh, that sensation. It is too strong. Too seductive.

He smiled and gulped down several mouthfuls of lager. Savouring the taste as he did the memories; already wanting more. To create, to experiment ... to perfect.

He had had fun with Stacey then.

Forget the sex!

This was so much more ... satisfying. It was intense and raw and so much more ... just *more* ... than a simple exchange of bodily fluids.

And who would have thought it? That floating out here in his long-held idea of hell, he had found his own little corner of paradise.

If only it could never end. Imagine what he might achieve!

A climax so grand they'd have to come up with a new name for it! Artistic, bloody delight; sensuous, exploratory physical grandeur like no man or woman had ever known!

Was he mad? Was this what madness felt like?

'Well,' he whispered to himself, 'bring it fucking well on, if it is.'

Out here was a world of untold possibilities. Untapped potential for a newly self-discovered life-form such as he. A place to create and to hone and to enjoy every excruciating and delightful moment of it.

Boom!

That sensation. It rattled his chest once more. Gripped him; shook him. He felt it pulsing between his legs; in his gut; and his pitiless heart.

It was growing stronger. His breaths quickened ever so slightly, but he needed to keep control. At least for a little while.

He wasn't too concerned about anyone finding Stacey anytime soon. He had taken a mobile phone from the little princess, in which she had very kindly created a group of all the friends joining her on this trip. Typing a message with little difficultly and adding the obligatory kisses at the end that he assumed Stacey would herself have added (she struck him as that kind of girl), he selected *Send to*, then *Group*, then *Hen Party*.

And it was done.

He had momentarily contemplated keeping the phone. Not something he would normally do, but it was so slim and sleek and shiny and far more advanced than anything he had seen before. It could do everything bar opening a tin of beans!

Which was good, as he didn't like beans.

He had immediately realised what a stupid idea that would be; what a mistake. And he wasn't about to risk getting caught for the sake of coveting a little piece — all be it a very desirable little piece — of technology. He wasn't about to give up this brave new world so easily!

Stubbing out the cigarette, he finished his drink, the bubbles sliding over his tongue and down his throat; bursting and tingling. An echo of that which tingled — even now — in his stomach and below; in every private place that desire can take hold.

Making his way off the open deck and down to the main reception area, he stopped at a map, a colour-coded schematic of the ship at all levels. He scanned it, quickly discovering that the engines and engineering section in general were coloured in a slightly odd off-green He followed the map and discovered that engineering was located several decks below and aft of his current position.

Aft! He smiled at how nautical he suddenly sounded.

Who'd have guessed it?

As he made for the stairs that would take him back into the bowels of the ship he heard a ruckus coming from the medical bay. For a moment he wondered whether they'd discovered Dr Drunkard.

Oh, he would enjoy watching that scene unfold!

But, the noise didn't seem … excited enough for it to be that particular event!

As he stared past the frosted glass divider that marked the outer waiting area of the medical bay, a uniformed man in his twenties with a shock of blonde hair and an armful of folders stumbled out of the doors that he knew — from experience — led to the room of stainless steel and bright lights. And freezers.

Distracted by the female voice shouting harsh instructions at him from the room within, the Blonde Shock staggered straight into him sending the pair crashing to the ground along with the tower of folders in his arms; spilling a sea of A4 across the floor.

'I'm so sorry.'

His initial reaction was to call the man a *dickhead*, drag himself up and continue on his way. But, he immediately thought better of it. It was obvious from his uniform that the guy worked in security. This could be a valuable opportunity. One he might not come across again.

He started picking up the pieces of paper that had scattered far and wide.

'It's no problem,' he lied, 'these things happen. Let me help you.'

'Thanks.'

'Sounds like you've got enough on your plate.' He said, nodding towards the medical bay.

'Oh, Dr Dildo's got her knickers in a right twist today — '

The Blonde Shock of Scouse cringed even as the words left his mouth.

'Dr — '

'Shit!' he cut in, 'Sorry. Please don't tell anyone I said that. She's just a bit pissed off. Shit! She'll kill me if she finds out . . .'

'Your secret's safe with me.' He laughed and continued to pick up the pieces of personal information, scanning them as quickly as possible, before slipping them into the nearest folder. They were mostly crew evaluation and medical reports from what he could tell. 'What's she so upset about?'

The blonde hesitated. For a moment. 'A member of her staff seems to be missing.'

'Missing?' he intoned. 'On a ship?'

'That's the worrying part.'

'So, what're you doing with these?' he nodded to the files, 'will they help you find him?'

The blonde eyed him once more. 'I hope so.' he said, slowly.

'I suppose it must be difficult. Being all self contained and what-have-you. You can't call in extra help like you could if you were on land . . .'

'Tell me about it.'

'And I don't suppose there's a lot of help in terms of forensics and stuff, eh?

'You're very . . . curious, aren't you?' said the Blonde Shock as he stacked the folders once more.

'Sorry. I've always been the same. My uncle worked on some crime scenes in Wales.' he said, not entirely lying. Without his uncle there would have been no scene to investigate! 'I've always been interested, you know. I wanted to follow him . . . but I didn't get the grades and . . . well . . .'

He fell to silence, allowing the young, blonde officer to make the next move. Would his story of unfulfilled dreams be enough to reel him in?

Silence.

Then.

'If I'm honest with you, it's not the best.' Jack pot! 'We don't even have a permanent database on the ship; no criminal records, forensic records, nothing! We have to log everything, send it back to the *Golden Star's* Central Investigations Unit, who then contact the relevant medical and police departments and what-have-you. *They* have access to all kinds of databases, but it costs too much — apparently — for us to have that kind of access at sea. Something to do with *Ocean Satellite* and their bandwidth prices. But, then, *Ocean* do have the monopoly on all that and, well, *Golden Star* are simply too tight to pay. Cheap bastards!'

It seemed as though the blonde security officer had been keeping that particular rant locked up for some time and once the tiniest drop had begun to leak, the rest was quick to follow.

He imagined this officer and his colleagues sat around a table discussing the hardships of their job and the piss-poor decisions of the penny-pinchers back at *Golden Star* HQ.

For him, however, this was delightful news. Just what he'd been hoping to hear.

'I'm sorry.' he feigned, 'it must be frustrating.'

The blonde nodded. 'And time consuming. I suppose they think that 'cause we're at sea the suspects haven't got nowhere to go, but that's not entirely true either. There's life boats and all sorts. If someone had enough knowledge about them ... you get the picture.'

He nodded.

'So, what do you do?' asked the blonde muscled man, standing now and dusting himself down absently.

Handing the last of the folders back to the officer, he smiled, 'I'm an Artist.'

'Yeah?' came the pleasant reply, 'We seem to have loads of artists on board this time. You'd think there was some kind of convention going on or something!'

'Is there?' he asked, suddenly. Eagerly.

'No. Not that I know of. Just some mad coincidence I suppose.'

He nodded, surprising himself with his own disappointment at hearing this news.

'Thanks for your help.'

'No problem.' he said.

'My name's Marc, by the way. Marc Davies.'

I didn't want to know your fucking name.

This — by all unspoken laws of polite society — meant that Marc now wished to know his name. And — under the same laws — it would be completely impolite and improper (not to mention suspicious) to not give a name in return.

Shit!

But then, recounting their conversation and feeling suddenly quite safe within the anonymity of this self-contained, tin world, he did something he'd never done with a stranger before.

'I'm Leigh.' he said, his heart pounding in his throat as Marc extended his hand and he — in an almost trance-like state — took a hold and shook it firmly.

'Nice meeting you. I hope to see some more of you. And thanks again.'

Leigh smiled, releasing Marc's hand. 'Yeah.'

As he turned to leave, Marc threw a glance back at Leigh; a full, sparkling white-toothed smile spread wide across his face. Leigh watched him move down the corridor.

What the shit just happened?

Had he, in fact, just given up his name — his actual name — to a junior member of the *Sea Police*? Yes. Yes he had!

And had that same fella — all be it a strikingly handsome young fella in a uniform — just openly come-on to him? Again, he'd have to go with *yes.*

Yes! He was pretty certain that between the exchange of names, the handshake, the glance, winning smile and the *see some more of you* comment that he had, in fact, just managed to pull a member — a male member — of the security team!

Well. That was different!

Turning towards the stair-well once more, something caught his eye. It was a missed piece of paper from the many strewn papers that Marc Davies had managed to spill all over the place. He picked it up.

It was a passenger list.

He scanned it quickly, but could not find his own name — though there were plenty of passengers named 'Lee' on there to satisfy Marc, were he to check. Vince had obviously got him on board using a fake name. The only trouble was that he didn't know which one was supposed to be his! Not that it mattered much; he could figure it out later.

But, looking at the list it seemed that the Aryan-looking Scouser had been right. There were quite a few names he recognised; artists, musicians, a couple of actors, wags and fag-hags.

Figures, he thought, sardonically as he continued to scan the names.

But on the plus side, with so many celebs about, if he were to be recognised it would be easy enough to convince people that his fame was derived from something other than his handful of true professions; Gangster / Drug-lord / Trafficker / General Crime Boss!

Besides, he was feeling the winds of change. A man could change, couldn't he?

And he had never felt more changed, yet — oddly — more true to himself than when he had announced to Marc Davies, only moments earlier, that he was an *Artist*.

Yes, Doctor Drunkard was bungled. Merely a first step. An overhasty experiment.

But, Stacey, she was his first true work and now — even now — he longed to complete a second. Here, inside this tin-can, adrift on the open ocean — his stomach protested even as he thought of it — he could form a great cannon of work.

He would be appreciated.

Scanning the list still, his eyes came to rest upon a name in the third of four columns. He smiled. He had found the one person who he knew would appreciate his work more than any other.

But, first things first.

He needed to stop the ship.

16:40

Saturday 14th May, 2011

After their breakfast-come-lunch-come-afternoon-tea, Kelly had left Christine with so many questions and, while she had been acutely aware of the psychologist inside her clawing to over-take their conversation, she'd managed to keep the intellectual beast at bay.

Though only just!

Now, alone on her balcony with her old friend, White Zinfandel, and her journal she could no longer contain the animal that longed to analyse the portfolio Kelly had kindly left in her possession.

They had talked for hours. About all sorts.

Even their more serious discussions concerning Kelly's own works, as well as those of other artists, had been punctuated with random conversation, small talk and memories. And Christine had given back as much as she had received, which was unusual for her. Normally she would listen and analyse — yes, analyse as always — but, would very rarely give anything back.

Then again, that was her job. Or had, at least, *been* her job for so many years now.

Had it simply become part of her?

It seemed that people had come to expect it of her and, oddly enough, it seemed that she was pleased to oblige. No doubt an extension of her in-built perfectionism; wanting always to do her best, to be the best that she could be and to please everyone, bar herself.

And why was that?

God! She was a psychologist's field day on her own!

But, with Kelly it was different.

Kelly expected nothing of her. Demanded nothing of her. She was one of the most calming, patient and — despite her outward signs of disregard for certain things — one of the most caring people Christine had ever met.

And yet her art was filled with incredibly violent images and ideas, devastating metaphors and allusions. Her use of colours, bold strokes, shapes and splatter-patterns were — from a psychological point of view — more than a little disturbing.

It concerned Christine. And not just in the usual psycho-analytical sort of way. It concerned Christine because she had already begun to think of Kelly — though she had known her for such a short time — as a friend.

If she were truly honest with herself, she thought of Kelly as more than just a friend. But she still wasn't certain of where she was going to go with that particular train of thinking and feeling.

She sipped at her wine and placed the glass back on the table. It caught the sunlight, sending a prism of colour across a piece of work entitled *Girl with Two Faces*.

The image was interesting to say the least. It cast one half of a young face in a dark blue graphite and ink shadow, while the other was physically lifted from the page using layers of paint that swirled together in a violent mixture of red and orange and yellow hues, punctuated with black streaks and slices.

This 'second face', a grimace racked with pain and guilt, seemed almost hideous in the light now cast by the glass. And yet it was pitiful and touching; crying out — absolutely — for help, for understanding.

For a friend.

'There you are.' Christine said.

She stared at the image for several moments before returning to her journal, where she began scribbling furiously once more.

17:12

Saturday 14th May, 2011

Gary Blakely; the emaciated, 29 year-old Deputy-Chief Engineer of the *Ianus*. He had been with *Golden Star* for three years now.

During a somewhat strained conversation that they had had a little earlier, Leigh had learned a fair amount about the particular engine system that powered the *Ianus* along with all the certain intrigues and odd little kinks it bore.

For example; were the engine room itself to become caught-up in fire it would seal itself off and fill with carbon-dioxide in order to contain, minimise and ultimately extinguish the fire before it could cause too much damage. Sensible.

Only, that feature on *this* ship didn't seem to work too well.

Actually, the way Blakely had told the tale, it was the opposite that was true.

Since the take-over of the new anti-smoking policy and the introduction of all the devices installed to enforce such a policy on all levels of the ship, the engineering 'lock-down' facility now worked a little too well. They'd already had several close calls.

Yes, it had been a very interesting conversation indeed.

Now, Gary Blakely lay whimpering in the corner of the of the small generator room. Bleeding, burned, branded and bruised, he shivered in his boxers and stained, torn t-shirt; bound and gagged with strips of old uniform.

Leigh looked down at him in disgust, pulling on Blakely's own blue overalls and pocketing his swipe-card. He would certainly be needing that.

From what Gary Blakely had — eventually — told him, the main smoke detector was situated at the far end of the engineering control room. He had also — with a little persuasion — been convinced to relinquish the codes and details on how to reroute control to the secondary computer in this outer generator room, which had apparently been built to act as a back-up control room in the case of the main room being sealed.

Normally this would all be done by Blakely or the Chief-in-Command, once everyone was evacuated. But, not today.

Leigh would have only the tightest window of opportunity in which to operate. It was literally do or die!

He swiped the ID card through the reader and entered the corridor, feeling completely giddy. The secret mission, the change of clothes, the codes and a man tied-up in the next room adding to the feeling that he was now starring in his own Bond film!

He worked furiously at the various keyboards for what felt like an age, avoiding the eyes of the engineers that passed him and noting how helpful and incredibly accurate Blakely had been in his descriptions.

The man certainly knew his stuff!

Entering the final codes, Leigh hit the command execute button and it was done.

All around him the computers began to lock-down.

Quickly, he struck a match and stuffed it inside the sensor housing above him before sprinting up the corridor towards the exit.

Surging past several engineers, he grinned, knowing what they did not yet know as they ran in the opposite direction to discover the source of the problem. They had a hint that it lay with the main computer room.

Little did they know that this really was the least of their problems.

In the next moment klaxons were screeching, warning lights flashing a terrifying red as Leigh rounded the corner and threw himself through the air-tight door that was already descending.

It crashed down behind him, almost on his heels, and he lay panting on the floor for several moments as the CO2 cylinders on the other side of the door began to release their deadly mist.

Climbing to his feet, he watched the rooms beyond begin to fill. He smiled once more as the engineers struggled back towards the door, towards him, begging him to help them as they drove their fists — pointlessly — into the reinforced glass window until their knuckles bled.

'You lied to me.' he said, re-entering the small generator room. He removed Blakely's gag, kneeling before the skinny engineer, stroking the side of his face before clamping his palm across his mouth and squeezing his cheeks tightly as he continued, 'You said I'd have nearly forty-five seconds, but that was barely thirty. Anyone would think you didn't like me.'

Before Blakely could answer Leigh struck him hard with the back of his fist, sending his head crashing against the iron wall. He bobbed and bled and slumped to the ground.

Leigh then turned his attention to the computer and, stepping into a phone-box-like booth, quickly set about typing in the codes and instructions that Blakely had — once again — so kindly revealed to him earlier.

As he struggled with the final sequence he happened to glance up and to his absolute surprise and horror, discovered that his reflection was not the only one staring back at him.

Ducking to the right and spinning, pressing his back against the booth, he kicked at Blakely who suddenly slashed at him with a small knife. He hadn't counted on that!

Stumbling from the booth, Leigh collided painfully with the floor. His thigh stung suddenly as a ribbon of blood spilt from the fresh wound.

The bastard had caught him!

Blakely was trying to stop the shut-down sequence.

No! He couldn't let that happen.

Throwing himself at Blakely, he drove the engineer's head into the computer screen, glass and plastic splintering around them. But it wasn't enough. Blakely shook him off, shooed him away like an annoying insect. He was certainly a lot stronger than he looked, this intelligent bag of bones!

Falling to the floor for a second time, Leigh's hand pressed into the sharp point of a solitary screw. He recoiled instantly, reacting to the pain. Then, taking up the threaded piece of metal, he jumped onto Blakely's back, tearing at his face with his hand before driving the screw into the engineer's left eye.

He screamed in agony, slashing wildly at his assailant.

But, Leigh was too quick. *Sentence structure is rough*

He ducked and weaved, catching Blakely's knife arm and twisting it suddenly, ferociously. He felt Blakely's shoulder pop as he dropped the knife yelping once more, stumbling, half-blind, out of the little booth.

Grabbing the knife, Leigh forced open the metal cabinet doors beneath the monitor and keyboard. Inside were the motherboards and cooling fans, the power supply and a thousand other things he didn't understand. Not to worry.

He picked up the broken Blakely, hurling him forward into the electrical Narnia with delight!

The brief lightshow that followed was an unexpected pleasure, causing Leigh to laugh out loud as he tore a sleeve from the blue overalls and bandaged his bleeding leg. Just a flesh-wound. Nothing to worry about.

Then — music to his eager ears — the ventilation system ceased to whir, the lights blinked to nothingness, the engines, pistons, injectors and propellers; all fell silent.

Absolute silence.

It was a beautiful thing.

In another moment the emergency power kicked in. Blakely's body twitched in the eerie dim light, his head firmly embedded in the powerhouse of controls; his melted face clinging to the boards around him.

Leigh cocked his head, admiring his work. Taking a mental picture. 'Man Machine.' CRINGE

He smiled, slipping his hand into his pocket and finding the piece of paper that he had acquired not so long ago. Though that chance meeting now seemed so strangely distant and unreal somehow.

Unfolding the paper, he scanned the list once more, finding his target without distraction. 'You'd like that.' he said, fingering the name, 'You'd appreciate a piece of work like this ... wouldn't you?'

Checking that the coast was clear, he slipped from the room. Slipped from engineering.

'Yeah, I bet you would.' He grinned, closing the door behind him. 'You'd get it, wouldn't you ... Miss Livingstone. You'll get it. Oh, yes you will.'

17:20

Saturday 14th May, 2011

'That's it! I've had it with that prick!' Andrews yelled, rounding on Prior as though it were his fault. 'I said he couldn't be trusted. You need people you can depend upon on a ship like this.'

'I understand, sir.' Prior said, clawing his opportunity to speak now that Andrews had finally paused to take a breath, 'He's been under some personal pressure recently. It doesn't excuse him. But, he has had . . . problems.'

'And now we *all* have problems. Stupid bastard.'

'Sir, with all due respect, he could be dead.'

Andrews stopped mid-pace. 'Don't you think I know that?'

'I think you're aware of the possibility — sir — but, I have to say that I find your sense of compassion for another human being to be somewhat lacking.'

'How dare you — '

At that moment the lighting on the bridge flickered, spluttered and cut out. The constant drone of the engines faded in a downward scale until it was little more than a bass hum. Then there was no more sound.

Only silence.

'What the hell is happening?' Andrews demanded.

Several moments passed and the emergency power kicked in. The engines did not.

'Sir, we've come to a full stop.' came the report from a fair-haired helmsman, 'The engines have been completely disengaged.' He moved from console to console, to screen, to control board and back again, checking and doubling-checking, trying to discover the reason for this, 'It looks like a fire broke out in engineering; the emergency procedure engaged and the seal is holding, but there's some sort of malfunction. The engines simply aren't responding.' he paused, confused by the readings before him, 'They've been taken off-line and locked. We're completely locked out of the system, Sir.'

not introduced as commander

'Who has the authority to do that?' asked Commander Roberts.

Prior shook his head, 'Rachel does.'

'Rachel?' Andrews raised an eyebrow, 'I didn't know you and the Chief were so close.'

At that moment he wanted nothing more than to smack Andrews right in his smug, lean face. But he refrained.

Instead, he met the Captain's querying stare with an equally iron resolve, thankful for the sudden decrease in lighting as his cheeks burned. 'Chief Adams and I spent some time together when we were on leave.' he said, 'Do you have a problem with that? Sir.'

The young Captain made a strange noise and a face that Prior couldn't help but notice smacked more than a little of jealousy. He stifled the overwhelming urge to grin from ear to ear.

'Get Adams on the phone.' Andrews said, turning away from him.

The fair-haired helmsman rushed to the corner of the bridge, lifting the receiver and dialling furiously. He waited. Tried a second time. Waited.

He shook his head. 'There's no response, Sir.'

Shoving his hand into the knee-pocket of his trousers, Prior pulled out his mobile; lucky number eight. He quickly flicked through the options to find Rachel Adams number and was holding the phone to his ear as the helmsman tried to reach engineering for a third time.

'She's not answering her personal phone either.' Prior said, listening to the opening syllables of her soft and alluring pre-recorded voice before hanging-up.

'What the hell's going on down there?' Andrews spat.

'Captain?' It was Roberts. 'I think you should take a look at this.'

Everyone in the control room crowded around the terminal that Roberts occupied. He pulled up various sets of numbers that looked, to Prior, like some sort of time indexes. Though he couldn't be certain.

'Look. There.' said Roberts, offering little help to the Security Chief as he watched one set of numbers count down into another. 'The timing sequence that automates the emergency seal-off hatch has been altered.'

'Drastically altered.' Andrews cut in.

'And then this.' Roberts continued, 'This is the delay on the CO_2 release sequence. Again, it's been radically shortened. And look,' he pulled up yet another screen, 'these are the codes that enabled the override. Now, I don't know what all of them correspond to, but this section,' he pointed to a group of numerical digits and letters embedded within the sequence. 'That's a personal ID code.'

'So we can discover who altered the timings?' Andrews asked.

Roberts nodded.

'Well, get on it then. I want to know who that code belongs to, Mr Roberts.'

'Sir.'

'And Prior.'

He was already at the door as Andrews called his name, but turned his head to acknowledge the young Captain.

'Go a find out what's happening down there.'

'Already on it. Sir.'

One thing Prior simply couldn't stand about Andrews was his *it was my idea* attitude.

It never failed to wind him up. But, he had other concerns right now.

Why hadn't Rachel answered her phone? Something wasn't right.

He suddenly felt that same bad feeling, that same churning in the pit of his stomach that he had suffered on the day of the ill-fated warehouse raid.

As he turned the corner he broke into a cautious jog, which then become an urgent sprint. He was eager to reach engineering. Eager to discover the crew busy and stressed out with trying to fix all of these anomalous problems; eager to find that it was so loud down there that no one had even heard the phone, let alone having the time to answer it. That that was reason for no one picking up the calls from the bridge.

But, again; that feeling.

He pressed his mobile to his ear, even as he raced down the central flights of stairs. 'Davies.' he said, 'get a crew together and meet me down in engineering.'

'Yes sir.' came the reply.

No questions asked. Just like that. Good, reliable compliance.

Prior smiled. Briefly.

Engineering still seemed to be miles away. Another corner, another set of stairs.

He was near the aft portion of the ship now and entering those sections that were the dominion of the crew rather than the passengers. Those parts that appeared more stark, more sparse and much more military.

His phone rang.

'Prior.' he said, answering the call.

Nothing.

Static.

He raced back up the stairs he'd just come down, panting as he went. Still nothing. He looked at the phone; all six bars of signal had disappeared and the telecom signal pulsed with a digital urgency.

'Shit.'

As he moved back to the steps that led down towards engineering Prior heard footsteps in the corridor before him. He strained to look up, scanning the darkness for further movement; to no avail.

Creeping forward and feeling his way with his hand, forced back against the wall by the impenetrable dark that seemed to gain in density with every single step, Prior found himself wishing he'd brought a torch!

The emergency lights that should have been guiding his way down here crunched in broken shards beneath his steel-toed boots as he struggled to press forwards. Who would smash the emergency lighting? And why?

There, again. Movement.

Ducking low, Prior did his best to keep quiet as he sprinted the hundred yards or so between them. At the last moment he dove forward, knocking the figure off balance and pinning him to the ground.

A painful fist in the face told Prior he hadn't secured him as well as he'd first thought.

The pair scuffled, rolling across the floor, crashing into unseen obstacles as each tried to gain the upper hand. Each trying to pin the other.

Why wasn't this guy simply trying to escape?

Prior suddenly found himself on his front, face pressed against the cold metal floor. He managed to swing his arm up and back, jabbing his elbow forcefully into the aggressor's abdomen. The hulk grunted and fell back, giving Prior enough time to flip onto his back and raise his legs, tucking them tight into his chest.

As the grunting shadow lurched forward once more Prior kicked out, sending him flying backwards. He crashed over a desk and into the wall as Prior raced forward to grapple him into submission.

'Fuck!'

He knew that voice.

At that moment a couple of junior security officers appeared in the corridor, LED torchlight blinding him.

And his assailant.

'Guv'?' The voice came from the man beneath him.

'Davies?' he questioned in reply, blinking as his eyes adjusted to the new light.

'Fucking hell, sir, you haven't half got a kick on you.'

Shit!

Releasing Davies, Prior pulled himself to his feet, dusted himself off and offered his hand to the deputy. 'And you've got a bloody good left hook. Near dislocated my jaw!'

'Sorry sir, I thought you — '

Prior raised his hand, stopping him. The junior officers continued to stare in disbelief. 'To be fair, I attacked you.'

'I thought I'd better get down here as quick as I could,' Davies said. 'I asked Collins and Edwards to follow.' The pair nodded at the mention of their names, 'Asked them to bring some Maglites with them.'

Prior began to smile at the almost comic hilarity of the confusion, which gave way to a bass round of laughter between himself, Collins and Edwards; Davies soon adding his own dimpled chuckle to the mix, a gleaming grin on his broad face.

'Are you ok?' he asked, eventually.

Davies nodded, rubbing his ribs absently as he did.

Prior took two of the heavy-duty LED torches off the ginger-haired Collins, passing one to Davies. 'You're a stealthy bastard, Guv'.' he said as they moved into the corridor and back towards the steps.

'Don't you forget it!' Prior smirked, leading the way, 'Did you try and call me?'

Davies shook his head. As did Collins and Edwards.

Sliding open the heavy iron, manual door, Prior pushed his way into engineering.

He was immediately hit by a wall of heat and scent; heavy, pungent. Sickening.

'Shit! What *is* that?' Davies said, pressing in behind Prior.

'I don't know. But, it doesn't smell good.'

The four security officers spread out; checking all the small, dark spaces, the changing rooms and the main operations centre. It was so quiet. Prior could hear his heart pounding in his head, feel it throbbing in his aching jaw.

Absolute silence.

To be stood in the normally-bustling central hive of a ship like that and not to hear a single, solitary sound sent shivers tingling up and down Jonathan Prior's scarred back. It was beyond eerie. It was out and out creepy.

Riiiing!

Prior jumped. Visibly. But so did Davies; now just ahead of him, sweeping left and right.

Riiiing!

'Fucking hell!' said Prior, picking up the phone. 'You scared the living shit out of me!' he continued, hoping — though only as an afterthought — that the recipient wasn't Captain Andrews.

'Prior? Is that you?'

It wasn't Andrews. Thankfully. It was Roberts.

'Yes. Yes sir, what's up?'

'I tried to call your phone, but something's happened. It's like the network's gone down or — '

'But that's not possible,' Prior cut in, 'is it? It can't just go dead like that. There are backups — '

'Not if it's been sabotaged.'

'Really?' Prior lifted his hand, signalling for Davies to wait for him. The deputy paused near the secondary control room, watching Prior in the dim light. 'You think that's what's happened?'

'Well, it would explain a lot. Like why the wall-phones work, but mobiles don't. Even the satellite systems are out; internet, tracking, positioning, radio, TV. All down. Nothing.'

'So, we have no communication with the outside world?'

'That's right.'

'That's shit. Do we know our current position? Does anyone else know it?' Prior asked.

Davies rolled his shoulders and stretched, clearly feeling sore from their scuffle. Prior watched him bobbing from one foot to the other, stretching his calves.

The lad really couldn't stand still for two minutes!

'We're working on it.' Roberts' voice snagged down the line, 'Have you found anything down there?'

Prior shook his head habitually, 'The lights are all smashed. And it stinks. There's no sign of anyone.'

'Well, that's partly why I was calling you. We isolated the ID tag within the override codes and tracked it back to . . .'

Prior watched Davies sniffing around ahead of him like a cat; something had definitely caught his attention. Though he couldn't see what it was from his current position, he could tell that it seemed to have the young security officer suitably perplexed.

'. . . Blakely.' Roberts continued, 'He was behind the override, his codes reduced the delay on the doors and the CO_2 release.'

'Why?'

Prior looked up to see Davies move into the smaller control room.

'I don't know, but I think he might have — '

'SHIT!!'

Davies fell back out of the control room, tripping over himself in terror; horrified and clearly distressed. Dropping the phone, Prior ran to his side.

'What is it?' he asked. No response. Davies was simply pointing towards the room, shaking as he mumbled in strange syllables that sounded like another language. 'What is it? Marc?' Prior continued, 'Marc, look at me.'

'I ... I think it's ... Blakely.'

Prior placed the palm of his hand on the control room door, easing it open. A fresh waft of stink hit him; warm and scorched. He lifted his torch, flooding the room with a bluish pool of LED light.

'Collins,' he said, 'get on that phone. Tell Roberts we found the source of the smell. We need a medical team down here.' he coughed, 'Now. And tell him Blakely won't be answering any questions.'

He stepped into the small control room.

The window of the small booth that housed the engineering back-up computer was streaked with blood; smeared and splashed. The reinforced glass was cracked, but unbroken. And in the bottom of the cube, merged with the contents of the open metal cabinet, lay Blakely's still-twitching, still-cooking, beaten and befouled body.

He was cut and bruised and had clearly been tied up at some point. His left eye was a pulped mass of congealing goo in his socket, a silver screw sitting snug amongst the remains of the optical organ; nestled down next to his bled-out tear duct.

What remained of Blakely's face and hair could barely be considered human. He was a screaming skull dipped in wax; a Madam Tussaud's reject!

This horrific monstrosity, this spectre that should have been a man, that had once borne Blakely's now-melted face, was dripping onto the once-pulsing heart of the pc like some futuristic Giger-esque nightmare.

Prior fought the urge to vomit.

He turned away, unable to face the smell of the atrocity any longer. It was then that something caught his eye.

Up in the corner.

The monitor. It was the CCTV for engineering.

The camera was angled to capture the length of the next corridor; that which was sealed off. Which led to the main engineering control room.

It was difficult to make out in the dim light, the camera struggling to focus, but it looked to Prior as though the corridor had been filled with bags or sacks. Was this thing capturing in real-time? What were they?

Prior stared at the human-sized bin bags ...

The *human* ...

A cold sweat broke over Prior's tense body as the awful realisation drained the colour from his face.

He dashed out of the secondary control room, leaping over Davies who was still quivering on the floor. He ran through the next room until he came slamming up against the seal-locked door. Holding up his torch, he found the glass hatch smeared with blood.

'Davies!' he shouted.

Though he didn't want to, Prior knew he had to check. Pushing out a battered breath, he peered through the glass. Past the blood.

Shining a beam of light into the room, he could see that the bags — as he had feared — weren't bags at all. Creeping slowly, as though it were unwilling to uncover the truth, his torch found boots, then legs and arms, then torsos, hair. Faces.

They were. They were bodies.

They were crew. Shipmates. Friends. Colleagues.

They were *their* bodies.

The light from Prior's torch continued to seek out the faces of his friends until it could move no further. It had stopped and he couldn't — for all the strength of his will — force it to move an inch further in any direction.

Haloed in the strange blue light of the torch, oddly angled and paler than usual, upturned as she struggled in a motionless frieze on her back, her eyes open and lips parted … he found the face of Rachel Adams.

Prior felt his knees begin to buckle, though he did not fall.

Rachel's arm was outstretched, her palm open willing him to take hold, to pull her through the glass and the steel of the door into his arms. To pull her back through time. Back to life.

Davies was at his side. Catching him.

His legs had given out.

'Rachel.' he whispered.

'Get this door open!' shouted Davies, his voice still trembling.

The room was suddenly filled with people. More members of Prior's own security team arrived with portable lighting rods, small petrol generators and hydraulic cutters. Medics arrived. He was pulled away from the door and propped up against a metal wall opposite.

A light passed before his eyes as the room descended into chaos. Someone was calling his name, speaking to him. But he couldn't hear.

He didn't want to hear.

And then the words punched through his numbed and grieving, semi-conscious brain. The words he had dreaded, but expected all along. How long had it been anyway? How much time had passed?

He didn't need to hear those words … didn't need them. He already knew.

If he was honest, he had known all along.

That was the bad feeling. The churning in the pit of his stomach; the clawing, gnawing, aching pulsing … thing that ate him up from the inside out.

'Sir, they're dead. They're all dead.'

Chapter Three

17:24

Saturday 14th May, 2011

Christine stepped onto the wide corridor that led to Kelly's lush and voluminous accommodation. It was a light corridor filled with pictures, paintings and plants. There were no plants in the corridors near her room!

And it wasn't as though her room was cheap, either.

She had Kelly's folder tucked under her arm and found herself leaning a little heavier than usual on the stick she hated to admit that she needed. She felt tired this evening.

As she pressed forward, Christine noticed that the door to Kelly's room was open. She paused, uncertain as to whether she should look in, knock, or simply turn and leave. The less confident and more self-conscious, unadventurous part of her opted to bolt as quickly away from the room as her stick could manage. She hated that side of herself. It had never existed before ... all that had happened.

Christine sucked in a breath and pushed her anxious, nervous other-self to one side. She moved towards the door, her heart racing. And peering through the gap she saw ...

Blink.

Flicker. Clunk.

Darkness.

The lights went out and, after a moment, she realised that the strangely comforting sound of the engines had also ceased. They had actually ceased several minutes earlier, though she hadn't really paid the absence any thought. But, now that the lights too had gone . . . that couldn't be right.

She felt her heart begin to flutter and pressed her back against the wall, becoming increasingly terrified. She could no longer stand the dark.

As she searched awkwardly with her hand against the wall, Christine knocked over a wooden plant stand. Along with the vase that used to sit on it.

She cursed silently and struggled on, relieved when the emergency lighting — for all the good it did — finally flickered into existence.

'Kelly?' she called, annoyed at tremor in her own voice.

She pushed the door a little wider, but found herself suddenly very reluctant to enter. And this time it wasn't a slightly anxious, nervous thing; something she could reprimand herself for and simply *pull herself together*. Now she was truly scared. There were no two ways about it. She was petrified.

The evening had already turned as dark as a winter night, though — again — she hadn't really taken much notice before.

But, being here in the darkness, she couldn't help but be confronted by the fact that it was unusually, even eerily dim both inside and out. She could see that beyond the glass and metal housing of the ship the sea was becoming increasingly violent.

But, then again, her stomach could have told her that much.

Thick and heavy storm clouds gathered and swirled beyond the French doors that led to the balcony. There were no stars twinkling and no moon. It was as though someone had reached up and tugged at an invisible pull-cord or flicked off some great, unseen light switch, plunging the skies into a vast and all-consuming shadow.

And it looked so much darker inside Kelly's room than it was in the corridor. And she really didn't like the dark. Not since that evening.

Janet . . .

She swallowed hard, trying to bite back the memory before it took a hold of her. But it was too late.

The tears that threatened to break from her liquid eyes were a mixture of pure, irrational terror and the violent torrent of reminiscence. It was stupid — she knew it was stupid — even as she fought to control her breathing, as her heart raced and her chest heaved and her mind screamed out, begging her, spurring her to turn and run. Just run.

She knew there was no way that Thomas Butler could be inside that room.

Even still, the mere sound of his name rattling around her skull made her nauseous.

Hello Sweetheart . . .

'No!' she screamed, clawing at the wall to keep her balance as the ship dipped and rolled suddenly. Struggling, she released her grip on the folder, spilling the contents across the floor as she fell into Kelly's room. 'I will *not* allow myself to be ruled by the memory of you.' she whispered, crawling on her stomach.

Afraid to lift her head, but unwilling to accept the rule of her fear she pressed forward, hand after hand deeper into the room until with a sudden sickness she felt the slick warmth of something like oil on skin.

And she knew from experience that it wasn't oil.

'Kelly?' she whispered, reaching out to touch the cool flesh once more. She looked at her hand, rubbing her forefinger and thumb together and knowing the sickly scent of blood without the need for sight.

Suddenly the skies cracked electric blue as an epilepsy of lightning sheeted across the charged particles trapped within the dense and darkened atmosphere. A momentous clap — hot on the heels of the flash — soon turned to the deep boom of a bubbling roar that continued to roll even as another burst of silver-blue lit up the soupy sky.

Through the noise and the confusion and the haze of shock at seeing such a sudden and entirely uncalled-for meteorological out-burst, Christine raised her head to look out of the glass door. She caught sight of a group of variously sized canvases that stood in the corner of Kelly's room.

Each was covered with painted strokes of some violent detail or other. Several were close to completion, while others had clearly been discarded.

Momentarily shocked at the shear brutality and horror of the images before her, Christine found herself unable to tear her gaze from the paintings, straining her eyes as the stormy illumination gave way to darkness once more.

It was only with another streak of hot, blue lightning and the rolling boom of thunder that accompanied it, did Christine's eyes finally discover Kelly, confirming what her hands had already felt and her olfactory senses had already guessed at. The incredible terror of the realisation that her fears were not unjustified hit her like a bucket's worth of ice in the pit of her stomach. It was not an irrational fear of *something* lurking in the dark, but of *someone*. Someone with intent to harm.

The soft skin of Kelly's cupid's bow lips had been split and streams of blood were now drying around her mouth and button-nose; crusting amongst the nest of bruising that fell across her face and cheek. Her left eye too looked swollen, even in the dim light.

She was wearing a pair of dark shorts and a matching top that looked more like a sports-bra than anything else. Her lean, muscular torso that showed — by its definition — her commitment to the gym, was now a collage of paint and blood and swollen bruises. Her left hand was cut to shreds, as were her arms and legs.

She was a mess.

Christine pulled herself up next to Kelly. Leaning over her she searched for any sign that she was breathing, praying that she would find it.

She ran her hand gently through her short, black hair, pulling her shimmering fringe — also slick with blood — back from Kelly's battered face.

'Kelly?' she said, biting back tears. She couldn't do this again. Couldn't watch this happen again.

The ship bobbed suddenly, throwing Christine a little off balance. Something moved in her periphery and an intensely cold shiver shot up and down her spine.

'Who's there?'

The door slammed shut.

17:35

Saturday 14th May, 2011

Prior had done his best to pull himself together.

He'd bolted from engineering several minutes earlier, only just making it into one of the public restrooms on the floor above before throwing-up the contents of his stomach. Which, wasn't much. His muscles contracted time and again as he retched over the lavender-scented bowl.

He fell to a sitting position on the floor of the tiny cubicle, reaching up to pull the handle. He listened to the swoosh of the water and the cistern filling once more. He pressed his head back against the flimsy divide, his eyes brimming with tears every time he thought of Rachel.

He could think of nothing else. Could see nothing but her face ... drained of colour. Her arm outstretched. Reaching out. To him.

He smashed his head back repeatedly against the cubicle wall, his ears filled with an alien sound of desperation, agony and disbelief as it roared from his lungs. He jumped to his feet, pounding his fists into the door, kicking it and near ripping it from its hinges in a helpless fit of despair and utter uselessness.

He crossed the room, raging like a madman as he ran the tap; the water trickling slowly into the sink.

He swilled his mouth, spat and splashed his face. He drove his fist into the reflection of his own tear-drenched, bruised and sopping countenance as it stared defiantly back at him.

The mirror shattered.

The outer door pushed open and Marc Davies stood in silence, watching him; concern etched into every corner of his young face. Prior pulled a splintered shard of glass from between his knuckles. It wasn't deep. He couldn't feel it anyway.

He couldn't feel anything.

'Sir?' said Davies.

Prior looked up at the officer who — he knew — admired him so. He felt a twinge of guilt that he was somehow letting Davies down; that he shouldn't see him behaving this way. But, then again, how *should* he behave? How *should* he deal with this?

Davies shook his head, silently apologising for the intrusion. 'I've been meaning to report that broken mirror.' he said.

Prior managed a small half-smile even as the tears stung his eyes once more. Davies was kind and thoughtful, he was trusting and honest; a true and loyal friend who never pushed him and clearly cared for him. And yet, Prior had never even revealed the truth about his relationship with Rachel to Marc Davies.

Then again, he hadn't had a chance.

A second twinge of guilt stabbed at his heart as the silent mention of her name threatened to break him all over again. He felt his knees give a little.

His head was spinning and he was shaking uncontrollably.

Davies stepped forward and, before he knew what was happening, Prior had been enveloped in the young man's strong arms.

He held onto Prior, letting him ball the shirt on his back into tight fists as he continued to shake, sobbing into his shoulder without the need for explanation.

Under different circumstances such an embrace in a setting like this could have been wildly misinterpreted, but Prior didn't care. He needed this. If he was to be of any use to anyone else anytime soon, he needed this. Now.

A silent understanding passed between the pair; Davies bearing Prior, Prior holding Davies. Who let him. Without judgement, desire or motive.

And Prior was suddenly very glad that — despite the *keep your distance* attitude he had developed over the years — he was fortunate enough to have earned the friendship of the strong, but sensitive Scouser he now embraced.

17:35

Saturday 14th May, 2011

Shona froze high up on the rig. She shouldn't have even been up there, she'd been warned before, but there was nowhere quite like it for clearing off the cobwebs of the mind and getting a new perspective on things.

She liked sitting up here on her own. Away from the twirlies and drama queens. She had never really counted herself as one of them and preferred the company of the technicians — the lampies and the noise-boys (and girls) — any day.

That's how she had come to find this spot.

She had smiled only moments earlier, recalling the sensual memories of stolen moments with Heather; with Jack; with Craig and Carly.

But, then the lights had cut out. Just like that. She had no idea how or why this had happened, all she knew was that it was ridiculously dark inside the cavernous theatre and she was treacherously high up.

'Shit!' she cursed out loud.

It had suddenly turned quite cold and she was glad of the warmth her thick grey and pink hooded-top provided to her mid-riff and upper body. Glad that she had picked it up after all!

Her bare legs, however, had suffered in the tiny denim cut-offs and, though beautifully tanned and superbly crafted by her profession, they were now awash with goose-bumps in the dithering cold of the upper platform.

Reaching in to the front pocket of her hoodie, Shona pulled out her phone and using the light from the LED screen as a torch, navigated her way slowly across the rickety platform and back to the steel wall ladders.

Stuffing the phone back into her top, she scuttled down the ladder one rung at a time, reaching the stage floor some forty feet below with an audible sigh of relief.

However, being alone in the dark can do strange things to a person. Shona knew this and forced herself to try and remain calm even as her mind began playing terrible tricks. Though she knew the Dionysus Theatre like the back of her hand, she couldn't help but feel the heavy palm of fear pressing down upon her chest; quickening her heart and causing her breaths to become short and sharp.

Despite the fact that there was a little more light down here, Shona still couldn't see clearly and, worse still, she suddenly felt a cold bead of sweat trace a slow course down her long spine as she came to realise that her fears were not unfounded.

That she wasn't alone.

She pulled out her phone for the second time, diving straight into the calls menu. Kelly's number appeared at the top as they had spoken earlier, arranging to meet for a bite to eat before the show. Though it was now looking very doubtful that there would be any performance at all tonight.

She looked at the display.

Shit!

No signal.

Shona shook her phone, then tapped it against her thigh. She threw it in the air — not too high — to try and 'catch' a signal. But it was no good. She usually had four bars in here.

Something stirred to her right, causing the legs — the wing drapes — to ruffle and sway in a breeze of movement.

Her heart was thundering now, pounding like fists against the inside of her chest as her small, quiet breaths clawed their way to escape her lungs. She tried to use the phone's screen as a torch once more, despite the overwhelming fear of what she might find. But, by the time she had organised herself and aimed the face of the phone in that direction, there was nothing to see.

Nothing there, but the swaying leg.

Turning, Shona was prepared to bolt from the stage and through the auditorium when she slammed into a wall of flesh and a tight, masculine grip. The thumbs of the unseen force-to-be-reckoned-with pressed painfully into her arms, causing her to let out a small cry.

Instinctively, she brought her knee up to connect with her assailant's groin.

It worked.

He released her, falling to his knees, unable to speak or make any other sound as he rolled around on the floor, clutching himself.

Shona wasn't about to hang around and had reached the main doors by the time he found his voice.

'Fuck! Fuck!' he spat out, sucking in breath as he did. 'You ... fucking ... Oh, god! Why did you do that?'

She knew that voice.

'Mike?' she called.

'Who ... the bloody hell ... did you think it was?'

He continued to wince and writhe on the dark stage. She still couldn't see him, but knew his position from the noise he was making.

'You scared me to fuckin' death, you prick.' she said, anger replacing the fear she had felt only moments earlier, 'What the fuck did you think you were doing? Why didn't you answer me when I called?'

'I thought I'd ... scare you.'

'Well, congratufuckulations! It worked.'

'I think you knocked my balls up into my stomach!' he said, struggling.

Shona couldn't help but smile, briefly. 'Well, that's what you get!.'

'I'm fucking dying up here. Aren't you going to come and help me?'

An icy chill washed over her as sudden as an April shower. 'No.' she said assuredly, 'You really scared me, Mike. And you hurt me too.'

'Hello?' he returned, sarcastically.

'How was I supposed to know it was you? When you grabbed me ...'

'I'm sorry. I shouldn't have done that.'

'Instinct just kicked in.'

'That's some fucking instinct!' he said, 'I wished it'd have kicked somewhere else though.'

She could tell from the change in the height of his voice that he had now managed to scramble to his feet. She lifted her phone, angling the screen towards the stage. She supposed that after relocating his bollocks to his abdomen, lighting the way as best she could to ensure that he didn't also fall and break his neck was the only half-decent thing she could do.

But, as the light from the screen found him it bounced, reflecting off something slim, sleek and metallic. Something that flicked and clicked away into nothingness as he shoved his hand sheepishly into his trouser pocket.

Shona gulped, trying to pretend that she hadn't seen the sharp, metal object. Fighting the urge to ask him what he had just had held in his hand. Though, she already knew the answer.

'I've got to go.' she said as he struggled his way slowly towards her, each step clearly as painful as the last, knocking the wind from him.

'Shona ...' he called, his voice a mixture of pain and anger, 'Why don't we get some ... food? A drink?'

She shook her head in the darkness, pushing through the door as he approached. There was something in his eyes. Something she just didn't trust.

'I'm meeting someone.' she called, letting the heavy door fall shut behind her, breaking into a run and taking the dimly-lit stairs three at a time as soon as she was clear of the theatre.

In the pitch black of the *Dionysus* Theatre Mike drove his fist into the dark wood of the door. He slumped back against the cool wall and stuffed his hand into his trouser pocket. Pulling it out, he felt the comforting weight of the object he'd been forced to hide.

He fingered the smooth, rounded handle — crafted from a mosaic of colourful enamel — that housed the blade of his flick-knife.

He relaxed and smiled, breathing a sigh of relief as his stomach began to settle, though his balls still throbbed with a sickening pain.

'Nearly.' he whispered to the darkness.

17:42

Saturday 14th May, 2011

After spending some time in the strangely comforting arms of Davies, Prior cleaned the wound on his hand once more; washing and drying it with care. He splashed his face with another handful of cold water and looked up — instinctively — at the empty space where the mirror should have been.

He grunted and shook his head, annoyed that he had lost control like that.

Then, leaving the sickly, lavender-scented men's washroom behind, he locked the door and, in passing, informed a maintenance crewmember of the broken mirror.

Now, as the pair pressed on towards the medical bay, torchlight guiding them, Prior tried to organise his thoughts into some reasonable, logical course of action. He wasn't entirely certain of how he should proceed, but, anticipating Captain Andrews' inevitably vague instruction to simply *get to the bottom* of things; he chose to take matters into his own hands.

Immediately.

'We need to speak to Dr Matthews.' he said, 'I think it's fairly obvious that those . . .' his voice tailed off as he came to a full stop, his feet unable to take another step. He'd wanted to say 'those people', but then, they weren't just people.

They weren't simply unknown victims; nameless with numbers and temporary ID tags in place of any true identity. They weren't just bodies. They were friends.

'I think it's obvious,' he continued, clearing his throat, 'that the CO_2 canisters released and . . .' He couldn't do it. Couldn't bring himself to say the words suffocated . . . killed . . . murdered. Not yet.

All efforts to try and describe the sequence of events that had culminated in the horrendous discovery down in engineering only brought the image of Rachel Adams — *his* Rachel; with her soft, milky skin and fiery red hair; her incredible topaz eyes and honeyed voice — crashing, along with the reality of losing her, down on the shores of his agitated brain.

Davies nodded, placing a firm hand briefly on his superior's shoulder, squeezing his support, before releasing him once more. 'Dr Matthews should be able to tell us for certain.'

Prior pursed his lips together, his eyes filling once.

This time they did not spill.

'Did you manage to get hold of the medical records for the crew earlier?' he asked.

Davies gave a short, sharp nod, the smallest hint of a smile spreading over his boyishly handsome features. 'I didn't know who half of them were ... even with pictures. I don't know how you do it, Guv'. How you keep a track of everyone.'

'I have too much time on my hands. And I don't have any real hobbies.'

Prior flashed that same half-smile at Davies, who returned a subdued chuckle. 'I don't believe that for a second. I know what you're like. You're thorough. And maybe even a tiny bit of a workaholic, but that's just you. Just who you are, and people feel ... comforted knowing that. Knowing that you've got it all covered.'

'But, I didn't. Did I?' Prior said, turning to face Davies, his voice low and shaking. 'If I'd had it covered, something like this — '

'Sir, you can't blame yourself for this. No one could have known ...'

'I should have!'

'No.' Davies said simply. 'No. You shouldn't.'

'She'd still ...' Prior stopped, squeezing his eyes as tight shut as his clenching fists, swallowing hard, 'They'd *all* still be alive if I'd have been more ...'

'There's nothing you could have done. No one could have seen this coming.' he said, forcing Prior to look at him, 'This really isn't your fault. But, we *will* get whoever is responsible. I promise you.'

Slowly, Prior shook his head in the silence of the dark corridor, 'I didn't tell you about me and Rachel.' he said finally.

'You didn't have to.'

'What do you mean?'

'You're a very private person. I get that. And — no offense — but, sometimes you can be a little ...' Davies hesitated, tilting his head this way and that, before abandoning the sentence completely.

'Grumpy?'

Davies grinned, giving a single nod, 'But, not recently, sir. Nah, you've been totally different. A new man. Cheerful. You know, with a skip in your step and all that ... I saw you and Chief Adams having dinner one night. I put two and two together. You looked happy. You *both* looked very happy. And I was pleased for you. But, I knew you wouldn't say anything until you were ready and that you wouldn't appreciate me bringing it up before that.'

Prior choked back tears once more, recalling the too-few dinners that they had shared; the long evenings they had spent together. The way her golden-red hair would spill across his pillow and the scent of her would linger in his bed long after. The way her eyes sparkled, creasing at the corners when she smiled. The way she felt in his arms; small and warm and soft.

And now she was gone.

Simply ... gone.

Ripped from him before he had even had a chance to really explore this strange new feeling; this unplanned thing that he had reluctantly begun to accept and even refer to as an actual, real, genuine relationship. Rachel had laughed sweetly at him, mocking him that it was all downhill from here.

'Right.' Prior said, making a small coughing noise in the back of his throat that signalled a return to the matters at hand, 'Even if Blakely's codes were used, I don't think he's our man somehow.'

Davies agreed.

'So, I'd like you to go grab the personnel files and head up to the bridge. I'll meet you there shortly. You can fill Andrews in — '

'Aw, thanks, Guv'.' Davies said, sardonically.

'You're welcome.' he continued, a wry smile just about curling his thin lips, 'I'll join you up there shortly and we can go over everything we have and everything we know. I want you to get hold of a passenger list too and as many two-ways as you can carry — I don't know how many are fully charged — but we're going to need them to keep in touch.'

'Yes sir.'

Davies gave a small nod in acknowledgement and turned from Prior. The elder man caught his arm briefly, almost as an afterthought. 'Thanks Marc.' he said quietly.

Davies' eyes were friendly as he bobbed his head a final time, before moving swiftly down the corridor.

Sucking in a deep breath to steady his nerves Prior turned the corner, marching resolutely towards the medical bay.

'Prior?' called a familiar, feminine voice, 'Mr Prior?'

He recognised the soft accented tones instantly and turned to find the dark-haired woman he had been sat next to at the dinner table the night before.

Christine Kane.

She was struggling towards him in the low light, dragging another human figure along besides her, a left arm draped around her neck to secure them in place as she inched her way along the corridor using the wall as a support.

'Dr Kane.' he said, rushing to her side.

He took the blood-soaked body from her, realising only as he scooped the sagging bulk into his arms that it was Kelly Livingstone. 'What happened to her?' he asked, looking down at Kelly's injuries.

Christine struggled to catch her breath as she continued to lean on the wall for support. Her beautifully crafted, dark-wood stick nowhere in sight. 'I went ... to see Kelly,' she breathed, 'to return some work ... the lights went out and ... I think someone was in her room ... I found her like this on the floor.'

Prior raced her through the doors of the medical bay and straight into the back room where the gurneys and the freezers lived.

There was more dazzling, false light in this room than he'd experienced in the last half an hour and his eyes complained at the sudden brightness. He placed Kelly down on the first bed he came to, turning on his heels to go back and help Christine.

'What is this?' Dr Matthews clipped in irritation.

'This is Kelly Livingstone.' he shouted back as he exited the room, jogging from the medical bay to find Christine not four steps further than when he had left her. Reaching her, he extended his arm.

For a moment she looked dubious, resistant and even a little hurt. He knew it was her pride preventing her from accepting his help and ordinarily he wouldn't have pushed, but he was concerned for both her and Kelly. And time was of the essence.

'Please.' he said, quietly.

Releasing her grip on the wall, Christine Kane slipped her arm through his and leaned her gentle weight on him as he assisted her through to the harsh, bright room.

Once at Kelly's side, he left Christine only for a moment while he found a blue, plastic chair and sat it next to the bed. 'They're not the comfiest.' he apologised as Christine sank into the awful mould.

She winced briefly, trying not to let it show, before relaxing against the back of the horrid plastic thing.

'It's fine.' she said. 'Thank you.'

In his haste Prior hadn't noticed just how busy it was in the room whose light still hurt his eyes. He found himself straining his green gaze as if he were looking out across a bay on the brightest of cloudless days somewhere in the Med.

All around him nurses and technicians hurried about checking over the unending stream of bodies that poured through the doors. Searching — hopelessly — for any small sign of life; peeling back the lids of those whose eyes were shut and passing a small light before their pupils; pressing at their wrists and throats to find a pulse, to discover any small sign that their defiant little hearts were still trying to pump the cooling haemoglobin around their bodies.

They searched, knowing it was futile. But, they searched all the same.

'What's happened?' Christine questioned, following his gaze.

Prior shook his head. 'We're not entirely certain.'

As Prior made his way towards Dr Matthews he caught the bedraggled sight of Kemp — looking more wild than usual and even a little terrified — thundering his way towards him.

'Prior!' he shouted over the clamour.

What? No Jon-Boy? It must be serious.

'Nurse Kemp!' Matthews interjected, joining Prior, 'I will not have you screaming and shouting across my medical bay, can't you see what a — '

'I'm sorry.' he cut-in, shaking visibly. 'But, you haven't seen what I've just seen.'

It *was* serious.

Pressing Kemp into another blue plastic chair, Prior signalled for a glass of water. When the pathetically small paper cone of H2O arrived he shook his head a little and handed it to Kemp.

He waited for him to drink it down and catch his breath.

'Now, what is it?' he asked.

Kemp opened his mouth, but no words came. Only the tiniest sound — a strange sound that conveyed only his horror and disbelief as he tried to translate his thoughts into language — managed to escape his lips. He shook his head over and over, seeing something in his mind's eye that Prior could not access.

'Adrian,' Prior said patiently, as the man began to sniff, his eyes filling with tears, 'I can't help if you don't tell me.'

'I don't know how old she could have been.' he whispered.

'Who?'

'The girl … in room fifteen-thirty-four. She … she's dead, Prior.'

'What?' he exclaimed, equally unnerved and intrigued by Kemp's statement. 'Did it look like suicide?'

Kemp shook his head gravely. 'It looked like a bloody horror movie. Like a … butcher's shed.' He struggled to finish the sentence, before violently throwing up the contents of his stomach across the bleached linoleum floor.

Dr Matthews expelled a sharp grunt in annoyance, before clawing at one of the junior nurses to fetch a mop and bucket.

And an extra bucket for Kemp in case it happened again.

Prior caught Mathews gently by the arm, 'She needs looking at.' he said, nodding towards Kelly.

For a moment it seemed that Matthews would argue the point with him. But, she did not. Instead, she reeled off a list of names and called for equipment, medicines and an IV drip as she finally turned her attention to the battered and bloodied body of Kelly Livingstone.

'Well, she's alive.' she said, almost nonchalantly. Christine raised an eyebrow as Matthews began checking over the artist. 'She's lost a fair amount of blood . . . and has certainly taken a battering . . . hmm, her ribs might . . . no, I don't think they're broken. She'll need stitches though . . .'

Her voice trailed off as she continued to press her palms against Kelly's beaten body. Christine looked away, catching Prior's eye.

'Are you alright?' he asked.

She nodded, shakily. 'Do you need . . . is there anything I can do?' she said, her eyes flicking towards Kemp who was still shaking and vomiting intermittently, his head hung low over a small, grey plastic bucket that sat on his knee.

He looked lost. A still and tortured thing misplaced amidst the chaos of the medical Marathon that swooned around him.

'I didn't think you'd want to get involved.' Prior said, without cruelty.

'I probably don't. But, I'd rather be helping you. I'd rather be useful. If I can.' Her gaze fell on Kemp once more, 'If I don't . . . and more people . . .'

The words seemed to catch in Christine's throat, but Prior understood perfectly. He'd been there.

In that same position.

Torn between fear and self-hatred; carrying both the tortured burden of survival and the knowledge that if he chose to turn away from helping out with a case and more innocent people paid with their lives, that he would only have to carry a heavier, guiltier burden along with him in the future.

He nodded and extended his arm as before. This time Christine slipped her arm through his without hesitation, but still with a reserved sense of defiance, trying not to wince as she rubbed the false knee joint once more.

'Take care of her.' she said, her eyes narrowing with concern as she spoke to Dr Matthews.

The physician glanced up, even as she continued to check over Kelly's bruised ribs for fractures and brakes. 'Wait,' she said, turning suddenly from Christine and Prior, her tightly bound blonde pony-tail bobbing ferociously as she moved quickly about the room; her severe features pulled into a firm frown as she shooed people out of her way.

She spoke briefly to yet another young nurse who nodded and rushed out of sight as Matthews returned to Christine with a small box. 'Diclofenac Sodium.' she said, 'Take two now and another two in three to four hours time. It'll help with the pain. Have you eaten?'

Christine nodded — slightly bewildered — as Matthews popped two tablets and thrust them into her palm. She stared at the ugly brown pills for a moment before popping them into her mouth and swallowing.

She'd never had trouble with taking tablets and rarely needed a drink to wash them down. Though, she soon wished she'd taken *these* tablets with a very large glass of water, struggling with the acrid taste that now coated the back of her throat and trying not to let the look of disgust show on her face.

She didn't succeed.

'Thank you.' she said, coughing.

Dr Matthews smiled a small, tight smile and gestured to beyond Christine and Prior. They turned to see the nurse that Matthews had spoken to only moments earlier hurrying back into the room. She carried an ugly-looking metal walking stick that she presented to Christine as if it were a trophy.

Christine breathed out an irritated sigh, gritting her teeth.

'I thought you might need this.' Matthews said.

Inhaling slowly, Christine forced herself to smile as she thanked the nurse and Matthews alike.

It wasn't Matthews' fault, she told herself. She was only trying to help. She didn't know — couldn't know — just how deeply she was wounding her fragile pride.

Prior picked up on Christine's irritation and the awkwardness that was now pressing down upon them like stale air. His reaction was stereotypical of his sex, brushing off the moment with a jolt and three small words as he turned towards the exit; 'Come on then.'

Christine nodded, twisting awkwardly as she tried to find a comfortable position and range of movement with the horrid, grey stick. It was a little too short for her liking, causing her to stoop on her initial few steps towards the door. But once she had found her feet, she straightened her spine; stretching out and enjoying the satisfying crack that followed.

She would not stoop!

'Are you ok?' Prior asked.

'Yes. I'm fine.' she snapped, a little harshly. She was immediately sorry for this and he seemed to understand and accept her silent apology. 'So, how do we find this room?'

Leaving the medical bay was like stepping out of the sunlight and into the darkest of dark winter nights. Both Prior and Christine blinked, stunned for a moment by the sudden intensity of the shadows that blanketed the inner deck; the low-level emergency lighting doing little to aide their quest for vision.

'This way.' said Prior, taking the lead and turning to the left down the vast corridor. It was surprisingly clear considering all that had gone on.

Obviously, the passengers didn't yet know about the atrocity in engineering. Only a handful, including himself, had any idea about that. But he had, in all honesty, expected to be confronted by a wide-spread panic following the sudden loss of power.

Maybe there had been a certain amount of chaos. Earlier.

Perhaps he had missed it.

Perhaps Andrews had actually managed to organise his crew and contain the alarm. Contain the panic before it really set in.

Prior couldn't fight the small grin that curled his lip at the corner as he thought of Andrews actually taking charge of something like that; *Well, stranger things had happened!*

'So,' Christine said, cutting through the meandering trail of his thoughts, 'are you going to tell me what you know?'

He looked at her, admiring her courage. Knowing how she must have suffered, though he was aware of only a fraction of the details surrounding the Butler ordeal.

'A man was killed in engineering.' he said, 'The deputy-chief. Gary Blakely. Someone used his codes and . . .' his voice became small again, barely audible even in the relative silence of the unmoving ship, 'they changed the time sequences on the emergency lock-down facility. It's used to contain and extinguish any fires that may break out in engineering. Only the time delay and code sequences guarantee the crew the time they need to evacuate the area.'

Christine stopped, feeling the gravity of his words as if the atmospheric pressure had increased three-fold, pressing down on her chest, making her fight to catch her breath. 'Those people in the medical bay . . .' she whispered.

'The engineering crew.'

'I'm sorry.' she said as they pressed slowly forward, 'I'm so sorry. I . . . was there no way of resetting the system or aborting the command from inside the lockdown area?'

Prior shook his head, 'There wasn't time. The delays on the lockdown and the CO_2 release were specifically designed to prevent anything like this from happening, but they had been tampered with . . . and it was Blakely's codes that authorised the alterations.'

'Do you think it was him?'

'If it was, he didn't do it willingly. He was a mess. Merged with the backup CPU.'

'Merged?' Christine asked breathlessly as they reached a flight of stairs.

Prior stopped; turning to look at the petit psychologist as she hobbled along besides him.

A handful of her soft, brown hair bounced in a tangle of curls about her face, having escaped the constriction of the taut bun that sat at the base of her skull.

She was an attractive woman; there was no doubt about that. And she had a natural grace about her that made her seem elegant and refined even whilst struggling with the monstrous stick Dr Matthews had provided. She looked closer to her early thirties than her early forties, younger still when she smiled.

Prior felt a pang of guilt and his heart ached as his mind was flooded suddenly with thoughts and memories and the image of Rachel Adams. Even just noticing how attractive Christine Kane really was felt like a great betrayal.

How could he do that? How could he do that to her?

'Blakely's face,' he continued, shaking off the thoughts of Rachel, 'and most of his body were ... melted to the CPU.'

Christine let out a small gasp, but retained her composure.

Prior strained to look down the stairwell, it seemed clear of obstruction. 'Can you manage — '

To his surprise and delight, he saw that Christine was already making her way down the stairs, a step at a time, before he could even finish his sentence. Or make an offer of assistance. This was a woman who clearly didn't accept aid lightly.

As Prior moved to follow, he felt a large hand on his shoulder. He jumped, tensing; ready to deliver a short, sharp jab to the mid-riff of the owner of that hand.

It was Davies.

Didn't he ever tire of jogging up and down this ship?

'Guv', he breathed, 'you left this.' He held up the large torch that Prior had somehow managed to leave behind him in the medical bay. 'Thought you might need it.'

Prior nodded, 'Thanks. Did you speak to Captain Andrews?'

'Yeah. Briefed him and Roberts … they're looking through the crew files and passenger lists now.'

'I bet that pleased them. Trawling through papers like a couple of ensigns.'

'Yeah. I told 'em it was your idea!' Davies sniggered.

The lad truly was an insatiable ball of energy that simply couldn't be contained, with a smile that was more than contagious, it was epidemic! You simply couldn't dislike Davies. Even if you wanted to.

'Thanks for that.' Prior said, as he flicked on the LED torch and the pair made their way down the stairs behind Christine, 'You might as well come along with us now that you're here.'

'Where are we headed?'

'Room fifteen-thirty-four.' Prior said. He made a gesture towards Christine and was about to introduce the pair. But, as they turned the corner that brought them onto the main corridor of that level, they were immediately confronted by a crowd of people gathering around the two young men that had been posted outside the closed door of room fifteen-thirty-four.

As they approached, several women in the crowd surged forward, shouting and clawing at the stifled maintenance officers. 'Let us in!' they cried, 'We want to see Stacey.'

'I need to see my sister!' called another, as she scrambled to grab the cardkey attached to one of the officer's belts.

With a precise slight-of-hand and an awesome speed, the feisty, young blonde had slipped the cardkey through the reader and thrown open the door before the officer had even had a chance to react.

There were gasps of horror and repulsion as the door swung back. This was followed by a moment of sickly silence when all the sound seemed to dissipate as if it had simply been sucked out of the lungs of the spectators and the gossips gathered before the suddenly exposed scene.

Strung up on the metal curtain pole opposite the door was the bloody, naked body of a twenty-something year-old girl; her arms spread wide. It seemed that several torn pairs of nylon tights held the girl aloft, while the bloodied drapes that fell in symmetrical arcs below her arms looked like open wings.

Her face was a battered, bloody mass of pulped and spongy flesh. Pieces of her shattered left cheekbone protruded from the mess; white and gleaming as though they had been polished up. A trophy on a mantel piece.

Bite marks covered her thighs, her naval and breasts, while another chunk of flesh had been torn roughly from her neck — near her throat — releasing the river of blood that had cascaded over her young, tight body, coursing its way over her cooling skin as gravity dictated.

Now it dripped, like a leaky tap, from her flapping foot as she hung lifelessly in the air. Dripping in the silence before the crowd.

Drip. Drip. Drip.

'Oh my — ' was all that Christine could manage before the silence was pierced by the heart-wrenching sound of sorrow that sprang from the blonde who had opened the door.

Stacey's sister.

She moaned and howled as all around them the crowd broke to murmurs and mutterings that quickly became shrieks and shouts and exclamations of terror and panic.

Unable to support herself, the sister slid towards the ground. Prior rushed forward, catching her as she fell. She twisted in his arms, hysterical and howling still. She seemed unaware that the noise was in fact her own as she looked around her blindly, seeing no one; searching for her sister.

'Get everyone out of here.' Prior shouted to the officers, as he pressed the girl's head to his chest and pulled the door closed.

The maintenance officers, under Davies' guidance, began to usher the passengers through the corridor as even more spilled from their rooms to catch a glimpse of the great commotion. Prior lifted the blonde's head and tried to look into her eyes.

She still didn't see him.

'Davies!' he shouted, pulling her close to him once more. She wrapped her arms around him, sobbing and pleading nonsensically. 'Marc!'

Davies swam through the crowd, clawing his way back towards Prior and Christine in time to see the girl in Prior's arms vomit a vibrant blue emulsion down the front of his dark uniform. Prior didn't flinch, though his face creased in revulsion as his own stomach heaved. 'Guv'?'

'Get her up to medical.' he said, easing the girl back from his now lubricated torso; the alcoholic vomit mixing with the wool of his ribbed, black jumper. He tugged at the high neck feeling suddenly very claustrophobic and unwell himself. 'Don't leave her side. If you do move, let me know.'

Davies nodded, unclipping one of the half dozen two-way radios he had attached to his belt.

Exchanging the radio for the girl he wrapped his arm around her cautiously, trying to keep as much distance between himself and her as possible.

As he turned to lead the distressed blonde from the scene, Prior called him back. 'Give me another radio. For Christine.' Davies unhooked the two-way and chucked it at his superior. 'Keep in touch. And get someone down here with a camera.'

'Yes, sir.' he said, disappearing down the corridor.

Alone now, Christine stared at Prior. He handed her the radio that he was certain had been nowhere near the human bile. 'Are you ok?' he asked.

She nodded slowly.

'You're sure?'

'Yes. I'm fine.' she snapped off. She paused, regaining some modicum of control before attempting to smile at Prior, apologising silently, once more. It wasn't his fault. It wasn't even him she was angry with. 'I'm not the one wearing my enzymes on the outside.' she said.

Humour. The classic defence mechanism.

Prior snorted a short laugh, looking down at his chest. The stench of bile and alcohol scorched his nostrils. He swallowed hard and choked back a cough. 'To be fair, they're not my enzymes.'

'And is that supposed to make it better or worse?'

'Oh,' he gagged, 'it's much worse.'

With another brief smile and a long sigh, he pulled out the overriding master cardkey that he always carried with him. Sliding it through the reader on the door he glanced at Christine, waiting for the confirmation that she was certain she wanted to do this.

The small affirming nod came without hesitation.

Prior opened the wooden door and together they stepped inside.

18:51

Saturday 14th May, 2011

After the strange run-in with Mike, Shona made had her way towards the *Grande Central*.

She would have gone up onto the open deck — she had wanted to and desperately needed to feel the fresh air on her face — but, the weather had suddenly turned; a dark and stormy night had descended seemingly from nowhere. Thunder and lightning and torrential shite pouring from the sky!

Besides, she felt safer somehow in the midst of the jostling crowd.

She was supposed to have met with Kelly for dinner in here nearly an hour earlier. She had been a little late with everything that had gone on. But, she hadn't been *that* late.

She had been more than prepared to apologise and divulge the unnerving tale and the reason for her tardiness. She had looked forward to indulging in a quiet drink — or three — and much more besides, with the rock-star-hot artist who looked more like the lead singer in some sexy, emo-punk band than a professor and tutor at some stuffy university.

But there had been no sign of Kelly when she arrived.

There was *still* no sign of Kelly.

Shona huffed, pressing through the crowd, back towards the bar. 'Jimmy,' she called, catching the attention of the white-haired, white-stubbled man serving there, 'you couldn't rustle me up a stiff Americano could you?' she said, winking as he nodded, 'Cheers honey. Oh, and I mean cocktail, not the coffee!'

The older man smiled; pleased with the attention he was receiving from the Latino-looking beauty. He quickly set about completing her order, ignoring the customer in front of him.

Shona continued to squeeze and squirm through the sea of people and eventually settled onto the padded bar-stool near to the Christmas-faced man she had called Jimmy. She pulled a straw from the polished wooden dispenser and began chewing on the black plastic.

In the darkened restaurant, lit only by torches and mobile phone screens — which had been rendered as little more than glorified torches themselves — along with the pointless low-level emergency lighting strips that ran along the floor, Shona absently peeled the label from a stray beer bottle as she contemplated the evening she had had in mind.

She considered the mystery of the sudden loss of power only as an after-thought; rating it not too highly on her list of personal priorities. Certainly it came after the strange encounter she had had with Mike and was far from significant when taking into account the missed encounters she had hoped to have with Kelly.

'Ah well,' she sighed, 'Your loss, Kelly Livingstone.'

As her drink arrived she raised it high, toasting the air before her. Then, parting her full and glistening lips, she allowed the delights of the liquor to pass and wet her eager taste-buds.

'Your loss.'

In the darkness he watched her. In the darkness he waited.

Unknown. Unseen.

The low-level lighting and throng of thirsty passengers obscuring him; allowing him the luxury of a comfy seat and a delightful view to boot.

He stared at her; at her strong thighs and her soft lips, imagining those lips pressed against his, wondering what they would taste like now.

He hadn't been close enough to hear what she had ordered, but it didn't matter. He would give anything to be that glass tumbler; her warm, sensual lips wrapping around him. Her soft, slender hands caressing him.

Or the liquid. He would gladly be the liquid itself.

He smiled at the thought of sliding over those parted cherry lips to trip on the tongue and then be inside her mouth as she savoured all of him.

He suddenly ached with wanting her; the denim of his trousers stretching tight across his crotch. And not for the first time that day.

'Patience.' he whispered. 'Patience.'

19:15

Saturday 14th May, 2011

The hands of the junior security officer shook as he tried to photograph the scene.

Prior sighed, thinking, *He shouldn't be doing this.*

He felt Christine's hand on his arm. 'None of you signed up for this.'

It was as though she could read his mind.

He shook his head, agreeing with her. 'And you,' he said after a moment, staring into the distance somewhere between the body of Stacey Atkins and his own thoughts, 'I'm sure this is the last thing you needed at the moment.'

Christine shot him a look, her intense gaze snapping him suddenly from his trance. He met her dark, chocolate stare with one of equal, unmoveable determination. There was an intensity there; a fire burning behind the glass of her eyes.

And he knew the cause.

He longed to question her about the night that Thomas Butler had escaped custody. The night that he had tracked this strong and brilliant Criminal Psychologist and followed her to her sister's house.

Prior's was not a morbid curiosity. He was not merely fishing to bite at a juicy tit-bit of lurid detail from the living memory of the traumatised woman by his side.

He had read the papers, seen the news reports and tutted time and again at the senselessness of it all; the mistakes of the Cheshire West Police force; the violent tortures inflicted upon Christine and her sister; the death of Janet Kane; the insensitivity of the media who — even now — continued to hound her.

No wonder she was so quick to throw up her guard.

In a strange way he felt like he knew her. And yet he knew — absolutely — that he did not. He knew nothing of her in the living flesh; only the words that he had read.

But, he had felt for her — even then — reading of her plight and her suffering.

And then he had come to meet her. And she was no longer a picture in a newspaper; a distant character of media print that might exist *somewhere*. She was real. Human.

She was soft and warm and attractive; living, breathing, tangible and *here* on this ship. His ship.

She was strong and secretive and yet she was so very fragile; the cracks of that fragility threatening to break at the smallest tap.

That was when she threw up her protective, concrete walls.

From the moment he had first heard her speak at the dinner table with Captain Andrews and Dr Matthews and the rest of them he had known that he felt something for her. Something strong.

The desire to protect.   *Gross.*

He had wanted to protect her even then; though it wasn't his place do so. To shield her from the onslaught of questions and judgements; from his crewmates and his commanders sat at the table; from the relentless world of media that he knew had been harassing her constantly since the original trial.

From the whole world.

Knowing her a little better now, it was clear to Prior that Christine Kane would not accept the offer of such protection lightly. She was a very proud woman; independent and determined. And he couldn't help but admire her, though he doubted he would ever be able to voice this high regard without Dr Kane misunderstanding the intent of the sentiment.

Without her believing it to be some misguided placation routed solely in a sense of sympathy for her inflicted circumstances and enforced condition of disability.

Yes, the attractive ex-profiler was quick to take offence.

But he understood why.

He wasn't certain whether it was simply some psychotic reaction to losing Rachel so suddenly or something else entirely, but the desire to protect Christine had gripped him with an astonishing and redoubled intensity ever since he had spotted her outside the medical bay supporting Miss Livingstone earlier.

She was just incredible.

Prior realised that Christine was still watching him and met her eyes as she opened her mouth to speak. The fair-haired officer, still photographing, the scene interrupted before she could begin.

'Sir, I think you should take a look at this.'

He was standing close to the still-mounted body of the girl, Stacey Atkins, and leaning in to the right-hand side of her. He clicked the digital box in his hand and the flash — once more — illuminated the room with several bursts of silver-white light that left Prior momentarily blinded.

'What've you found?' he asked, moving closer.

'Look here, Sir. Along her ribs. I didn't notice it at first ... I only saw it with the flash.'

Prior brought the torch shining up onto Stacey's limp and battered body. There was so much more bruising than he had first realised; the harsh white-blue light revealing the extent of her suffering; disclosing the unspoken record of all that had occurred.

He shook his head involuntarily, feeling Christine fall-in at his side.

There was something comforting in her being there, knowing that she was seeing this too and — as odd as it sounded — simply knowing that she too would be cataloguing the information as he was; building up a sequence of events in the seemingly cold and detached manner they had each been trained to.

They were a pair; she and he. Born through their previous experience. And now they were sharing, comparing; working together.

An invaluable collective of living knowledge.

Yes, as awful and as selfish as it may have been, he was glad to have her there.

'You've worked crime scenes before?' he questioned, already knowing the answer. It seemed the politest way to break the stifling silence.

Christine nodded as the light from the torch continued to crawl over the now cold flesh of Stacey's body, exposing more and more of the secret tale that had concluded with her being strung up crucifixion-style; the tangled, taffeta-drape angel-wings billowing from her arms in a gruesome display of creativity that seemed to mock the scene itself.

'What's that?' she asked, pointing.

Prior focused the light steadily onto the area. It was the same patch that the young officer had just pointed out. They stared at a series of roughly cut scratches that had been carved into the skin above Stacey's ribs.

He frowned suddenly as he realised they weren't just random scores meant to torture the poor girl. They were words.

'Not . . . My . . . Type.' he whispered, reading.

'Looks like they were carved post-mortem.' Christine said. 'The body hasn't tried to heal itself.'

He nodded thoughtfully.

Out of the corner of his eye Prior saw Collins stooping near the bed. The young man was struggling to bag something; dry-wretching as his awkwardly angled, latex-gloved hand trembled. He seemed to be trying to pick up a small, blood-soaked piece of material and deposit it into a clear plastic bag as quickly as possible.

'What've you got there, Collins?' he asked.

'Looks like underwear.' the flame-haired officer said, struggling from the floor, trying not to disturb anything else, 'I don't think they've been worn from the way they were folded. But they're covered in blood.'

'Let me see.'

Standing, Collins made his way to Prior, handing him the plastic evidence bag.

'Do you know what it reminds me of?' he said, staring intently at the garment. He didn't wait for a cue, 'It reminds me of a rag I used to have for waxing and polishing the first car I ever bought. I was so damn proud of that car.' he continued, almost smiling as he gave himself over to the strength of the memory, 'I used to polish it up every weekend. Regardless of whether it needed it. Look at the fold,' he said, holding the bagged garment up in the torch light, 'You can see where it's been sat around his finger, as he ... worked.'

With a steady hand that made the movement seem strangely and disturbingly elegant, Prior shifted the focus of the torch so that the stream of light now fell silently on what remained of the left quadrant of Stacey's face. On the horridly white cheekbone protruding through the pink gelatine blend of muscle and flesh.

'He was proud of this.' said Christine, a small tremble in her voice.

Prior nodded and returned the bag to Collins. 'You sound worried.' he said, 'But, they say pride comes before a fall. Maybe he's slipped up here. Left something behind that'll lead us to him.'

Christine shook her head, 'It's not that. And in any case, I don't think he's worried about being caught. If this is the same person who took out the engineering crew, who managed to bring the ship to a total standstill and disabled all communications with the outside world ... they already know they have nothing to fear. They know they're in control and, yes, they took pride in creating this ... display. And that makes me wonder whether this isn't the first time they've done something like this. I mean, this level of brutality isn't just something that happens; it's something that you work up to. And, as awful as it sounds, I don't think he's anywhere near finished.'

'What makes you — '

Prior was interrupted as the two-way, now attached to his belt, crackled with static.

'Davies to Prior.'

'I'm here.' Prior answered, holding in the call button on the side of the radio, 'Go ahead.'

'Guv', I think you should come back up to medical.' Davies said, his voice crackling over the channel, 'We've . . . .' he paused, 'Well . . . we've found Dr Cunningham.'

Found.

Prior exchanged an ominous look with Christine and in the dark of room fifteen-thirty-four, he silently conceded that her bleak and undesirable forecast may just have been correct.

19:15

Saturday 14th May, 2011

Leigh's head throbbed with a fury.

He turned over on the bed, eyes still pressed tightly shut against the pain of the kettle drums being pounded in a relentless rhythm under his skull. He groaned as he leaned a little too heavily on the leg that Gary Blakely had caught.

Bastard.

He had been a tough one, that Blakely. Deceiving, really.

There hadn't been much to him at all; no great, obvious muscle mass. He was a fairly tall bloke and of a slim-to-scrawny build. Or rather, he *had* been.

But there had been power in those arms when the pair of them had fought and — for a time — Blakely had thrown him around like he was merely a rag doll. An amusement.

But, then again, he *had* been in the process of murdering most of Blakely's friends and companions.

Adrenaline.

It could make you do crazy things; give you an almost inhuman strength.

For a time.

He remembered reading an article in a paper somewhere about a mother who had lifted a solid section of wall after it had fallen on her child. Three men couldn't shift it. But the mother, hell-bent on saving the sprog she had popped out only five years earlier, had raised the still-cemented bricks while her neighbours had pulled the kid to safety.

Then, she had turned to check that her child was safe. She had smiled, seeing that he was. And had promptly died of a massive heart attack.

Adrenaline.

He pushed out a long breath and turned again — onto his side this time — propping himself up on his elbow. He reached over to the bedside table where he found the packet of tablets that the accommodating, latte-licious whore had pressed into his pocket up on the open deck that morning.

So much had happened since then.

Lost briefly in remembering, his eyes found the beautifully crafted handle of the flick-knife that now sat next to the ibuprofen. Blakely's knife.

He licked his lips; his thoughts returning — suddenly — to the dark-haired dancer. To that delightfully tight, little button arse that she seemed to enjoy showing off as she paraded around the upper deck.

Popping two of the pills into his mouth he swallowed them down without a drink.

Yes, a lot had happened since that morning.

But the night wasn't over yet.

Slowly, he sat up and swung his legs over the side of the bed. His thigh stung as he flexed the healing muscle. He winced silently, examining the wound. The stitches were holding at least.

He had made a good job of them; each stitch sewn individually as his brother had taught him. Individual stitching made it easier to cut them out later.

A travel-sized sewing kit was never too far from his weapon of choice these days.

He jumped up, immediately regretting the action and paused, bent — almost doubled-over — in pain for a moment, sucking in quick, small breaths. It wasn't just his leg, his ribs ached too; the muscles around them pulsing with every heart beat.

And his face, God, his face was sore! He could only imagine the bruising as he ran the tips of his finger over his swollen cheeks in the darkened room.

And it hadn't been just Blakely he had had to contend with today.

There had been Stacey too.

She had scrambled about a bit, trying to hold on; not managing to inflict any real damage on him. But, still.

She had twitched and writhed as he had dragged her from the bathroom, but there was no real fight left in her by then. Life and sense were ebbing from her in the dark red gush that sprang from her shattered, little face.

A broken china doll.

She had flailed in his arms, striking wildly at him as he had nibbled at her neck; tasting her young flesh. Then, the nibbling turned to biting and then, suddenly, he had been tearing soft, pink chunks from her.

He couldn't say whether she had been conscious when he had torn out her throat.

He hoped so.

And then there was the artist; Kelly.

Jesus, she was tough for a bird! What a scrapper!

She had been busy painting when he had found her and was in an almost trance-like state, moving from the pallet to the fresh canvas and back again in a quiet fury of fluid movements.

It was odd to say the least, but enticing and he found himself watching her from the shadows for some time before finally revealing himself to take control of her.

Watching her work he had realised, all of a sudden, that he had encountered the strange, inky-haired artist — who reminded him of something from the Goth scene back home — once before.

The night before, in fact.

She had been the sickly sack of scrawny-looking bones that had staggered from the theatre not too long before he himself had given up on the cacophony of moral dogma.

Funny how things worked out.

He had imagined — for the briefest of moments — the pair of them working together.

He was well acquainted with the work of Kelly Livingstone. He had even visited a gallery to see it! Though, he had never previously known her face before this surreptitious boat trip.

Initially, Vince had *made* him visit the gallery; dragged him there — almost kicking and screaming — muttering something about culture.

Ha! He pissed fucking culture!

Back then he had been so reluctant.

Why the fuck would *he* want to go looking at a bunch of sappy paintings by stuffy, bloody, self-involved artists?

But Vince had insisted.

And the twisted, old bastard had been right.

He *had* enjoyed himself. Kelly's work had given him a lot to think about; it had given him a semi just to look at it, if he was honest!

After that particular excursion he had enjoyed a very interesting evening with a homeless girl — who remained a missing person to this day — revisiting the savage imagery of the paintings he had enjoyed most. Recreating them in his very own *very* physical style.

Never-the-less, it was thanks to Vince that he had been introduced to the brutal work of the enlighteningly morbid artist who now laboured before him; creating new works in his unknown presence.

Watching her, his breath had quickened.

He admired the vicious honesty and wild passion of Kelly's work. He adored it in a way that made him want to fuck the canvas; to just be fucking part of it!

But that simply wouldn't do.

And besides, he didn't work well with others. And he knew it.

In the brief time between him revealing himself and her realising that she was no longer alone, their artistic differences had caused a rift to open up between them, forcing his hand towards the action of having to knock her the fuck out.

She had struggled — hell, she had given him a fucking good run for his money — but he had his way in the end.

He only hoped he hadn't gone too far.

He couldn't recall everything, but knew he had become rather excited by the whole ... affair. What if he had gotten too carried away and ...?

Still. Never mind.

He had been exhausted afterwards and crashed out on the bed for ... he didn't really know how long. But now he was refreshed and ready for action.

He pulled his trousers back on and stumbled over to the re-stocked mini-bar that was no longer locked.

Unfortunately it was no longer cooling the contents either. The first real downfall he had encountered since cutting the ship's imaginary power cord. Still, you couldn't make an omelette ...

If he was honest with himself — and he generally was — he hadn't really expected it to work. And certainly not this well!

He grinned, taking a small bottle of Spanish beer from the mini-bar, pleased to find that it was still fairly chilled.

He popped the top using the edge of the dressing table, slamming his hand down hard, before shaking it off as the excess bubbles danced over his fingers. Bringing the bottle to his dry and swollen lips he downed the liquid in several gulps before tossing the bottle onto the floor.

He stretched slowly, feeling every cut and every bruise complaining as he did.

He was becoming more and more accustomed to the feel of the ocean beneath his feet and even the ever-growing storm had done little to dampen his heightened spirits and cheery mood.

Tapping his pocket to locate his cardkey — though he doubted he would be needing it anytime soon — he gave a small nod; confirming to no one but himself that the key was safe.

He began whistling the tune of an animated film he had seen as a child as he returned to the bedside table unit, grabbing Blakely's knife and pushing it into his free pocket.

Moving back towards the door he reached for the handle.

'It's off to work I go.' he grinned as he stepped into the corridor, closing the door behind him.

19:30

Saturday 14th May, 2011

Christine struggled to keep up with Prior as they entered the medical bay for the second time that evening. The doors closed behind her and she found herself momentarily blinded as before.

Her mind rattled as she tallied the death toll that this unknown killer had managed to rack up in only a few short hours; Gary Blakely, twenty-three members of the engineering crew (that she had counted), Stacey Atkins and now Dr Cunningham.

And they were still no closer to discovering his identity. Neither did they have any idea why he was killing in such an apparently sporadic and disparate fashion.

Why he was killing at all.

Christine couldn't help but feel that had she not offered her assistance earlier, she would still have been receiving a knock on the door right about now from the green-eyed Security Chief, Jonathan Prior. She could just imagine the conversation; the awkwardness and his eventual imploring of her to join him and offer her professional opinion. She could see him in her mind, cautiously inviting her input whilst he tip-toed around the issues of her recent past.

The more she thought about it, the more she realised that there was in fact nowhere else she would rather be at a time like this. Regardless of her fears and her somewhat shattered confidence, this was what she did; it was who she was.

She would much rather be aiding in the investigation than be sat in the dark of her room, climbing the walls in terror and self-loathing. Or drowning her sorrows and trying to numb the sense of panic and pain with a nice bottle of rosé.

I do drink far too much. She thought as they approached Dr Matthews and the handsome, blonde-haired ox that was Davies.

Matthews looked undeniably shaken. If it was possible she looked even paler than she had earlier and her hands shook whenever she unclasped them. On the table before her lay the undeniable outline of a body covered by a thin, pale green sheet. Seeing Christine and Prior she opened her mouth to speak.

Silence.

She gave herself a moment before she tried a second time.

'He was in the mortuary freezer.' she stammered.

Christine shifted her weight, stretching out her stiffening left leg as Prior lifted the sheet before them.

The sight that greeted them seemed a quiet Sunday afternoon compared to the body they had just left. And yet it was no less horrid.

The only visible injury was located in the centre of the deceased doctor's forehead, just above the line of his eyebrows. It was an open wound that looked to extend at least an inch deep into his skull. The hollow gash was merely millimetres thick, but appeared to have done the trick.

Christine leaned in, visually examining Cunningham; inspecting the bruising around the site of the wound.

It was dark and distinct; a deep blue-black contusion with edges that were crisp rather than diffuse. Such a defined pattern indicated that the blood from the ruptured vessels beneath the surface of the skin hadn't had much opportunity to seep into the wider tissue area. It was what she would have expected from such a mortal-looking injury and she anticipated that the bruising appeared so sharp due to the fact that the blood had ceased pumping around Cunningham's body shortly after the injury had occurred; which in turn, indicated that the damage had been sustained peri-mortem.

'This was the cause of death?' she asked, confident in her silent deduction.

Dr Matthews nodded, 'He doesn't seem to have suffered any other external injuries. But, I'll know more when I ...' Her words trailed off to nothingness as she fought to control the emotion that quivered in her voice. 'They say you shouldn't carry out a pathological examination on someone you know. Have known.'

'I hate to say it, Dr Matthews,' Prior said, his voice quiet and almost as lost as hers, 'and I hate to be the one to point it out and sound completely heartless here, but I have a feeling that you're going to be quite busy with post-mortems.' he paused, touching her hand, trying to comfort her, to make a human connection, 'And most of them will be concerning people that you ... that we, all of us ... have known. And loved. I need to know that you can cope.'

Christine stared at him, feeling for him and knowing that he was right. And that Dr Matthews was now the only one who could do this. The only one qualified.

'What happened to you?' she asked, noticing the shining bruise that was beginning to show across his cheek, blackening the skin below his left eye. Then she recoiled, clearly catching the scent of vomit from his ribbed, wool jumper. 'And what is that smell?'

'Davies' he said, pointing to his cheek. Matthews looked concerned for a moment and threw a daggered glance at the blonde ox, but Prior shook his head, grinning. 'Nothing to worry about. A simple miscommunication.' Then he pointed to his jumper. 'The Atkins girl. The sister. Is she still here?'

Matthews nodded her head towards a separate room. The room she had discovered Cunningham's almost-empty wine bottle in earlier that morning. 'She's talking to somebody now.'

'It might be easier you know, Doc. Having more autopsies to ...' Davies' voice tailed off as he continued to stare at the body of Dr Cunningham. Matthews' eyes locked him suddenly with a daggered glare.

Christine could see that he immediately regretted airing the statement and wished that he could take it back; that he had been trying to bring some sense of alleviation to both the awful situation and the hawk-like doctor in the only way he could think of.

All he had managed to succeed in doing was to incite a visible rage in the tall, angular woman, whose light blue eyes — though glistening with tears that threatened to breach her severe exterior — had turned suddenly dark as the storm outside, flashing with a white hot anger.

'Easier!' she snapped, turning on the blonde bull, 'You think that having *more* people to cut open and catalogue and try to determine a cause of death for; that having *more* human organs to weigh and dissect and label and store will be *easier?*'

'I just thought it might, you know, keep you busy — '

'*Busy?*' she repeated, furiously.

'I thought that if you were just going through the motions it might be more — '

'*Going through the motions!*' she interrupted a second time. 'This isn't like mopping up the floor at the end of the night, Marc. Or getting your paperwork in order, or fucking tidying your room in case you pull, you know!

'I ... I Know, I just ...'

'What was the mechanism of death?' Christine cut in, trying to divert Matthews' frustrated attention away from wanting to throttle Davies.

Matthews shook her head in clear irritation. 'He ... I can't be absolutely certain until ... but, from the looks of the bruising around the wound, I'd say death occurred within minutes of him being stabbed.

The instrument entered just above the procerus muscle and penetrated the skull.' She pushed out a heavy sigh before continuing; slowing her words as she began to come down from her rage, 'There's clear evidence of sharp-force trauma; a single, swift delivery by some sort of blade. He's most likely suffered an epidural bleed.' Matthews paused, eyeing Christine coldly, 'But, like I say, I can't be absolutely certain at this time.'

Christine nodded.

She glanced around the room, which finally appeared to be settling in terms of noise and hustle, despite the fact that it was still bursting at the seams with bodies and medical staff.

She couldn't help but notice the mortuary freezers at the far end of the room and found herself contemplating the limited amount of space that would be on offer to house the ever-increasing number of cadavers needing to be stored.

Christine couldn't bring herself to air the question. Thinking of Matthews' reaction to Davies words only moment earlier made her slightly nervous and she flicked her eyes up to meet Prior's. He gave a small, but resolute nod, seeming to know her thoughts.

Scanning the medical bay once more, Christine suddenly frowned.

'Where's Kelly?' she asked.

Matthews stared at her for a moment, but before Christine could push for an answer a team of two security officers and two medical staff — none of them older than twenty five — burst into the light of the medical bay, each shielding their eyes as they did. They pulled between them a large, deep, squeaking laundry trolley; an off-white and blood-stained blanket covering the mass of oddly angled shapes beneath it.

The lead security officer, a tall lad with broad shoulders and short-cropped black hair clicked off the torch in his hand and — seeing Prior — made his way towards the Security Chief.

'Sir.' he said, pausing to take in the bruising that now adorned his commander's face as well as the stench of the drying vomit that had become a crust on the wool of his top. He chose not to mention them. 'We've done all we can down in engineering, the medical teams tried to revive the victims trapped inside the lock-down area.' He paused a second time and shook his head, gnawing his lower lip for a moment as he pushed back the emotions that were clearly beginning to overwhelm him.

'It's alright, Stratton.' Prior said, 'You're doing fine.'

The man named Stratton pushed out a long breath and continued to shake his head, his dark eyes glassy as he stared into the space between Prior and Christine. 'There were so many, Guv'.'

'What's that?' Prior asked, nodding towards the trolley they had just wheeled in.

Christine couldn't help but feel for the young man who seemed suddenly younger still. A boy lost in a wood of terrifying clinical chaos.

'That's Blakely, Sir.' he said, trembling, 'We did our best, but he's still ...'

Prior put his hand on Stratton's shoulder, reassuring him. 'Did you take pictures of the scene, check for evidence?'

Stratton nodded.

Digging down into the knee pocket of his black trousers he produced a small, silver digital camera. 'I took the pictures myself. There wasn't much evidence to be collected. Nothing at all in the lock down area itself, aside from a match; burnt out in the sensor housing near the main console. I don't think the crew even knew what was happening until it was too late.'

'Good work.' Prior said, taking the camera from Stratton. 'Davies, will you take this and the other evidence — '

'Can I see the pictures?' Christine cut in, pushing herself forward amongst the men.

Stratton looked at her, momentarily horrified, then hurt and swiftly after; angry. 'They're not happy holiday snaps you know.'

Christine contained her initial response, pressing her lips together for a moment. It wasn't Stratton's fault; he didn't know her from Adam. Or Eve. He was struggling to come to terms with the horrors he had seen and she knew that — in his own young, sweet way — he was actually trying to protect her.

A quality she seemed to be inspiring in her newly acquired male colleagues of late.

'I know Mr ... Stratton, is it?' she said flatly, 'I've worked alongside various police departments on more than a few crime scenes in the past. It's sweet of you to be concerned, but if we're going to catch the person that did this I need to see the way they work. I need to try and understand them, or at the very least try and understand why they are doing the things they are doing and see if I can find some sort of pattern to work from. Anything that might help us to identify them.'

'Stratton, this is Dr Christine Kane.' Prior said, opening his palm towards her, 'She's a Criminal Psychologist.'

The tall, dark-haired Stratton eyed Christine for another moment. She cocked her head slightly, trying to read him even as he tried to read her.

'So, I guess you see stuff like this all the time.' he huffed, finally.

She shook her head and managed a small, friendly smile. 'Fortunately not.'

Stratton snorted a short laugh before Prior took him and Davies to one side.

Though she couldn't hear their conversation, Christine could see that Prior was — once more — taking control of the situation; giving orders, making plans. They were fortunate to have a man of his experience on board, especially considering the average age of most of the crew and their inexperience in dealing with anything like this.

Then again, how exactly would you go about training people — training young, happy-go-lucky, see the world, cruise-liner crew type people — to deal with a situation like this?

'Oh, your *friend*; Kelly.' Dr Matthews' clipped voice sliced neatly through her thoughts, 'I had someone take her back to her room. There was no a need for her to remain here. And to be honest there simply wasn't the space to keep her.'

Christine restrained the urge to scream into the miserable doctor's severe, angular face *She's not a fucking puppy!*

Though only just.

Matthews had covered Cunningham back over and was now busy scribbling short-hand notes into a pocket-sized pad, unwilling to offer any further information on the subject of Kelly Livingstone. As though her previous statement should have been enough to satisfy the psychologist.

'So, she's stable then?'

'I'm sure she'll be fine.' Matthews said, looking up at Christine, 'With rest, she'll be just fine. She needed a few stitches. There was a lot of superficial bruising, some smaller cuts.'

'Did she mention anything?'

Dr Matthews shook her head. 'She barely came round.'

'And you sent her back to her room?' Christine blasted, angrily, 'What if she has a head injury? She already suffers with severe migraines.'

If it was possible, Dr Matthews' face became momentarily tighter, her nostrils flaring in annoyance. 'I am *confident* that she has not suffered any great head injury and that she will recover in her own time with rest and painkillers. You are welcome to check on her yourself. I'm sure you won't find it too much of a hardship.'

Matthews had snapped off the final sentence and spun on her heel, marching swiftly towards the newly arrived trolley that contained the remains of Gary Blakely, before Christine could even muster a reply.

'What's that supposed to mean?' she called after her.

Matthews didn't answer.

She was beginning to wonder whether Dr Matthews had known all along just how much that hideous metal and grey rubber walking stick would injure her pride, after all. That she felt somehow threatened by Christine and wanted to put her down in any way she could. That she had purposely gone out of her way to rile her up and embarrass her.

The one thing she could be certain of was that — though she had no idea how or why — she appeared to have found herself on the wrong side of the friend-or-foe fence when it came to dealing with the fierce-faced doctor.

What was her problem?

Was she threatened professionally? Maybe.

Christine ran her tongue over her teeth, feeling the little nick of the small chip at the front. She watched Matthews as she busied about the medical bay; as she flitted here and there working her way towards the group of security officers.

Towards Prior.

Christine smiled, noticing that Matthews' eyes rarely left the tall and attractive Security Chief for more than a moment. Suddenly, she understood.

Seeming to sense her, Prior looked up at Christine. He began moving back towards her and she instantly felt the envious stare of Dr Matthews cutting through her like a Martian beam. She shook her head softly.

'What?' he asked.

'Nothing.' she returned, 'I'll tell you later.'

He shrugged, a little confused and held up the digital camera along with several evidence bags and an SD card. 'I think it's time we grabbed a coffee. I don't suppose you'd happen to have a laptop with you, do you?'

Christine nodded, drawing an instant smile from the ruggedly handsome, emerald-eyed ex-copper. She could understand why Matthews found him attractive.

It was an easy thing to do.

'I didn't have you down as the *leave your work at home* type.'

'Got me in one.' she said, 'Can I ask a favour though?'

'Of course.' Prior said, stuffing the camera into his pocket.

Christine leaned the metal walking stick against the table, taking a moment to steady herself. 'Might I lend an arm?'

Much to her surprise, Prior appeared to blush as he nodded and extended his arm for her. She took hold, feeling the taut and powerful muscles of his solid bicep.

It was a little childish she knew, but she would not be the slave to another woman's jealousy. And, after all, it was Dr Matthews who had thrown down the gauntlet, not she.

'So,' she said loudly enough for Matthews to hear, 'back to mine, then?'

Prior nodded.

'Although, I think I could do with a shower.' he said, unaware of the jealous doctor as they made their way towards the doors, 'I don't know how much longer I can stand the stench or the sensation of someone else's vomit on me!'

'I'm sure I can spare a towel.'

Christine laughed as Prior coloured slightly for the second time and they moved through the doors of the medical bay, leaving a seething and almost steaming Dr Matthews behind them.

19:42

Saturday 14th May, 2011

He had been at the table for only a few minutes. Rotating a cold and bubbling pint of golden lager between his cupped hands he savoured the thrill of the icy wet glass on his palms. It seemed a small slice of something divine in the close humidity of the dark and crowded bar.

Drinking deeply and savouring every delightful mouthful he scanned the dim room that seemed so much smaller now as it swarmed with people eager to take their minds off the situation *he* had created.

Though they, of course, had no idea of the part he had played so well.

Passengers, punters and potential pickings pressed against one another, clawing their way towards the bar, to a chair, a table or even a spare patch of wall; theirs to lean against.

All ripe to be plucked, he thought. Each of them puckering up, opening themselves to him and the twisted new appetite he seemed unable to satisfy.

Over in the corner sat a girl with brown hair; frightened and looking to make a friend. And then here, opposite him, was a lonely string-bean of a boy intently focused on completing the next level of some idle game offered up to him by the harsh light of his phone.

Either would have been an easy target.

But, he hadn't yet decided upon his next masterpiece.

Should he be making vast sweeping statements? Should he simply let his art take him wherever it might? Become lost in that dark creativity he was only just discovering he possessed.

Or rather, was possessed of.

He chuckled quietly to himself, drawing a look from the gangly gamer.

The boy raised an acidic eyebrow, but didn't speak and swiftly returned his attention to the phone, lost once more in the two-dimensional world of the game. A slave to the screen.

'Do you mind if I join you?'

The sudden and sultry feminine voice slipped through his thoughts even as her warm, lithe body slid onto the padded bench-seat next to him, not waiting for a reply.

She wore a slip of incredibly expensive-looking turquoise silk over her bare, pale skin. Even in the shadowed room the garment revealed the curve of her tight, unhindered breasts as she leaned across the table to pick up a worn beer mat. She set it down in front of her, then rested the large glass of white wine she had held in her slim, almost skeletal hands upon it.

'Be my guest.' he said ironically, as she made herself comfortable.

She appeared tall for a woman, her height exaggerated by her slight frame. She was dripping in diamonds and white-gold, her fingers glorified with enough rocks to sustain a third-world country for at least half a century!

His eyes traced over her bejewelled hands to her bangled arms and still further up her long body. At her throat was a large topaz stone surrounded (once again) by a multitude of smaller sparkling stones that he was certain could be nothing less than diamonds, set — as with the other pieces — in a rich bed of high-carat content white-gold. Teardrops matching the necklace centrepiece pulled at her earlobes, catching and reflecting the smallest amount of light and lengthening an already elongated face.

She was not unattractive despite the odd angles of her slight and lengthy, bedazzled body, and although her face was surgically taut — thin in places with her natural age and needle-plumped in others — she appeared to be no older than forty. Still, he had the feeling that he should add an extra decade to that estimation.

But, she was pleasant enough to look upon in the darkness.

Her lips were botox-thick, her nails freshly manicured and her teeth — when she smiled — were unnaturally white and straight as a pin. The only natural asset visible to the naked eye appeared to be the shimmering lengths of silver-white hair that fell linearly down her back, spilling over her bony shoulders like the crest of a wave against the blue of her dress.

'I'd offer you a drink,' he continued eventually, 'but you seem to have that covered.'

'I do.'

She sipped at the wine in her glass and smiled felinely.

'So, how might I help you?' he asked, partly intrigued and slightly bored with her obnoxiously rich facade. She seemed to be the animated juxtaposition of a Druid wise-woman and a character from *Desperate Housewives*.

He stifled a smile.

'I was thinking we might help one another.' she breathed, her voice like treacle in the darkness; sweet, thick and bitter.

'Oh?' He turned his head from her, scanning the room for a worthy prize, but feeling the heavy gaze of the rich druidess pressing upon him. She continued sipping at her wine even as she drunk him in, in great gulps.

The minutes came and went without a word passing between the pair. He half expected to see her gone as he turned back to his pint, but she was there — as before — sipping from the sweet glass; the intensity behind her pale blue eyes boring a hole in his skull.

He shifted in his seat, manoeuvring to escape the weight of the glare, pressing the balls of his feet into the thick, carpeted floor as he made to stand. 'Look, I — '

He felt the sudden pressure of her skeletal hand on his knee, her bony digits pressing into the flesh, holding him as she pounced.

'I know.' she hissed, her tongue licking at his ear with the sudden proximity, 'I *know* who you are.'

His heart pounded furiously while his stomach began doing back-flips just as it had in the theatre. He felt his temperature plummet and imagined the colour draining from his face, thankful for the darkness. He considered bolting from his seat, but knew it would draw too much attention, even in such a dimly-lit room.

Quickly he considered his options and pressed his clawing hands into the brush of the harsh material beneath him, keeping himself in the seat; forcing himself to remain calm.

This was why he needed Vince.

Why he listened to him.

Vince had always said not to kill on your own patch, not to cause havoc where you could be directly connected, where there was the smallest possibility that you might be identified.

Shit!

Vince would have disposed of this Makeover Misfit in one swift move and no one would have been the wiser. But *he* was not Vince. And Vince was not here.

Shit! Shit! Shit!

His head began pounding and he found himself struggling to contain the shake of his hands or the way his stomach seemed to beat violently, making him want to vomit. Discretely he began to search for the pocket knife he had acquired from Gary Blakely.

'I don't know what you mean.' he said in a low voice, his eyes unable to meet hers.

She seemed to smile at this, enjoying the obvious power she knew she held over him.

'Is this your doing?' she said, sweeping her arm up in a needlessly dramatic gesture that caused the game-boy to break his concentration once more and glance their way. 'I've ...' she paused once more, whether simply for effect or specifically to choose her words he couldn't tell, 'I've seen your work before. Experienced it. Lived it, you might say. There was a time ...' she broke off suddenly, white-hot anger simmering to the surface even as she struggled to push it aside. 'I lost everything. You took it from me. But, it would seem that Fortune has put you in my way for a reason.'

'And what might that reason be?' he asked, the slightest caress of curiosity prickling beneath his skin. He had no idea who this woman was or how he was supposed to have wronged her, but, then again, so much was done in his name — even when it had very little to do with him — that it was near impossible to keep a track.

Whatever had been done to the gold-dripping druidess in the past, it clearly didn't affect her current bank balance and the fire behind her eyes suggested that it was far more personal than money; more close to home.

He racked his brain searching for any clue as to her true identity and more importantly the reasons for her knowing his. Nothing came to the surface and he was forced to wait at her pleasure.

'You have particular skills that may be of use to me.' she said eventually, pausing once again and taking a long, slow drink from the large glass before returning it to the table.

He tilted his head, still waiting, his brain still working furiously beneath his skull when a thought suddenly struck him.

It may have been the case that his brother was — in fact — *wearing the crown* at the time of this woman's tragedy. People often tied his and Matty's deeds and debts together. That would account for his not knowing her, while she appeared to know him so well.

And it wouldn't be the first time it had happened.

'You have a job for me?' he said finally, raising an eyebrow.

'I would pay you. I have cash on board and if that isn't enough I can have money wired to any account you like. That is, when we can once more communicate with the outside world.'

She smiled at him, carnivorously, and he understood that she knew far more than she was letting on. At the very least, she had made her guesses so close to the truth regarding his involvement in disabling the ship, as to almost have witnessed it first-hand.

But just how much did she know?

Really.

'I don't think there'll be any communication for a while.' he said, returning her smile as he remembered all that Blakely had told him about the total shutdown procedure.

However, this old druidess could have her uses and — with a little convincing — might even be willing to act as a decoy for him when the time came to depart; something he hadn't really contemplated as of yet, but which would need to be executed with precision when they eventually neared a port.

'Four-thousand in cash then.' she said, 'For the full works.'

Keeping his face neutral he lifted the pint to his lips, drinking in the golden bubbles and enjoying the cold and bitter taste that washed over his palette.

In his experience 'the full works' meant not only a hit, but disposal as well.

The druidess seemed not only completely aware of this, but also almost uncontrollably eager to see it done. He stifled a laugh, thinking it over. It made sense — he supposed — that she should approach him concerning a hit when there was chaos all about and bodies piling up anyway.

He supposed another one wouldn't hurt. And she was offering a reasonable amount of money for it. In cash too! That would come in very handy when he finally landed.

'You're a very forward thinking woman,' he said. 'Considering everything.'

'Considering my age you mean.'

Though it had crossed his mind earlier, at that very moment there had been no ageist sting in his words. No. No thought of it at all.

'No.' he said, looking into her eyes for the first time since their conversation had begun, 'I take it you want this done at sea.'

'Oh, yes.' she said, craning her neck, 'As soon as possible.'

'And who is the lucky guy?'

Her eyes darkened and she pulled her hand from his knee; the sudden rush of cold air in the absence of her warm flesh reminding him that it had been there all this time.

'Don't mess me around. I thought you — of all people — would understand.'

He opened his mouth to speak. Then closed it once more.

'It's me.' she said with only the slightest quiver in her voice, 'It's what I want and — '

'You?' he whispered, leaning in.

'Do you really find prospect so horrific?'

He shook his head slowly, though he had to admit he wouldn't — in a million years — have placed a bet on that being the answer to his question. 'It was just ... unexpected.'

'I'm dying.' she said, the sobering words having the effect of slapping him in the face. 'I've never really been in control of my own life, never taken the reins ... and now it's drawing to a close without me and I won't have it. I want to be remembered. No. I want to be immortalised.' She paused, taking in a deep breath, slowing the rise and fall of her skeletal chest, 'I want my name tied dangerously close to yours so that when people think of you or speak your name or even hear it on the wind, they won't be able to avoid speaking mine and thinking of me too.'

He was dumbfounded.

'You're sure about this?' he asked, a strange and unexpected emotion — something like respect and desire — swelling in his chest, stifling his own breath. In the last few minutes he had become quite fond of this odd, silver-haired siren, and now she was asking him to destroy her. 'You're certain that this is what you want?'

'Want.' she echoed, tears filling her eyes, 'What would you want when faced with so little time? A second chance? A miracle cure?' she shook her head, 'I just want to *feel* again.'

She reached for her wineglass, swallowing the remaining contents down in one gulp before tapping the rim forcefully against the edge of the table.

He heard it chip, though the sound seemed to be swallowed by the darkness before anyone else could notice.

Placing her arm flat on the table, the druidess began dragging the chipped glass across her skin. She pressed against it firmly drawing a steady line of red from the neat tear as she guided the glass over her thin flesh.

She did not flinch.

He stopped her hand and taking the glass returned it to the table, looking into her strong face; her determined, misty eyes.

'Please.' she pleaded, 'Help me to feel something one last time.'

He nodded, touching her face with a tenderness he had forgotten he might even posses. He watched as a tear of relief broke from her ice-blue eyes, flowing over the defined contour of her cheek.

'It would be an honour.' he said, surprised to hear his own voice speaking the words, 'What's your name?'

'Call me Nona.'

'Nona?' he asked.

She nodded, 'It's what my brother used to call me. He was young.'

Standing, he took her hand in his, 'Well then Nona. It seems I am yours to command.'

20:50

Saturday 14th May, 2011

Christine had struggled not to gag as she had leaned against Prior on the way back to her room.

It really wasn't his fault, but being quite a tall man the sticky, crust of alcohol-infused vomit that still clung to his ribbed jumper was just at the right height to waft directly into her nostrils with every step they had taken.

He had been busy explaining about the emergency power distribution as she had swiped her cardkey through the reader on the frame. He had already covered the logistics of the emergency lighting and air-filtration, the door-locking mechanisms, navigation and basic amenities and Christine couldn't help but smile at his meticulous enthusiasm as they had entered the room, the door clicking softly shut behind Prior.

'But you see with the satellite and communications relays taken out the little control we should have had on positioning and navigation has been all but lost and with the engines off and the amount of time we've had to drift, not mention this weather — '

'We really can't be certain where we are.' Christine had finished for him.

He had nodded at her, smiling.

Then she had proceeded to usher him into the shower, telling him to rinse his jumper in the sink before closing the bathroom door and crossing the suite to fetch her laptop.

The thin, light-weight world of technology had a soft lilac glaze and sat closed on the dresser near the balcony doors. The sky was miserably grim and dark and a small sigh had escaped Christine's lips as she had finally sat down and powered up the computer, her thoughts returning to Kelly every so often.

She wished she could just phone her. Speak to her. Check she was ok.

She wasn't at all happy with the way Dr Matthews had ejected her from the medical bay; the way she had simply *removed* her to her room. She could understand the awkward and angular woman's reasons; all twenty-three-plus of them.

And yet, Kelly had been attacked in her room.

No. Sending her back there just wasn't right.

Christine sighed.

She had hooked up the camera and inserted the additional SD card and was now scrolling through the litter of grotesque images that popped up before her, but all she could see was Kelly sprawled across the floor; battered and bleeding in her mind's eye.

As she had been when she'd found her.

The room was warmer now and as Prior stepped out of the bathroom — post-shower — and he smiled to himself, thankful for the warmth. He had dried and dressed as best as possible, but was unavoidably exposed from the waist up and seemed to apologise for his nakedness as he hung his jumper and t-shirt on the small radiator. 'It went right through.'

Christine smiled, 'I'd like to say I might have something for you to borrow, but I just don't think cashmere would stretch cross those shoulders.'

'That's ok.' he said tentatively, making them both a cup of coffee and pulling up a chair next to her. 'At least I don't reek of somebody else's insides anymore.'

Although her eyes had adjusted somewhat to the darkness, working at the laptop had had the effect of once more destroying Christine's night vision and it wasn't until Prior sat down next to her that she spied the claw of finger-like scars on his shoulder.

He caught her looking and shrugged; a small half-smile on his face. 'It's nothing.'

'Well, I wasn't going to mention it.' she said, 'But, now you've made me all the more curious.'

'Another time then.' he returned, his green eyes still managing to sparkle even in the dim light of the room. 'For now, we have more pressing matters.'

Christine nodded, though she couldn't help but think that the smallest of reasons would had been enough for Prior to try and lock her out.

But that was his choice and she had to respect it.

She understood it.

'Listen, before I tell what I think I've found, I need you to do something for me.'

'You're worried about Miss Livingstone.' Prior said, sipping at his coffee. 'I heard that Dr Matthews had had her taken back to her room.'

'I don't think she should be alone. And certainly not after being attacked.'

'I agree with you.' Prior said evenly, 'It wasn't one of Dr Matthews' better decisions. And I can understand you wanting to go and check on her, but — '

'What if whoever attacked her comes back.' Christine pressed, 'We don't even know why she was targeted.'

'And we won't have any idea until she comes around enough to answer some questions.'

'And what if she doesn't come back round at all?' Christine spluttered, gnawing on her lip involuntarily, her eyes stinging suddenly at the thought.

'Hey,' Prior said, taking her small hand in his, 'that isn't going to happen. She'll be fine once she's rested up a bit.'

'And if the attacker comes back in the mean time?'

Prior smiled softly, 'I had Stratton and Collins form a detail outside her cabin. I told them not to disturb her, but to keep their ears open and inform me as soon as she's awake. They're under strict instruction not to let anyone enter her room until we get there.'

Christine almost threw her arms around the handsome, green-eyed officer, holding back only at the last moment.

Instead, she squeezed his hand, thanking him as she did.

'I need you. Here.' he continued, raising his finger and pressing it gently to her temple, 'I need that keen mind of yours focused on the evidence. Focused on building a profile. I can't do this alone. Not today.'

She gave a small nod, her dark eyes meeting his in a silent understanding. Then, breaking from his gentle grip, she turned back to the computer screen and the deathly images that waited patiently as the laptop whirred in the quiet dim of the room.

'Well,' she began, layering several windows one on top of another, 'I took a look at the pictures from Stratton's camera. There's not much more to add to what we already know about what happened down in engineering. The bodies appear to have been starved of oxygen.' She scrolled through the pictures as she spoke, not wanting to linger on any for too long, knowing how painful it must be for Prior. Without warning he stopped her hand, preventing her from flicking to the next image.

The subject of the photograph was a woman in her thirties. Her red hair spilled over the shoulders of her dark blue uniform, a strange look of terror and acceptance in her glassy blue eyes. 'Knowing the circumstances and the conditions they were found in makes it easier for me to identify the cause of death, though I won't pretend to understand the hurt you'll be feeling now, Prior. I know nothing I can say will make this any easier.'

'I don't want it to be easier.' Prior growled softly, reaching out to touch the face of the woman on the screen. 'I should have stopped it.'

'You really couldn't have known.' she said, echoing the words that Davies had offered so many hours earlier.

'People keep telling me that. But it's my job, isn't it.' He was struggling to keep a semblance of control over his voice as his body trembled. He couldn't bring himself to look Christine in the eye. 'It was my fucking job.'

'This isn't about blame. It cannot be about blame if we're going to move forward and catch whoever's responsible before they hurt anyone else.'

Prior shook his head involuntarily, his mouth moving without sound.

'Prior.' Christine continued, shaking him gently, 'Prior ... Jon.' His head snapped round and he stared at her for the longest time without moving or saying another word.

Eventually, he seemed to shake off the distress that cloaked him so well, a single tear shimmering over his cheek as he finally spoke with a distant voice. 'She was the first woman I'd really fallen for in a long time. We'd been taking it slowly, but I never thought ... you never think that ... if I'd have known — '

'But, that's just it,' Christine said, 'we never *can* know.'

'I'd have held her all night long. Every night.' he said, sniffing, 'But, you think you have all the time in the world. And the first week into a voyage is always hectic, especially for engineering. Rachel stopped in her own quarters. I stopped in mine.'

'And that was her choice. You can't control everything. And you can't torture yourself for not anticipating something that no one could have predicted.'

'But, that's ... my job, Christine. My job. That's what I'm supposed to do.'

'No.' Christine said firmly, slightly taken aback at hearing him use her forename for the first time. Though — she supposed — she had started it.

For a man like Prior who — not unlike herself — enjoyed the formal use of surnames as a mechanism for keeping people at arm's-length, that simple change in courtesy had instantly opened up a whole new uncharted dimension of their relationship. With that small change they had grown infinitely closer.

'No,' she said, 'I won't accept that.'

'But — '

'No buts. That's it. Do you think Rachel would want to see you this way?'

'D'you think I wanted to see *her* this way?' Prior shouted suddenly, bounding from his seat; stalking back and too across the room. 'When I find out who's done this … who's doing this, I'll tear his fucking head off with my bare hands.'

'You will not.' Christine said forcefully, 'but, we'll cross that line when we come to it. And in that regard we're not going to get very far with you stomping around like a gorilla in a zoo. You said you needed me. Needed my help. Well, I can't do this alone either, so make yourself useful and go top up my coffee while you're on your feet. Then, come and sit down and help me. Help me solve this thing so that we can avenge Rachel and everyone else.'

Prior eyed Christine for some time and for a moment it seemed that he would continue in his rant. Then he took the mug from Christine's hand and, downing the remainder of his own drink, made each of them a fresh cup.

He returned to his chair, feeling the psychologist's eyes on him as he stared at the screen.

'You can go onto the next photo now.' he said by way of apology, his voice sounding suddenly small in the darkened room.

'I know it's difficult,' Christine said, closing the windows that concentrated on the engineering lock-down victims and opening a set that revealed the injuries sustained by Gary Blakely. Prior simply nodded at her words, allowing her to continue without interruption.

'Gary Blakely seems to have suffered a whole mass of different injuries, some only moments before death, some minutes before and others . . . perhaps an hour or so before he died.'

Christine clicked through the photo flick-book of injuries as she spoke, Prior cocking his head or nodding his agreement and understanding from time to time. 'I think you were correct in saying that Blakely's codes weren't taken willingly. There was ligature mark bruising around his ankles and his wrists. Left quite a furrow too; I'd say electrical wiring or something similar. Something thin enough to leave a smooth impression, but not so thin that it would just slice through the skin.'

'You think he was hog-tied?'

Christine nodded, 'Looks that way.'

'How'd he escape?'

'Well, if it was electrical cable that was used to bind him it could have slipped enough for him to wriggle free over time. But, not before he was repeatedly beaten and branded across his shoulders and back with what looks like the 'V' end of a crow-bar.'

'Shit.' Prior gasped taking in the sight of Blakely's battered body. The mass of blue and purple bruising spread across the deputy's back was indeed interspersed with red, raging V-shaped blisters, 'And he was alive when this was done?'

Christine nodded. 'I believe so. These blisters are very different to those on his face, which I am quite sure occurred peri-mortem. These have already begun healing. Dr Matthews should be able to tell us for certain, but I'd say yes. Yes, Blakely was very much alive throughout the ordeal.'

'It looks like he was beaten with the crow-brow too.' Prior said, pointing to the image, 'I'd be very much surprised to find that he didn't crack a rib. Or two.'

Christine sipped at her coffee as she brought up the next two images. 'So, it looks like Blakely was definitely tortured; most likely for the information his murderer needed to cripple the ship, disable the communications systems and trap those who remained in engineering.'

'Taking the lives of those he trapped in engineering.' Prior seethed.

Christine conceded a small nod, 'But, I don't think that was the whole story. I think the architect behind all this enjoys the torture aspect, which would indicate that whoever killed Blakely is also likely to be responsible for the murder of Stacey Atkins.'

'You're sure?' Prior asked, hoping that her guess was right and that they were dealing with only one psychotic lunatic; praying that the ship hadn't in fact descended into absolute and murderous chaos.

'I understand your concern.' said Christine, seeming to read his mind, 'And again, it's just my opinion. But I'm quite confident they're connected; that these two murders are indeed linked by the torture inflicted upon the victims. But that's not to say that there couldn't be a second culprit involved in all of this.'

'How d'you mean?' Prior said, stretching his back. He hated to sit for too long and could feel his lateral muscles beginning to seize up.

'This picture shows a distinctive ligature mark across the victim's throat. It wraps around the neck completely.' Christine said, pointing at the picture on the left before moving to the image of a feminine throat on the right. 'That was Gary Blakely, but look here. This image shows the throat of Stacey Atkins ... with the same mark. Exactly the same mark.'

'A chain of some sort?'

'Looks like.'

'So, that's further evidence to link the killings, isn't it?'

'Yes.' Christine said, 'But, there *are* differences. Sure, both of these victims bare distinct — I'd say identical — ligature marks. But a pair of killers working together might each own one of these chains.' She paused, gathering her thoughts and looking into Prior's eyes, ensuring that he understood her, 'By openly wearing the weapon used as part of the killing process — part of the fantasy — the killer, or killers, are exhibiting an incredible display of boldness. A confidence, as I said before.

'And yet, while they appear to be displaying the weapons for all to see, taunting — I don't know — us, authority ... they're also using it as a shield. Hiding behind it; actively using the chain to physically take on the identity of a killer. Do you understand?'

Prior nodded slowly.

'And,' she continued, 'if there *are* two of them the chains could also unite them symbolically as much as they literally bind them together. A totem that empowers them.'

Prior shook his head, wearily.

He liked Christine, enjoyed her company and her insights, but it had been so long since he had worked on a case with a psych. He had forgotten just how much hard work it could be ... analysing every angle. Trying to understand the reasons and the motives of the monsters he just longed to put away and forget.

He pushed out a long breath, rubbing his eyes. 'So, what is it that makes you think there could be two? I mean, I can't just ask my men to start to cataloguing every piece of jewellery brought on by the passengers on board.'

'Of course not.' Christine snapped, 'that would be absurd. And I never said I conclusively believed that there were two, but that we shouldn't exclude the possibility.' she paused, her voice softening once more, 'The good news to take from this is that *if* there are two killers, they will be working together; rather than non-conjunctive individuals taking out random targets. They'll discuss their marks, choose them for specific reasons — '

'Such as?' Prior asked.

'Sexual desire and gratification,' she said, with a shrug, 'the need to assert power . . . a power they feel they don't necessarily possess at other times. Don't forget, in most successful killing partnerships there is a dominant and a submissive. One egging the other on until the need to increase the brutality of the fantasy emerges so strong that it is too much for the sub. The sub feels the guilt for both parties; they bear the weight of the crimes and when that happens — as much as it may drive a wedge between them in terms of emotion — they will find that they become more and more dependent on one another. And that may be the key to their undoing. That is, unless, the dominant chooses to dispose of the submissive to cover his tracks.'

Christine opened another window containing a stream of images from room fifteen-thirty-four; the room of Stacey Atkins. 'Putting aside those that died en-masse in engineering, there are similarities and differences in the manner, style and cause of death of the three individual cases we have.'

'Blakely, Atkins and . . .'

'Dr Cunningham.'

'I wouldn't have thought the little details we know of Dr Cunningham's death had much in common with the other two.' Prior said, drinking a gulp of hot coffee from his mug.

'Why?' Christine asked, 'In all three cases the perpetrator seems to have used whatever was to hand. With Blakely it was electrical cable or something similar and — if I'm right — the crow bar too. With Stacey Atkins it looks like he used her broken cardkey to inflict some of the injuries; to slice and carve the words on her body. He used *her* stockings to tie her up for display.'

'And Dr Cunningham?'

'I think he used a scalpel. The dimensions seem to match those used on board.' Christine said, zooming in on the open wound, 'I heard one of the nurses talking about finding traces of blood on one such implement and in the area around the large cabinet; though our killer did seem to do his best to mop up after himself.'

'Why didn't Matthews say anything?' Prior said, agitated.

'I think she's been a little distracted. And, to be honest, I don't know that the nurse had even got round to telling her yet. She's not exactly the most approachable person, is she?'

Prior flicked his eyebrows, agreeing with her.

'My point is that he's taking advantage of whatever is there.'

'He? As in one guy. Not two?

Christine sighed.

She could see that Prior was a man who liked to keep things simple. Good and bad, black and white. No grey. A give me a gun and point me in the right direction kind of guy.

For her, it was never that simple.

'*This* sort of consistency is indicative of a personality trait; one person actively thinking on their feet because they are used to doing so. No matter how much you might plan as a team, you cannot *plan* spontaneity. You can't plan adaptability. So, I don't know ...' she said, sipping at her coffee and watching as Prior sifted through the images. 'And then, there's the differences in ... style. There's cruelty; the enjoyment in the torture being inflicted here. And then there's necessity. There are some incredibly bold statements that are a complete counterpoint with the shrinking and swift dispatching of Dr Cunningham. There's — I don't know — a plan ... a desire. An overall driving force. The need to gain the information from Blakely that would disable the ship, for example.'

'Hold on.' Prior pressed, sitting forward, 'What if *that* is it? What if he — they, whatever — what if the torture is an aspect they enjoy, but the necessity has forced their hand. You know; *I want to have a little fun, enjoy myself, but time is of the essence.* That kind of thing?'

Christine nodded.

'We need to find out how he heated the crow bar.' he continued, 'And whether he did just take advantage of what was lying around or if he had truly planned the torture aspect. See just how much of this whole thing was planning and how much was thinking on your feet.'

'That would help.' said Christine. 'That would help us a lot. I mean, timescale-wise we've got these three individual murders occurring within a window of about twelve hours. That's vast for one or even two killers. And that's not including those who died in engineering, even if they were merely a necessity to the plan. That in itself — in some ways — is so much colder than the rest. It's more of an indicator of true psychopathy even than the specific cruelties inflicted upon Stacey Atkins and Gary Blakely.' Christine shook her head, 'We've got Dr Cunningham who died almost instantly through sharp-force trauma resulting in a suspected epidural bleed; then there's Gary Blakely, who is hog-tied and tortured for around an hour before some sort of struggle ensues and he ends up as a permanent fixture of the engineering CPU; and finally, Stacey Atkins ...'

'There was no sign of forced-entry into her room.' said Prior, even as the thought occurred, 'So, it would seem that she knew her killer. Maybe even let him in. She was wearing an engagement ring, but her fiancée's not come forward as of yet.'

'He might not be on board. It was her sister that was kind enough to throw-up all over you earlier. She seemed dressed to party and had already been drinking. It could be a hen do.'

Prior nodded in agreement, flicking to the next photograph. It was a close up of the flesh that covered Stacey's bruised and battered ribs; that bore the scratched-out words *Not My Type*.

Christine shook her head again, involuntarily. Her hand covering her mouth as she mentally sorted through the catalogue of injuries that accompanied that stark message. 'We need to know whether or not she was sexually assaulted; pre or post mortem. And if so, we need to know whether that was conventional or object rape. This is clearly a sexual attack, despite the words he chose to carve.

'Everything about it is sexual. He was facing her when smashed her face into the side of the bath,' Christine said, pulling up the photo of the blood-spattered tub besides the first picture. 'and looking at the angle of it, he must have been in the bath with her when he did it, which also indicates that he's left handed. Afterwards he polishes her up like a trophy, he displays her with pride, takes time to create a whole scene ... but carves *Not My Type* into her flesh?' she sighed, 'I don't get it.'

'Could it be mockery?' Prior ventured, 'Imagine that all the violence that took place here was energy geared towards sexual conquest. Then, at the last moment he chooses not to rape her. That could be a way of showing us that he's in control. Even in the heat of the moment. Right? A way of proving that he's in charge. Like you said before.'

'Perhaps.' Christine said, thinking, 'Or maybe he simply can't do it. Maybe he *can't* perform sexually, despite his fantasy. So after getting in this deep he can't simply back out, he has to try and take *back* the control. Maybe that's why he wrote it. Suggesting that she wasn't his type is an excuse for his lack of sexual performance. He's putting the blame on her to try and protect his shattered ego.'

'Maybe she insulted him.' Prior said. Christine cocked her head, her eyebrows flicking up as she thought it over. She looked at him with interest.

'You suggested that she might have known him. Well, maybe she did. But maybe she insulted him in some way. Turned him down. Rejected him.'

'It's a thought.'

'What I don't get,' Prior started, before finishing the last mouthful of coffee that remained in his mug. He swallowed. 'Is why there would be surgical instruments sitting around sterilising overnight anyway. Going back to Dr Cunningham. It might sound stupid, but there's not — usually — a great demand for emergency medical attention on a ship like this. Certainly not something that's likely to pre-emptively require a scalpel!'

Prior stood and crossed the suite to return the mug. When he turned to face Christine once more he gave a brief, nervous smile that seemed completely at odds with the confidence he had exuded moments before. Christine watched as he rested his back against the edge of the side unit, folding his arms across his still bare chest.

The psychologist returned his smile, instantly realising the source of his discomfort.

Even in the dim light of the room, she had found her eyes drawn over and over to the scar that snaked across his shoulder. As he had moved away from her, she had managed to glimpse the damage that extended across his back to form a physical atlas of memories that were clearly too painful to discuss for such a private man.

She mentally rebuked herself for making him feel so self-conscious, knowing all too well the pain and the humiliation of bearing a physical scar; something that turned heads, drew whispers and reminded you — everyday — of how you had failed those that had put their trust in you. Those you were supposed to protect.

'Well, maybe that's just it.' she said, returning to his comment as she began closing down the images on her laptop, 'You mentioned that *Golden Star* liked to keep their costs down as much as possible. I suppose if there's not a great demand then it makes sense to have the instruments and the sterilising fluid rather than single-use, disposable packs that have to be replaced by a certain date, regardless of whether they've been used or not.'

Prior nodded. 'I suppose. But, why were they being sterilised last night? It doesn't make sense. Unless they'd been used in the evening — and as far as I know there were no emergencies — the only other reason I can think of for them being there is that someone was anticipating needing them.'

'What do you mean by that?' Christine said, frowning.

'I don't know.' Prior said, rubbing his eyes groggily as he crossed to check the progress of his drying t-shirt and jumper. They were still damp, but they would do. 'I don't know, I'm sorry. I'm tired and I'm hungry ... I can't concentrate when I get like this.'

'That's ok.' said Christine, shutting the laptop and returning the SD card and camera to their respective evidence bags, 'I'm the same.'

She struggled to stand, using the chair-back to help her, rubbing her false, aching knee even as she stretched it out and manoeuvred it painfully round.

'It still hurts quite badly, doesn't it?'

Christine felt the heat rising through her chest and flushing her face bright red in response to the attention. 'It's not so bad.' she lied.

Prior flicked a sincere half-smile at her as he pulled on his t-shirt, wriggling as the cold patches of damp material clung to him. 'How long has it been?'

'Eight months since the pins. Nearly nine since ... the event.'

He nodded. And didn't push.

'I was wondering,' she said with a small cough, a typical sign that she was changing the subject, 'I know you don't have the greatest CS equipment onboard, but did anyone manage to find any fingerprints? Any at all? Only I haven't come across any pictures or any other evidence bearing a single print so far. Not even half a print.'

'No. Me neither.' said Prior, 'which ticks more boxes in the meticulous and calculated category.'

Christine found her herself forced to agree. None of this was half-hearted or spur of the moment; the perp knew what they were doing. What they wanted to achieve.

'He or they must have come into contact with at least ten different surfaces in engineering alone.' she said, 'I mean operating the keyboard for crying out loud!'

'Yeah, but, along with about a hundred other people in engineering ...' Prior shook his head, 'Trying to isolate one print from that jumble would be . . . well it would be exhausting if nothing else. And certainly not conclusive or even reliable.'

'Ok, so what about in Stacey's room? The bathtub, surely that might offer something?'

Prior exhaled, pulling his jumper over his head. He knew what she was doing, she just wanted some sort of a lead, something that might stand and stick if — no, *when* — they caught this guy.

He admired her persistence, but the truth was that whoever was responsible for the murders of Stacey Atkins, Gary Blakely, Dr Stuart Cunningham, Rachel Adams — his Rachel — and the majority of engineers on board the ship had gone to great lengths to remain anonymous, leaving them — quite literally — in the dark. Still, what could he do? Give up?

Taking the two-way radio from the deep pocket on his thigh, Prior pushed the button on the side, 'Prior to Davies.'

The radio crackled static for a moment.

'Davies here, Guv'.'

'Anything to report?' Prior asked.

Christine listened as the sound of a chair scraping and then a door clicking shut accompanied the now familiar and friendly Scouse husk of Marc Davies' voice, 'I've just finished taking a statement from Stacey's sister, Lauren Atkins. She's still quite distressed. But, then again, who wouldn't be?'

The two-way bleeped the automated *over* sound and Prior nodded.

The image of Stacey hanging there, framed by the open door washed over Christine with a suddenly painful and personal twinge. She felt for the drunken sister. She knew how she would blame herself now and for the rest of her life; that she would tell herself she should have been there to stop it. That she should have known.

It was all futile, of course.

'Right.' Prior continued, 'What has she said?'

'She doesn't seem to know why anyone would want to hurt her sister. From what Lauren says, Stacey was a pretty likable girl . . . always surrounded by friends and admirers. There's a party of girls come away together. Seems Stacey was due to marry . . . two weeks after we dock back home.'

Prior looked at Christine who returned his thoughtful gaze, spying a stifled sadness behind those shining, spring eyes.

She reached out, touching his arm, though the action felt immediately alien and electric all at once. She felt herself swallow hard as she continued to watch him, feeling strangely conflicted by this man — this strong and handsome man — who worked so hard to bury the feelings that danced plainly before her well-trained eye.

You might fool others . . . She thought, sadly.

'Do you have the name of her fiancée?'

'Michael Copina.' Davies replied, his voice crackling through the radio's speaker, 'Investment banker, mortgage broker . . . business entrepreneur by the sounds of things. He's American. Lauren says his granddad's Argentinean, but that he moved the family north as soon as possible. They settled in New York ... made their money. The American fucking dream, eh?'

'Davies.' Prior cut in, chiding him.

'Sorry, Guv. According to Lauren, most of his family live in L.A. now. But he's been in the U.K. for about six years.'

'And were they happy?'

'Sir?'

'Were they happy? Michael and Stacey? What did the family think about the marriage?'

'You think this could have been a set up? Think he might have wanted her dead?'

Prior shrugged involuntarily, 'I don't know. But I think we've got to look at every angle.'

'Pretty expensive set up, though. The bride-to-be and nine members of the hen party on an all-inclusive cruise?'

'Which shows that he has the money to organise a hit. If that's what this was. And — if it *was* Michael Copina that planned all this — he would have the perfect alibi and could appear as the devastated and doting husband-to-be upon hearing the news; a man who spared no expense on the woman he loved. I want you to find out all you can about their relationship.'

'Yes, Guv.'

'And Marc, have a team go back over the scenes as best they can. See if Dr Matthews can spare anyone. We could do with some forensic evidence if we're to stand a chance of positively tying these murders to somebody. DNA, fingerprints, anything.'

'Guv.'

With that the automated *over* signal bleeped a final time and as he clipped the radio onto his belt, Prior found Christine's eyes locked on him once more. She raised a questioning eyebrow.

'You really think that Mr Copina had Stacey Atkins murdered?'

'To be honest,' he replied, 'probably not. But, the name rings a bell. And, I don't know, there's something familiar about all this.' he looked at Christine, who waited patiently for him to continue, 'I know that sounds bizarre and I don't want to be so cliché as to say *I have a feeling*, but ...'

'You have a feeling about this.' Christine smiled, handing over the evidence bags for Prior to deposit them once more in the deep, side-pockets of his black combat pants.

He returned her smile, even as he shook his head, 'You already know me far too well.'

With that he moved to the dresser, next to which he had spotted an ornate cane that appeared to be cut from a single piece of white marble. The neck was marked with a double ring of gold, while the handle was carved with a colourful scene; a girl sat beneath a willow.

'That's my ... spare.' Christine blushed.

'It looks expensive for a spare.'

'Which is exactly why it *is* the spare. I'm scared to use it. Scared of breaking it or losing it. But, I like to have it with me.'

Prior nodded, holding the stick. It was heavier than he had expected.

'Well, I think you're going to need it. At least until we recover the other' he said, handing her the cane. 'Unless you'd prefer that awful grey thing from medical?'

Christine felt a small laugh push past her lips as she took the stick from him, leaning her weight cautiously on it though she was fairly certain that it would not give way.

'So ... dinner?' said Prior, holding the door for Christine. 'I think we could use some dinner!'

'Yeah, but, half ten at night. Do you think they'll still be serving?'

'Stick with me kid.' he laughed, letting the door click shut behind them.

23:32

Saturday 14th May, 2011

After he had finished with Nona he had polished every surface he could find before discarding the rags — torn pieces of a flowery dress previously belonging to Nona — out of the balcony door and over the side of the ship.

It was much easier to slide back the glass door and confront the ocean in the dark. When he couldn't see beyond the wooden decking and the patio table; when he couldn't tell the ominous night sky from the depths of the murky water beneath him.

He shuddered suddenly at the thought.

Nona's room was spacious and luxurious enough to rival his own nautical accommodation. On top of this it was also nicely stocked, as her mini-bar — he was delighted to find — had not been nearly so ravaged as his.

The biggest difference between Nona's room and his own had to be the bathroom.

It was larger than his for a start, and featured a king-sized corner spa-bath, perfect for soothing the aching muscles he had worked so hard over the last two hours.

No, the last two days.

He relaxed back into the warmth of the now rose-coloured water that lapped at his somewhat battered body. The scented bubbles burst and soothed and threatened to drag him down into a dangerously all-consuming state of relaxation, but part of him didn't care.

He knew no one would come looking for Nona.

She had suggested as much.

And even if she wasn't entirely alone on this trip, it didn't matter. For those few, relaxing minutes nothing mattered.

This was to be her final voyage before her long list of illnesses could wrap their toxic fingers around her soul and squeeze. Those incurable conditions that crawled beneath her flesh; clawing at her lungs and other spongy organs.

When they had arrived at her room, Nona had taken a small, silver tin from the suitcase at the foot of her bed. Opening the tin she had smiled sweetly at him, revealing the treasure within; a wealth of unburned, purple tea-light candles. Then, with a care and devotion that was almost hypnotic to watch she had set about placing the candles around the room; their fragrance soon clouding the air with a sweet, lavender scent.

She seemed ever more the wise druidess as she continued to create what she had called the *perfect atmosphere*, humming light melodies to herself and muttering words that could quite easily have been the invocation of some ancient rite.

At first he had tried to stop her, explaining about the heat and smoke sensors. For, as atmospheric as it may have been, he really didn't want to be interrupted by some eager-beaver, busybody crewman when in the midst of the act he most enjoyed engaging in; the taking of human life.

Nona had laughed at him then and for a moment a bitter rage had taken hold; contracting his hands into tight, solid fists as an uncontrollable surge of anger bolted through his frame. He had been laughed at before and it wasn't something that he was in the habit of taking too kindly to.

But somehow, with her, it had been different. Her laughter was soft and without judgement and — despite the pussy-whipped way it sounded as he replayed the moment in his mind — he had melted into her as she had taken his face in her long, skeletal fingers and pressed her botoxed lips against his.

'They don't work.' she had whispered softly, 'Not since your little trick with the power.'

He had neither confirmed nor denied her statement, but had sat on the bed and watched — simply watched — in plain awe as she had moved about the room producing all kinds of exciting toys for him to play with.

Whatever Nona's true identity, he was beginning to think that the lithe and mysterious wisewoman could have easily have been re-christened *Ann Summers* with the stock she carried around with her.

Still, he wasn't complaining.

'I just want to feel. You understand?' she had said, pressing him back onto the bed.

He had caught a glimpse of her arm and the deep gash made by the broken glass that had caused no discomfort to her at all. It was then that his heart and his mind had truly begun to race. With ideas of blood and nerves and sex and flesh.

Of pain and pleasure.

'I guarantee it.'

'Good.' she had replied, her hands moving across his chest as she unbuttoned his shirt with expert ease, 'And then you can make me immortal. You'll find the money in my top draw. I want you to take it in payment.'

He had barely nodded his reply before she had stifled him with a passionate meeting of lips, which quickly became parted lips; with the introduction of a particularly gymnastic tongue.

A flurry of kisses across his throat had then led to the nibbling at his ear. The nibbling turned to biting and soon he had felt the passion rise in him with such strength that before he knew what was happening he had taken the lead in the game of teasing and pleasing.

But this was a deadly game. Both could play and both could win.

But only one would survive.

Now, in the quiet tranquillity of the bath he sipped the expensive champagne from a miniature bottle, checking the state of the stitches in his leg.

She had smacked down hard on the wound — several times — in her final moments, but he had made her a promise and he would not relent.

He had sworn to be as strong as she needed him to be; that he would finish what they had started. No matter what.

The pain she had wrought in the graceless struggle at the end had been impressive, thrilling him and filling him with pure, pumped-up, ready-to-rock adrenaline. She had been a deceivingly tough nut; and impressively skilled in ways of pain and pleasure.

She had utilised these skills until the last, teasing and testing him, drawing blood and salt from him even as he carved it from her. The final moments were still a blur, though he knew he had held the chain around her throat.

Ah, yes.

His legs had buckled under the pleasure of his delight as he had spilled across her tight and naked buttocks, his torso pressed against the cool flesh of her back even as they fell to the blood-stained bed in that final, eternal embrace.

'Immortal.' he had whispered, finding — to his amazement — that his face was soaked, not with blood or sweat, or bubbling water, but tears.

Yes.

He was weeping for the deceased druidess!

Champagne drunk and body cleanly soaked, he pulled the plug, releasing the pink water to swirl from the bath before dressing quickly in the dying remains of the candlelight. He dried the bath, removing any stubborn signs of congealing evidence as he went.

He thought about the last few moments of Nona's life as he played the part of the maid in the bathroom, hoping he had given her what she had wanted, when he was suddenly interrupted.

Knock, knock.

He froze in horror and confusion wondering whether he had actually heard the sound or simply imagined it.

Knock, knock. Knock.

He had heard right.

It was really real. There really was someone at the fucking door!

Shit!

'Are you in there?' came the call of a muffled and effeminate male voice.

Making his way across the bedroom-come-living-space, he barely had time to comprehend what was happening before he heard the swift exchange of a cardkey swiping through the door-mounted reader.

Shit, shit, shit! You have to be kidding!

The door unlocked instantly, leaving him dumbfounded. Fortunately his natural sense of preservation kicked-in just in time and he flung himself into the confines of the mirrored wardrobe just as the short, garishly dressed, dark-haired, male intruder entered to room.

What the fuck?

The Midget was now stood before him, taking in the scene that *He* had worked so hard to perfect. The lasting image that he had created.

Just for her.

He watched as the stranger struggled to comprehend what his eyes were telling him lay before him. Was it a trick of the dark?

No. No it wasn't.

The man opened his mouth; the small sounds of an unbelieving shriek forming as he took a step backwards.

With a well-practised flick of the wrist, Leigh slipped his faithful chain over the man's head, letting it drop around his throat before pulling it tight. Twisting it to gain that extra measure of tension.

It didn't take long.

The newcomer struggled only for the briefest time. And really only half-decently when his body's natural reflexes finally kicked in. It was an uneventful death. Over in seconds.

Not like hers.

She had been beautiful. And in her final moments she had been glorious.

Just glorious.

Slipping the chain back into his pocket he stepped over the new body, unable to tear his eyes from Nona, committing every detail of the scene — of her lithe and pale body, her long white hair — to memory.

He knelt before her, remembering how he had laid her out so carefully after they had finished their game.

Now, pressing his lips against her forehead for the final time, he was surprised to taste the salted water of the tears that had apparently continued to carve a rapid path across his face.

Shaking off the emotion he wiped at his eyes.

He looked up at the mirrored wardrobe, though he could no longer see himself.

Perhaps that wasn't such a bad thing. Why, would he want to look at something so weak and pathetic?

You really are pathetic. A familiar voice whispered in his ear.

Anger catapulted through his chest as he surged forward, taking up a metal-studded leather paddle from the table of goodies. He straddled the chest of the short-statured, short-lived, pointless, deceased little man who had interrupted him and — with a rhythm that became more seductive with every beat — he began whipping the waxy manikin across the face. Playing him like a drum.

Like the drum that beat inside his head.

That throbbed and pulsed and pained in him. That plagued his sleep and made him twitch. That lived beneath his skin, driving him ever-forward, tolling out the progress of his life.

Shaking himself as if waking from a nightmare, he forced the percussion into momentary submission. He stood, his gaze falling on the pile of money that Nona had left for him.

He shook his head. He couldn't take the money now.

How could you put a price on this?

Smiling, he contemplated the idea that something profound had just occurred. It was the closest thing he had ever felt to morality.

It was an almost angelic sense of delight.

As strange as it sounded, it made it seem all the more rewarding to ignore the stack of twenty and fifty pound notes staring him in the face. It felt . . . righteous.

Yes. He was a righteous messenger of the Druidess.

The ancient, mystical wisewoman.

The Midget was the scavenging thief in the night; the faceless unknown, to be forgotten by time and the history of man.

She would be immortal.

And he . . . well, he was content to be righteous.

Chapter Four

Christine fluffed the pillow behind her head for the umpteenth time. She turned her head to the right. Wriggled. And turned to the left.

She huffed and opened her eyes. It was no good. She couldn't sleep.

She was tired enough. She was bloody exhausted, in fact, but try as she might she simply couldn't sleep. Her mind just wouldn't stop whirring.

But, then again, there had been a lot to take in. So much had happened today. Too much ... especially considering that *this* was supposed to be a well-earned holiday!

She had always been the same when working a case. She couldn't just 'switch off' as so many of the other officers and detectives she had worked with seemed able to.

She couldn't just go home and relax, nor could she play pool, cards, video games or commit to drinking vast quantities of alcohol in the hopes of eventually passing out. She had always been far too aware that the case would still be waiting in the morning; staring her in the face, greeting her with a twisted, impish grin that would need to be met with an eye of sobriety.

She had known back then that she would need her wits about her if she was going to save lives. If she was going to make a name for herself and prove herself; prove that she really did know what she was talking about. That her methods, her research and her reasoning were valid. Valuable. And that they led to arrests and convictions.

She had been mulling things over since her late dinner with the ever-intriguing Jonathan Prior.

Now, there was a conundrum.

He had opened up a little as the evening — or rather night — had progressed. She now knew a little more about his relationship with Rachel Adams; how they had first come to notice one another. How and when they had first acknowledged the spark between themselves.

His voice had been so soft when he had spoken about Rachel that, at times, he had been barely audible; the oceanic green of his eyes clouding with yet more salt water tears. They had sparkled then in the lick of the flames from the many candles that adorned the tables in the restaurant and Christine had wanted to reach out and hold his hand. To reassure him.

But what could she say?

And the candle light. Candles, fine food and wine. It could almost have been a romantic dinner for two. An intimate evening of spectacular culinary foreplay.

But it wasn't.

So why was she having to remind herself of that?

Perhaps, she had simply been alone for far too long.

It seemed it was all that she thought about, lately. And it wasn't just the sex, or even the idea of the contemplation of the sex! Not really.

But, then again, she wasn't so self-deluded as to try and deceive herself into believing that it was merely *companionship* or any other nobler sounding prerequisite that now occupied her racing mind.

No, despite her better judgement she had found herself becoming more and more drawn towards the handsome Security Chief.

But, what if this was all just a bizarre reaction to Dr Matthews' odd behaviour earlier; her jealous claiming of the man? Surely, she wasn't so suggestible as to become attracted to him merely because another woman had showed an interest.

It would certainly be a formidable comment on her current state of mind if that was the case!

In all honesty Prior was an attractive man.

Physically.

And though he did seem to have some issues with trust and secrecy — a few skeletons in the closet, maybe — he was of a personality type that she had always found agreeable; attractive even.

He was thorough, dependable, meticulous. He was always presentable and clean shaven. They even shared a similar sense of humour.

But, this was exactly the problem at hand!

Why was she lying in bed cataloguing his qualities *at all*?

'Get a grip, Christine.' she whispered, turning onto her side and rubbing at the knee that had ached almost constantly today. Perhaps that was what it was . . . the pain distracting her. Maybe that was what was keeping her awake.

She nodded to herself, not buying into the idea at all, but preferring it to the other truths currently rattling around her brain.

Pulling back the covers, Christine slid out a cautious left leg, followed by a steadier right leg. She stretched out, reaching for the painkillers and the tumbler of water that sat on the small bed-side table.

In the back of her mind she knew why she was trying — so desperately hard — to distract herself.

She hadn't seen or heard from Kelly since she had left her in the clutches of Dr Matthews earlier that evening. It all felt like a lifetime ago now and she had certainly had mixed feelings about having to leave her in the medical bay at the time.

But she had felt guilty as hell when she had realised that Matthews had simply patched Kelly up and returned to her room as soon as she could!

Christine couldn't help but feel that she had somehow abandoned Kelly; though sense and reason told her that this was not the case.

She had wanted to visit her after finishing her late-night meal with Prior, but he had eventually swayed her from this course of action. And rightly so.

She knew Kelly would need to rest. She did not need a barrage of people bombarding her with questions. She would have enough of that to contend with in the morning.

Still, the whole saga saddened Christine and continued to pull at those heavily-waxed strings of guilt and conscience. And desire.

Desire.

That was the crux of it.

And she couldn't help but acknowledge the fact that she might just be inventing the idea of a romantic attraction to Prior simply to put-off having to deal with the obvious — if not confusing and somewhat all-consuming — feelings she was rapidly developing for Kelly.

And none of them needed that. Not Prior. Not Kelly. Not her.

Certainly not now.

'Christine?'

She jumped at the unexpected sound of her whispered name as it exploded from the two-way radio and sliced through the dark and the silence of her room. The pain in her knee amplified with her sudden tensing, sending an aching twinge shooting up and down her leg as she hobbled towards the radio.

She swore before pressing down the button to respond.

'Prior? Is that you?' she asked breathlessly.

'Yes. Are you ok?'

The radio bleeped.

'I'm fine. You just scared me, that's all.'

'I'm sorry.' came the reply, 'I didn't know whether to contact you now or leave it 'til morning, but . . . I thought you'd want to know. Miss Livingstone . . . she's not in her room.'

The radio bleeped again. Then silence.

Christine shook her head, disbelieving the words she had just heard. 'What! What do you mean she isn't there? Where else could she be? What's happened?'

'I think you need to see this.' Prior's voice crackled through the anxious energy that had suddenly filled the air, 'Shall I come and get you?'

'No.' Christine replied angrily. 'No, I can manage.'

She should have known better than to ignore her gut. The pangs of guilt that she had felt all evening had been leading her to this, that little voice in the back of her mind that had kept on at her, whispering to her; *Go and check on Kelly.*

It had been the same with Janet.

Why hadn't she listened?

23:58

Saturday 14th May, 2011

'You've got some nerve.'

Kelly shook her head, steadying herself against the door frame as her vision blurred in and out of focus. Her face throbbed with the sting of swelling and bruises. Her head pounded and rattled as though an intrusion of scarab beetles were scuttling around beneath her skull.

'Shona?' she questioned, her eyes desperately trying to adjust to the dim and the shadows. Why was it so dark anyway? 'What's going on?'

'Going on? How the hell should I know?' Shona bit back her words, dragging her hands through the dark lustre of her hair in a gesture of clear irritation. 'You're the one knocking on my door at stupid o'clock!'

Shona's frustration was nothing compared to the confusion and dull, but absolute and aching pain that Kelly was feeling at that moment. Her stomach lurched as her legs seemed to give under her.

'I ... knocked ...?'

Kelly's head spun violently. She seemed to blink out of time and space as the darkness began closing in on her.

'Kelly?'

She heard Shona's voice, but it seemed so far away. She felt the warmth of the dancer's firm body press against her, felt her long, deceivingly strong arms around her; pulling her. Supporting her. She felt the soft cotton of the quilt that covered Shona's bed hugging her suddenly tired and depleted muscles.

A light passed before her closed eyes. She tried desperately to open them, managing eventually to peel back her lids, though she still couldn't focus.

Any momentary anger or resentment Shona had felt towards Kelly had now fled from her voice, which rippled only with the soft sighs of

213

concern and disbelief. 'Kelly, what have you done? What's happened to you?'

As she slipped from consciousness Kelly could hear the battered and tortured cries of a girl she had once known echoing inside the depths of her own mind. Her chest ricocheted with a great sob as she recoiled from the underscore of a bass and guttural laugh. A voice she had tried so hard to forget.

'He's here.' she whispered as she fell further into darkness.

00:03

Sunday 15th May, 2011

Christine pushed past the guards that stood either side of the door leading to Kelly's room. She shook her head absently and the two men stiffened as she made her way inside.

'What the hell's going on?' she said, addressing Prior, 'I thought you said they'd let us know when she was awake, not allow her to go wandering round the ship!'

'Christine. I can understand you being upset — '

'Oh, you haven't seen me upset. This . . . is not upset! I can't believe it. I can't believe Dr Matthews moved her here in the first place.'

'You saw the state of the medical bay. There just wasn't enough room back there.'

'With all due respect, Kelly was the only one brought in with a pulse. She shouldn't have been pushed aside like that.'

Prior opened his mouth, but did not speak.

Christine watched his chest rise and fall, his fists clenching at his side as he struggled to control his breathing. She knew how her words would sting him and for the briefest of moments she didn't care, she knew she was right.

But almost instantly she regretted her choice to share that particular opinion.

Prior pushed out a sigh, nodding. 'You're right.'

'Jon . . .'

'No, you're right. She should've been in medical being observed . . . I should have checked in on her earlier. She'd been attacked after all . . . I just, I got caught up — '

'Jon.' Christine said, placing her hand on his arm, 'You did what you thought best. I'm as much to blame.'

'But, you didn't post the two idiots who were unable to follow simple orders outside her room. I did.'

'What do you mean *unable to follow orders?*'

'That pair,' Prior said, nodding his head towards the door. 'Stratton went to get them a sandwich and a drink about an hour ago.'

'Right,' Christine said evenly, sensing there was more to the story.

'Only, while he was away Collins decided he couldn't hold on another ten minutes for a cigarette break.'

'He did what!'

'Believe me, I can't tell you how angry I am.' he said, before lowering his voice, 'And I'm going to make sure this is the last voyage he makes with this company. But, for now I need every man I've got if I'm going to keep some semblance of control on this ship.'

'Why? What else has happened? What am I missing'

Prior shook his head, an irritated look in his eye, 'Apparently Andrews made a general announcement earlier, updating the crew on all that's gone on. But with the way things are with communications and what-have-you ... well, he basically broadcast it to the whole bloody ship, didn't he.'

'What?'

'Yeah. It went out across the PA systems in every bar and restaurant on the ship. So there goes our chance of keeping things quiet.'

'Oh, my God. What did he say?' Christine said, in disbelief, 'And how do you even make a mistake like that?'

'It's easy enough I suppose when you appoint a pup as the lead-dog!'

'Okay, I noticed that you could have cut the tension between the pair of you with a knife the other night. But, that's a little harsh, don't you think?'

'You tell me Christine. I mean, the kid's broadcast everything we know about the deaths of the engineering crew. He more or less openly connected it to the loss of power and outside communication. People aren't stupid. Come morning we're going to have an epidemic of panic and confusion on our hands. Those who don't already get that something's very wrong, will know soon enough. And we can't stop it, or reassure them in any way, because what do we have? Nothing.'

'Did he mention the other murders?' Christine asked, mentally assessing the damage this revelation could do. Even if the general populace of the ship didn't know that the engineering crew had been murdered, the idea that they had died in a massive accident which had rendered the ship powerless and adrift was not something anyone was going to take lightly. But, it was certainly better than it being public knowledge that someone had murdered them specifically toward this end.

'I don't think he overtly spoke about the individual murders or that that was the case in engineering, but it won't take long for people to start putting two and two together. I mean there's the Stacey Atkins' hen party for one thing. You see, Blakely and Cunningham were crew; practically faceless unknowns to the passengers. We can contain the details about their deaths. But, Stacey?' Prior shook his head, sighing, 'You saw how many people were in that corridor. How many glimpsed the inside of that room. It'll spread like wildfire.'

'If it hasn't already.' Christine pushed out a long breath, glancing around the dark room. 'And now Kelly has disappeared too. Do you have anyone looking for her?'

Prior shifted his weight awkwardly, meeting the hard stare she had pinned him with. 'I'm doing my best, Christine.'

'Your best? So, I take it that's a *no* then, is it? No. No one is out searching for the woman who was targeted and attacked in her own room around the same time that everything started going to shit.'

'Christine — '

'Don't.' she said, throwing her hand up to physically stop his words. 'Don't try and tell me everything will be ok, or that it could all just be coincidence or that she *might* just be fine. Don't. Because, do you know what? That's exactly what they said about Janet.'

Biting back a sob at the sudden flood of raw emotion that rippled through her, Christine turned from Prior, her hand pressed firmly against her lips as she drew in breath after stifled breath trying desperately to regain control.

After a moment she felt Prior's firm hand on her shoulder, though she could not yet bring herself to face him.

'I *will* find her. I promise you.'

'I just hope we're not too late.'

Christine felt Prior move away from her, the absence of his strong hand leaving her cold. She composed herself, wiping at a stray tear that had managed to breach her self-imposed defences. 'You said there was something you wanted me to see.'

'Yes' said Prior, switching on the torch that Christine hadn't even noticed he had been nursing in the dark. 'You're familiar with Miss Livingstone's work?'

Christine nodded, but as the silence stretched out — and uncertain as to whether he had noticed the slight movement or not — she added, 'Yes. She let me take a look at her portfolio, though I don't how recent it all is.'

'I can guarantee it's not as recent as this lot.' Prior said, his voice suddenly filled with unease.

As he shone the torch into the corner of the room Christine heard herself gasp as her eyes beheld the wonder and horror of his concern. Resting against the legs of a collapsible easel were two wild and grotesquely colourful paintings.

Christine's stomach churned uncomfortably as she approached, the gold gild of her ornate stick reflecting the light of the torch as Prior moved in besides her.

The picture on the left was entitled *Doctor Death* and revealed a good — if not somewhat artistically tweaked — likeness of Dr Cunningham. His face was deathly hollow, with a bluish tinge to his cheeks and flesh; his lips an odd purple. He smiled leeringly from the canvas, his head cocked to the side as he raised a glass of what looked like red wine. But as she continued to stare at the painting, Christine realised that the liquid inside the glass had an incredibly live and vivid impression of movement. Her eyes traced up to find that the dark red of the fluid pouring into the clear goblet came, not from a painted bottle, but from the gushing wound in the centre of Cunningham's forehead.

'Oh my God,' she whispered, looking to Prior for reassurance.

'It gets worse.' he said, offering none. Shifting the light to focus on the canvas to the right of *Doctor Death*, he waited for Christine's eyes to adjust to both the visibility and the shock of what she would find there. 'This one's titled *Man/Machine.*'

'That's … that's Blakely.' she said, staring at the horrid blend of flesh and metal; of bone and blood and computer components melded together in paint as vibrantly realistic as the photographs she had been looking at not two hours earlier.

In some ways this was worse. Almost *more* realistic in its twisted surrealism.

'And then there's this.'

Moving the light once more, this time to a canvas clamped in place on the easel, Prior revealed the most graphic painting she had ever encountered. There were hand-sized images — almost snapshots — of Stacey Atkins in variously lewd positions surrounding a larger icon that occupied the centre of the canvas.

In each of the smaller portraits Stacey bore some new wound as she was assaulted by unseen hands; her battered face; the bite marks that covered her body and throat; the ligature marks; the words carved into her ribs. Each small image almost sneering *Are you ready for your close up?*

The look of terror on the face of the young bride-to-be gave way to defeated acceptance as Christine's eyes moved from one image to the next.

They reminded her, in some strange and twisted way, of the 'Stations of Cross'. But, then, perhaps that was the desired effect. For, at the centre of the painting, gleaming and glorious in its brutality, was an all-too realistic depiction of Stacey as they had found her in her room; hoisted up, head bowed and arms spread out in a crucifixion-style pose.

But unlike the pictures they had taken, this central image had an almost angelic glow about it — created in paint and wholly inappropriate, but angelic none-the-less. In accompanying the apparently religious theme there was a wooden-looking plaque worked into the painting above Stacey's downcast, battered and bleeding head.

It was not unlike the tablet that sat above the image of Christ on the cross in so many religious tableaus, bearing the letters INRI in mockery of the 'King of the Jews'. Only, this tablet bore the title of the painting.

Christine cleared her throat, struggling suddenly to find her voice as she spelt out the letters, 'W.H.O.R.E. Whore.'

Prior nodded slowly, 'So, as you can imagine, I'm just as eager to find Miss Livingstone as you are.'

Chapter Five

08:38

Sunday 15th May, 2011

Feeling herself begin to fall, Kelly jumped up with a start.

She found herself sitting in an unknown bed. Her heart was racing, her breaths rapid and shallow as she struggled to take in the unfamiliar surroundings. Trying to figure out where she was. And why.

The room was light and inviting; the air warm and filled with the smell of toast and coffee. Somewhat smaller than her own suite, it seemed far better equipped for living. There was a kitchenette opposite the bedroom-come-living area, which, though small appeared fairly spacious and open. Sliding mirrored panel-doors masked a built-in wardrobe space that ran the length of the wall facing her; from the arch of the little kitchen they disappeared down a narrow hallway that led to the front door.

To her right, Kelly noticed another door leading to what she imagined must be a bathroom; the scent of fragranced steam and a cleanly hint of bleach aiding in this determination.

Three dark-wood shelves floated on the outer wall that housed the bathroom, displaying books and magazines, ornaments and a wealth of photographs set out in a multitude of mismatched frames.

Pushing herself up, Kelly let out a stifled cry as a sudden surge of pain seemed to electrify her body. She couldn't determine the epicentre. She just knew that everything hurt. Every limb, every muscle, every sinew and nerve seemed to complain as she continued to pull herself gingerly into some sort of a comfortable position.

Her brow wet with beads of pain and frustration, Kelly forced herself to move extra slowly, tentatively shifting her weight from one cheek to the other as she walked her buttocks up across the mattress.

After what seemed like an age she finally fell back against the wooden panel that was the headboard, panting and sweating.

'Hello?' she said. Her voice was quiet and hoarse; her throat dry. Aching. She shook her head, blinking as the dull thumping pain she was fast becoming accustomed to made its presence violently known once more. 'Shit.' she whispered, rubbing her hand over her eyes and the bridge of her nose.

She winced feeling the bruised tenderness of her face with her fingertips.

'Good morning.' The soft, familiar tones spilt out from the kitchen, cutting through the haze of the pain. 'I was starting to worry.'

'Shona?'

'I was beginning to wonder whether I should go and fetch someone from medical, but then I didn't really want to leave you alone either.'

The lengthy-limbed dancer eased her way across the room to take a seat on the bed next to Kelly. She eyed her for a moment before pressing her hand to Kelly's forehead. 'You're still very warm. How are you feeling now?'

'Like shit.' Kelly managed.

Shona smiled, pouring a glass of water from a jug on the bedside table. 'Your throat sore?' she asked, passing Kelly the glass.

'Like I swallowed a bee-hive. Bees included!' she replied, before drinking down the water, 'And thirsty. God, I'm so thirsty!'

'I'm not surprised. You had quite a fever last night. I was really worried, Kelly. Had to put you in the shower at one point just to try and cool you down.'

'Any excuse.' Kelly said slowly, trying her best to smile even as her face throbbed.

Returning the smile with a beam of her own, Shona refilled the glass and handed it back to Kelly, who, taking another long drink, found herself gasping when she finally parted the cool glass from her swollen lips.

'What happened?' she asked, trying to focus on the big, brown eyes that seemed suddenly devastated with concern for her.

Shona shook her head. 'I was hoping you'd be able to tell me. You turned up like this in the early hours. You were bloody and bruised ... the stitches in your thigh were seeping — '

'I have stitches?' Kelly interrupted, pulling back the quilt cover to inspect Shona's claim and noticing, for the first time, that she was wearing only an oversized T-shirt that was clearly not her own. Her mind raced as she tried to recall the events of the previous day, though nothing seemed to jump out. Until, 'We were supposed to meet!' she said, as the recollection of their dinner plans abruptly perforated her swirling lack of memories. Shona nodded. 'But, we didn't?' Kelly ventured.

'No. I waited for you, but you didn't show. I was really pissed off. And freaked out too, but then with all the power cuts — '

'The what?'

Shona stared at Kelly. It seemed she was trying to read her, to judge whether she was simply messing her around. 'The ship lost power yesterday.' she said in a questioning tone. 'Early evening?' Kelly shook her head, none the wiser. 'There was a storm too, which I had thought might have had something to do with it, but ...' she paused, taking hold of Kelly's hand, 'you really don't remember any of this, do you?'

Kelly shook her head slowly, feeling the heat of tears sting her eyes and trying her best to beat them back. She really wasn't used to revealing her emotions and was certainly less-used to actually, physically crying in the presence of another human being! Particularly when it was someone she found herself attracted to and had had plans to try and seduce!

'What *do* you remember?'

'I don't know.' she sniffed, 'I think . . . I remember being in my room and . . . I don't know. I remember the darkness. I was . . .' she shook her head again, covering her face as the tears broke free. The mixture of pain and exhaustion and broken memories was simply too much.

'Hey,' Shona said softly, wrapping her arms cautiously around the tenderised artist, 'Come here. It's alright.'

As she rocked her gently back and forth, Kelly found herself slipping into the seduction of simply letting her emotions flow. Shona didn't seem to mind her sobbing against her shoulder. She didn't make her feel that she was any less of a person for opening up and spilling her tears against her soft, warm flesh.

'It's not alright.' she whispered eventually, sniffing and pulling out of Shona's rich embrace. 'It's not right that I don't remember anything. That I'm battered and bruised and feverish . . . that I have stitches I know nothing about! It's not ok that I somehow came to be knocking on your door at some ridiculous time of night, before crashing out and leaving you to clean up the mess! None of that is alright!'

'Is that what you're worried about? How this looks? That you've somehow embarrassed yourself in front of me?'

Kelly flicked a small shrug at Shona, 'That's not *all* I'm bothered about, but . . . yeah. I suppose I'm a little embarrassed.'

The biggest smile Kelly had ever seen spread across Shona's face as she leaned in, making a small *awh* noise before planting a full kiss on Kelly's inflamed lips. She winced at the small bolt of pain that surged through her muscles as she suddenly tensed, but it was a pain she was more than happy to bear. 'You are *so* cute.'

'Don't tell me I'm cute.' Kelly said, playfully, 'I'm not fucking cute! What's cute about a puffy, broken face and amnesia?'

'Just that.' Shona said, pushing a strand of Kelly's jet-black hair back from her face, 'And the way you got all defensive about crying in front of me. It's … sweet … it's endearing.'

'Endearing?'

Shona nodded.

Wiping gently at her eyes, Kelly removed all evidence of her tears. 'Well, if I'd have known that's all I had to do to get you into bed . . .' she said, grinning.

'Somehow, I don't think it'd have worked the same.'

'Still, it kind of makes me feel like I should go and shake the hand of whoever beat the shit of me last night.'

'Hey, I didn't just do this out of kindness and sympathy, you know. I'm an incredibly shallow and egocentric person when you get to know me.' Shona joked, 'Not to mention cranky when woken in the middle of the night. It's a good job you're a looker or I'd have left you out there 'til morning.'

'I don't believe that for a second. Have you seen this face!' Kelly replied, smiling though it made her facial muscles ache and the pounding in her head amplify massively. 'Still, if you're as shallow as you're trying to make out, I have to ask … what exactly was it that you hoped to gain in return for taking me in?'

'Only your gratitude.' Shona rolled the words around her mouth as she traced her finger gently over Kelly's jaw and her neck and still further down until she reached the barrier of the quilt, 'When health and strength allow.'

Feeling her heart quicken, Kelly found her mouth suddenly dry once more and made a small coughing noise in the back of her throat.

Shona grinned impishly, clearly enjoying herself.

'Right,' she said eventually, doing what Kelly seemed unable to by stringing several words together and moving the conversation steadily forwards, 'I say we should get you dressed and take a trip up to medical. I don't really think a big blank canvas in your memory is something that should be over-looked, do you?'

'You're the boss.'

'And don't you forget it.'

Shona stood as Kelly pulled back the quilt and swung her bruised legs out of the bed. The dancer offered her hand, which she accepted gladly. Then Kelly felt Shona's free arm slip around her waist, steadying her as she pushed up to stand cautiously on her feet.

'I'm sure I can manage to dress myself,' she said, wincing as they made their way round to the bathroom.

'You say that now,' Shona replied, 'but you didn't see the nightmare I had trying to get the bloody things off you.'

Kelly raised an eyebrow.

'What? I told you, you were feverish. I was scared.'

'And in the face of fear you usually strip people naked, do you?' Kelly teased.

'Not ... people.'

Shona pushed the door open and a renewed wave of lemony-bleach-scented bathroom air hit Kelly as she felt the soft lustre of the carpet give way to the pitted linoleum of wet-room flooring. 'I've already seen the goods. So, you needn't be shy. Or embarrassed. You have nothing to be embarrassed about anyway.'

Feeling her face flush slightly, Kelly laughed and tugged at the oversized shirt. 'In that case, why did you subject me to this?'

'Well, you weren't conscious *before* and I thought you might freak out — even more than you did — if you woke to find yourself *naked* in my bed with no knowledge of how you got there. Especially, as I know that you don't drink. You might have thought I'd drugged you or something.'

'You remembered.' Kelly said.

'Of course I remembered. It's good for business. People tip you better when you make the effort.'

'I'll have to remember that. But, still.' She tweaked at the garment again and Shona stopped, her face blank and suddenly very solemn.

'It was mine.' she said, 'Before I lost the weight.'

Kelly could have kicked herself and was suddenly quite glad that someone had already done the job for her.

Why did she have to do that? Why had she gone on about it? Now, far from showing any gratitude to the woman who had helped her and nursed her through the night, she had wound up insulting her and making her feel like shit instead!

Nice one.

After a moment a child-like grin spread across Shona's face as she began to giggle. 'I'm only pulling you're leg. It belonged to one of my ex's. He was a professional rugby player.'

Kelly's relief was plain to see as she perched on the side of the bath and finally exhaled,

'I don't wear anything in bed.' Shona continued, 'It was the only thing I had that I thought might be comfortable. Oh, and on that note, you didn't *get me into bed*. I slept on the couch.'

'Your such a gentleman.'

'Somebody has to be. God knows blokes bloody-well aren't these days!'

Kelly laughed as Shona disappeared before returning with the clothes she had arrived in. 'I gave them a wash. Like I said, you're stitches had started to seep and there was blood … a lot of blood. Fortunately they're all quite dark so it's not too bad.'

Kelly didn't flinch as Shona lifted the professional rugby ex's t-shirt over her head. She slipped her arms into the straps of her bra and only stiffened slightly as Shona leaned in, fastening the clasp behind her. Turning her head, she caught a glimpse of herself in the long mirror. Her ribs were bruised and cut, as was most of her face; her lips were as swollen as they felt; her left eye too was puffy and looking more than a little blood-shot.

God, I'm attractive! She thought sardonically.

As if hearing her thoughts, Shona stroked the side of her face gently. She opened her mouth, but didn't speak. Instead she smiled and turned to pick up Kelly's jeans, holding them for her to step into.

'So, tell me about Mr Pro Rugby Dude. Was it serious?

Shona laughed, 'Does it look like it was serious?'

Kelly smiled, wincing slightly as they worked together to pull the jeans up and over her slender, but battered thighs. Slipping the brass button through the button-hole, Shona drew up the zip of the dark, stonewash denim; the tips of her fingers lingering at the soft pink flesh of Kelly's tight abdomen.

'This all seems a bit back to front, doesn't it?'

'All good things . . .' Shona whispered; her lips only millimetres from her own. Her dark-chocolate gaze beguiling and bewitching Kelly as she became very aware that her mind was now racing towards exploring the possibilities of those soft and nimble fingers as they continued to caress her navel in delicate little circles.

'Thank you.' she mustered with another small cough. 'Thanks for taking care of me.'

'The pleasure's all mine.' Shona said, before turning away from her and bending to pick up the dark blue shirt.

Kelly cocked her head, then instantly rebuked herself as the beautifully crafted dancer turned back to face her, slipping the shirt over her arms and buttoning up the front.

I doubt that. she thought, smiling into Shona's warm eyes. *I doubt that very much!*

08:45

Sunday 15th May, 2011

So far, Prior's morning had been the total antithesis of his normally organised and ordered routine.

He had hardly slept following the revelations in Kelly Livingstone's suite, not to mention the fact that the woman herself was now missing thanks to the incompetence of the two officers he had made the mistake of posting outside her door.

There were so many questions he wanted answered. And most of them involving the elusive Miss Livingstone and the query of whether she could actually commit to the acts alluded to in the twisted images that littered her work. So, right at the top of his list of was the necessity to locate and question her.

And fast.

He had been correct in his suppositions that come day-break the ship would be awash with rumour and panic. The most terrifying part of this, however, was that a majority of the *rumours* flying around bore more than a marked resemblance to both his and Christine's own deductions of the events that had occurred since the previous afternoon. This could only aid to inspire further panic and confusion and potentially hinder their chances of apprehending the culprit. Or culprits.

At first he hadn't really bought Christine's idea of there being two killers working together, but the more he thought about it the more — he reluctantly supposed — it made sense. Still, he wasn't entirely convinced and reserved the right to stick to his guns until absolutely persuaded otherwise.

He had met with Captain Andrews just before eight and updated him on everything that had happened so far, only just managing to hold his tongue when Andrews mentioned the *technical error* that had occurred during his transmission to the crew the night before.

'I heard.' he said, clamping his mouth shut and sucking his teeth as Andrew's continued to debrief him on the bizarre intricacies of this unusual situation.

The only positive thing he had managed to take away from his meeting with Andrews was a magazine called *Artist Profile* that had recently featured an article on Kelly Livingstone and her work. The head-shot colour photo on the first page of the article was exactly what he had hoped for and should have been more than enough to give his team a clear idea of who they were looking for.

After leaving Andrews, he had made his way down to the stuffy, little staff canteen on E deck. He had spent some time that morning transforming the place into a base of operations for the growing number of medical staff, security and the many other varied and now otherwise-unoccupied members of the crew he had gained as a make-shift investigative team.

He had managed to snatch two fully-charged laptops and had also acquired some presentation boards from the far more luxurious conference lounges dotted about the ship. He would have liked simply to move the operation into one of these rooms, but had been back-heeled — unsurprisingly — by Captain Andrews.

Apparently all the conference rooms and theatres on the ship were now being used in various ways to maintain order by providing family entertainment, distributing food and drink and generally distracting the populace from the chaos of the unexplained.

So his new *team* got the E deck staff canteen along with the cabbage and dish-water smell that haunted the place no matter how many times it was cleaned down.

'Right,' he said, striding through the crowd who slowly hushed to silence. Standing before the now-cluttered presentation boards — or evidence boards as they had become — Prior waited patiently, looking around the room at the sea of faces, many of whom seemed excited to be involved in something they could only equate to the fabled and glamorous televisual world of *CSI*.

Inwardly, he cursed the programme. And not for the first time.

'You've all been brought up to speed on why you're here.' he said, pausing to allow for the nodding heads to confirm this, 'I know that many of you have little-to-no experience in this field, but you're here. And as long as you apply a bit of common sense and do exactly as I instruct then I am confident that we can stop this dangerous individual before they take another life.'

'I heard a rumour there was more than one killer.' said a broad-shouldered man near the back of the cramped room. Prior recognised him as Alfie Dean, the ship's Chief LX and Technical Director of the *Dionysus* Theatre.

'We can't be sure. But, with the scale and the pace of everything that's happened it's certainly a possibility.' Prior paused for a moment as people began to murmur. He saw a figure move slowly in his periphery; entering the room. He turned his head to see that it was Dr Kane. Christine.

Slinging a small brief smile her way, he nodded his head for her to join him. 'This is Dr Christine Kane.' he said, extending his arm as she continued to make her way gradually through the crowd. 'She's a Criminal Psychologist and has — '

'Hey, I know her!' piped a skinny, overly-scouse Scouser in front of Prior, 'She's that one what got her sister killed 'cause she didn't do her job right.'

Feeling a spike of anger pinching the base of his skull, Prior sucked in a breath. All around the man people began to whisper and nod, spurring him to continue. 'Yeah, some fella — shoulda been sent down, like — got time in a nut 'ouse before getting out for good behaviour. All because of her!' Pointing his finger like the Witch-Finder General at Christine, the lanky Scouser — that Prior now remembered to be Dave Graham — grinned, enjoying the glory of the crowd's attention.

'Dr Kane has worked successfully with police departments nationwide to provide the workable profiles of countless violent criminals, including those of a number of murderers and rapists.' Prior said, squaring up to Graham, 'Her profiling skills and intuition have led to the apprehension of some of the most dangerous and deadly killers this country has seen in recent years. Many that otherwise would have gone undetected for ... who knows how long?'

Prior shot a look around the room before finding Graham's pointed face and small, too-close eyes once more, 'In short,' he continued, 'she's saved the lives of an innumerable amount of people and deserves your attention and respect. Right now we have very little to go on. We're self contained here. Cut-off from the world with a killer on the loose and little-to-no chance of identifying them using the limited CS equipment we have on board. So my advice is that you listen to everything Dr Kane has to say. And that you bear that information in mind as you proceed in this investigation.'

Prior held Graham's rat-like stare until the latter faltered, taking a step backwards and bowing his head. Letting out a slow and steady breath, Prior returned his attention to Christine, placing his hand on her small shoulder for only the briefest of moments as she cleared her throat to speak.

'Thank you Mr Prior,' she said, seeming to draw strength from the formal use of his surname.

She straightened and began to address the crowd of mismatched investigators, quickly filling them in on the details surrounding the deaths in engineering and the individual murders of Stacey Atkins, Gary Blakely and Dr Cunningham. As she continued, she pointed out some of the photographs now pinned to the evidence board, ignoring the noises of horror and disgust along with the tittering of those who didn't know quite how they should react.

'There are some definite similarities between these murders,' she said confidently, 'and Dr Matthews has suggested that Dr Cunningham was the first to die, while the state of rigor mortis and lividity in the other victims points to Stacey being the most recent casualty. Gary Blakely was most likely killed around the same time as the other members of the engineering crew, but his body showed evidence of torture by various means and methods over the course of about an hour or so.'

'What happened to the Atkins girl?' asked a fair-haired woman, 'I was trying to comfort her sister, but I didn't really know what to say. She was in bits. I mean totally devastated.'

Christine nodded slowly, taking in the woman's genuine concern. 'She was unfortunate enough to glimpse the state in which the killer had left her sister. It's the kind of thing you never quite get over.' Christine said, her gaze locking onto Dave Graham, who at least had the decency to lower his eyes in shame. 'But, listen there are a few things I want to make clear,' she continued, shaking off the momentary resentment she felt, 'I strongly believe that *all* the murders, including those of the engineers — who are absolutely being treated as homicide victims — are connected. Whether this is someone flying solo or several people working together there are certain aspects within each of the crime scenes that lend themselves towards a distinctive signature and also therefore a certain pattern and mode of behaviour.

'For example, Dr Cunningham, Blakely and the engineering team all appear to have been killed out of necessity. Whilst, whoever killed Stacey took their time. Enjoyed themselves, walking a fine line between planning and experimenting and — as with Blakely — torture played an all too obvious part in Stacey's final hours of life.' Christine paused, turning to

Prior who gave an approving nod. 'However, Dr Matthews has said that there's no evidence of Stacey being sexually assaulted either pre or post mortem. Which is good.'

'*Why* is that good?' asked an unknown voice.

'Why is that *not* good?' came an unseen reply.

There was a subdued roll of nervous laughter.

Christine smiled. 'It's good because rape is very rarely about sex. It's about control. It's about violence and humiliation. Often the attacker is only able to complete the sex act part of their attack due to the sense of dominance they feel they gain over their victim during the attack. However, this said; Stacey's body did show signs of sexual trauma. Not to mention the many sexually explicit injuries that were inflicted on her, both before and after death.'

'So what does that mean?' Prior asked quietly.

'It means that this attack was very much about sex.' Christine said, 'Yet, our killer didn't feel the need, or — rather — was unable to bring this to fruition. He couldn't carry out the act itself. He didn't try to conventionally enter her and neither did he use an object to achieve this. Not even after death. Now, whether that's because she held no further sexual interest for him once the life had left her, I can't say for sure. But, there didn't appear to be any traces of semen present inside Stacey or anywhere in the room. Not on the bed or in the bath, nor on the clothes she had been wearing.'

Christine moved back towards the evidence board, pointing to the photo of Stacey's ribs. 'And this,' she said, 'is the really interesting part, because these words — Not My Type — were carved after death. Now, is that frustration? Is it mocking? Is it a message for us?'

'How should we know?' someone shouted.

Prior's eyes searched for the owner of the voice, angry at the outburst and the blatant disrespect. He felt Christine's hand on his forearm and exhaled slowly, his eyes flicking to her determined face as she continued to address the crowd. 'That is my point.' she said, 'You have to question everything. You cannot assume *anything* at all. You need to know this evidence board and the information contained therein like the back of your hand. It's like a giant jigsaw puzzle and at the moment there are pieces missing . . . there are pieces that don't seem to fit because the picture is so distorted, but so too are there sections that seem to fit even when they don't.'

Christine paused looking around the room at the countless pairs of eyes that seemed to have clouded over like the evening sky in the previous night's storm.

'I think what Dr Kane is trying to say is that *everything* is important.' Prior said, stepping in, 'and the better you know these details here, the easier you'll make connections with any new evidence we discover and the quicker we can catch the perp.'

Christine nodded as a rustle of murmuring swept through the room.

'Now listen,' she said, awkwardly manoeuvring herself to the next board and pointing out several pictures, 'identical ligature marks were found around the necks of Gary Blakely and Stacey Atkins, categorically linking the two murders via the use of the same weapon.'

'Couldn't it just be coincidence?' asked Dave Graham, regaining some of his former confidence.

'If we were in a big city or something there might be a chance that this was coincidence. But, I think we're far too contained here for that to be the case.' Christine looked to Prior who nodded in agreement once more. 'So, I want you all out there talking to people. Asking questions. See if anyone noticed anything odd, heard anything, saw anything. Particularly in the area surrounding engineering between four and five pm yesterday.'

'Before you go,' Prior interjected, 'I want you all to take a look at this picture.' He held up a magazine opened at a page displaying a nice colour head-shot of a Caucasian woman in her late twenties. Her blue eyes sparkled — though she did not smile in the picture — and picked up the tints of blue in her otherwise jet-black hair, which was then swept into a scruffy bob. 'Her name is Kelly Livingstone. She's currently missing and wanted for questioning.' he said, feeling Christine's cold stare hit him and hold him like ice. 'Her hair's slightly different now, shorter at the back. And she may be confused. She was possibly attacked yesterday and has stitches in her right thigh.'

Pinning the magazine to the board, Prior concluded the brief. Then, he signalled to a handful of milling bodies, taking them to one side as the rest of the *team* began to filter out.

'Officer Marc Davies is up in the Security Office trawling through the limited crew files that we have on board the ship. Now, while I say *limited* there's still a lot of boxes up there and many of the files will be out-dated since the transference to digital so he's going to need a hand in sifting through what's useful and what's not.'

The small group nodded — some of them reluctantly — and made their way out of the canteen. Now there was nothing to keep him from ignoring the icy cold stare that Christine had still pinned him with.

'There was no call for that.' she said.

'For what?'

'You know what. You're making it sound like she's part of this.'

'Well, she is part of this. Isn't she?' Prior said, walking away from Christine and trying to make it appear as casual as possible. He reached a long table laid out with four immense, industrial-catering, push-top tea and coffee pots; a mass of take-away cups; sugar and milk. He set about fixing himself a coffee, holding the cup under the nozzle as he pressed down.

'It's *possible* she was attacked?' Christine continued, '*Possible!* We know she was. Jon, I was there for Christ's sake!'

'Christine,' he said, shovelling three sugars into the coffee along with a dribble of milk, 'I know you feel a ... closeness to Miss Livingstone — '

'What do you mean by that?'

'I know you want to protect her.' He began stirring, a maelstrom of coffee almost spilling over the lip of the white cup with every rotation. 'But, I think your feelings may be clouding your judgement. I'm just not convinced that things are as simple as you'd have them seem.'

'What exactly are you suggesting?' Christine said, leaning against the table and flexing her hand, aching already from a busy morning on her stick.

'Can you be certain that there was someone in the room with her?'

Christine opened her mouth to answer; to shout 'Yes! Of course I'm sure!' right in Prior's infuriatingly handsome face, but, found herself clamping her jaws shut once more. She shook her head in annoyance; gnawing her lip and feeling the chip in her tooth nick the fleshy inside.

She tasted blood.

'I don't want to hurt you, Christine. I don't mean to question your judgement, but you've suffered a lot lately. I can understand you wanting to save her.'

'This isn't a replacement thing, Jon.'

Prior held up his hands, 'If you say so. But, besides that, I know that Miss Livingstone brought a set of artist knives on board with her. She could have caught her own leg during some sort of artistic frenzy and not realised. Passed out from the blood-loss.'

'Is that what you really think?' she asked, trying desperately to hide the pain in her voice, 'Or rather is it that you think she took those knives and went on a merry little butchering spree about the ship last night?'

Prior didn't answer immediately. When finally he did it was with a soft and measured tone. 'Either way I want to recover the knives. And Kelly. Andrews never should have — '

'I didn't expect this of you, Jon. How can you think . . .'

'I'm just doing my job.'

'But, I'm incapable of doing *mine?*'

'*This* isn't your job.' he said, instantly regretting the statement, 'That's not what I meant. And you know how highly I respect your judgements.'

'Aye. Enough to tear them apart in front of a crowd of strangers and amateurs.' she said angrily.

'Now that's not fair.'

'Not fair? Why did you even ask for my help if you don't think I'm up to the task?'

'I don't think that.' Prior said, 'Not at all.'

'Well, you could have fooled me.'

Christine turned from Prior, making her way painfully towards the door she had passed through not-so-long ago.

'Christine.' he called.

She didn't stop. She didn't look back.

Prior's two-way radio bleeped as he watched her struggle through the remaining crowd. 'Go ahead.' he said, rubbing his eyes wearily.

The static crackled for a moment before he heard a familiar feminine bark.

'Prior? It's Dr Matthews here.'

'Doctor. What can I do for you?'

'It's more what I can do for you.' she said, cheerfully, 'You'll never guess who just walked in — or rather, hobbled in — through my door.'

Downing his coffee, Prior jogged out of the canteen, following the path Christine had taken. He caught her as she struggled up the last step in a flight that led to the next deck.

'Christine,' he said, catching a gentle hold of her arm, 'Christine, I'm sorry. Please. Listen to me. I know where she is.'

09:17

Sunday 15th May, 2011

The medical waiting room was so much brighter today, if not a little overcrowded. The cloudless blue skies — such a blessing after the dark and ominous, torrential brooding storm of the night before — allowed for plenty of sunlight to penetrate the stuffy, open-plan room.

On her previous visit, Christine hadn't really had a chance to notice the large rectangular windows that punctuated the length of the hull along this deck creating a corridor of natural light on a day like today. Overhead a series of sun-trap window lights added to the illuminating effect, bathing the deck with a warm and much appreciated glow.

Rounding the frosted glass divider that separated the waiting area from the general corridor, Christine felt her heart skip a little as she caught sight of Kelly sitting awkwardly in a blue plastic chair.

She felt Prior draw up besides her, spotting Kelly too, though she doubted his reaction would have been anywhere near as joyful as her own. He didn't move a muscle and after a moment she took her cue, realising that he was holding back to allow her a moment alone with Kelly.

She leaned gently on her white marble stick, crossing with purpose and delight towards the sable-haired artist who had somehow managed to capture her absolute attention with such ease.

As she drew closer, Kelly looked up, noticing her for the first time. A moment of doubt seemed to cloud her eyes, then it was gone and her face radiated only her joy at seeing Christine. She scrambled awkwardly to stand and greet her.

'Christine.' she said, embracing the psychologist who, without thinking about it, pressed her lips against her cheek.

Realising the forwardness of her actions and becoming suddenly aware of their physicality, Christine stiffened, cutting short the embrace.

She felt her face begin to flush and smiled a small girlish smile at Kelly, who continued to hold on to her arm.

'Kelly,' she smiled softly, 'You're ok. I was beginning to fear that ...' She couldn't bring herself to finish the sentence. She knew what she feared; there was no need to air the nightmarish thoughts that had plagued her as she had tried to sleep.

'Hey,' Kelly said, 'Don't worry about me. I — '

'Am I interrupting?' A soft and sultry voice danced near to them, her joking words loaded with just enough venom to serve as a quiet warning.

'Not at all.' Christine replied. A little quicker and a little louder than intended.

Leaning on her stick she took a heavy step backwards, allowing the tanned and tight-bodied beauty to move in close to Kelly, passing her a cardboard cup that smelt of strong, delicious coffee.

The attractive, dark-haired, young woman eyed Christine suspiciously and locked her in her sights though she appeared to speak to Kelly. 'You like black, right?'

'Thanks.' Kelly said, taking in the aroma of the cup, seemingly oblivious to the sudden awkward tension, 'Shona, this is Christine Kane. A friend of mine. A bloody saviour in fact.' Christine beamed inwardly. 'She's agreed to help me out with a publication the University's forcing me into.' The beam faded. 'Christine, this is Shona. She was in the show. She helped me out last night.'

Christine felt a strange mixture of jealousy, disappointment and disbelief twist in the pit of her stomach, making her want to throw up the handful of cornflakes she had managed to force herself into eating at around six that morning. 'Really?' she managed through a clenched smile.

'Oh, I wouldn't say that.' Shona said, holding Kelly's gaze for some time before turning to Christine so as to clearly articulate her position and intent. 'I mostly just put her to bed and kept an eye on her throughout the night.'

'You don't remember anything from before that?' Christine asked, trying to keep the desperation from her voice.

Kelly shook her head.

'She was in a pretty bad way.' Shona intoned, 'As you can see.'

Christine nodded a short, sharp nod and became suddenly aware of Prior — once more — standing beside her.

How long had he been there?

'Miss Livingstone.' he said evenly, 'I'm very glad to see you. We were worried.'

'You were?'

Prior nodded.

'Am I missing something?' Kelly asked.

'I – or rather, we – have some questions we'd like to ask you.' he paused a moment as Kelly looked between him and Christine anxiously. 'If you wouldn't mind coming with us.'

'Jon?' Shona questioned, but he simply shook his head.

Kelly handed her coffee back to Shona, turning to follow Prior. As Christine hobbled passed the dancer, she couldn't help but feel a small twinge of satisfaction.

He hung back, beyond the frosted glass divider. Watching them.

His heart seemed to pound in his ears as he forced himself to slow his breathing.

You must stay calm. You must stay calm . . . or they will find you.

He nodded to himself. Sweating profusely.

Cautiously, he peered around the frosted glass one more time. He cursed as his gaze found Shona leaning in to kiss the dark-haired one on the cheek. The older woman — the one with the stick — stiffened, unable to tear her eyes from the bitch.

Then he watched as the trio stepped into the adjoining room, leaving Shona behind.

She took a seat, leaning back against the wall and stretching out her legs.

You're not supposed to sit down!

She was supposed to leave. Alone.

He cursed under his breath and turned. Seething, he quickly retraced his steps along the corridor he had followed them through.

Feeling a sudden cold shudder, Shona glanced up. She leaned forward, craning her neck to look around the glass divider. There was no one there.

The elderly gentleman in the seat next to her raised his heavy, grey wiry eyebrows questioningly.

'D'you ever get the feeling that someone's just walked over your grave?' Shona asked.

He smiled, 'More often than not when you get to my age, lovely.'

He laughed a rasping, happy laugh; which in turn led to a spluttering, wheezing cough.

Shona couldn't help but think *Please don't die on me!*

'And that's when you found the paintings?' Kelly asked, dismayed and clearly upset, 'In *my* room?'

'Yes.' said Prior, matter-of-factly.

They had excused their way through the first GP-style office, settling into a smaller room located just behind it.

In truth, it was little more than a converted broom cupboard; a desk — a quarter of the size of its companion in the adjacent room — took up most of the floor space. There was one high-back, leather-look swivel chair that Kelly herself now occupied and an outdated computer; the tower whirring noisily, eating up the medical bay's emergency power, as it struggled to load the images from Prior's SD card.

'Where are they now?'

'They've been removed.' said Prior, 'As evidence.'

Christine shot him a cautionary look.

'Evidence? Evidence of what?'

Prior didn't answer.

'And you think *I* painted them?'

'Wait 'til you see them. Then tell me what you'd think if you were in my shoes.'

Kelly looked at Prior in disbelief. 'And just when am I supposed to have done this? I don't know if you've noticed, but I'm a little worse for wear. How many did you say there were?'

'Three.' said Christine, seeming to study every movement Kelly made as she squirmed uncomfortably in her chair.

'Somehow, I don't think I was in much of a mood for painting last night, judging by the way I feel today. Besides, whatever else might have happened to me, I obviously made my way here at some point.'

'*You* made — ' Prior began.

Christine shook her head in a small, but determined motion.

'Yeah. I mean, I've got eleven stitches in my thigh, for fucks sake!' Kelly said, indicating with her hand, ignoring fact that her dark jeans currently masked that detail. 'Surely the doctors keep a record. They'll be able confirm that I was here and give you a time. Give me an alibi.'

Christine stepped forward, 'Kelly, no one is accusing you — '

'Really?' she retorted angrily. 'I don't know *what* it is you're accusing me of doing, but I know what an accusation sounds like, Christine. And even if — by some bizarre streak of chance — I did happen to paint last night — which, I seriously doubt I could have done in this state — that *is* what I do. I'm a fucking artist. And as far as I'm aware there's no law against art!' she shot Prior a withering look, 'Unless it's another of your maritime security issues.'

Prior seemed to growl, staring through Kelly more than at her. 'The issue is in the subject of the paintings. And, yes we know where you were, Miss Livingstone.' he paused, drawing in a long breath as he slowed his speech; regaining some semblance of control. 'That is, we know your whereabouts for part of the evening. You were — as you say — here in the medical bay ... from sometime just before six o'clock last night. Dr Matthews tended to your injuries and checked you over,' he hesitated, 'before moving you back to your room. Within the hour.'

'Seriously?' Kelly said, physically agitated by this news, 'You mean she just patched me up and sent me out? Was I even conscious then?'

'Not so far as we're aware.' Prior sighed.

'What kind of half-arsed, idiotic doctor would do that? I could have fucking died!'

Prior sucked in a breath, his green eyes set. As rock. Locked on Kelly. She watched him, silently daring him to say something. But, it was Christine who eventually spoke.

'Kelly, I know this must be difficult for you to process. Dr Matthews should never have discharged you like that and I'm certain,' she said, though she wasn't, 'that under ordinary circumstances she'd never have done anything so irresponsible. But, last night was no ordinary night.'

'You mean the storm?' Kelly asked, watching Christine as she shifted her weight absently, flexing her injured knee, 'Shona mentioned something about it messing everything up. She said we have no communication. No satellite, GPRS, WIFI, stuff like that. Is that true?'

Prior and Christine exchanged a knowing look.

'Yes and no.' said Prior.

'What d'you mean *yes and no?*'

'There was a storm last night.' Christine began, 'A bad storm, yes. But, it wasn't responsible for the … casualties that arrived in the medical bay around the same time you did. Neither was it responsible for loss of power and communication.'

'So, what was?'

'Not *what.*' said Prior, 'Who.'

'Who?'

Prior nodded. 'Last night the communications and main-power functions of the ship were sabotaged remotely from an emergency station in engineering. Dr Kane and I agree that whoever was responsible for this is also more than likely to be behind the other crimes that were committed both last night and Friday evening. The crimes so vividly and perfectly captured in the paintings that were discovered in your room in the early hours of this morning.'

'Crimes?' Kelly asked, genuinely concerned.

Christine nodded slowly, her solemn air ensnaring Kelly completely, forcing her absolute attention as the pictures from the SD card eventually began to creep across the screen besides her. She could see a blur of tangled colours on the periphery, though her eyes were locked onto Christine, whose dire expression sent chills up and down her spine in expectation of her next words.

'Last night twenty-three members of the engineering crew died of anoxic asphyxiation. They were sealed in a room that was flooded with carbon dioxide.'

'Shit.' said Kelly, 'And it wasn't a mechanical fault?'

'We don't think so,' Christine continued, 'another engineer, the Deputy Chief in fact, was tortured and brutally murdered.'

'Oh my God.'

'As was Dr Cunningham.'

'The guy that was sat at the table with us on Friday?' Kelly asked. Prior nodded slowly. 'Oh my God, that's horrible. I — '

'That's not all.' Christine said, inching her way across the tiny room, 'A young Bride-to-be was also killed and mutilated. Mutilated and killed. Both in fact. And all these incidents occurred within the space of about sixteen hours.'

'What? How?' Kelly struggled, 'How did the girl die?'

'Take a look.' Prior said in a low bark, 'the painting's quite an accurate depiction of the scene we were greeted with last night. It even includes some snap-shots of her degradation and demise along the way. The parts we didn't get to see.'

Kelly turned to face the screen, her stomach sinking, heavy and ice-cold as she beheld the digital representation of a painting entitled W.H.O.R.E.

Prior leaned in close to her as her eyes continued to dance about the screen, scanning the image; the artist in her appreciating the quality of the work; the human being in her wanting to vomit at the knowledge that the sorry state of the model in each snap-shot was no mere artistic representation and creation. It was real, brutal destruction.

'Do you recognise the style of the work?'

Kelly nodded slowly, unable to tear her eyes from the screen or even rebuke the Security Chief for his not-so-quiet accusations. Flicking to the next image, she felt her stomach lurch again as she was confronted by the blood-soaked, amalgamated horror of an image that wouldn't look out of place in a post-apocalyptic, Giger-inspired sci-fi graphic novel. She shuddered and moved on to the next image, gasping as she came face to face with the clearly deceased, yet tauntingly jovial facade of Dr Cunningham. She brought her hand to her mouth, stifling a small sob.

'Kelly?' Christine said, resting a supportive hand on her arm, 'Are you ok?'

'How can I be?' she said, tears in her eyes, 'This is *my* work, Christine. Look at it. It's my style, my technique.'

'Technique can be mirrored.' the psychologist said softly, finding Prior's green, narrowed eyes as she spoke, 'Style can be copied.'

Kelly shook her head, unable to form words.

Prior's radio bleeped suddenly, cutting through the silence with a jolt that made them all physically jump.

'Prior.' he answered.

'Sir ... we've got a bit of a situation in the *Seraphim Suite*.'

Kelly recognised the voice as belonging to the pointless, ginger creation that had rifled through her bags two mornings earlier.

'What kind of situation, Collins?' Prior said, a hint of irritation in his voice.

'There's ... there's two more bodies. Sir.'

Prior shook his head and cursed under his breath, annoyed that this exasperating message-bearer had managed to taint his natural reaction to such tragic news; the mere sound of Collins' voice pissing him off beyond belief.

He looked to Christine, feeling her eyes already on him.

'You can stay here if you want.' he said.

She shook her head, a half-smile curling the corners of her mouth.

'And leave you stumbling around in the dark?'

Kelly felt Christine touch her shoulder once more. She sighed, releasing a long, slow breath and looked up at the psychologist who she already held in such high esteem.

'You'll be okay, won't you?' she asked, in those warm Scottish tones. Kelly nodded, feeling wholly unconfident in her silent testimony. 'Have a nurse check over your stitches and bruising now that everything's had a chance to settle down. Okay? I don't know when you'll be allowed back into your suite, but if you wanted to go — '

'It's ok.' Kelly said, 'If someone's already been in there once … some murdering, bloody psychopathic, impersonating freak …' she sighed, 'What's to stop them getting in again? I don't even want to think about it.'

'If we feel that someone is targeting you, Miss Livingstone,' Prior said, 'I swear I'll do everything within my power to protect you.'

Kelly turned on him, 'If you *feel*? Does that mean that you don't think I'm involved anymore? Did I pass your test?' she said, trying not to spit her words at him.

'I had to check.'

She gave a firm nod in answer as she pulled herself to her feet, clenching her teeth as a fleeting pain stabbed through her thigh where the fresh stitches had snagged on the denim of her jeans.

'I don't think you should be on your own.' Christine said, stopping her before she reached the door.

'I won't.' Kelly returned, without looking at her.

'I can assign someone to — ' Prior offered, only to be cut short.

'That's ok. Shona's said I can go back to hers.'

Kelly heard Christine release a short, quiet breath; but, more than this, she seemed to *feel* her deflate. For a brief moment she appeared fragile, doll-like; a young girl dealing with rejection. Then, in an instant, any sign of vulnerability was gone. Dissipated. Walls up once more. 'Am I free to go?' she said.

'Of course you are.' Christine answered, softly.

Kelly turned the handle and stepped out of the room with an awkward hobble, quickly closing the door behind her.

Christine watched Kelly leave, a cocktail of confusing emotions rattling her heart and her head. She wanted Kelly to be safe. And yet the thought of her in the arms of that vainglorious vixen she had seen outside set her teeth on edge.

She was so sure of herself, that one. The type of woman who knew exactly what she wanted and was rarely denied.

Yes, she was beautiful. But she knew it.

And she had a callous competitiveness about her, a look in her eye that was almost animal. Like a she-wolf warding off any other's interest in her mate with a silent snarl.

'Christine?'

She turned back to Prior, flashing a poor attempt at a smile as she tried to mask her thoughts.

'Come on then.' she said, 'It's probably best if you lead the way.'

10:14

Sunday 15th May, 2011

Kelly hadn't hung around in the ever-filling waiting room. She no longer cared to be checked over by any member of the medical staff, particularly not Dr Matthews.

She had many words she would like to say to the good doctor, though none of them were particularly pleasant. And yet she knew she should be grateful for the fact that Matthews had tended to her injuries at all, even if her later judgements had not been the best.

She was still seething by the time she reached the cloudless blue and the cool breeze of the top open deck, Shona racing to join her.

'Hey!' she called, 'What's wrong with you? Where are you going?'

Kelly felt a firm hand on her shoulder trying to spin her round. She knew it was Shona. Knew that she wanted only to help. Knew she was indebted to the dazzling dancer for all that she had done already. And yet she shook her off like a sulking teenager, folding her arms across the white, painted rail and resting her chin on them, pressing her face into the wind and enjoying the refreshing onslaught of sea air as she tried to organise her thoughts.

'What happened in there?' Shona asked, drawing up besides her.

'What do you know about the storm last night?'

'What does that have — '

'Did you know that it wasn't responsible the power loss? Or the casualties?'

Shona turned her body, pressing her back against the safety railing and leaning in close, forcing Kelly to look her in the eye. 'What do you mean *casualties?*'

Kelly didn't reply. Where should she begin?

'I heard people talking when I went to get milk this morning, but I didn't really — '

'So *you* left me alone too!' Kelly raged without thinking.

'I nipped to the shop to get a pint of milk, Kelly. It's like ten steps away from my room. Literally!' Shona replied, 'It's not like you were going anywhere and — anyway — I'm not your babysitter!'

Kelly shot a look at Shona, feeling the heat of all her rage rising inside as her chest swelled and her hands balled suddenly into fists. 'I know you're not my babysitter! I don't need a fucking babysitter! Alright?'

In her mind Kelly was transported back to a place she thought she had managed to obliterate from her memory completely. A place too painful to exist.

She was nine years old and standing in the blackened remains of her family home. She could still taste the bitter smack of the thick, blue-grey smoke that had engulfed the small, detached house. That had filled her little lungs.

She had been in hospital for nearly a week, recovering from severe smoke inhalation and several minor injuries. This had been the first time she had been allowed outside.

The white plastic band on her arm had itched and she had known — even then — that they would be coming for her soon. But, for those few, short minutes she was home.

In some ways it hadn't mattered that it was only a shell. And yet it had nearly destroyed her to see it that way.

Barren. Decimated. Cold.

From out of nowhere she could suddenly hear the militaristic voice of her Gran grating against the chalk-board of her memories.

A formidable woman of five foot seven inches and built like a brick shit-house, Kelly's Gran was not a woman with whom any sane person would ever willingly trifle. She was calling her name with the same tone of absolute disdain she had always made it so clear she held her granddaughter in.

It was clear as the day.

She remembered the beating she had received that night for running away from the hospital.

Well, they hadn't specified where she could and couldn't go. They had said she was allowed out. Stretch her legs. Not her fault that they didn't clarify!

You are so selfish, her Gran had informed her between beatings, the wooden spoon catching her thigh and her calves as she had tried — unsuccessfully — to run, *Do you have any idea how difficult this is for me? I don't have the time to organise this funeral and work a job and babysit you twenty-four hours a day, you selfish, horrid little brat!*

That had been the moment that Kelly had snapped, lashing out at her Gran though she knew she would eventually pay for it with her pound of battered flesh when the beastly woman finally caught up with her again.

She had jumped up, catching her Gran off balance and butting her square in the nose; feeling it burst across her father's mother's face with a satisfying crunch.

Try explaining that one to the W-fucking-I!

I don't need a fucking babysitter! she had shouted, running as fast as she could out of the prim and proper kitchen, through the 'perfect family' portraited hall to heave open the twisted, splintered and decaying front door.

Then she was away.

Pulled suddenly, as though she had been abruptly dropped back into her own shoes — her own skin and life, here and now — Kelly trembled as she readjusted to the reality of what was happening.

She watched a confused and irritated Shona take a step back, her mouth moving though her words were inaudible through the buzzing haze of mixed-up memories that continued to assault Kelly's senses.

She hadn't thought about that day in years. Or any of the days preceding.

If she was honest, most of her young life was a black-hole. And that in itself scared her.

Catching hold of Shona's arm and blinking back to the here and now, Kelly shook her head, trying frantically to speak, but unable to form any words for what felt like an age.

'I'm sorry.' she said eventually, 'Shona, please. I'm sorry. I didn't mean to ... that wasn't aimed at you. I'm sorry. It's all ... messed up. Please ...'

Shona eyed her for a moment, leaving Kelly to wonder whether she would turn her back completely. But she didn't.

'Let go of my arm.' she said in a quiet, but commanding tone.

Kelly did.

'I didn't mean — '

'Forget about it.' It was an order rather than a request and there was no sense of forgiveness in the statement. Just, that it was done. 'So, you so said there had been casualties. What kind of casualties?'

Kelly felt a lump in her throat as she recalled the images she had seen on the computer screen. They mixed with the rapidly resurfacing memories, tossing her emotions up and under on a sea of reminiscence that was almost too much for her to bear.

'The mortal kind.' she whispered, staring out across the ocean that now bobbed them about so freely. 'People are dead, Shona. Members of the crew; engineers. That doctor. Cunningham. And a girl too.'

'What?'

'I saw them.' Kelly sobbed, 'They showed me these paintings that — '

'Paintings?' Shona asked, looking confused.

Kelly nodded. 'They thought I was involved!'

'Who did? Jon? That woman?'

'Christine, yeah. I suppose they're just trying to do their job, but . . . how could they think . . . how could *she* think . . .'

'Kelly, you're not making any sense.' Shona said, taking her by the shoulders and forcing her to look her in the eyes. 'What's happened?'

'They're not just dead. They've been murdered.'

'What? No. That can't be . . .' Shona struggled, 'Murdered?'

Kelly nodded slowly. 'They thought I was . . . I don't know . . . involved or something.'

'How?'

'It doesn't matter. I'm not.' Kelly said, her azure eyes glistening with moist emotion as Shona continued to stare at her, inquiringly. She sniffed and wiped at her eyes. 'I'm fine.'

'Is that why you're like this, then?' Shona asked, waving her hand frantically before Kelly's battered body, 'That's not fine, Kelly. That's far from fine. That's someone trying to do to you what they did to those other poor souls.'

'But, why?' said Kelly, a strangled sob catching in her throat, 'What have I done?'

Shona shook her head, pulling Kelly into a tight embrace; kissing the top of her head as she rocked her, gently. 'I won't let anything happen to you.'

Kelly smiled through a haze of tears, allowing Shona — after a moment — to hold her face and wipe the tracks from her cheeks.

'I know.' she whispered, 'And I'm sorry.'

Feeling the soft warmth of Shona's hands still cupping her face, Kelly smiled as the curvaceous coryphée leaned in, pressing her full, plum lips against her own.

Relaxing back, she gave herself willingly over to the kiss.

He watched. And seethed.

His heart breaking and skipping all at once as he eyed the pair locked in their lascivious embrace.

His pulse quickened as his shallow, rapid breathing thrust him into a sudden light-headedness. He found his trousers becoming all too tight and highly uncomfortable, making him wish he had brought his camera along to capture this moment and relive it at a later date.

He watched as Shona pulled the woman towards her, whispering in her ear and smiling. The pair of them laughed, slinking off down the steps and out of sight.

'I won't miss twice, lovely.' he whispered to no one but himself, 'I won't miss twice.'

10:15

Sunday 15th May, 2011

Prior and Christine arrived at the *Seraphim Suite* in time to see Adrian Kemp stumble out of the door, fanning himself with a small stack of plastic evidence bags as he blew out a long breath; his face almost purple.

'Kemp,' Prior called, striding towards the male nurse, 'You ok?'

Sweating profusely, the young and wild-looking Adrian Kemp shook his head involuntarily as he struggled to catch his breath. Then, as if only just hearing Prior's question he nodded. 'I'm fine Jon-Boy. I'm fine.' he panted, 'It's just . . . not that nice in there. You know?'

Prior nodded, recalling from conversations with the Neolithic-looking nurse that Kemp had not long buried his father and that the suddenness of his death had hit him hard. He was still trying desperately to come to terms with the *whys* and the *hows*.

Mostly the whys.

Why had it happened? Why had he been taken from him? Why in such a manner?

Prior too knew — from experience — that facing such a reckless and wanton destruction of life in the wake of losing someone close could destroy a man completely. He had known enough officers — good officers — driven from the force after losing a partner or a member of the team. He had seen many men and women torn apart by trying to rationalise the gruelling insanity of the needless loss of life that stalked their profession.

His old profession.

'What are you doing down here?' he asked eventually.

'Dr Matthews told me to come down and collect evidence.' Kemp said, holding up the bags for Prior to see. 'She had me go back over room fifteen-thirty-four too. The girl wasn't there anymore, but it still felt . . .' the words stopped as Kemp's voice trembled.

Prior placed a hand on the younger man's shoulder, unable to keep the small, disapproving noise from the back of his throat as he thought of Dr Matthews ordering the nurse down to the room; sometimes she seemed to have absolutely no grasp of the meaning of the word *sensitive*.

Out of the corner of his eye, he saw Christine flick a subdued, but friendly smile at the male nurse and for a brief moment felt his chest expand at her natural inclination and compulsion to care; to show compassion. She was a true juxtaposition to the severity of Dr Matthews, for whom the caring profession — at times — seemed to be just that; a profession. A job.

Sans care.

'I'm sorry.' Kemp said quietly, 'I'm just not built for this sort of stuff.'

'No one is.' said Christine, 'But, you're doing brilliantly.' Kemp looked unconvinced. 'You're helping us to catch whoever's responsible for these sickening crimes, helping to stop them from hurting anyone else. You.'

He nodded slowly, sniffing.

'So, what have you found?' Prior asked.

'I've not been here long,' Kemp said, shaking his head, 'but, I might have had some luck in the other room.' He pulled yet another bag from his pocket. Black marker pen had been scrawled across the top identifying the date and location of collection.

15.05.2011.

Room 1534.

'I still couldn't find any prints. And I tried, I really tried. But they just weren't there.' he said, handing Prior the bag, 'so I went back over the floor and the bed and found this.'

'A hair.' Prior said, passing it to Christine.

Kemp nodded. 'I know it's not much and it's a long shot at most, but the girl — Stacey Atkins — and her sister, they were both blonde weren't they? This is dark. Short, dark, straight. So I bagged it.'

Christine eyed the single hair through the clear plastic bag, noting an approximate length and thickness before returning it to Prior. 'Well done.' she said feeling — for a moment — as though she were congratulating a child. 'Someone else might have missed it.'

'Someone else did miss it.' Prior said. Kemp straightened a little at the praise, a small, but proud smile flickering across his tired face. 'You're better at this than you give yourself credit for.' He paused a moment, allowing his words the time they needed to be properly digested. Allowing Adrian Kemp another moment to collect his thoughts and ready the mental tools he would need to put himself through the hell of returning to the room behind him. 'Do you want to walk us through what you've found so far?'

'Want to? No. But I will.' said Kemp, his chest swelling as he took in a great lungful of air before pushing open the door.

A strange, sickly scent cascaded from the room, engulfing the trio and beckoning them all at once. Prior gave a small cough and shook his head, 'Lavender?'

Christine nodded, taking in the heavy aroma as she struggled to manoeuvre about the dishevelled room.

It was littered with more sexually explicit paraphernalia than she thought it possible for one person to own. It looked as though the trunk of a specialist travelling salesman had literally ejaculated across the otherwise immaculate — if not more than a little blood-stained — suite.

'Well,' she said, taking in the scene, 'this is definitely not what I expected.'

In the stifling, windowless heat of the mid-ship Security Station, Marc Davies and his new team of researchers struggled through the seemingly endless stack of crew files.

It was slow-going; difficult to know what — if anything — they were looking for. Besides this was the fact that they were essentially investigating their friends and colleagues. Searching for the slightest clue that someone they knew — someone they worked with, drank with, played with, even slept with — *might* be responsible for the devastating string of murders as well as the sabotage to the ship.

How did you even begin to separate those that you thought might be capable of such a thing from those that you decided would be totally unable to commit such horrendous crimes? What did you look for?

Davies wiped his brow and felt the damp tingle of sweat on the back of his hand. The central air conditioning system hadn't been working since the power cut.

Power cut.

Like it was simply a mechanical failure!

He silently rebuked himself as the terrifyingly real images of the engineering crew, so still and lifeless — almost peaceful, yet, disturbing with their open, staring eyes — bombarded his mind once more.

It had been no accident. Of that he was all too certain.

He had managed to prop the doors to the security office open earlier on. Jammed the bastards open! But, it didn't seem to have made much difference. There was simply no air in the tiny room.

He struggled to follow the words as they danced about the page of the latest report. He rubbed his eyes wearily and tried to refocus. It was no good. He leaned back in his chair, stretching out his arms and his spine, triggering an involuntary yawn.

Feeling all eyes suddenly on him, Davies stood up, rubbing his face. 'Why don't we take a ten minute break?' he said, 'I know I could do with some coffee and a blast of fresh air.'

The suggestion was welcomed by all and he watched the group languidly filter out before following them and removing the small wooden wedges he had driven in between the set of sliding doors and their housing. The tinted glass panels slipped back into place, sealing the room.

Pushing out a long breath, Davies reached up above the door, inserted a small key and turned it a quarter to the right. He heard the lock click and looked up out of habit to check that the room was now alarmed. The green light that usually blinked above the door was not even lit.

But then it wouldn't be. With there being no power.

Feeling less-than-energised, the ordinarily bubbly blonde pulled himself up the stairs that led out onto the lower open deck, gulping in the fresh sea air despite the lack of breeze.

He looked over to his right where there was normally a steady stream of people queuing about this time to grab a drink and a hot breakfast panini from the ever-bustling cafe, *Hestia's Kitchen*. But, not today.

Hestia's was closed.

Typical.

Frustrated, Davies turned on his heel, wondering where he would be able to get a drink and a quick bite to eat. There was nowhere else near-by on this level.

Shit.

He had planned to avoid going back inside until the last possible moment, but — he supposed — needs must.

Making his way back across the deck, he spied a lonely figure dressed in white leaning against the railings and staring out to sea. He paused, double-checking that the image his eyes were relaying to his brain was, in fact, correct.

The figure seemed captivated by the blank canvas of the distant horizon, unaware of Davies watching him as he brought a slim roll of white paper to his lips and lit the twisted end with the fierce blue flame of a slim, metal, stormproof lighter.

'Captain?' Davies called, noting how Andrew's back and shoulders tensed up before he finally turned to answer. It seemed he was debating whether or not to ditch the smoke before he addressed his officer.

He chose to hold onto it.

'Marc.' he said, a weak smile on his thin, but handsome face. He looked older today. Much older than the charismatic, thirty-four-year-old, success-story that Marc Davies knew him to be.

The dark rings below his eyes lent a gaunt and almost spectral air to the man. It didn't suit him at all. He looked as though he hadn't slept in days, which — like Davies himself — he probably hadn't.

He hoped he didn't look as bad as Andrews.

The exhausted Captain beckoned him over, inhaling another long drag as he waited. 'Bet you think I'm a right hypocrite, don't you?'

Davies shook his head slowly, breathing in the sweet scent of the curling smoke and silently confirming that it contained more than just tobacco. 'No, sir. I think everybody's trying to deal with this as best they can.'

Andrews laughed, offering the joint up to Davies who, again, shook his head even as his hand twitched and he reached out, accepting the Captain's offer. He stared at it for a moment, watching a slither of smoke drift slowly up before bringing the paper wrap to his lips and inhaling deeply; holding it in his throat a while before releasing a small cloud of his own.

'You seem to be keeping it together ok.'

Davies took another long drag, already feeling the effects of the first. He handed the joint blindly back to Andrews, looking out across the vast blue that was the North Atlantic Ocean. 'It's all just appearance, isn't it?'

Andrews nodded, letting out a great sigh as his eyes filled with tears of genuine sorrow and distress. 'I'm fucked Marc,' he whispered, his voice shaking, 'Forget appearances. I can't take this. I'm a mess. Did you hear the message I broadcast ... to the whole, fucking ship apparently!'

'I heard it, Sir.'

'I had a meeting with Prior this morning. He didn't say anything about my mistake, but I could see him seething behind that perfectly unruffled fucking facade of his. He thinks I'm completely incapable. Doesn't he?'

'What makes you say that?' Davies asked, stalling for time, fighting the obligation to answer truthfully. After all, he knew he was a terrible liar.

'It's in his eyes. In the way he speaks to me. I know he has no respect for me or my position.' he took another long pull on the joint before rubbing his eyes and his temples, 'And maybe he was right.' Andrews shook his head and made a small coughing noise in the back of his throat. 'He gets people, doesn't he? Understands them in an instant. He's a good judge. If I'm honest — and let's face it, I might as well be — he's a bloody good officer. A decent fella, you know?'

'I do, Sir.'

'I managed to round up a small crew of junior technicians. Those lucky few who happened not to be in engineering when ...' Andrews' voice tailed off to be swallowed up by the ocean and the gentle breeze once more. Davies gave a small nod and waited patiently, eyeing his Captain without judgement. 'They've come up with a way to reboot the system and get us back on track. Full power to the engines; communications; satellite; geographic location tracking. The works. They said, so long as the dishes, the antennas — whatever they are — as long as they're still physically intact and undamaged ... we should be back in business in the next twelve hours. Roberts is overseeing it all; the man has a wonderfully technical brain. Much better than me.'

'That's brilliant, Sir.' Davies said, but Andrews didn't seem to share his enthusiasm. He continued staring out to sea, swaying with the bobbing motions of the ship, his lips parted; moving, but wordless. 'Captain?'

'There's no way of by-passing the wall that's been created using Blakely's codes — '

'I thought the chiefs-of-staff each had an override for their department and that the Captain held overall countermand codes and control authority. I thought you could — '

'You thought I could just type in a code and save the day? Don't you think if I could do that I would have done it already?' Andrews said, a slight hint of irritation in his voice.

'Well, I didn't think it'd be like restarting a pc, Sir. But, yeah.'

Andrews snorted a laugh. It wasn't a harsh noise, but something else. An audible recognition of the conflicting emotions that warred on the other side of the thin glass sheet that was his self control; that threatened to shatter at any moment.

'Ah, Marc . . .' Andrews sighed, 'If only that were true. But, no. Most of that shit is pre-programmed and executed remotely. *Golden Star* could sail us like a radio-controlled ship on a boating lake if they wanted. But not with the communications out. No, if we're to stand any chance of regaining control of the system we have to shut down everything.' he said, slowly, 'Everything. No emergency power; no lights; no electric; no heating . . . and no cooling facilities.'

'No cooling?' Davies raised an eyebrow, concerned by his Captain's tone.

'Why do you think *Hestia's* is closed?'

Davies shook his head. 'The power cuts, I suppose.'

Andrews turned his whole body towards the compact blonde, his sharp, brown eyes narrowing as he spoke. 'No. There's enough emergency power going into the place. But, it's not open, because it's not serving food. And it's not serving for a very good reason. The food has been removed.'

'Removed?' Davies said, beginning to tire of Andrews' cryptic sentences. Only professional respect — or something like it — kept him from gripping the man by his collar and shaking him until he began to make some kind of sense.

'It's been redistributed to the other restaurants and diners throughout the ship.'

'Sensible. I suppose.' Davies said. He really didn't know what else *to* say.

'Isn't it though? After all, we wouldn't want any cross-contamination, now. Would we?' Andrews pushed out a bitter laugh that — this time — did not succeed in covering the obvious distress in his gruff voice.

An uncomfortable wave of realisation began to creep over Davies like a cold shadow; like the bony fingertips of an unwelcome visitor tickling the hairs on the back of his neck.

'What do you mean by *cross-contamination*, Sir?'

Andrews shook his head, wiping his nose with the back of his hand. His eyes were suddenly full once more; the salty tears about to breach the dam even as he fought — fiercely and angrily — to keep them back. 'You probably don't know this but, *Hestia's* has the second largest walk-in freezer on the ship. The one in *Grande Central* is only a couple of foot deeper, really.' he sniffed, 'It was the only place big enough to hold them all. The medical bay just isn't equipped for this kind of . . .'

Davies felt his stomach somersault inside him as he glanced over his shoulder towards the closed-down cafe. He shook his head involuntarily, the disbelief plastered clear across his face.

'The crew?' he whispered, almost shaking. 'They're in there? In a walk-in fucking freezer?'

Andrews shot him a disarming look. 'Yes. They are in there.' he said, 'And if I give permission to go ahead with the total shut-down procedure we'll lose all emergency power, including that which is currently keeping the freezers cold. You understand now?'

For several moments Davies found himself unable to form words. Even if he could have spoken in that time, what would he have said?

How did you go about trying to comfort a man bearing such a heavy weight alone? Where should he even try to begin?

'I'll back you, sir.' he said eventually. 'Whatever your decision, you have my support.'

Andrews smiled, nodding, 'Thank you. That really means a lot.'

'Does Prior know?'

'How am I supposed to tell him?' Andrews said, looking suddenly lost. 'He really is a good man. And despite what he may think, I admire him. But, this ... he's going to hate me more than he already does.'

'He's quite an understanding kind of guy when you get to know him.'

'Somehow, I don't think he's ever going to want to get to know me after this.'

Davies drew in a long breath, releasing it slowly as the seconds ticked by. 'So, you've made your decision then.'

'I never really had a choice. Did I?'

'Will you do ... anything ...' Davies didn't really know how best to finish the sentence, so left it open.

'A service I think.' Andrews said, his eyes on the ocean once more, 'Don't you? Commit them to the sea.'

'They might ... They might be ok. I'm no expert, but ...'

Andrews shook his head, silencing Davies. 'The heat out here, even in that room — that freezer — after three or four hours ... it won't be nice. After twelve ...' he pushed out another long breath, 'I don't want to make things worse than they already are. No. I don't see another option.'

Davies agreed; the last thing they needed now was some plague-like epidemic breaking out across the ship. After a moment, he placed his hand on Andrews' shoulder. 'I'll be reporting my findings to Prior in a while. Would you like me to ...'

He didn't finish the sentence. He didn't have to, Andrews was already nodding; the appreciation clear on his emotionally weathered face. 'Yes. Please.' he said, a thankful half-smile flickering across his lips. 'What have you found so far?'

'Nothing really.' Davies began, unconsciously drawing himself to attention as he reported his findings. Or lack thereof. 'Turns out Gary Blakely could be a bit of a nutter, but that hardly helps us and it seems a bit tight bringing it up as the man's now dead, but . . .'

'What do you mean by *nutter?*'

'That he could be a bit of a psycho, sir. I found evidence of repeated reprimands and disciplinaries from the Captain and the Security Chief of the ship he'd worked on a few years back.'

'How come I didn't know about this?'

'I don't think anyone did, sir. The hard-copy file was amongst a load that had been archived. My guess is he just slipped through the net.'

Andrews turned to face Davies, 'But I know Prior wouldn't let something like that slip past him. He's so ... thorough.'

'That he is,' Davies said, smiling, 'But he's also human. I think maybe Blakely got a recommendation off somebody that — I don't know — put him at the top of the pile for candidates. And the man *was* good at his job. That much is bloody clear.'

Andrews laughed. It was short, but it was the first time Davies had seen any real light in the man's eyes since they had begun talking. 'Yes, too bloody good.' he sighed, 'Anything else?'

Davies shook his head, 'Surname wise, I'm up to the J's now. I think. And I've got a small team helping me out, who — shit!' he said, checking his watch, 'They'll be waiting to get back in the office now! I'd better — ' he took a step back from the bleary-eyed Andrews, who caught hold of his arm for a moment.

'Get back to them.' he said.

Davies nodded, but Andrews held on to him still. 'Thanks Marc.' he said, eventually, 'Keep me informed.'

Releasing Davies, he turned on his heel and made his way up the nearby steps.

Davies smiled, feeling rightly pleased with himself at being able to help ease the man's conscience a little.

He began retracing his steps, returning to the security office the way he had come.

But so much had changed now.

In the last few minutes the whole world seemed to have been completely shaken up and back down again.

And he still hadn't had any bloody coffee!

10:40

Sunday 15th May, 2011

They had established that the suite had been booked in the name of a Mrs Fiona Jenkins and there were more than a few pieces of evidence within the room that identified this latest female body as being the woman herself.

Christine had felt conflictingly both more and less shocked when finally viewing the scene that the killer had created for them this time.

But then, if you removed the creeping odour of the early stages of decomposition, the battered corpse of the short, unknown man with the obliterated face and the fact that Fiona Jenkins *had* been murdered and was now, in fact, little more than a cooling cadaver, the room actually had quite a peaceful air about it.

The suite appeared to be of a similar lay-out to Christine's, making it easier for her to navigate and to try and build up a chronological picture of events. She knew, for example, that the room situated opposite the massive king-sized bed was the bathroom.

Her own featured a large, corner, hydro-spa bath and had been the reason for her choosing that particular type of suite, despite the price. She knew how much she would appreciate the warm water-therapy on her aching knee joint of an evening.

Not that that particular feature was working at the moment.

At the foot of the immense bed stood a deep-fill, russet-coloured travelling chest, the old-fashioned kind that you would have expected to find in an expensive suite on board the Lusitania or the Titanic, not a city-sized ocean-liner of the twenty-first century. It was a glaring anachronism in the ultra-chic modernism that engulfed the rest of the room.

Christine shuddered as it suddenly dawned on her that neither of the two ships with which she had drawn a visual comparison in her mind's eye had survived to enjoy the honour of an official decommissioning.

The first had been torpedoed by a German U-Boat, with devastating effect. The latter — rather more famously — had not even completed its maiden voyage; the drastically damned and fated fictional romance of Jack and Rose that ended in short, sharp whistle blows and the ironic words 'I'll never let go', suddenly assaulting the cinematic screen inside her mind. The warbled whir of Celine Dion's most recognisable verse infested her brain before she could prevent it nesting.

Great. I'll have that stuck in my head all day now.

The room had been immaculately well-kept before the top two shelves of a speciality sex shop had apparently rained down upon it. The luxurious — if not a little blood-stained — white satin sheets had been straightened, the quilt meticulously folded back to the foot of the large bed and the pillows neatly plumped. It almost felt like a particularly diligent member of housekeeping had called round in the early hours, but had somehow failed to notice the anathema of the two corpses degrading inside the suite.

The travelling chest had been furnished with a line of purple tea-lights, all of which had long since burned away their small wicks. Christine suspected them to be responsible for the heavy lace-scent of lavender that hung in the air above the unmistakeable slow stink of decay.

Beyond this, elbows resting on the chest and kneeling upright as if in prayer, was the carefully moulded corpse of Fiona Jenkins.

Dressed in a thigh-length nightgown of fine silver silk, she appeared almost animate in the strange, other-worldly ambience of the room.

There were various marks running up her arms and over her shoulders; bruising, bite-marks, slices, blood-spots. Winding around her throat and neck was a ligature pattern that appeared — visually — to match those found on both Stacey Atkins and Gary Blakely. Christine suspected that there would be a whole host of other injuries beneath that nightgown for Dr Matthews to explore once they finally moved Mrs Jenkins up to medical.

It was going to be no easy feat moving her discreetly in the daylight, especially now that the whole ship was buzzing with rumour, intrigue and conspiracy theories. But then, moving her at night would pose its own problems; the darkness being one major issue, the fact that she would then have been dead for a further ten hours being another.

And that wouldn't do at all.

No, moving her at night was not an option.

Struggling, and with an awkward and almost clumsy progression of movements, Christine lowered herself to her knees before the rigid cadaver.

Fiona Jenkins' eyes were closed, while her mouth fell open to form a soundless scream. Her long, white hair spilled over her shoulders, straight as a pin; a healthy shine and lustre still present in the colourless fibres. Had it been brushed after death?

Christine inspected the lengthy locks, reaching out with a gloved hand, feeling the weight of it as she took a closer look. She might even go so far as to suggest that the hair had been *washed* and brushed, then left to dry post mortem.

She raised an eyebrow, releasing the hair as she pondered.

She found herself thinking about how — for hundreds of years — religious images bearing saints and persons of Christian canon importance had been painted, drawn and carved by artists. The saints were ritually depicted kneeling with their hands clasped in prayer and bound by the beads of the rosary. In the same manner and style of such religious works, their artistically twisted assassin had created yet another icon; binding the hands of the late Mrs Jenkins.

Only, hers were not rosary, but florescent pink anal beads.

Christine didn't quite know what to make of it all. Clearly there was a certain amount of mockery in the scene; an ironic undertone that was completely wasted on her and Prior and their small team, if not also on the cooling and inanimate Fiona Jenkins.

But what disturbed her most was the amount of care and almost tender attention that had been paid to this poor, deceased sculpture of a woman, while across the room — no more than ten feet away — an unknown male had had his brains smashed in; his face battered to a bloody pulp.

And yet, he too bore the same ligature marks around his neck.

Christine shook her head; what did it all mean? She pressed one palm down onto the bed and the other on the ornate cane that she feared so much might break. As she tried to gain the leverage she needed to winch herself up onto her feet once more she was suddenly aware of Prior standing beside her. Feeling his strong hand take hold of her arm, supporting her, she stiffened.

She was still angry with him, even as he helped her to her feet.

Especially because he was helping her.

'Look, are you going to stay mad at me all day?' he whispered close to her ear. She stared at him. 'I've apologised once already, Christine. And I meant it.'

He had apologised and they had moved on, but that didn't mean she had to stop being mad at him. Still, the handsome, green-eyed Security Chief did seem to have a way of getting under her skin and really there *were* more pressing matters at hand.

She knew what the problem was. It was simple. She had allowed herself to trust someone for the first time in a long time. She had allowed herself to become close to this man and then ...

She knew she was making far more of this than she really should, but still. After everything, beginning to trust Prior even a little, opening up in the slightest . . . it was all a major step forward for her. It *was* a big deal. So much so that it made the smallest of disagreements or confrontations feel like betrayal.

A huge betrayal!

She knew it was ridiculous to react the way she had; to feel the way she now felt. She could reason it logically; she was — after all — more than accustomed to the intricate and irrational workings of the human mind.

But that didn't stop her from feeling rejected, undervalued and betrayed.

Forcing herself to smile up at Prior she stretched out her leg, rubbing the knee joint that was cold and metal and alien to her body. 'You did apologise.'

'So?' he said, 'Are we ok? I want us to be ok.'

'We're ok.' she replied weakly, watching him watching her. 'I only have guesses so far. What I can see. But, the state of rigidity suggests she that was killed within the last twenty-four hours, at the most thirty-six, but I'd say much less than that. Her body shows signs of both blunt and sharp-force trauma; there's a chain pattern of bruising around the neck and throat, indicating that she was strangled with a similar — if not the same — instrument that was used on the others. Though her tongue is not protruding, so I doubt she died of asphyxiation. Whereas he,' she said, nodding towards the second body, 'his tongue — or at least what's left of it — is. His eyes also show evidence of petechial haemorrhages, and — while I realise that could be a result of the battering he received post mortem — taken with the chain marks that appear around his neck and his protruding tongue, I'd say cause of death was ligature strangulation. With a splash of gleeful over-kill afterwards. What did you find?'

He gave a nod even as the brief flick of a smile played on his lips. 'You're good at this.'

'Oh, aye. It's a wonderful talent to have!' she said, ironically. 'My favourite party trick.'

He chuckled and it was only in that moment that she realised just how greatly important it was to him to have received her forgiveness.

Though she knew it wasn't *her* forgiveness in particular that he sought and in his own way — though completely without his realising — he was simply using her to ease his battered conscience. To patch up his damaged sense of self-worth.

But she understood.

'Right, well the fella over there is one Merko Solich. Croatian. Mid-to-late twenties. Kemp discovered a photo album in the bottom of one of the cases. I tell you, this Mrs Jenkins didn't believe in travelling light!' he paused a moment and Christine couldn't help but smile as Prior scratched his now lightly-stubbled chin, 'Anyway, he's in loads of pictures with her. Though I can't really say whether he was her toy-boy or if she was his fag-hag. It's all a bit ... confusing.'

This time Christine laughed out loud causing Adrian Kemp and the other two security officers currently sweeping the room for evidence to pause in their quest to look up at the psychologist.

'Well, with all the gear strewn around here I think it's safe to say that Mrs Jenkins was not only clearly sexually active, but also more than a little open. I'd even go so far as to say extrovert when it came down to the physical, so I don't think we can rule *anything* out on that front.'

Prior nodded, a look of bewildered terror plastered across his face as he scanned the room once more. 'I'd have to agree.'

Christine stifled a second giggle.

'What?' he asked.

She shook her head, smiling softly. 'You do make it hard to stay mad at you.'

'Good.' he said, grinning with a renewed enthusiasm as he led Christine around the side of the bed and held up a small black-light torch, 'Now, it's plain to see that there's blood on the sheets, which — by the way — are not standard sheets for this type of suite. In fact, I doubt there's a room on this ship that has silk bed-linen as standard! These obviously belong — or rather belonged — to Mrs Jenkins herself.'

'The lady certainly liked her home comforts. And had a high standard of living, by the looks of things.'

Prior nodded, 'But, look here,' he said, clicking the switch of the torch so that the odd-coloured light beamed brightly across the bed; highlighting luminous pools that spanned the sheets and pillows 'there's traces of other bodily fluids here.'

'Well, I'd have been surprised to find there weren't!'

Prior gave her a mock-withering look and continued, 'I was thinking we might finally have some DNA evidence. And, if it matches that of the hair that Kemp found in room fifteen-thirty-four, we might have a good chance of positively identifying the killer and tying them to these two murders at least. Makes it easier to build a multiple-homicide case, you know. Evidence.'

'Yes, sir.' Christine said with a sarcastic grin as she pulled a small salute.

'And,' Prior continued, striding across the room and stepping carefully over the late Merko Solich, 'look at this.' He point his gloved finger at a nice, thick pile of crisp twenty and fifty pound notes neatly stacked on top of a set of drawers. 'Now, there's a few grand sat there. In plain sight. And he didn't take it. Why didn't he take it?'

'It could be a statement. I mean, look at what he's done with Mrs Jenkins. Religious overtone isn't in it. And, if we take that in conjunction with the painting of Stacey, that's two separate scenes flooded with obvious religious connotations.'

'That's true. But, does that necessarily mean that this has anything to do with religion? Or is it more to do with the fact that these are simply powerful, recognisable images. Images that conjure different emotions and meanings for each individual person that encounters them?'

'The way art evokes different emotions in each admirer, you mean? Allowing them to draw their own conclusions whilst still making a bold and powerful statement?' Christine said, thinking.

Prior nodded.

'You're right.' she continued, 'This might have nothing whatsoever to do with religion. It might be that some aspect of some organised religion played a major part in our killer's childhood. But, then again, it may have absolutely nothing at all to do with the religion or religious aspect itself. It may or may not be specifically related to Christianity, despite the image being heavily Christianised.'

'Either way, that still doesn't account for why he left the money.'

'Perhaps money's just not important to him.'

'You think he might be well-off? Like Michael Copina well-off. Or at least somebody being paid by the man?'

'Michael Copina?' Christine shook her head, 'We have nothing to connect Copina to this, or even to Stacey's murder if we're honest. But let's say — hypothetically — that Michael Copina was involved in and perhaps even behind Stacey's murder, why would he want Fiona Jenkins out of the picture? Do we have any evidence to suggest that they even know each other? Or rather, knew each other.'

Prior smiled.

It was a wide, boyish grin that flashed a perfect set of pristine, white teeth.

'Well,' he said, 'I'm glad you asked that.'

Making his way back to Christine, he picked up the photograph album that Kemp had discovered and opened it in reverse; handing it to her.

There in the back, tucked into the transparent sleeve that wrapped itself around the album was a single, oddly sized picture.

The photograph appeared to show a large, multi-racial family celebrating Christmas. It looked as though it had been taken a few years previous.

Glancing at the picture, Christine spotted Fiona easily. She was stood to the left of a tall man with olive skin and grey hair, her own long, white hair was plaited to the side and sat over the shoulder of a royal blue gown like a thick length of rope. She looked entirely respectable in a subdued and repressed kind of way. Merko Solich was nowhere to be seen.

She scanned the picture further, but didn't recognise anyone else.

Then, all of a sudden she realised that the picture wasn't central. The family in the miniature portrait were all shunted to one side.

Pulling the photograph free from the album and feeling with her fingers, Christine discovered that the right-hand edge had been folded back behind the picture.

Drawing the previously hidden flap forwards, she looked up at Prior quizzically.

The family were now central in the picture and had been joined by a young couple. A pale-skinned, youthful girl with dark hair and light-blue eyes leaned into the suited chest of a tall, tanned and handsome figure who wrapped his arm around her, flashing a dazzling smile at the camera.

'Turn it over.' Prior said eagerly.

She did.

On the back, scribbled in a corresponding order to the image on the front were the forenames of every person on the photo, including the disgraced young couple; Stacey and Michael.

Christine sucked in a breath in open surprise as she turned the picture over once more to study the face she now knew to be Stacey's.

'No.' she whispered, still unable to believe that the youthful, innocent-looking girl in the picture was the young woman she had seen so recently; firstly strung up in room fifteen-thirty-four, and then laid out on a cold, steel gurney. Her hair had changed, yes. And she was certainly older, but it was definitely her. 'This is . . . it's just so . . . how did you find this?'

'I'm just good.' said Prior, 'This is what I used to do for a living. Remember?'

'Yes, but . . .'

'It's a link, Christine. It's a lead, something tangible that we can follow up on.'

'But, it doesn't make any sense.' Christine said, handing the photograph back to him. 'If this is revenge or a family feud or even some extreme reaction to getting cold feet . . . it still doesn't account for Blakely, the engineering crew or Dr Cunningham.'

'But it does.' he smiled, 'You said yourself that they seemed to be the unfortunate victims of circumstance. And Blakely was blatantly tortured and killed for the information he had. Information that would disconnect us from the outside world.'

She shook her head slowly. 'I don't know.'

'Chris — '

Before Prior could launch into the debate he had been mentally preparing for the past twenty minutes, the animated face of Adrian Kemp suddenly appeared on the opposite side of the bed.

He had apparently been couched between the bed and the wall for some time, searching around and underneath the king-sized sleeper.

And he seemed to have just hit the jackpot.

'Jon-Boy,' he shouted. Christine noticed the flicker of a cringe on Prior's face as they both turned their attention to the excitable male nurse. 'I think I've found something.'

Prior scooted around the eerie cadaver that had once been Fiona Jenkins and knelt down next to Kemp. Reaching under the bed with his left arm he seemed to be at full stretch even as his right hand dived into his trouser-leg pocket, tearing out a clear plastic bag.

'Ha ha!' he laughed triumphantly as his gloved fingers teased the object forward and into the bag. 'Good work.' He clapped Kemp on the shoulder and climbed to his feet, crossing swiftly back to Christine.

'Still don't think it's possible?' he said, holding up the evidence bag.

Taking it from him, Christine examined the contents without removing the object.

It was a pocket-knife.

About four inches in length when extended, the blood-stained blade was clearly sharp enough to have been responsible for the many cuts that now adorned Fiona Jenkins' arms and body. It had an elaborately carved and decorated handle that was embedded with what looked to be enamel and semi-precious stones.

Stones that formed one, undeniable letter in the centre of the handle.

'M'.

Chapter Six

Kelly rested her head on her arm, which in turn was pressed against the white plastic tile-effect panel, steadying her as she finally began to relax, enjoying the rivulets of warm water that streamed over her hair and face.

She had turned the temperature of shower right up; she had felt so cold. She had been shaking. With anger. With horror, revulsion and fear. With the fever that Shona had told her she had suffered the previous night.

She had flushed red hot at first.

It had felt as though her skin would blister under the internal heat that had suddenly sprung into combustion. Then, as quickly as it had come upon her it had washed away, leaving her desperately cold and dithering.

It seemed to have taken an age to warm all the way through; for the heat to penetrate that icy core. She must have been stood in the shower for forty minutes now.

Opening her eyes, Kelly blinked through the pressured droplets that continued to spill onto her face. The room was wall to wall steam. It looked as though an unruly smoke machine had made its way into the bathroom and flooded the place for dramatic effect.

As if she didn't feel disturbed and nervous enough already!

Turning the handle on the shower, Kelly stopped the water and reached for the white, fluffy towel that hung on the chrome rack besides the bath, the gold-threaded letters *GS* garishly intertwined near the hemmed edge.

She stepped out of the bath cautiously, still aching; still battered, bruised, cut and all too aware of every single, painful injury. The healing scar on her leg looked red-raw and seemed to throb visibly as she took a moment to catch her breath, perching her naked backside on the edge of the bath as she had done earlier.

When Shona had helped her to dress.

She rubbed her hair with the towel, her scar still pulsing as her head too began to bang.

I need some air.

She stood gingerly, feeling a little light-headed from the heat and the steam.

Suddenly something caught her eye.

There in the mist.

Near the sink.

Something — no, someone — was watching her.

She didn't want to look, but neither could she look away. She could see it. See him. Moving in her periphery. He was staring right at her, watching her. Laughing at her. His cold eyes staring through the fog; callous blue eyes.

He pounced.

A noise that Kelly couldn't even have imagined trying to make — something that sounded completely non-human — escaped her throat as she leaped out of his way.

Losing her balance, she slipped back into the tub; her head crashing to meet the enamel corner with a brutal force.

She couldn't move.

She blinked. And blinked again. But still could not move.

She blinked. She saw only light.

Then. Darkness.

11:30

Sunday 15th May, 2011

In the overly-harsh white light of the medical bay backroom, Dr Matthews stared at the yawning great linen trolley that now held a prominent position amongst the disarray of metal gurneys and tables.

Parked next to this was the body of a short, tanned man whose face was noticeably absent. The faceless man and the contents of the linen trolley were the latest additions to ever-increasing roll-call of victims taken by the *Cruise-Ship Killer*. As he had now been dubbed.

Matthews tutted in annoyance at the absurdly obvious epithet even as she contemplated the others currently doing the rounds.

There were more than a few passengers and members of the crew placing their money — so to speak — on there being a murderous dynamic duo in their midst. Amongst the most popular of the colloquial titles for the pair was the unimaginative *Gruesome Twosome*, the slightly higher-browed *Ianus Asphyxiators* and of course, *Jekyll and Heidi*.

She had to admit she rather like the last one.

Pulling back the long, white linen sheet that had been draped over the trolley, Dr Matthews made a conscious effort not to breathe in. Still, it did not stop the waft of urine, faeces and general organic decay from assaulting her olfactory senses. She wrinkled her nose.

Matthews didn't mind admitting that she had no idea where to begin with this one. The woman in question was knelt in a prayer position, elbows raised, clutching a set of bright pink, oval-shaped anal beads.

What the hell would they bring in next!

'Right, I need her up on that table.' she barked, thrusting a pair of latex gloves into the hands of the two security officers that had rolled the trolley through the doors only minutes earlier. They stared at one another, a silent scream of horror and revulsion passing between them. 'It's ok, she's in the rigid stage; that means she shouldn't turn to jelly in your hands anytime soon ... although,' Matthews said, taking hold of the woman's jaw and manipulating it gently, 'some of the muscles *are* beginning to look a little flaccid. So you might want to hurry.'

A brief smile flashed, like a shadow, across Matthews' stern face as she watched the pair attempting to lift this latest cadaver. They struggled and heaved, trying desperately to avoid coming into contact with the late Mrs Jenkins as best they could.

It certainly wasn't an easy task, but was oddly amusing to watch as Dr Matthews began setting up for the latest post-mortem.

While she was under no illusion that she would probably suffer some sort of psychological break-down when this ordeal was finally all behind her and — though she loathed to admit it — she had discovered to her astonishment that Marc Davies had, in fact, been correct in his earlier assumption. At least to a certain degree.

She *was*, no matter which way she looked at it, becoming more accustomed to death. To dealing with the dead.

To stripping down those pieces of meat that had once been human beings.

To cataloguing all the fine and tiny details that aided in revealing the mechanism, manner and cause of death.

Oddly enough, the thing that got to Matthews the most about the whole dissecting and recording routine was the *preferred method* of establishing a core temperature. It was one aspect that she hoped she would never become any more accustomed too or accepting of.

The idea of inserting a thermometer four or five inches into the rectum of the deceased just didn't sit well with her. It simply wasn't right!

She hadn't been able to bring herself to use that particular method on any of the bodies to pass through her somewhat trembling hands thus far. And she certainly wasn't about to start now.

Not with this one!

Her own feelings aside, it would look positively indecent!

As she was lining up her equipment Matthews realised that she wouldn't be able to open the woman up properly until she returned to a flaccid state, anyway. And that could be anything up to another twenty-four hours.

Changing tactics, she picked up a slim, silver digital voice-recorder and began reporting her first visual observations. 'Fiona Jenkins.' she said, examining a brown file that contained little of any other useful information besides the woman's name. 'Caucasian female. Early to mid fifties.' She paused the recording so as to better hiss at the still-struggling security officers without receiving an earful of feedback later, 'You'll have to lay her on her left!'

Taking up a scalpel, Dr Matthews sliced a neat incision above the liver and thrust a lengthy thermometer into the cooling organ.

She pressed record once more.

'Hair; white. Eyes,' pausing once more, she peeled back the left lid, 'Blue. No clouding, suggesting victim died within the last twenty-four as suspected. The cadaver is currently in a state of rigor and is set in a kneeling position; arms raised in a prayer-like posture; elbows out and away from the body. Hands are clenching a chain of pink ...' she swallowed and sighed before turning suddenly on the two, wide-eyed security officers, barking at them once more. 'You can go now, you know.'

They did not need a second invitation. Nor did they hang about to wait and see if the temperamental doctor would change her mind.

Matthews set the recorder down on the metal table, rubbing her brow and the bridge of her nose. This was too bizarre. It wasn't anything like the voyage she had thought she would be experiencing.

It was mostly minor injuries on a ship like this. Six to eight major incidents per year.

Per year!

In the last three, in fact, the most flexing emergency she had had to deal with had been an older gentleman of a somewhat larger build who had suddenly collapsed in the gym. Poor guy had suffered a heart attack on the rowing machine.

Apparently he had just kicked a forty-a-day smoking habit and a lifetime of fried breakfasts. He had even given up cream cakes and *real* butter.

And that's what you get for trying to make a sudden healthy change to your big, fat, unhealthy lifestyle! A big, fat heart attack.

But, at least he had tried.

And at least *he* had survived!

Matthews leaned on her elbow and pushed of a long sigh, her eyes coming level with the hands of the late Mrs Jenkins.

She cocked her head noticing for the first time a rather sickening anomaly. The woman's right index finger was bent sideways. From above the knuckle.

Matthews picked up the silver box and began recording once more. 'Right hand; middle phalange of the index finger appears to have been dislocated. Lack of contusion or any pooling of blood suggests injury occurred post mortem.' She pressed paused. 'You weren't holding these when you died, were you? And he . . . struggled . . . to mould you. Didn't he?'

The thermometer jutting out of Mrs Jenkins' liver bleeped quietly, as though it too was slightly afraid of Matthews; afraid to break her concentration.

She pulled it out and looked at the reading.

79.2.

That meant that the body had cooled around nineteen point four degrees, which in turn indicated that she had been dead for around thirteen hours only.

Thirteen hours. Yet the body was already showing signs of returning to a flaccid state. The general rule of 12:12:12 — being 12 hours to achieve maximum rigor; 12 hours remaining in that state; and 12 hours to for the muscles to relax, thus completing the cycle of rigor mortis — didn't seem to apply here.

But why?

Snatching up a pair of scissors, Dr Matthews quickly cut open Mrs Jenkins' nightdress, making a rag of the once-expensive silk garment without apology. She toured the body swiftly; uncertain of what she was looking for in particular. Apprehensive of what she might find.

'Body shows signs of lividity under the arms, just behind the elbow,' she said, noting the deep-purple pools beneath the skin, 'and the same on the shins and the tops of the feet. This is consistent with the way the victim was found, though I do not believe she died in this position. There is some superficial bruising on the upper arms and legs. These bruises are small and round and are consistently spaced finger marks. This evidence, taken with the patterns of livor mortis and the rapid rate of rigor suggest that she would have had to have been moved and repositioned almost immediately after death.' she paused the recording once more, 'But, why the sudden rigor? What caused it?' she asked of no one but herself.

Moving around the corpse, she noted the many shallow nicks and slices; the small, patterned bruises that looked as though the victim had been beaten with something studded. 'Were you a party to this? Did you agree to it?'

Doctor Matthews pressed record once more and continued reciting her observations, noting the size and pattern of the speckled contusions and suggesting a studded paddle or something similar as the culprit. She recorded the lengths and depths of the superficial lacerations that littered Mrs Jenkins body; all similar in depth; all caused by the same instrument.

All but one.

The one anomaly to the lacerations ran lengthways along the forearm from the wrist. This cut was deep and jagged; the skin torn rather than sliced.

Matthews determined that the majority of lacerations had been carved with a small blade; most likely the pocket-knife that had been brought in along with the laundry trolley and the additional male body.

She had forgotten about him — the faceless man — for a moment, but glanced up now to check on the unenthusiastic senior nurse who was currently taking his core temperature and preparing him to be opened.

At least he was in a fairly flat position. Only his arms were raised; his fists clenched near his throat. Though *his* body had not been 'positioned' in the same way that Mrs Jenkins' had. Rather, he looked to be the victim of a cadaveric spasm.

Cadaveric spasm!

The recollection of the term jolted Dr Matthews, propelling her suddenly back into her student days; in particular to the study of death and dissection. She had done her best to bury these lessons in the back of her mind as they had made her feel queasy at the time and really quite anxious about the point of it all.

Life.

But now was not the time for a theological, philosophical or even existential meltdown.

She had already known the course of her professional life; the direction and route that *she* had wanted to take.

And pathology was absolutely not her north.

Neither was it her south, east or west.

In fact, it had no bearing on her compass what so ever!

But now, in the bright white glow of the medical bay, she was thankful that she had tucked away the knowledge she had gained in those horrid classes and not discarded the memories completely.

She moved her hands over Mrs Jenkins' body, feeling along the taut muscle that was the Gluteus Maximus; the largest muscle in the human body. It was solid, the sinews tight with rigor; like a solid sculpture layered with cold clay to give only the impression of flesh.

Striding back to the far end the examination table, she reached out once more to test the pliability of the facial muscles; taking hold of her lower jaw and manipulating it with ease.

She picked up the recorder and mused for a moment. 'Rigor may have set in so rapidly due to a lack of adenosine triphosphate in the muscles; particularly the larger muscle groups. This would most likely occur as a result of some excessive muscular activity prior to death. With so little ATP left, rigor would have set in very quickly indeed in the smaller muscle-groups and could also have taken anything from only a few short minutes to several hours to take hold of the larger muscles. All changes will be monitored and recorded, but — at this time — theory appears to be consistent with the current state of the muscular rigidity present in the cadaver.'

Dr Matthews clicked the tiny digital recorder triumphantly, ending her report for the time being. She wouldn't be able to access the data hidden within the deceased woman's organs until she had returned to a manageable state.

'I suppose I better see to your mate then, Mrs Jenkins.' she said, pushing out a laboured breath as the fleeting sense of achievement left her once more.

It was going to be another long day.

The room was cold and damp.

You could feel the damp crawling over your skin, taste the dank, fetid air as it forced its way between your lips. As it clawed and tunnelled up through your nostrils.

It really is a horrid place and I wonder, suddenly, why am I here? How had I ever come to be in this depressing, rot-infested hole?

I run.

Abruptly and without warning. I'm running, running, running. Faster and faster, but I'm not getting anywhere. And the walls are tumbling now.

And the weeds are clawing at my feet, scratching my skin. Catching my ankles.

It hurts. I bleed.

I'm crying out. I'm screaming and howling as the tears carve a route through the sodden dirt that clings to my face.

And now I am the earth. I had no choice in the matter. But, I am — none-the-less — the teaming, streaming, retching, screaming Earth.

Covered and choked and torn apart. Born and reborn. And dying all the time.

I am just an eye.

An eye with a basic knowledge of this world; looking up from beneath the strangling weeds to a carrion sky and a sun that burns bright with maggots. Writhing. Writhing in the endless chasm that we are taught to believe is a grand and ever-creating universe.

But, all I see is a tomb.

And faces. So many faces.

Ravaged by the decay of time and the grotesquely gnarled claw that moves at my command.

That moves because it is mine.

11:30

Sunday 15th May, 2011

Prior had quickly figured a way of adapting his stride and the speed of his steps to accommodate Christine's slower, but no-less determined pace. Better yet, he had seemingly managed to accomplish the alteration without offending the warm and attractive psychologist.

At least so far.

Leaving the *Seraphim Suite*, Prior had managed to steer them past one of the smaller lounges that were currently serving breakfast rolls and strong coffee en masse. Only upon seeing the sheer number of people waiting to be served, did he break from Christine, his stride lengthening once more.

He pardoned his way to the front of the queue and picked up two *All-Day's* on white, before moving to the end of the counter to order a coffee and a tea, deciding that he would have whichever Christine didn't want.

The sausage, bacon and eggs that seemed to be flowing in abundance — most likely due to the perishable nature of the food now that there were only two large working refrigeration units on the ship — were being cooked camper-style on portable gas stoves attached to small butane cylinders.

'There you are.' Christine said, a little out of breath.

'I thought you might be hungry.' he replied with a smile, handing his food card over to the fair-haired young lady skilfully manning the till. 'I know I am. And talk about thirsty!'

'Men.' she said, rolling her eyes. 'Always thinking with your stomach.'

He had to laugh. 'An army marches on its stomach. Isn't that what they say?'

'I'd hardly say we constitute an army. You and I.'

Prior conceded with a grin and pulled a floury white bap out of the white paper bag in his hand. He opened the lid to reveal butter and yolk melting across the well-cooked strips of salty bacon and sliced Cumberland sausage. Grabbing the plastic bottle of brown sauce from the counter, he zigzagged it across the mega meal of a bun, a satisfied *mmmm* escaping his lips as his did.

Refitting the bun lid, he turned back to the fair-haired till operative to receive his food card along with two white cardboard cups; one containing hot black coffee and the other, hot black tea, the teabag floating on the murky surface of the water.

'Which do you want?'

The look on Christine's face was a picture. Though precisely what emotion the picture was supposed to represent, he couldn't quite be sure.

'What?' he asked, 'Oh, don't tell me you're ketchup girl? Is that what this is? 'Cause, I can tell you now, it's never going to work if you are. It's the only kind of red I can't stand.'

Christine was very quiet.

'That was a footy reference, by the way. Not anything sick, like ...' he struggled, 'obviously I don't like blood and guts and gore and — '

'I get it.' she said, raising her hand and halting him mid-sentence. 'But, I think for sure that I'll be giving the breakfast barm a miss, if you don't mind. That cup of tea would hit the spot though.'

'Tea it is then,' he said, placing the drink on the counter before Christine.

He watched her add a dribble of milk and one sugar to the throwaway cup, before stirring the teabag around and squeezing it out, then discarding it into the plastic bowl set aside for the specific purpose of teabag disposal.

Similarly, he attended to his coffee and grabbed two lids, handing one to Christine. Then, breakfast barms in one hand and his coffee in the other, Prior led the way through the bustling lounge and they continued on their way towards the security office.

He struggled to resist the call of the deliciously hot and tasty baps that he now laboured to carry without squashing.

Stacked with care in their separate paper bags, the salted and savoury scents taunted him like Sirens as he cautiously navigated his way through a small sea of people.

Finally, seeing the doors to the office wedged open, Prior called out to Davies and took a seat in the reception area just beyond.

Christine followed Prior and seated herself opposite just as Marc Davies' cheerful face appeared between the glass doors. He grinned from ear to ear as he watched Prior set the bags down on the small glass-top table, already guessing their contents.

The Security Chief shook out his arm, wincing as a dribble of hot grease and brown sauce seeped through the paper, burning him. He caught the oozing bubble, mopping it with the tip of his finger and popping into his mouth.

'Awh, Guv', Davies said, approaching them, 'Is that for me?'

Prior's eyes flicked to Christine, checking that she had not changed her mind and was still dead-set on not consuming the mouth-watering bag-full of grease and carbs. She gave a small, almost indiscernible nod, which Davies didn't notice, being too mesmerised by the lure of the breakfast bin-lids.

Prior nodded and indicated for Davies to sit down and join them.

'Cheers, sir.' he said, his hand diving into the bag as he sat. A stream of yolk began to leak from the bap and Davies twisted his arm around, his tongue striking out; preventing the escape. 'You're a star. I haven't eaten yet. I'm starving!'

The young officer tucked into the breaded feast hungrily as Prior watched him, smiling. He followed suit with a slightly less-ravenous air than his colleague, speaking in between mouthfuls.

Christine sipped at her tea.

'So, what've you found then?' Prior asked. 'Anything useful?'

Davies motioned with his head; his mouth still full. It was neither a confirming nod indicating that he *had* found something, nor an out-and-out dismissing, negative shake suggesting that he had not.

'I found some stuff on Blakely,' he said swallowing the mouthful, 'Stuff that had been hidden away. Archived.'

'What kind of stuff?' Prior asked.

'Well, there were records of incidents. Violence. And threatening behaviour. I think the fella must have had issues, you know? Anger management and things like that. There's a psych report in the folder, it's a few years old now, but it might go some way to explaining why the file had been archived in the first place.' Davies paused and took another bite, chewing the mouthfuls of food and savouring the tastes, 'I mean the guy was clearly bright as a button and meticulous too. But, from what I've read, he had real trouble trusting people. Didn't like to get too close to anyone, didn't like talking about how he felt or why according to the report. And when he was pushed, he'd just react violently.'

'Hmm,' Prior said, digesting the information along with his late breakfast, 'He didn't seem ... But then, I suppose he did keep himself to himself. Though I never noticed a violent streak in him.'

'Then again, I don't suppose you ever provoked him. Did you?' Christine asked.

Prior shook his head.

'Interestingly though,' Davies said, 'There is mention of some sort of incident involving Blakely and another man several years ago. It was before he came to work on this ship and whatever it was, he's somehow managed to have it all but expunged from the record. Most of the document's just black marker now.'

'What?'

Davies nodded. And tore off another mouthful.

'So who else was involved? And what did they do?'

'Well, that's just it, Guv'. We don't know. He's not named.'

Prior deflated in a huff of frustration.

'But,' Davies continued, chomping on another medley of sausage, egg, bacon and soft floury bread 'I took a look at the date on the report, which was 18th November 2006 — the date of the incident itself had been removed. I went back a couple of months and ...' he paused, leaning in, drawing Prior and Christine in as he did so, 'I don't know if you know or not, or whether you'll remember, but, the end of August beginning of September 2006 a girl went missing off the *Stratum*, one of *Golden Star's* Med-bound Ocean-liners. I remember 'cause a mate of mine was the Chief LX. The ship was held up at Livorno for days — there was an inquiry and everything that continued well after — but, there was no sign of the girl. And no sign of her body. And by the end of the week the passengers were starting to become a bit ... restless. Hard to control.'

'That's nice and understanding of them.' Christine said.

Davies nodded.

'That's human nature.' Prior said, swallowing the last of his breakfast and taking a long drink of his coffee, 'Everyone's understanding and helpful until events begin impeding on *their* time. Then everything suddenly becomes a hassle. And nothing you do is good enough.'

Silently they all agreed.

'She did eventually turn up though, this girl. A month and a half or so later. She'd been stuffed in a metal barrel at the back of a little tavern near the port.'

'Oh my god.' Christine whispered. 'And you think Blakely had something to do with the murder?'

Davies shrugged. 'I can't point a finger at him for sure with the central online system being down, but I might have found something that connects him to it.'

'Go on.' Prior said, patiently.

'While I was working my way alphabetically through that mess in there, I came across something in Mike Jones' file. It's some sort of corroboratory report concerning a statement he gave back in September 2006. Now, I know for a fact the Mike Jones was working on the *Stratum* at that time, and this report — though it doesn't mention his full name — says that Mike backed up and confirmed 'GB's' version of events. 'GB'.'

'Gary Blakely.' Prior said, nodding.

'Who is this Mike Jones?' asked Christine, 'And, if you don't mind me asking, how do you know he was working onboard the *Stratum* at that time?'

Marc Davies blushed.

Instantly and completely; from below his collarbone — visible above the low, v-cut neckline of his figure-hugging, black t-shirt — it crept over his muscular neck and right the way up to the rows of bleached follicles that guarded his high forehead.

He looked away and laughed. Though, it was brief snort of laughter, devoid of any humour.

'Marc?'

Prior continued to wait patiently, his eyes flicking to Christine for a moment. She had finished her tea and was watching Davies keenly.

'Because, I'd had some holidays owed in the July and my friend — '

'The LX?' Prior asked.

Davies nodded, 'Yeah, Abbey. She convinced me to go on the med cruise.'

'Bit of a busman's holiday, isn't it?'

'Well, to be honest, I would have just been sat at home, anyway. I didn't really have the money to do much else, but, with working for *Golden Star* for a while, I'd built up my discount so it only cost me about two-hundred quid in the end.'

To the right of Prior, Christine made a small, surprised noise. It wasn't quite a choked cough, but an expulsion of air that conveyed her honest astonishment, revealing that she had forked out a hell of a lot more than two-hundred pounds for this trip.

'I, er ... I saw Mike rehearsing for one of the shows and I ... well, I thought he was quite hot. So I left Abbey in the lighting box and I went down to speak to him. There was no one else around at first and he seemed quite pleased with the attention. He was giving me all the right signs and everything ... so I asked him if wanted to go for a drink.' Davies paused, his eyes clouding over for a moment as though he were so lost in the memory that he might never find his way back. Eventually, he pushed out a great, long sigh, seeming to shake himself back to the here and now. 'Anyway,' he continued, 'He turned out to be a bit of a dick after that.'

Davies looked at Christine and apologised before continuing. She smiled at him and for a moment Prior felt that same, odd sense of paternal pride for the young security officer.

It almost made him laugh out loud. But, he controlled himself.

And continued to listen.

'Yep, I'm afraid Mike Jones is one of those most fabled and mythical creatures that you hear tell about, but rarely ever see.'

'Oh. And what's that?' Christine asked.

This time when Davies laughed a bright smile broke across his face as he raised an eyebrow and said in his best *David Attenborough*, 'The little-known and Lesser-Spotted Straight Male Dancer.'

Prior's gruff laugh came in sweet counterpoint to Christine's surprised chuckle. He watched her relax for a moment; dropping her guard and even revealing the chip in her tooth as she grinned. He was pleased to see her making no attempt to hide the beautiful imperfection.

In the time he had spent alone with Christine there had been only a couple of times that she had dropped her defensive shield in such a way; allowing him to step in close.

And she had been keeping him at an almost painful distance since he had managed to disappoint her with his misjudgements of Miss Livingstone and the foolish, unthinking comment he had made about this not being 'her job' earlier that morning.

Now she was laughing and smiling again. Seemingly without a care.

With both him *and* Davies.

Marc Davies; the lad could charm the sparrows from the trees; charm the defences from the battlements and bring the walls crashing down.

Again, that feeling of paternal pride swelled his chest. It took the form of an almost audible voice somewhere deep down inside of Prior. 'Good lad.' it seemed to whisper.

'So,' Prior said, shaking off his sentimental other self and returning to business. 'Would you say Mike was violent?'

'I don't know.' Davies said, 'He's got a temper and, like I said, he's a bit of a . . . well, he's not the nicest of guys. I've hardly spoken to him since he's been on the ship. I think he's avoiding me.' Davies grinned impishly, drawing yet another smile from Christine.

'Which one is Mike?'

'You'd know him, Guv'. He's the Numero Uno, Prima Ballerina; the one that kicks-off when he doesn't get a nice, big, juicy role in whatever they're doing. He doesn't seem to have been too bad, lately. Only 'cause he got the lead, like.'

Prior nodded, searching his mind, trying to picture the dancer. 'Was he the one Shona was seeing for a while?'

Davies shrugged, 'Could have been. Like I said, I haven't really spoke to Mike since the incident on the *Stratum*.'

'And Shona?' he asked, an urgent tone creeping into his normally steady voice.

'She hasn't really said anything to me about him, but ...'

'No,' Prior said, distracted, 'but, she did to me.'

He stood and, noticing Christine beginning to follow suit, resisted the urge — this time — to rush to her aid. Davies too was on his feet.

'I want you to go back through Mike's file. And Blakely's too if you need to.'

'What am I looking for, sir?' asked Davies, nodding.

'Any oddities. Connections. Like the one you've already made.' Prior said, moving around the table. 'I need to speak to Shona.'

'Shall I come with you? Or am I better off here?' Christine asked.

'No offence, Dr Kane,' said Davies, lowering his voice as he spoke, 'But, it's already crowded in there. And more than a little bit ripe. I don't think anyone should have to put themselves through that if they've another choice, really.'

She smiled and glanced at Prior, 'Looks like I'm with you then.'

Davies began clearing the waste from their breakfasts into the nearby bin. He returned to the table and picked up the half-full, still-warm coffee that Prior had been drinking. 'Do you want the rest of this, Guv'?' he asked spritely.

Prior spotted the glimmer of hope in the younger officer's eyes and laughed. 'Go on, you can finish it.'

'Cheers, sir.' he said cheerfully, making his way back towards the claustrophobic office.

'Keep in touch.' Prior called as he and Christine began to move through the desolate reception area.

'Oh, Guv'!' Davies shouted just as they had just rounded the corner. Prior popped his head and shoulders back into view. 'I need to speak to you ... in a bit. It's kind of important.'

'Okay.' Prior said dubiously, 'Do you want to tell me now?'

Davies shook his head. 'No.' he said quickly, 'No, sir. In a bit. When you've spoken to Shona.'

Prior nodded and watched Davies return to the office before following the path Christine had cut across the open room.

'What was that about?' she asked.

'I don't know.' he said, honestly.

He didn't like not knowing.

12:04

Sunday 15th May, 2011

Kelly had managed to knock herself clean out for a good fifteen minutes.

She had been lying in the long, slim bathtub at an odd angle when she had finally come to and discovered the pillow shoved awkwardly under her neck and a blanket thrown over her damp body.

Shona told her that she had considered moving her, but didn't know whether that would do more harm than good and so she had simply tried to keep her warm and comfortable instead.

Kelly had thanked her, though her head pounded furiously and the crick in her neck that had developed over the fifteen minutes was ridiculously painful.

Still, a couple of ibuprofen later and an intensely sensual neck and shoulder massage — which quickly developed into a full-body massage — at the tender and experienced hands of the deliciously surreptitious Shona made it seem almost worthwhile in the end!

Shona had kneaded and gently pounded the knots from Kelly's aching muscles, working small circles with her thumbs up and down the length of Kelly's taut calves and thighs.

Kelly remembered nothing from before the fall and had apologised in soft moans as Shona had continued with the circles up and across her lower back, skilfully avoiding the bruises that already covered most of Kelly's lumbar region.

'I'm not normally this ... clumsy.'

'I like you this way.' Shona said, kneeling before Kelly as her head bobbed over the foot of the bed. 'Don't ever change.'

Kelly laughed, 'You hardly know me.'

Shona cocked her head at the statement, smiling, 'And still, you're in my bed for the second time in so many hours.'

'Technically, I'm on your bed.'

'Technically, you're wearing a lot less then you were the first time.'

Kelly nodded, conceding the point.

Earlier she had worn only the over-sized t-shirt that had once belonged to an ex-boyfriend of the olive-skinned, aphrodisiac woman who — she was so glad — had now decided to play on her team.

A cold chill ran suddenly over Kelly's naked body as an important question perforated her thoughts; *What if she's still trying to choose a team?*

That would put the pressure on.

Not that she was worried at all.

But there was no way she was going to allow this wonderfully seductive and seriously sexy woman to slip through the net! No, she was as resolute as though she had been charged by Sappho herself!

A wide smile drew across Kelly's lips as a flurry of images rolled out across the plains of her mind. All were at odds with the traditional aphorism 'Lie back and think of England' and yet there was something strangely seductive, if not preposterously imperial in the idea of the ancient Sappho calling her to arms to do her duty.

For Sappho, and Lesbians everywhere!

She laughed and Shona looked at her quizzically, making Kelly realise that she had been lost in thoughts of conquest and liberation for several moments.

Propping herself up on her elbows, Kelly leaned forward, contemplating her next move. A Chess Master studying the board. 'Technically,' she said, 'You're right, but — '

'Fuck technically.' Shona interrupted, taking Kelly's face in her hands and kissing her fiercely. Eventually she broke off and held her gaze for a moment before continuing,'I know what I want. And I think I've gotten to know you pretty well in the last few days, Kelly Livingstone. So, whatever else may come, I welcome it with open arms. But you really are fit as! Cuts and bruises and all. And I think we've done enough talking for now, don't you?'

Well, if there had have been a ball, which had at that moment been in Shona's court, the dexterous dancer would — in Kelly's mind — have just slam-dunked her way into the finals.

Before she could react or think or try and even muster some kind of witty reply, Shona had flipped Kelly onto her back and was now perched on top of the injured artist, staring down into her ocean-blue eyes.

With her luscious and lengthy legs comfortably straddling Kelly's naked frame, the dancer eased back to sit, resting her slight weight against Kelly's pubic bone.

Kelly sucked in an excited breath, feeling suddenly dizzy and overwhelmed.

Smooth, mocha calves grazed against her own lightly-tanned and freckled thighs, sending shivers up and down her spine, causing her heart to race and the fine hairs on her arms to prick up instantly; goose bumps all over her body.

Oh, Shona was no mere supporter.

No bystander or cheerleader.

Though that particular image — the vividly alluring idea of it, pompoms and all! — made Kelly's heart skip quite suddenly and she gasped a little, drawing a smile of quiet confidence and delight from Shona.

She was clearly an active and practised player, this woman. Well accustomed to and more than comfortable with a female form that was not her own. Her wandering hands had already revealed that much!

Shona's tongue flicked out, the tip of it touching the bow of her upper lip as she brushed an unruly lock of ink-black hair back from Kelly's face, tucking it behind her ear. Kelly pulled up to engage those sensual, teasing lips, catching Shona by the chin and locking target. Kissing her hungrily only to be pressed back down onto the bed.

Her own hands now worked their way up Shona's firm thighs, squeezing and massaging and drawing soft, but gratifying sighs from the dancer even as their tongues continued to explore and devour one another.

Shona clearly enjoyed the idea of being in control and caught hold of Kelly's wrists, pinning them up behind her head so that when she eventually broke off the kiss, Kelly found herself completely immobilised. At Shona's mercy.

She smiled.

'I didn't expect you to be so ... dominating.'

'Really?' Shona said, her eyebrow arching as she tightened her grip with her left hand, leaving her right free to roam.

No, not really! Kelly thought as Shona's fingers began tracing circles — yet more delightful circles and swirls — across her chest.

'I think most people would say I'm ... driven. If not a little bossy.'

This didn't surprise Kelly at all.

You didn't get to be the lead in anything in this life on pure talent alone. You had to push. But she played along, enjoying the soft press of Shona's bare flesh against her own.

'No. You?' she said playfully, wanting more of that flesh.

Realising that Kelly was winding her like a clockwork mouse, and longing to be the cat once more, Shona pounced.

Laughing, she slapped her hand across Kelly's bare ribs in mocking admonition before falling on her once more, kissing her with a renewed fervour as her free hand began moving steadily south. With purpose.

Kelly's back arched in delight.

Sappho would be proud.

12:29

Sunday 15ᵗʰ May, 2011

Coming face to face with yet another set of stairs, Christine rested her hand on the railing and paused for a moment. Bending slightly at the waist she took in a long, deep breath and exhaled.

The pain in her knee was so much worse today than it had been in a long while. It was physically exhausting.

She pushed out another slow breath through pursed lips before sucking in another lungful of air, feeling a little light-headed now, but better for it.

'Are you alright?' Prior asked.

She could tell that he had been keen to ask her that same question for some time now. But he had pressed his lips tight shut each time and she had noticed just how much the muscles around his jaw — not to mention those in his neck and shoulders — contracted when this happened.

She smiled and this time did not dismiss him or brush him off with her standard answer of *I'm fine*. Always a lie.

'I'm just a little sore this morning.' she said.

'Is there anything I can do?'

She looked at him properly for the first time since their discussion in the canteen that morning. She had been too blinded by anger, too defensive earlier to notice how tired he was looking. It wasn't a rough and rugged tiredness that dominated his superbly carved countenance, though it was clear he had cut shaving out of his routine this morning.

No, it was something else. Something like sorrow. And battened-down despair.

Her heart felt suddenly heavy looking at him. To see such sadness bottled up in such a seemingly strong, but fragile oak of a man like him was really quite devastating.

'Do you mind if we stop for a moment?' she said.

Prior gave a small nod. His splendid green eyes were now red around the edges and shimmering as much with fatigue as with the effort it took to restrain the medley of emotions that he was trying to hide from her and all the world.

'Can I get you anything?' he asked, offering his arm to Christine as she lowered herself to sit on the top step.

She shook her head, tucking her hand into the pocket of her chocolate, linen kick-flair trousers. 'I'll take one of these and I'll be fine in a few minutes.'

She popped a mustard coloured tablet from the blister-pack strip that Dr Matthews had given her the day before and swallowed it without a fuss; managing to hide her revulsion through mere anticipation of the taste.

Prior shuddered.

'I don't know how you can do that.' he said, 'I have to have at least half a pint of water whenever I take a tablet.'

'Really?'

'Oh, yeah. I'm terrible.' he said, settling down next to her. 'I blame my mum. She made swallow a paracetemol once, when I was little. I had some apple juice and tried to use it to wash the tablet down, but ... d'you know when it gets stuck on the back of your tongue. Eugh!'

He shuddered a second time. This one more forceful than the last, rippling through his body from his toes up.

Christine smiled, 'There's nothing worse is there?'

'I now can't stand apple juice either!'

'Oh, she really tortured you. Didn't she?'

'Traumatic is what it was! Though *Barnardo's* didn't seem to think so.'

The pair of them laughed a little and smiled and it felt to Christine like they were beginning to regain some of the ground that had shattered beneath them earlier.

She cleared her throat as the laughter subsided.

A small group of passengers — young women and men in their mid twenties — approached and passed them, pulling into an efficient single file on the stairs as they did. Prior turned his head, watching them amble along the corridor that he and Christine had just come down.

Christine watched him.

'You're a good man, Jonathan Prior. A very good man.' she said her eyes becoming ever so slightly glassy, 'And I shouldn't have bitten your head off earlier. You *were* just doing your job.'

'And so were you.' he said, 'I didn't mean to upset you. It was thoughtless ... careless of me. I probably shouldn't have mentioned Kelly either, but — '

'No, you were right.' she said, pulling a loose thread from her long-sleeved, lime, cotton shirt and balling it between her finger and thumb, 'Those paintings were disturbingly accurate and heavily stylised. It did look like Kelly's work.'

Prior said nothing and Christine was thankful for his silence. His patience.

'I know that only by questioning her could you eliminate her as a suspect, but,' she paused, drawing in a great breath as if trying to gather some strength from the stale air that filled the wide, but muggy corridor, 'I think I was a little blinded by my emotions.'

He gave a slow, single nod, but remained silent. Not unlike a confessional priest.

'But, I'm not trying to replace Janet.' she said, smiling, 'I'm not trying to save Kelly, because I couldn't save my sister. That's not what this is about.'

'So, what is it about?' he asked.

'I'm sure it will come as no great surprise to hear that I have apparently developed some ... unresolved feelings towards Kelly. It seems like everyone else realised before I did, really. And, I have to admit, it's come as quite a surprise.'

'I might have picked up on something between you ... But, actually ... no. I don't think I noticed at all.' Prior said, smiling.

Christine returned the smile. 'No? Well, Dr Matthews made some scathing remark when I asked about Kelly last night. You know, when she'd had her moved.' Prior nodded. And waited. 'Oh, I don't know. I don't really know *what* it is that I feel anymore. But I do know that I can't stop thinking about her. Is that stupid? It's stupid, isn't it?'

'No. Not at all.' Prior said, 'That's how I ... that's how it was with Rachel. I couldn't get her out of my mind. Whether I was on duty, in the gym or lapping the pool, she was never far from any other thought. Still isn't.' He coughed and shifted his weight, 'But no, it's not stupid.'

'It is a little silly when the object of your affections doesn't reciprocate your feelings.'

'And you think she doesn't?'

'Well, I thought she might have. But perhaps I read it all wrong. You know, seeing signs that weren't really there, like Marc said.'

'Miss Livingstone does seem to have a certain charm about her. The type of person who could make you believe she's interested ... even if she wasn't.'

Christine found herself nodding emphatically. She felt slightly ridiculous, but couldn't stop bobbing her head. 'Exactly.'

'But, then again, you know ... you met with her for breakfast and dinner — '

'We never got to dinner. That was when I found her in her room.' she said, rubbing her knee absently, 'That's probably why I'm such a wreck today. Dragging her halfway across this bloody ship!' The full-weight of her subtle accent compressed into the last three syllables as she laughed to herself.

'She's owes a lot to you, Christine.'

'She doesn't even know it was me. Thinks the first I knew about it was when we saw her this morning. She was so wrapped in that other girl. Shona. I mean, how do I try and compete with her? There's no way.'

'Don't be so hard on yourself,' Prior said, turning towards her and taking her hand in his, 'And don't be comparing yourself to people like Shona. There's a world of difference between the two of you.'

'Aye, that's the problem.' she smiled.

'You know what I mean.'

A moment of silence followed. But it was a comfortable and thought-collecting silence during which Christine eventually became aware of Prior watching her; searching her.

Meeting his gaze, she nodded.

'Shall we make a move, then?' he asked.

'Why not.' she said, allowing him to help her up. 'So, have you given anymore thought to your hunch? Any ideas?'

Prior raised an eyebrow at her as they began descending the stairs. 'Yes and no. That name, Copina, it struck a chord that I couldn't quite place. But it was the murders themselves that finally jogged my memory.' he paused, allowing Christine to steady herself at the foot of the stairs before they continued. 'I worked with the National Crime Squad for a bit. Back when you actually got involved. Before they merged it with all those other organisations and moulded and mangled it into some sort of public-owned, target-driven agency that's flooded with managers and accountants and more paper work than . . .' he paused and looked at Christine, who smiled sweetly back.

'I understand.' she said.

'I don't mean to rant.'

'Everyone's allowed to rant sometimes. I mean, I've just sat and winged to you about the confusingly strong feelings I have for another woman. So, I'd say we're good.'

Prior chuckled heartily and threw a cheeky glance at her as he continued. 'Well, during my time with the NCS I was involved in an on-going investigation which finally came to a head back in ninety-nine. It wasn't pretty. That's when I got my scar.' he said, drifting for an instant, before snapping back to the here and now.

'I'm sorry.'

'No, don't worry' he said, throwing his guard back up again, 'part of the job isn't it.'

Christine didn't believe that at all and had the feeling that Prior didn't believe it either, but remained quiet for the moment, making a mental note to revisit the issue with him at a later date.

'There were several gangs involved and it was big. Drugs, human trafficking, money laundering, smuggling. You name it, they were doing it.' He stopped Christine in her tracks, 'One of the guys involved was a Copina. Now, I can't say for sure that it was Michael Copina, but it might have been a relative or something. I mean it's not like it's the most common of names. Especially not 'round Merseyside.'

Christine nodded. 'It could just be coincidence.'

'You're right.' Prior said, much to her surprise. 'It could. But, this fella — this Copina — he was the go-between for some local mobsters of the time. There was one gang in particular, a real family affair, fancied themselves as the new Krays. He worked for them a lot.'

'And *was* he a local lad?'

Prior shook his head. 'No. I don't quite know where he was from originally. He had a bit of an odd accent. There were enough incidentals in his pattern of speech to indicate that he'd spent a good few years in and around Liverpool. But, he was definitely an outsider. I think, in the end, he was starting to feel that way too. The last time I saw him alive he was really freaking out. He said the family knew he'd been picked up by us on a few occasions and that that had put him on *The Scalpel's* watch list.'

Christine had picked up the pace ever so slightly now that the pain was slowly subsiding. She was also beginning to feel more at ease with the ornate cane that Janet had pre-emptively bought for her.

Almost as though she had known that Christine would one day need it.

Though, that — she thought, swallowing hard — was nonsense of course. It was simply coincidence. Janet had bought it for Christine because it was a thing of beauty, because it had been so carefully crafted and was totally unique.

They had been antique bargain-hunting in Camden. Just for fun.

Christine smiled as the fond memories of the day — the sights and the scents — spilled across the canvas of her mind, blurring her vision.

They had each had a budget of a hundred and fifty pounds to spend on any 'treasure' they wished to buy for the other.

Christine had found a dusty old, gramophone in desperate need of some TLC.

It had had the original lily horn still attached; sky-blue with a polished brass edge and a medley of hand-painted pink and white cabbage roses splashed across the inside of the beautiful, open mouth.

It didn't work when she had bought it, but Janet had always loved to tinker and had soon restored it to its former glory.

It was now sat in Christine's garage in Harrogate, collecting dust once more.

And she was here, hobbling around this damned cruise-liner, aided by the stick that Janet had deemed beautiful enough to spend almost a hundred and twenty pounds on.

Christine smiled sadly, thinking how strange it was the way things had a way of working themselves out.

'Sorry,' she said, reeling back from the powerful memories along with the sudden and uncomfortable thoughts of an ever-expanding destiny beyond all human control, 'What is this scalpel?'

'Not *what*.' Prior replied, '*Who*. A guy named Vincent Keating. He earned himself the nickname for his handiness and almost surgical precision with a knife. Or any tool really.'

'So he tortured people?'

'Yeah. He worked with the Simmons' — '

Prior's two-way radio bleeped loudly, cutting him off mid-sentence. He stopped and Christine watched as he unclipped the handset from his belt.

It bleeped again.

He held down the call button and spoke with renewed authority into the receiver, 'Is someone trying to reach me?'

The reply was garbled and crackled with static. They could only just identify the caller's voice as belonging to Marc Davies from the brief snippets they managed to catch, along with a distinct '-vies' during the mangled transmission.

'Marc?' said Prior, 'The signal's really bad down here. I don't know if you can hear me any clearer than I can hear you.'

Again, the reply was more static than words, but they listened.

'I . . . searching . . . file . . . Mike . . . Guv' you need — '

Bleep. Silence.

'Repeat the last.' said Prior

Static. Bleep. Silence.

'Davies.' he said, as a bead of sweat trailed his forehead. He hadn't even noticed the creeping heat down here in the bowels of the ship until the moment he was wiping his now sopping face, 'Repeat.'

'Jones . . . for . . . Blakely's cous — '

Bleep.

They waited.

'Copina.' said Davies anxiously. Then more static. Bleep.

Silence.

He was gone.

Prior turned swiftly on his heel as Christine struggled to follow his lead. 'What was that about?' she said.

'I don't know. But it didn't sound good.'

They were on the move once more and, though it was certainly with more urgency this time, it seemed that Prior was still accounting for Christine's difficulties, holding back a little even now.

She was grateful and yet she couldn't help but feel that she was more of a hindrance than a help at that moment. She tucked her head down and threw all her energy into picking up the pace.

'I think the sooner we speak to Shona, the sooner we can find Mike Jones and get to the bottom of this.'

'Why? What's so important? What does she know?' Christine asked, breathlessly.

'Shona and Mike were together for a while. They had an awkward split and Shona wouldn't talk to me about it. She wouldn't say anything about him after that. Good or bad.'

Why would she talk to you about her relationship with another man?

Christine was taunted by the thought, but didn't dare voice it for fear of the answer. She was beginning feel like a bit of a third wheel when it came down to this Shona girl.

A third wheel left in the garage.

The unused spare on this ship that liked to share.

She supposed that that made Shona the bike and found herself smiling as she allowed the idea to saturate her brain. She did, after all, get the impression that when it came to matters concerning Shona everyone seemed to have enjoyed a ride!

12:35
Sunday 15th May, 2011

Shona's naked body was a true wonder to behold and Kelly found herself drinking in her beauty inch by inch as they lay entwined atop the now-somewhat dishevelled bed.

Her eyes followed every contour of her new lover's body; from the beautifully balletic stretch of her arching foot, over her calves and all of her curves to the delicately soft and sweetly curled mounds that were her perfect breasts.

It seemed that Shona had been blessed in every conceivable way.

There was not a blemish on her skin, nor any kind of mark to suggest anything other than complete perfection. She was a smooth-skinned nymph, shaped and cast by the ancient Gods. She was desire and pleasure and action without words.

Without the need for words.

She was Eros; hand-crafted and confident in a glorious feminine form.

Kelly ran her fingers through the soft mane of Shona's thick and silken hair, noticing — though not for the first time — how every inch of this woman seemed to appeal to her senses and her appetite. Almost as though she had been designed and created for a specific purpose; to lure and to please.

Kelly was in no doubt that Shona took as much pleasure in her actions as she granted to her lovers and noted with a grin that she herself had drawn no complaints — though, plenty of moans — from the mocha beauty during time together that morning.

She pulled Shona towards her, kissing her with a renewed hunger; wanting her all over again. To taste her. To feel her.

To be inside her once again.

As if brought to life by Kelly's touch, Shona sprung into action once more, clawing impatiently at her freckled shoulders and guiding her hands.

Within moments Kelly felt Shona's body sigh against her as they fell into a natural rhythm of desire and reward. She felt Shona's lips form a smile as they pressed against her own. Felt the dancer's slender hands creeping over her hip and down to her thigh.

Kelly winced and pulled back; breaking from the chain of kisses that poured from Shona's sweet lips. Her leg was throbbing suddenly as she twisted in her arms.

'What's wrong?' the dancer asked, breathless with delight.

Kelly shook her head, unable to organise her thoughts for a moment. She had felt a bolt of white hot pain tearing through her muscle.

She had felt it earlier as well, but had been too otherwise engaged to care.

Shona shifted her weight, a strange look of fear and confusion casting a twisted shadow over her perfect face. Kelly continued to watch her until it became clear that her eyes were now locked onto the source her bewilderment and, following the line of her lover's gaze, she saw for herself.

'Shit.' she said, seeing Shona's hand covered in blood. 'What's happened? Are you ok?'

'Kelly, it's *your* blood.'

'What?'

She twisted her body, sitting to gain a better view.

Shona was right.

The blood that now coated the dancer's hand had also managed to soak through a small patch of the quilt on which they lay.

And its source; Kelly's injured thigh.

With the stitches cleanly burst, the wound had proceeded to spill an unnerving amount of blood into the recently grey and white, rose-patterned cover.

Kelly gasped.

It wasn't that she hadn't believed Shona. But, had she not seen the wound — gaping and pumping the way it was — with her own eyes, she doubted she would even have realised that anything was wrong at all.

At least until she passed-out from severe loss of blood.

'Shit!' said Shona, leaping suddenly from the bed and grabbing the towel Kelly had used to dry herself earlier. 'Put this on it. Press it tight.'

She thrust the towel into Kelly's hand.

'No, it'll wreck it.' Kelly said, obeying Shona none-the-less.

'Don't worry about the bloody towel!' she cried as she stumbled into the bathroom, running the hot water and washing her hands before returning to the living-slash-bedroom space. She stepped back into the tasty denim shorts that she had discarded earlier while pulling on a previously floored white vest-top in an impressive and almost singular motion.

You've done this before. thought Kelly.

'Why didn't you say something?'

'I didn't notice!' Kelly said, honestly.

Shona had plucked Kelly's shirt from the handle of the bathroom door and was now holding it open. Gingerly, she slipped one arm, then the other into the dark sleeves, noticing the rounded movement under Shona's dangerously thin vest-top.

Kelly struggled to tear her gaze from Shona's perfect breasts as they scuffed against the material; her dark nipples becoming suddenly very stiff and all the more appealing. She shook her head, trying to focus.

'How can you not notice yourself bleeding to death?'

'I was distracted.' Kelly said, pulling Shona to sit on the bed before her. The dancer was now holding a dark pair of jeans that Kelly recognised as her own. 'I want you — no — I need you to calm down. I'll be fine. We'll go back up to the bastard medical place and tell them I've burst my stitches. They'll have a good laugh and sort me out. But, I'm going to need your help, so you need to calm down.'

Shona nodded, appearing not unlike a fawn in a wood. All doe-eyed with concern.

Kelly touched Shona's face and drew her into a soft kiss that seemed to melt on her lips. She smiled and released her. 'Though, I don't think I'll get those on without a struggle.' she said, 'Have you got a loose pair of shorts or something?'

'I see, borrowing my clothes already are you?' Shona said, something of her cocky, old self returning, or at least trying to mask the quiver in her voice, 'My, you do move quickly!'

'What's the point in hanging around, eh?'

Kelly became suddenly aware of a light-headed dizziness and a slight blurring of her vision as she struggled to button her shirt. A moment later, Shona handed her a pair of torn-off grey shorts that had once been joggers.

'They're my warm-up pants.' she said, almost apologising.

'They're perfect.' Kelly said, pulling on the shorts. Then, her left arm around Shona, her right hand still compressing the towel against her thigh, Kelly struggled to her feet.

At that moment there was a knock at the door.

No, there was a pounding on the door. The kind of impatient thumping that demands an immediate answer.

Kelly looked to Shona, who answered her unspoken question with a small shrug and called out, 'Who is it?'

Another round of blows rained down upon the wooden door and, for a moment, Kelly thought the thing might simply cave under the pressure. But it held.

'Stay here.' Shona said, releasing Kelly.

Fuck that! Kelly thought, hobbling forward behind her.

Shona reached out, throwing the safety chain on before unlocking the silver mechanism and turning the handle. 'What the fuck?' she said, opening the door just a crack. 'What the hell do you want?'

Leaving his small, newly acquired team behind in the security office, Marc Davies tore through the corridor dodging passengers and crew as best he could whilst travelling at an almost dizzying speed.

Unable to confirm whether Prior had managed to receive and decode his garbled transmission, Davies had been unable to sit still any longer. This was too important.

He knew where Prior and Christine were heading. Knew Shona's quarters well.

If they had had as much trouble in understanding him over the radio as he had them, he doubted that they had clinched the true gravity of the situation.

He bounded down the stairs three at a time.

Not far now. Just two more levels.

He stopped. Doubled over, panting.

He sucked in a lungful of humid air and pushed on.

Kelly crept forward even as she watched Shona recoil from the door, which at that very moment burst open; the links of the chain seeming to bend then split like a series of paperclips under the brute force that shouldered its way into the room.

Standing in front of the doorway — blocking their escape — was a man of similar height and age to Shona. He had light brown hair that looked as though it had been styled at some point that morning, but had since been blasted by the wind and sea air to create something quiffed and lifted and manic. This only served to add to his crazed demeanour as he stood before them, huffing and puffing like a bull in the *Plaza de Toros de Las Ventas*.

His eyes burned with hatred and desire as he stared at Shona. Then Kelly. Before settling on Shona once more.

In his left hand — which had been momentarily obscured from her view — Kelly could now see the bejewelled handle of a knife or dagger; its exposed blade about three inches in length.

Her head already spinning from the blood she had lost, she struggled to steady herself and stifled a yelp as she finally managed to wrap the towel around her thigh and tie a small knot. It hurt like a bitch, but she didn't want to draw any further, unnecessary attention to herself.

Under different circumstances, Kelly would have laughed out loud, realising that she was now reacting as the kids in *Jurassic Park* had done in the hugely memorable T-Rex sequence. She could almost hear the voice of Sam Neil — the fictitious Dr Grant — telling her not to move; *He can't see you if you don't move.*

'Mike?' Shona struggled; the sound of clear and absolute terror ringing through the singular syllable. 'What are you doing here?'

Mike.

Sextus Tarquinius.

From the show Kelly had struggled to sit through on the first night of their voyage. It all seemed so long ago now. So far away.

Mike closed the door without turning his back on them, flicking it shut with a single shove of his powerful arm. 'That wasn't a very warm welcome.' he said, his voice like sandpaper.

Shona shook her head. Struggling to muster a reply.

'You knew it was me, right?' he continued. His speech slow and weighted.

He was in no hurry.

'I . . . I didn't realise at first — '

'But, when you did,' he said, cutting her off as he idled the knife around with small rotations of his wrist, 'you didn't seem that pleased to see me. Maybe, it's because you were already busy . . . entertaining.' He sneered at Kelly, though his eyes never left Shona, 'but, that's no excuse for the way you spoke to me just now. Or for what you did to me. For what you do to me, you prick-teasing, little whore!'

Mike took a step towards Shona, who backed off a pace as Kelly struggled to make her way across the room, shouting as she went.

'Oi! Who the hell do you think you are?'

Mike turned to her; a strange, amused look draped across his reddened face.

'Kelly, don't.' Shona begged.

But she continued to move towards him.

'Who the hell am I?' Mike said, cocking his head, 'Who the hell are you! I'll tell you. Nothing more than Little Miss Latest Thing in a very long line of conquests to that bed. That's who you are! Another notch on the bedpost for that slag, there. Nothing special.'

'Shut your stupid fuckin' mouth!' she said, knowing it wasn't the strongest of replies and feeling slightly like a child in a playground.

But still, she had managed to distract him long enough to place herself between him and Shona. She either really liked this woman or the adrenaline had simply kicked in and was now working overtime!

'Well, aren't you the knight in shining armour.' He laughed cruelly, brandishing the knife before him. 'You don't look too well to me.' he said, his eyes moving over Kelly's body then to the bloodstained bed and back again, 'You look like you need a doctor.'

'She does, Mike.' Shona cried.

Kelly felt her take a step towards the pair of them, felt an intense heat at her back. Instantly she threw out her arms; making more of an obstacle of herself. Intent on keeping Mike as far away from Shona as she possibly could.

'You!' he spat, 'You shut the fuck up! You fuckin', little whore!'

'Hey, dick-face!' again, Kelly knew it wasn't the greatest of comebacks, but it caught his attention, 'I told you to watch your stupid fuckin' mouth. Now, tell me what the problem is.'

It seemed to have worked.

For the moment at least.

Mike look intrigued and smiled as he stepped closer to Kelly who instinctively pushed Shona back, holding her at arm's length.

'You want to know what the problem is?' he asked, his sickly sweet, vodka-laced breath warm on her face.

She refused to turn away, despite wanting to wretch.

Instead she nodded, slowly.

'Why not, eh? You don't look like you'll be conscious for too much longer, anyway. Sure, let's kill some . . . time. Tell us a story, Jackanory!' He grinned an awful, evil, twisted grin and Kelly could have sworn she felt Shona shudder.

'Go on then!' she said, trying to disguise her sudden breathlessness.

'The problem lies in Shona. And girls like Shona. The ones who know they're pretty and flaunt it and tease guys like me. They go on and on, making us believe they're gonna let us see the treasure; hit the jackpot. They get us all riled up and then . . . they say 'stop'.' He eyed Kelly for a long moment, 'Do you know how difficult it is for a guy like me to simply stop?'

Have a bit of bloody self control! she thought.

'So, Shona turned you down? Is that it?'

'No!' Mike shouted, 'She didn't fuckin' turn me down. We were together.' Kelly resisted the urge to eye Shona and question her silently as Mike continued ranting. She was finding it difficult enough just to remain standing, never mind trying to turn her head without falling on her arse. 'We were together and I really thought you might be the one, Shona.' He flushed suddenly redder still as his eyes flooded with tears of rage, his words slurring as he spoke, 'But, no! You had to go and ... humiliate me! And then all this lesbian nonsense! I mean, come on. Really?'

This time Kelly couldn't keep from laughing.

Despite the pain and the blood-loss and the dire nature of the situation, she laughed. She laughed out loud.

'What the fuck are you laughing at?' he asked, staggering a little; this way and that.

'I'm sorry.' she said, really quite breathless now, 'I'm ... actually I'm not sorry at all. You're such a pointless piece of shit! I mean, did you actually just hear yourself? Can you hear what you're saying? You sound ridiculous.' Both Mike and Shona appeared momentarily shocked into silence. Both stared at Kelly as she continued to sway; spilling her words and her blood into the room. 'I just love how *guys like you* can never seem to get your fat, stupid heads around the idea that a woman ... because that's what she is Mike, she's a woman, not a girl ... That a woman as fit — as delicious, talented and as beautiful — as Shona would choose to be with another woman rather than a man. That she would choose me over you.'

'You're just the latest fuckin' trend! Don't think you're anything fuckin' special.'

'What's next?' asked Kelly, 'It's just a phase?!'

'If it was, that slag's had plenty of opportunity to decide what she really wants.'

'Stop saying that!' said Shona. 'If anyone's a slag here Mike, it's you.'

'You're pathetic.' Kelly joined in, 'A sad, little boy who likes to throw his weight around. Why don't you do yourself a favour and just piss off.'

Kelly had no idea where her sudden burst of courage had come from, but it was strangely intoxicating. It was delightfully self-feeding and she found herself instantly hooked.

The more she stood up to this pointless, little man — despite his stance, his rage and the knife he still waved at them — the more of a kick she felt; the more it tingled beneath her skin. It was wholly addictive and far too difficult to turn her back on now that she had begun.

'Sad, little boy?' he said, rolling his shoulders back, 'we'll see about that when you're lying in a pool of your own blood and piss watching me show her exactly what she's been missing.'

'Over my dead body.' Kelly said, knowing — again — that is was a pretty crappy comeback. The worst, most obvious and overused of all comebacks really, but still. It wasn't as though anyone was keeping score.

'If you like.' he said calmly, before swiping the knife in front of Kelly's mid-riff, clearly hoping to catch some flesh or more with the blade.

To her own astonishment, Kelly managed to dodge the knife by twisting back to her left as Mike thrust forward. Somehow she continued the twist, which then became a sort of roll along his knife-arm until she reached his shoulder where — despite landing heavily on her injured leg and wincing in pain — she was still able to grab Mike in a sort of head-lock before he could realise what had happened.

Appearing momentarily unaware of the fact that Kelly had now clamped onto his head and seeing only that a gap had opened between him and Shona, Mike attempted to step forward. Kelly threw all her weight back and yelped in agony as she hit the deck with Mike crashing painfully down on top of her.

Her arms were now tightly locked around his neck and it finally seemed to be making a difference, though Kelly didn't know how much longer she could hold on before she herself passed-out.

At that moment a blur of noise exploded through the room as the door was sent crashing back against the mirrored wardrobe doors, the glass splintering instantly.

Then Mike was off her and Kelly fell back into the warm and inviting pool of oblivion. Unconscious once more.

Chapter Seven

12:50

Sunday 15ᵗʰ May, 2011

Davies crashed though the swinging doors of the medical bay backroom.

'Dr Matthews!' he called as went, 'I have a patient here in need of some attention.'

Replacing the coronation chicken sandwich — that she had finally sat down and attempted to start eating — back onto the white side plate, Dr Matthews climbed labouriously down off the metal stool and made her way across the room.

'Where is everyone?' Davies asked.

'If by *everyone* you are referring to the limited number of staff I actually still have working with me — physically here — in the med bay, I sent them for a lunch break now that things have finally started to quiet down ... or rather *had* at least appeared to have quietened down.'

She stopped suddenly and Davies looked up to see an expression of irritated disbelief slapped across the physician's face.

'I don't believe this.' she said, letting her fingertips touch the cold rail of the mobile bed. Lying there — blood-soaked towel tied roughly around her thigh — pale and unconscious once more was the raven-headed artist, Kelly Livingstone. 'This woman's been the bane of my life recently. What happened this time?'

Davies shook his head, 'Some sort of altercation with Mike Jones.'

'The dancing lad?'

'Yeah. I got to Shona's room just in time to see Prior press his face into the ground and cuff him. He asked me to bring Miss . . .'

'Livingstone. Kelly Livingstone.'

'Kelly?' Davies asked, raising an eyebrow.

'I think I should know her name by now, Marc. I've had to write it down enough times in the last few days.'

'To be fair, she does look like she's been in the thick of it lately.'

'And don't I know it.' Matthews said, sucking her lip.

Davies didn't like Matthews' tone.

He didn't like her attitude or way she was currently eyeing her patient. It was a look of exasperation and disgust, as though tending to the poor woman involved far too much effort on Matthews' part.

However, a single withering look from the stern doctor informed Davies that it really wasn't his place to comment.

'Dr Kane and Shona are on their way up.' he said, at a loss for anything else to say.

'Oh, great!' came the reply from the woman who for whom the solemnity of this whole situation seemed to have had no physical impact what so ever.

Unlike himself, Prior, Christine Kane and even Captain Andrews, Dr Matthews appeared completely dislocated from the reality and the horror of everything that had happened recently.

Not a single hair was out of place on her white-blonde head. No, every last one had been neatly pinned into the typically caricature scraped-back bun that they had all come to associated with her.

'That's just what I need.' she continued, 'More bloody drama. Well, no thank you. They can wait outside.'

'Yeah, well good luck with that.' Davies said dismissively.

He had had enough of Matthews and needed no excuse to leave.

He had done as he had been charged in delivering the injured woman into her cold, sterile hands for some much-needed medical attention.

Prior had instructed that with that done he should make his way down to the brig and ready one of the small and stifling interview rooms for Mike Jones to be questioned.

He turned on his heel and heard Dr Matthews make a noise that was something between a sulky huff and a high-pitched, nasal 'humph'.

She clearly wasn't impressed.

He smiled to himself as he went, letting the doors swing shut behind him.

Leaving the miserable Matthews alone.

12:50

Sunday 15th May, 2011

Christine had to admit that this was the last place she would have wanted to be.

Arm in arm with the woman who had just been enjoying the woman that *she* was apparently — and unexplainably — attracted to. Typical.

Though, to give credit where credit was due, Shona appeared to be genuinely concerned for Kelly. She even seemed to have taken an interest in Christine and — much to the psychologist's surprise — had fallen in step with her rather than racing on ahead towards the medical bay, leaving Christine to struggle along on her own as she had expected her to.

When Prior had first asked her to escort the somewhat-shaken dancer she had been more than a little apprehensive, but the professional in her had soon taken charge; which only aided in making her feel that her initial reaction had been somewhat self-involved and even a little infantile.

And perhaps it was.

Prior had been almost forceful in his instruction that they 'stick together', but, despite the strange show of obedience that had befallen Shona at the time, Christine had whole-heartedly expected to be dropped at the earliest opportunity.

And yet, she hadn't.

And now Christine found herself wondering whether she had perhaps judged Shona too harshly, too soon.

If so, it seemed that she was beginning to make an annoying habit of it.

The delicate and irritatingly perfect dancer had slipped her arm through Christine's, linking them together as they made their way down the corridor, following the path that Marc Davies had scorched as he had raced through only minutes earlier, clutching Kelly like a newborn babe.

She couldn't decide if this linking of arms was due to Shona feeling that she should support Christine or that she needed the support herself.

She quickly decided that it didn't really matter.

However, Shona did appear to need a physical, human connection. A closeness and warmth gained only through actual, physical contact. Though, Christine mused as they turned another corner, it could just as easily have been the shock setting in.

'Does it hurt?' Shona asked. Her voice was quiet, but managed to shatter the previous silence as though she had hollered the question up and down the corridor. 'Your leg. Is it painful?'

Christine turned her head and found herself staring into a set of dark, liquid orbs that appeared full to bursting. Shona's eyes were red around the edge; her mocha-coloured flesh mottled as she struggled to contain the raw emotion that ebbed and flowed beneath a delicately stitched surface.

Ready to tear at the slightest snag.

'Sometimes.' she said, quietly.

Shona nodded and sniffed. She opened her mouth, but no sound escaped and Christine noticed that her breathing had changed. That her hands had begun to shake.

Shock.

'It's my knee.' Christine said eventually, deciding that the pressing silence was probably doing neither of them any favours. 'Or what's left of it.'

'What happened?'

'It's a long story.' she said, trying not to sound too dismissive.

'We have plenty of time.' Shona replied, without pushing.

Christine smiled at Shona's seemingly natural ability to manipulate a situation — or a person — with ease.

No, manipulate was too strong a word, really. Too harsh.

It implied that Shona was actively trying to draw something from her or — at the very least — that she was aware of her unseen power; her charm. And now that she had actually been forced to spend some time with her, Christine found herself contemplating the idea that that might not be the case after all.

In fact, she thought ruefully, it was probably that same charm — or whatever it was — that was responsible for placing the attractive, young dancer directly in the path of the kind of trouble they had discovered her in only minutes earlier.

'Why don't you tell me about you and Mike?'

'What's to tell?' Shona said, a small hint of defensive irritation screaming through a tone of otherwise subdued restraint. 'I thought he was an alright guy. We got together. He was a dick. We split up. That's it.'

But it so obviously wasn't.

Shona shrugged her shoulders in the silence as though Christine was still questioning her. Perhaps in anticipation of those questions still to come.

Christine knew she had to be careful or Shona would shut down completely.

Prior had seemed convinced that she knew something of importance. Something relevant to the case. If that was true then she needed to be careful. She needed to tease it from the dancer as cautiously as she could afford to, but as soon as possible.

'And yet, you still work with him.' she said, 'What's that like?'

'It's just work, isn't it. You do what you have to do.'

'But, what you do is very physically demanding and even intimate at times.' Christine said before pausing, thinking; trying not to overweight her words, 'I know that Jon's worried about you.'

Shona stopped.

She turned to face Christine, a lump clearly catching in her throat as she tried to speak. Her eyes filling up once more. Only, this time it was anger driving those tears.

'Do you know what it's like trying to fit-in in a place like this?' she said. Christine shook her head, remaining silent. 'It changes you. Forces you to change. Everyone. Even the wonderful, unfaultable Jonathan Prior.' Her voice broke as a single tear paved the way for the many more that threatened to follow even as Shona stubbornly wiped them away. 'Because, on a ship like this there's always somebody who knows your business, or thinks they know your business. Someone who thinks that gives them the right to comment on your life. On your choices and your decisions and ...'

She finally broke.

Falling back against the wall and covering her face to hide her sobs, she cried and cried as though she had been aching for the freedom to do so for a very long time.

'Shona,' Christine said, placing a gentle hand upon her shoulder, 'You can talk to me, you know.'

Shona leaned into Christine, who instinctively wrapped her arms around this young woman who seemed suddenly so much younger. There was a strange sense of innocence about her and Christine wondered just how much of the Shona that she had met previously was mere bravado. An invention to keep others at bay.

She understood the concept well enough; if not her particular strategy.

'The things he said, when he was my room,' she struggled through sobs, 'it was like I'd gone back a year ... I was suddenly back there with him and he was ...'

'Mike was abusive towards you.'

Shona nodded, 'But, he was sly about it. And it was mostly just words and stuff anyway, but ...' she broke off again. 'The things he'd say. I feel so stupid, crying over that bastard and his stupid, fucking words.'

'Words can be very hurtful, Shona. You don't need to feel ashamed. You're not stupid.'

Pulling back from Christine, Shona inhaled a great, lungful of air, trying to steady the rapid rising and falling of her chest; to pace the racing, fluttering sensation in her heart. 'I know.' she said, 'I just ... I can't believe how bad he made me feel, you know? I always thought I was stronger than that. I can't believe how easily I slipped right back into fearing him. Oh, my god! I'm so angry!'

'Why did you fear him? Did he hurt you? Physically?'

'A couple of times towards the end. Just before I finished with him.'

'Did you speak to anyone about it?' Christine asked, meeting Shona's dark chocolate gaze and holding her there. She shook her head. 'Why not?'

'Mike has a very good way of twisting things.' she said, slowly, 'He had this whole ship believing things about me that weren't true at all. Not in the least.'

'Like what?'

'It doesn't matter. It sounds stupid now, but it's hurtful. It gets to you, you know? If a guy sleeps around he's a hero. But, a girl ...'

Christine nodded, feeling a fist of guilt hit her — smack — in the mid-riff. She understood perfectly; she had drawn the same conclusions herself.

'I knew Jon would be devastated when he heard all that was being whispered. And I didn't want to hurt him.' Shona said, 'I never wanted to hurt anyone.'

They began moving once more, making their way in silence through the all-too-quiet corridors of the vast ship. It was only as they clambered up yet another flight of stairs that they began to encounter a steady flow of passengers as they busied about trying to find something to occupy their minds.

The sky had turned a splendid blue and was cloudless as far as Christine could see through the vast tinted-glass windows as they emerged on the next level. It was a far cry from the staff and crew rooms of the lower levels, which featured only small porthole windows. If any.

'So, you and Jon are close then?' Christine said, surprising herself as she listened to her voice echo in the small, light space around them. She had been mulling the question over in her head for some time, curious to know the current status and true nature of their relationship.

Though she didn't really know why.

She didn't understand this compulsion she had developed regarding Jonathan Prior and his past. Didn't know what had driven her to air the question at all.

And yet she had.

Why did it matter? Why did she care what their relationship was or might have been?

The feeling — or rather, the compulsion — was like that of sitting around a table, staring at a plate of biscuits. No. Cookies. A plate of cookies.

In her mind's eye Christine saw the plate. Saw the cookies. Saw that only two remained on a large, white, imaginary platter; oat and raisin and double-chocolate chip. And although she had known she which one she truly wanted — known right from the start — she had sat politely at the table, talking herself out of sublime temptation as she compiled her reasons for why she should really be choosing the oat and raisin.

In the meantime, someone else had swept in, swiping the double-choc chip from right under her nose. Someone who dealt in action.

Not thoughts and words and contemplation, as she did.

And now only the oat remained. And she didn't really want that cookie.

It was nice enough, but it just wasn't double-choc chip. And yet — for some reason — her imaginary self felt oddly compelled to understand the intentions of all others towards that cookie.

Had it previously been claimed? Should she simply seize it while she had the chance? While it was there.

But — again — it wasn't the oat and raisin that she *really* wanted. So why should it make a difference?

She couldn't say.

Had her imagined other-self dallied too long in her decision, because she knew that she was afraid? Because, she knew that she simply hadn't the courage to reach out, to grasp that cookie and allow herself to experience all that the delicious double-choc chip had to offer. Had she simply lingered in her choosing because of the invented eyes that she felt watching her? Judging her?

In this society obsessed with healthy living, fitness and appearance; with stats and norms and pigeonholing, had the oat and raisin just always been the safer option?

Christine shook her head; making her escape from the strange cookie quandary.

'We never used to be that close.' Shona said, oblivious to Christine's cerebral interlude, 'I've known him for years, but, you know ...' Christine didn't, but nodded anyway. 'Then there was the wedding.'

'The wedding?' Christine exclaimed, now completely bemused.

Shona nodded and opened her mouth to continue, but at that moment Marc Davies came into view at the end of the carpeted corridor and — seeing the pair — called to them, a wide grin on his young, tanned face.

Shona waved, throwing a brave smile in his direction, abandoning the sentence and leaving Christine's queries unresolved. Leaving her more than a little confused.

'You like Kelly, don't you?' she asked suddenly, as they waited for Davies to reach them.

Christine didn't quite know what to say. It was a simple enough question with an obvious enough answer; yes, she did like Kelly. Very much, in fact.

But when it was so painfully obvious that Kelly and Shona had moved beyond the realms of mere friendship, she couldn't help but wonder whether or not it was really worth opening up to admit the truth of her feelings. Or should she simply bury them back beneath the surface?

Shona smiled softly, seeming to read Christine with an ease that made her slightly uncomfortable. 'You do. I know you do.' she said, without malice. 'She likes you too, you know. Thinks a lot of you.'

Great! Christine thought. It had the same effect on her already low-altitude balloon of confidence as being told 'You're a good friend.'

It stank!

'Hey, Shona. Dr Kane.' Davies said, nodding to each of them. 'I dropped Kelly off in medical, but I wouldn't advise that you go down there just yet. Dr Matthews isn't really a people person at the best of times — as I'm sure you've both discovered — but, right now I think she might actually be in the running for some kind of anti-social behaviour award!'

His smile drew a mirrored grin from both Shona and even Christine herself.

'I know that Jon wanted to talk you,' he continued, addressing Shona, 'He wants you to make a bit of a statement and stuff. We could go and do that now if you wanted. I can always check in with Dr Matthews in a bit.' He held up his two-way radio.

Shona eventually nodded. 'Why not.' she said. 'Might as well get it all out of the way.'

'Are you coming along, Dr Kane?'

Christine too found herself nodding in answer to the lad's question.

She lifted her stick several inches from the ground and rotated her wrist, mentally preparing herself for yet more walking about this seemingly never-ending vessel. 'So long as that witch doesn't simply patch her up and send her back out like she did last time, I'm happy to come along.' she said.

Davies laughed and turned to lead the way. Shona followed and Christine took a moment to stretch out her spine, twisting this way and that. Wanting nothing more than to climb into a hot, bubbling bath and rest her aching joints.

They reached the brig within ten minutes, which Christine thought was good going, despite the fact that she was now more than slightly — and quite obviously — out of breath.

'I can't wait until they get the power back on,' she said, panting, 'And the bloody lifts are working again.'

She sat down on a long, metal bench that was bolted to the floor.

The whole area was windowless and looked a lot more like a standard constabulary waiting area than she had expected; if not a little more stripped down.

Due to the 'windowless' aspect of the space and the overhead square panel lights being out, someone had dotted three massive LED torches along the floor of the corridor. Each had a face circumference of about a foot and had been stood on its end so that it directed a wide beam of light up towards the ceiling.

It went a fair way to illuminating the place, though Christine would have been lying to herself if she didn't admit that the spectacular blue-white up-lighting effect didn't lend a distinctively creepy air to this largely abandoned portion of the ship.

'Does anyone want a drink?' Davies asked.

Shona declined, but Christine was thirsty after the walk and asked for some water or whatever he could find. The blonde tank of a security officer nodded and, taking a smaller torch from his belt, made his way — solo — down a particularly dark and daunting corridor.

'Well, he's a braver man than me!' Christine chuckled as Shona took a seat besides her.

'Yeah, I don't think I'll be heading down there on my own anytime soon!'

A silence fell between them as they waited in the relative, eerie darkness. There weren't even any informative posters on the walls to distract them.

Not, Christine noted, that they would have been able to read them anyway!

'How long have you known?' Shona asked; the first to break the silence once again.

'Known what?' Christine said, already guessing at the topic of Shona's eager inquiry.

'That you were into women?'

Into women.

Now, this one wasn't as simple a question to answer. This was not like Shona's previous prying into her feelings concerning Kelly. And she didn't immediately know how to even attempt to make an answer. Or how she should react.

As far as she was consciously aware, Kelly was the first woman she had ever actively noticed herself being physically attracted to.

And yet, the more she thought about it, the more she began reassessing her feelings towards those women she had previously thought she merely admired. Those she seemed to envy; those she should dislike and perhaps even *did* dislike, but found herself drawn to none the less.

Did *attraction* cover that? And could it explain the seemingly conflicting emotions she was fastly becoming more aware of? More accustomed to?

She supposed it could.

And could it *always* have been there?

Again, it might.

Christine pushed out a long sigh, buying herself some time to articulate her thoughts. Those she wished to share. And those that she did not.

'I think ... I noticed Kelly. Noticed that I had feelings for her. Feelings that I couldn't easily explain.' She paused, looking up to see Shona watching her; her eyes, her lips, every small movement of her face, 'But I don't know if that means I'm attracted to women in general. Or if it's just Kelly.'

Shona nodded slowly. She smiled at Christine and leaned her back against the wall. 'I remember when I was trying to figure everything out.' she said, 'I'd started — I don't know — noticing stuff, like you say; it was like suddenly everything was in HD! Like, I was paying attention for the first time and realising that I wasn't just seeing things differently, but feeling them too. It made me start to question whether I'd always felt that way.'

Christine kept quiet, not quite willing to admit that she had just been contemplating the very same thing.

'We were doing a run of *Les Miserables* at the time and — without realising it, at first — I totally fell for the girl playing Fantine. She was amazing. Jemma Forrester. But ... I was with Mike.' Shona paused a moment, shaking her head ever so slightly in the dark, 'We had a big party on the final night and I must have had enough drink inside me to give me a bit of confidence. To go over and speak to her. To tell her ... what I thought of her.'

'What happened?' Christine asked with interest.

'She kissed me.' Shona said, smiling; reliving the intimate memories, 'I was ecstatic! We spent the night together and everything. The next morning I was just ... oh, god! I was so happy ... and embarrassed and giggly! I was ridiculous, really! But Jemma didn't seem to mind. If I could have paused time there and then ...'

'But, you couldn't.'

Shona shook her head, 'No. I had to face the music. Go and break up with Mike. I didn't know where I was going to start, but — as it turned out — I didn't need to. He already knew. He'd seen us together, seen us — in his words — *slinking off together*. And, I think he might have taken some stick after that; you know what lads are like. It got back to me — later — about them taunting him; the stupid things they'd said.'

'Like what?'

'Just boyish, playground crap; like, that he'd succeeded in turning my eye from men. Like, that being with him was so awful that it had turned me gay. You know, the usual, ridiculous shit! As though it had nothing to do with *me* and the way I saw things. Or what *I* might want!'

'That's absurd.'

'That's blokes. Especially when they get together.'

'So, was that when he started ...'

'The malicious hate campaign?'

Christine nodded.

'Yeah, that's when it really took off.' Shona said, 'But I can understand why he did it, in a way. And that's the most annoying part. I should just be able to hate him, or at least violently dislike him. Or maybe not even feel anything for him. But I do. I understand him. The way he works; the way he thinks. The way he's scared and small and completely insecure.'

'Caring for people like that, the way you do, Shona ... understanding them ... I know it must seem like a curse sometimes,' Christine said, 'but, it's a gift you've got there. Use it. Own it. Make it work for you.'

She would have said more — would have liked to have said more — but was suddenly interrupted by the suitably eerie squeaking of hinges as a door opened further down the slim corridor and Prior emerged from the shadows.

His eyes fell first on Shona, who stood and went to him, meeting him in a tight embrace. He wrapped his arms around her, squeezing her tightly for a moment and kissing the top of her head, before releasing her once more.

The look slapped across his face was one of open joy and relief.

'I always knew you were too good for him.' he said. 'What did he think was he playing at? Breaking into your room? Threatening you! If he'd have done anything ...'

Shona touched his face, 'Don't worry about that now. I'm fine. It's a good job Kelly was there.'

Prior stiffened slightly, though Christine couldn't quite tell whether it was the mention of Kelly's name or the fact that Davies had just reappeared in the corridor.

He nodded to the Security Chief and handed Christine a bottle of water; which was when Jonathan Prior finally appeared to notice her.

'Christine.' he said, now slightly embarrassed. 'I didn't see you there.'

She smiled at him and waved her hand, 'That's ok. It's dark.'

He gave a small nod, before turning back to Shona. 'Are you ready to do this?'

She said she that was and he indicated to a small interview room that had been treated to the same make-shift lighting technique as the corridor. 'Dr Kane,' Shona said, pausing near the door, 'aren't you coming too?'

Christine looked up at Shona. Then her gaze fell on Prior as the strange white-blue light danced in his eyes adding a splendid luminosity and intensity to the already-vibrant jades.

'I just assumed you were coming anyway.' he said, almost apologising, 'unless you want to go with Davies and see what Mike has to say.'

'I'll do that.' she said, feeling the need to distance herself — for the time being — from both Shona and Prior.

Despite being the one who had requested her presence, Shona seemed happy enough to let Christine go. The psychologist watched the pair enter the small interview room and close the door behind them.

She felt Davies watching her as she continued to stare at the door.

'So,' she said after a moment, 'What's the story with them?'

'Shona and Prior?' Davies asked.

'She said something about a wedding, but I didn't quite get it.'

A wide smile spread across Davies' face, 'You thought they were married?'

'That they were or had been. I don't know.' Christine said, as she began to feel a creeping notion spider its way across her the back of her neck; that feeling that she had — once again — gotten things completely back to front, upside down and inside out.

'Nah, he's never been married, so far as I know.' Davies said, 'But, his dad has. Three times now.' He paused and Christine felt the spidering suddenly tingle to a flush of red embarrassment. 'Wife number three's name is Stella Jacobs.'

'Shona's his step-sister.' Christine said, closing her eyes and shaking her head, her face burning with the realisation of her mistake.

'And now he gets to be the big brother he always wanted to be; he gets to take care of Shona and sort everything out for her. And she now has a big brother to run to. Everybody wins,' he said. 'But no, they're definitely not married.'

'I think I must be overtired or something.' Christine said, 'I don't seem able to read anyone properly at the moment. I'm normally incredibly good at this. It's my job, after all.' Davies chuckled in a soft, friendly manner as she continued, 'But, I keep coming up with the wrong conclusions lately; seeing the worst in people. I don't know.'

'Don't worry about it.' Davies said, his accent flooding each syllable as ever, 'It's probably just all this — with the ship and what-not — getting to you.'

She nodded silently; glad of the darkness.

Glad that it hid her ever-reddening face.

13:12

Sunday 15th May, 2011

Down in engineering, Captain Andrews paced the metal flooring beyond the chamber that housed the main control system.

Three officers worked inside. Disconnecting, reconnecting and patching. He had tried to follow their progress, but really had little-to-no clue at what he was looking at.

He couldn't help but feel lost.

He was supposed to be the Captain of the ship; the man who would lead and guide and see it all through. But he was as much at the mercy of the machinery and technology as anyone else on board and it angered him to the point of distraction.

There hadn't been much in his life that he hadn't been able to achieve, no problem too large or too complicated to overcome if he set his mind to it.

But this. This he simply didn't understand.

It had been lucky for him — and all of them — that this small handful of engineering technicians had — one — managed to survive the incident that had taken the lives of the rest of their colleagues and — two — that they knew enough about the system to basically reconstruct it.

Andrews shook his head, feeling a renewed sense of annoyance.

With himself, with the situation. Everything.

And Davies hadn't been back in touch since their chat.

Neither had Prior.

Though, he didn't quite know if he felt better or worse for not hearing from his chief of security for the moment. He was on edge. Waiting for the radio to bleep; waiting to hear Prior's voice asking for him; calling him out.

And what would he say to the man?

What *could* he say?

'Captain Andrews.' one of the technicians called from inside the chamber.

Andrews paced back along the floor to stand in the open doorway where found himself staring down at a lad of about nineteen years-old. He had hazel eyes and brown hair, shaved close to his head.

He looked so young.

Andrews struggled not to think about the fact that had his shift pattern been altered only slightly the boy would now be in a body bag in the walk-freezer of *Hestia's Kitchen* instead of working to try and turn this tragedy around. He could so easily have shared the sad fate of so many of his colleagues.

His friends.

'We're ready to do this.' he said, 'You just need give the order.'

Andrews nodded his understanding, feeling a lump the size of a golf ball stick in his throat.

His eyes began to fill again and he clenched his teeth against the flow of emotion, balling his hands into fists behind his back.

'Do it.' he said.

The boy acknowledged him and the two remaining technicians began furiously entering codes into the system, while he physically altered levers and twisted knobs and kept a watchful eye on the pressure levels.

Andrews turned his back to them, taking a small torch from his pocket.

The lingering emergency lighting cut out without a flicker. The basic air-flow system ceased. Any small hum of power that had survived until this point now struck out; like the final 'tock' of an old grand-father clock.

He had made an announcement earlier. Advised people to go to one of the restaurants or conference rooms on the upper levels (where the oxygen would still flow naturally), but he couldn't force them. Could he?

In reality he hadn't the man power to instigate such an order.

He was also painfully aware that once the revelation dawned of the full shut-down procedure knocking out the automated locking system — the system that was used to secure the passenger and crew rooms — that he would have a battle to keep people from wanting to protect their belongings. He shuddered at the thought, though he knew that for some the need to guard their material possessions would seem oddly far more important than the need to breathe fresh, oxygenated air.

No, he wouldn't have it.

If there was even a small chance that leaving the safety of the designated rooms would cause more casualties amongst his passengers and crew, he had to make sure that no one left. And if that meant enforcing a strict 'no access' policy, then so be it.

He sighed, striding back towards the main corridor in the dark.

Now the real mayhem would begin.

13:12

Sunday 15ᵗʰ May, 2011

Davies had let Christine take the lead in interviewing Mike Jones.

She wondered, as she sipped at the bottle of water he had brought for her earlier, whether this was simply a courtesy due to some perceived chain-of-command between the pair of them, or whether it was because the athletic and handsome blonde actually felt somewhat less-than-confident in taking the reins in this matter.

Not that it mattered, really.

The room was large enough to not feel claustrophobic, but small enough to achieve the sense of intimacy needed in drawing out the truth; enough to put the suspect a little at ease and even create a sense — perhaps a false sense — of trust.

This environmental tool could be especially useful when the suspect was feeling like he wanted to brag. But, so far, Mike was not feeling this.

In the centre of the room a wide, metal table stood bolted to the floor; a metal bench bolted similarly either side.

Mike was sat opposite Christine, watching her as she took up her pen and began writing in short hand on the notepad in front of her. Davies was stood a little way off to her left, watching all.

'What you writing?' Mike asked, craning his neck to try and gain a better view.

Christine looked up at him and smiled slowly, before standing the pad upright and turning it around for him to see; judging the movements in his face as he tried to decode the shorthand manuscript.

He snorted.

'Is that meant to impress me?'

'Does it?' Christine asked, returning the pad to the table and the lid to her pen. She folded her hands, palms-down, one on top of the other onto the cold metal and waited.

'No,' he said, 'Not really.'

'Good.' she replied, 'Because, I'm not here to try and impress you, though you're clearly trying your hardest to impress me.'

'What makes you say that?'

'Oh, come on, Mike. Look at yourself, listen to yourself. Your tone, posture, attitude. You're desperately trying to make a statement.'

'Oh, yeah,' he said, playing right into her hand, 'and what's that, then?'

'That you're not scared.'

'Well, I'm not!'

Mike seemed to realise the — almost hilarious — futility of his statement and proceeded to make a big fuss of folding his arms across his chest. Huffing and puffing as he did. Christine curbed the smile that threatened her lips and continued to stare at him.

'So, do you want to tell me what all that was about? Earlier on.'

'All what?' he said, a smarmy look on his face.

Oh. He wanted to play *that* game, did he?

'Mike.' Christine said, drawing in a long breath and releasing it, slowly, 'We caught you, there and then. At the scene of the crime. Kelly's blood all over you; knife in hand.'

'Hey! I didn't cut that stupid dyke! Ok?' he said, viciously. 'She was bleeding when I got there.'

Davies chuckled in the corner and Mike shot him a cold look. 'Oh, that's brilliant, that.' he said, 'Yeah, I've heard some excuses before, but that one, that's . . .'

'It's the truth, you fucking hominid.'

Continuing the theme, it was obvious that Mike was now trying to rile Davies by throwing — what he believed to be — insults at him relating to own his sexuality.

Christine kept a poker-faced calm, despite the overwhelming urge to laugh in Mike Jones' childish face and inform him that all three of them, in fact, were hominids. That every other person on the ship; every single human being *in the world* was — in fact — a hominid! That that was what the word meant; only he was too stupid to realise it.

She resisted the urge.

Tearing a page from the pad, Christine scribbled a note and passed it to Davies.

'Marc,' she said, softly, her accented tones bouncing off the tin walls and echoing in the space around her, 'would you go and ask Prior if he still has these evidence bags, please?'

He took the note, his eyes on Christine, 'And leave you in here? With him?'

'It's fine,' she said, her eyes never leaving Mike 'You're going to behave now, aren't you?'

Mike frowned, looking from Christine to Davies and back again. He nodded.

'I'd feel better if you let me cuff him to the table.'

'Yeah, I bet you would.' Mike said.

Davies ignored him.

Christine shook her head and Davies sighed. 'I'll be quick.'

She heard the door click shut behind her and although she hadn't seen Davies leave, she felt the room suddenly absent of his somewhat larger-than-life presence.

'So, what is it that makes you so special?' she said, her accent and the timbre of her voice continuing to resonate almost liquidly around the metallic room.

'What?' Mike asked.

'What is it that makes you think you don't have to obey the laws that others do.'

'I don't know what you're talking about.' he said, nonchalantly.

'Oh, I think you do. All this violence, Mike. Did you think there'd be no retribution? That you'd just get away with it forever?'

For a fraction of a second, Mike's face clouded with doubt and fear. Then, like a wispy cumulus on a windy day, it was gone.

'I don't know what you're talking about.'

'Oh, but I know you do.' she said, relaxing back into her chair, 'I've sat across the table from many a seasoned life-taker. But everyone is different. What I want . . . is to understand. To understand why you do what you do. What drives you? What is it that *you* get out of killing?'

'Killing?' he said, the worry springing back to his face.

Christine remained silent, watching as he struggled to gather his thoughts, his alibis and his reasons. Watching him sweat.

'I haven't done anything wrong. Well, maybe I went a bit far bursting into Shona's room and . . . but I haven't *hurt* anyone. I haven't done *anything* to anyone else. I swear.'

Christine nodded slowly, hearing the door open behind her.

'We'll see.' she said.

Davies managed to hand over the evidence bags quite discreetly before returning to his position by the door. Christine thanked him, her eyes always on Mike.

She waited a moment before bringing the first of the evidence bags from her lap and placing it on the table.

'This is the knife taken from you when you were apprehended in Shona's room earlier.' She didn't ask him if this was correct. She didn't ask his to identify the weapon. She merely watched him. Watched every movement that his eyes made as they darted over the intricate detail from the handle to the blade. 'It's really quite beautiful. Isn't it?'

Mike nodded, almost involuntarily.

'But, I have to admit, I was more than a little curious about it,' she continued, lifting the still-bagged blade as she spoke, 'I mean, all this fine detail, the enamel; the stones, the mother of pearl; the silver. It must have cost a small fortune.'

'A fortune, yes. Small, no.'

'So why spend all that money on a knife? A knife that I assume is locked away most of the time.'

'Because, I wanted it.' he said, proudly.

'Like you wanted Shona?' Christine replied, 'But she couldn't be bought. Could she? She wasn't interested.' Mike slumped back, staring at the table. 'Do you look at the knife much? Do you take it out and hold it? Do you think about how it would feel to stick it into another human being? To twist it in and watch them bleed.'

'No!' Mike shouted, jumping to his feet. Davies stepped in close behind Christine. 'No! I don't do that! I don't dream about killing people. I never even wanted to ...'

Mike had started pacing the room, setting Davies on edge. 'Sit down!' he barked, but Mike ignored him. 'Mike.'

The male dancer turned his head to look at Davies, but remained where he was.

'It's ok, Mike.' Christine said, 'Come and sit back down.'

He looked back and forth between Christine and Davies for a long while before eventually yielding to sit.

'Thank you.' Christine continued. 'Now, you understand why I'm asking these questions, don't you? Understand why I *have* to ask these questions of you?'

He shrugged before answering. 'Because I attacked Shona and … the other one.'

'Yeah, for starters.' Davies snorted.

Mike's head swung round to look at Davies, his face burning with rage; his defensive eyes awash with fear and curiosity. 'And what's that supposed to mean?'

Christine had already raised her hand and — taking his cue — Davies remained silent.

'Come on, Mike. You're not stupid. I'd like to say that I *know* you're not stupid. Marc Davies believes that you're not.' She watched Mike's narrow eyes flick across to Davies once more, 'But, that knowledge is really only an assumption with a little common courtesy thrown in for good measure. And, I would be grateful if you extended the same courtesy now. And spoke plainly to the both of us.'

'I am speaking plainly. It's you that talks like a bloody text book!'

A small, soft smile played on Christine's lips as she gave a single nod, acknowledging his point. 'Tell me what you know about all that's been happening on this ship, recently.'

'What's to say?' he said with a shrug, 'It's gone to shit! Some big accident or something. It killed half the engineers and left us without power.'

'And that's all you know?'

'I heard something about a girl on a hen do. People were even saying we had our own *Jack the Ripper* on board. But there were so many different stories — you know — I just thought everything must have been blown out of proportion. Like that girl, for example, she could have died from alcoholic poisoning or something that, but with everything going tits up and a massive game of Chinese-whispers … well, the story just expands. Doesn't it?'

'Sometimes.' Christine said, scrutinising Mike as she spoke, 'Though, on this occasion, I can categorically confirm that that young girl did *not* die of alcoholic poisoning. Nor anything even vaguely related to any cause of death that might be considered natural.'

Mike seemed genuinely taken aback to hear this.

He was either a better actor than any of them had given credit, or he truly had no idea that Stacey Atkins had, in fact, been murdered.

And horrifically murdered at that.

'Let's return to the incident in Shona's room for a moment,' Christine said, changing tactic; hoping to draw Mike out. 'And to the weapon you used.'

'I've already told you, I didn't *use* my knife! I didn't stab anyone, I didn't slice anyone.'

'Did you intend to?'

Mike was silent for a moment, contemplating his answer. 'No. I think it was more for show.'

'To what ends?' Christine asked, 'To threaten? *Do as I say or I will ...*'

'I suppose.' he shrugged, 'but, I wouldn't have used it. Not on the ship.'

'And what do you mean by that? *Not on the ship.*'

'Well, I've used it when I've been hunting and stuff.'

'And what did you like to hunt, Mike?'

'Nothing big. Rabbits, cats — '

'Cats?' Christine said, horrified.

Mike nodded. 'Wild ones, yeah. In Greece, Morroco, Italy, places like that. Nobody cares about them. It's pest control out there.'

Christine managed to put a lid on the overwhelming revulsion she felt.

But only just.

Mike grinned sadistically.

'Did you hunt *birds*? Out there?' Davies asked, his words so weighted that they had an almost metallic edge to them, which cut through the sudden silence and strangely buzzing energy of the room like a machete through butter. 'Did you hunt in Livorno?'

The grin was wiped from Mike's smug face as though it had been slapped right off it and he began rising slowly to his feet once more. 'I don't like your tone — '

'Sit. Down.' Christine said, taking an iron-like grip of control over the situation before it could spiral.

Mike obeyed. Much to his own apparent surprise.

'Well, well.' he said, looking into her eyes, 'You can be quite commanding when you want to, can't you?' Meeting his gaze, Christine resisted the urge to use the clichéd double-negative *You ain't seen nothing yet!*

Instead she held the first evidence bag, dangling it in front of his nose before placing it on the table. 'So,' she said, 'you smuggled a knife on board, despite the fact you could be charged if discovered.' Christine turned her body towards Davies, 'What's the penalty for that, Marc? Anything up to ten years?'

Davies raised an eyebrow and nodded, his arms folded across his chest as he leaned coolly up against the door jam. 'Certainly is.'

'And that's before we add a charge of 'threatening use with the intent to harm'.'

'Wait!' said Mike, 'Wait a minute. What is it that you want from me? What do you want me to say? That I'm sorry?'

'Sorry won't bring back the crew. Or any of your other victims.'

'The crew? They're not my victims.' he said, raking his hands through his hair, 'I have no fucking victims! I told you, I haven't hurt anyone onboard this ship. You have to believe me.'

'But, how can we believe you, Mike? When — by your own admission, your own actions — you've proved to us just how much you wanted to hurt Shona. And Kelly.' she paused, folding her hands flat once more, 'When you've purchased a knife — yes an incredibly expensive and beautifully crafted knife, but a knife none-the-less — and smuggled it on board with the sole purpose of killing when you make port.'

'Rabbits and cats! God damn it! They aren't the same as people!' he said, the frustration in his voice ringing clear as a bell.

'No.' Christine said, 'They're not, are they? They're too small. They don't satisfy the urge, do they?'

'I don't know what you're talking about.' Mike flustered.

'Oh, I think you do.' Christine said, staring at him once again; her eyes locked like lasers on her target.

'I lied! Ok? I lied.' he said, throwing his hands up in the air, 'But, that's all I've done. Look, the knife's not even mine.'

'Really?' Christine said, playing her cards close to her chest, 'But, we found you with it. Your prints will be all over it.'

'But, I didn't bring it on board. I didn't smuggle it on.' He paused for a moment, trying to regulate his breathing, 'I know I threatened Shona and . . .'

'Kelly.' Christine said.

'Yeah, and that was fucked up and maybe I need help. But, I don't deserve to be locked away for ten years of my life. Please,' he said, 'you've got to help me.'

Christine turned herself slowly to look Davies.

'Is that what we've . . . got to do?' he said, smiling.

'What do you think, Marc? Without the smuggling charge, what could he expect for 'threatening behaviour'?'

'Oh, that all depends.'

'On what?' Mike pleaded.

Davies looked as though he was beginning to enjoy himself and Christine made a mental note not to let things go too far.

'You could get anything really,' he began, 'from a fine and stint of community service to two years in prison. It all depends. You have to think about Shona's statement and Kelly's statement, not to mention her injuries. Then, there's the hearing to consider. Judge, jury, all of that depends on the severity of the attack and perceived intent of the attacker by the victims.' he paused and looked at Christine, who nodded. 'Then again, Shona and Kelly might be kind enough to simply drop the charges. But, there's still the ownership of the knife, which — regardless of your protestations — does have your prints all over it. Even if Shona did choose not to pursue this, I doubt Prior would be so quick turn a blind eye.'

'But, what if I could prove that the knife didn't belong to me?'

'How might you do that?' asked Christine.

'Well, like you said, it's a posh knife. But, more than that, it's an identity knife, you know? Personalised. Beautiful, polished blade; individually crafted handle. Very expensive.'

'But, you could afford it if you wanted it.' Davies said, 'especially if you haggled for it in some of the shops off the beaten track. I mean, you've been all over. Haven't you, Mike?'

'Yes, but my point is this,' he said, his arms cutting wildly through the air as he spoke, 'Why would I spend all that money on *this* knife? Look! Why would I buy an identity knife that bore the wrong initial?'

'Initial?' Christine asked, appearing wholly curious.

'Yes.' he said, reaching for the evidence bag and turning it over.

Christine leaned in as Marc Davies too took a step forward. 'What is that?' he asked.

'That's a 'G'.' said Mike, tracing his finger over the scrolling, semi-precious stones.

'That could be anything.' said Davies, 'It's just a pattern, isn't it.'

Mike huffed, but didn't speak and Christine made a show of examining the knife, though she knew he was finally speaking the truth. 'I don't know.' she said, 'I suppose it could be a 'G'. But, it could stand for anything; Gaudy, Glamorous, Gorgeous. Give in to me.'

'Or it could be a name.' Davies added, playing along. 'Gareth, Glen, Greg. But, what does it prove? That you're a thief on top of a bully? Or that you own a knife with a swirl on the handle that vaguely resembles a 'G'.'

'No!' shouted Mike, 'That's my point! I'm not a thief! The knife doesn't belong to me ... it doesn't. But, I'm not a thief, either! This is one of a set.' he paused, feeling that he had said too much and quickly changed tactics, trying to double-back, 'I mean, surely, if I was going to own a knife like this and risk smuggling it on board, I'd have one made with up an 'M' on the handle, wouldn't I?'

'Would you?' Christine asked.

'Of course I would.' he said.

Bingo.

'Like this one, you mean?' As she asked the question, Christine produced the second evidence bag, laying it flat on the table before him.

Dried blood flaked about the inside of the bag and could be seen clearly staining the blade of this, a second knife — a twin of the first — bearing, in the same scrolling pattern of semi-precious stones as the other, the letter 'M'.

All colour drained from Mike's previously reddened and enraged face. He seemed to physically shrink back into his seat; deflated. Exhausted.

'Where ... where did you find this?' he stammered after a moment.

'It was found at the scene of yet another brutal crime committed on this ship.' Christine said, 'Do you deny that it belongs to you?'

He shook his head.

'This is mine. No. It *was* mine, but I haven't seen it for . . . years.' His hand wavered over the bagged knife for a moment, before he drew it back, his eyes engaging with Christine's. 'He's set me up! That's what he's done . . . he's set me up, the bastard! You have to believe me!'

'Sure, yeah.' Davies laughed, 'On account of you being so open, honest and up-front about everything, right?'

'Who set you up Mike?' Christine asked.

'I told him I didn't want anything to do with it. That I didn't work for his bastard family anymore! That I was done!'

'Who?'

'This family wouldn't happen to be the Copina's would they?' Davies asked, laying his hands flat on the metallic surface of the table.

'How did you know?' Mike said.

'Because, it's my job.'

Christine couldn't help but smile, hearing a little of Prior and even herself in Davies' now-commanding voice.

'It's your job to go snooping into people's pasts?'

'Well, kind of, yeah!'

'What does the 'G' stand for, Mike?' Christine asked, eagerly 'Who is 'G'?'

'Why don't you tell me.' he said, sitting back in his chair and folding his arms across his chest.

'Is it Gary Blakely?'

Mike made a small, snorting noise and nodded. 'I don't see why I should have to protect the little prick! I told him I was done with his family. And, if he's trying to set me up, anyway — '

'Gary Blakely's dead.' Davies said, with a look that conveyed the words; *you dick!* 'And he's been dead for while too.'

'Dead?' Mike echoed. 'Like, really dead? And gone. For good.'

Christine nodded 'He was killed at least twelve hours before this knife was found in the suite of a Mrs Fiona Jenkins.'

The name appeared to mean nothing to Mike, but that was really neither here nor there. Criminal families extended all the time. And if Mike was little more than a hired hand there was really no reason to expect that he *should* have known the late Mrs Jenkins. But, still.

'What was it that Blakely had asked you to do for him, Mike?' Christine said.

He hesitated. 'It wasn't for him. It was a job for his cousin.'

'Michael Copina?' Davies asked.

Mike nodded. 'Apparently he's getting married. But, their family can't ever be normal about anything, can they?'

'What do you mean?' Christine pressed.

'Well, he wanted me to go and chat her up. Try and get her into bed.'

'Why?'

'That's what I wondered.' he said, honestly, 'It was obviously some sort of test, but was it meant for me or for her? And what if I succeeded! What then? I doubt Michael would have clapped my on the back and said *Thanks for all your help mate, I knew she was a slag, but I had to be sure.'*

'What was the girl's name?' Davies asked, already knowing.

'He didn't tell me and I didn't ask. I didn't want to know. I didn't want to know anything.'

'Did you speak to Copina at all?'

Mike shook his head. 'Just Blakely.'

'And when was the last time you spoke to him?' Christine asked.

'Four weeks ago?' he said, thinking it over, 'maybe more. Yeah, maybe six weeks.'

Christine exchanged glances with Davies, feeling Mike's eyes studying the pair of them as they did.

'So, can I go now?' he said, suddenly much cockier, clearly believing that he was no longer in any danger of seeing the inside of a prison cell.

'Oh, no.' said Christine, 'You're not done yet. There's still the matter of this knife and the state of Kelly's health to consider.'

'I already told you I didn't cut her!'

'And yet she was bleeding. And there is blood on Gary Blakely's knife. The 'G' knife. The one that you threatened Shona and Kelly with not two hours ago.'

'That's old blood.' he said, before he could stop himself. Then, he shifted in his chair, reacting as every guilty person does when they come to realise that they have said too much. He fell silent; face flushed, looking suddenly very guilty.

Guilty as hell.

'What do you mean by that?' Christine pressed.

'Exactly what I said,' he stumbled, 'that it could be old blood.'

'You said *that's* old blood. Like you knew. Like you were absolutely certain. How could you be *that* certain, Mike?'

'I'm not. Ok?' he shouted, 'I was just saying that it could be! So what if it came out wrong?'

But it hadn't.

Christine picked up the evidence bags and pushed herself up to stand. 'Marc, can I speak to you outside for a moment?'

Davies nodded and followed her to the door, holding it open for Christine to pass through before joining her and closing the door behind him.

The hall seemed even darker than before and, for a moment, Christine was overcome with fear. She found herself holding back, hovering near the door. Ready to charge back inside to the sanctuary of the lightened space.

But she didn't.

'I don't know if what I said in there was correct.' Davies said in a hushed voice. 'Prior would have know exactly what the maritime penalties were for carrying a knife and threatening or assaulting someone, but me . . . I don't really know. I just guessed.'

'It's fine.' Christine said, 'We just needed to shake him up a bit and that's exactly what we did.'

'I'd say!' he said, smiling, 'Do you think he knows anything?'

Christine shook her head. 'He's not our man.'

'So, what was all that, just now?'

'He's certainly disturbed. An animal torturer; the little big-man,' she said without emotion, 'And he has admitted to working for the Copina's in the past.'

'That's what I was trying to tell you earlier; over the radio. I found out that Copina and Blakely were cousins. Which goes someway to explaining Blakely's expunged record.'

Christine nodded.

'I want you to go back in there and I want you to talk to him. I think he might have been more involved with the missing girl incident than we first thought. He wasn't just paid to provide an alibi for Gary Blakely. I think he was with him when she was killed.' she said, pausing to consider, tilting her head as she pulled apart her own thoughts, 'Now, whether it was Blakely that killed her or Mike, I can't say for sure. Maybe, they both played a part. But, he was scared in there. Really scared. Did you see how nervous he looked when he first saw the knife?'

'But that doesn't explain Blakely keeping hold of Mike's knife and Mike having Blakely's. Does it?' Davies said, feeling like he was missing something.

'It could have been a trust thing. Binding them together.' Christine reasoned, 'If each of the knives had a set of prints on them — one with Blakely's, the other Mike Jones' — and even a drop of the girl's blood, DNA, whatever . . . well, that's a pretty damning amount evidence in a case that has — thus far — remained unsolved.' She paused, staring at the door as though she could see into the room beyond; see Mike sweating out his reasons and his decisions. Reliving his actions. 'Swapping knives would have forced each man into a kind of silence. The kind of terrified silence we just witnessed in there. They'd be *forced* to trust one another.' she continued with a sigh. 'But, it goes beyond that. Like Blakely *asking* Mike to take part in the testing of Stacey Atkins' fidelity. I mean, Mike's initial conclusion when he saw the knife was that he'd been set up. Almost, as though he was expecting it.'

Davies nodded slowly, agreeing. 'Because he'd already refused Blakely.'

'Exactly.'

'What do you want me to do?'

'Keep him here. Try and get a confession. An account of everything that happened. He can't be allowed to get away with what he's done.'

'Yes, Ma'am.' he said. 'I'll do my damned best.'

'I'm sure you will,' Christine said, smiling briefly, even as she looked nervously up and down the darkened corridor, 'And can you also bring Prior up to speed when he's done with Shona?'

Davies nodded once more. 'Where are you going?'

'Back to my room. I need to think. And rest.' she said, 'Although rest can wait, I suppose. I might even go and speak to Dr Matthews if I absolutely have to.'

Davies chuckled, understanding her lack of time and enthusiasm for the less-than-friendly physician perfectly well.

Christine turned back towards the darkened corridor and hesitated once more.

Pulling the small LED torch free from his belt once more, Davies offered it to her. 'Here,' he said, 'you might just need this … a little guiding light to find your way.'

Christine smiled a sad, exhausted smile, taking the torch from him with silent thanks.

'Don't we all from time to time?' she said.

13:12

Sunday 15ᵗʰ May, 2011

He had been hiding for some time now. Enjoying the chaos that had been delightfully easy to set in motion. The chaos that he had helped to create, but which had now expanded into something even more spectacular than he ever could have imagined.

This was so much more than he could have hoped for.

And none of them suspected. Well, how could they? Why *should* they? Not with that testosterone-fuelled young amateur stepping up and catapulting himself so splendidly into the limelight!

And just in time.

He grinned from ear to ear as he lurked in the shadows.

He couldn't have asked for a better cover. A better diversion.

Couldn't have planned it better if he had orchestrated the frenzied, little farce himself.

This had bought him time.

Time to plan. To begin work on his final masterpiece before the big unveiling. Before he was *finally* able to reveal himself to the world. And then disappear once more.

The difficulty lay in deciding who should feature in such a grand finale; his opus magnum. There were — after all — so many players involved now.

Thus far, luck and lust had drawn him from one great work to the next. Granted, there had been some set-backs. There had been some surprises and some downright rude interruptions too! But he had persisted in his labour, evolving with each masterful stroke; with each cut and slice and spatter of scarlet delight.

He slipped the chain from his pocket, thumbing the tags where his brother's name had all but worn away.

Years of the same thumbed motion had nearly erased the lettering; the last of the deeply personal, physical evidence he possessed which accounted for his brother ever existing at all. And though he knew that that same thumbed action was responsible for the wearing of the engraved metal down to a flat, polished surface; it was also one of the few things in this pointless journey known as life that now brought him any real, tangible comfort.

Part of him — he realised with an ironic smile — was doing this — all of this — for Matty. In his name, so that he would *never* be forgotten.

While, the remaining parts of him were enjoying it simply for *him*. And him alone.

He looked forward to the day that he could finally wear his brother's tags with pride. When he had finally earned that right.

He had longed to slip them over his head on many a dark and lonesome night, when he had felt so alone, so ... lost.

But he hadn't dared. He knew better than that.

You have to earn something like this!

He heard the words as clear and crisp as though they had been poured directly into the chasm of his mind and remembered the first time he had seen Matty wearing the tags around his neck. The first time he had asked about them.

Had he been six?

Not quite six?

He had told how he had earned them through hard work; through physical training, mental torture and the spilling of blood.

He called them his 'ticket to ride', his free pass to kill and be thanked for it. And these tags, they came with weapons and ammo and enough moving targets to satisfy even Matty's thirsty, cavernous desire to spill blood.

Just so long as he signed on the dotted line; pledging his unfaltering obedience to his imperial den-masters.

At least, that's how he had seen it. Matty.

It was the grand old sceptred Isle — Great Britain, Britannia, The United Kingdom, whatever — that had originally paid his brother's cheques. Though there were many other soldiers that he had talked about who were earning more — much more — than he.

Soldiers far better equipped than those of his deprived platoon.

They were the well-paid pawns obeying the silent commands of the pointing finger that extended from the Don-like hand of the good old U S of A. That which pointed ever East; towards the oil.

Not that any of that mattered.

Not to him. And not to Matty.

But then there had been that inquest.

And the dishonourable discharge.

He boiled with a sudden anger. Striking out at nothing, but the yawning darkness. He didn't care what they said. What any of them said.

His brother was a hero.

To him at least.

And soon he could wear those tags with pride. And not for any half-arsed allegiance to some soulless nation. Not because he needed a 'ticket to ride' or to kill.

But simply because he had earned them. Because he was worthy of them; worthy to bear the legacy his brother had left behind.

But to honour the dead with the simple spilling of blood? Was that really enough?

He had — after all — been enjoying his merry, little self immensely. Enjoying the sweet and salted toil he had wrought.

It had hardly been a testing penance.

In any case, he was of his brother's ilk and killing came naturally to him. So, he had had no trouble in the 'spilling' part of that little equation, but honour ... now, that was another matter. Would honour really be satisfied with these sacrifices?

He had aided Nona, with her plea to *feel* something one last time.

He supposed that he had honourably assisted her in ending it all in a blaze of glory that would forever be connected to his name and that of his brother's. Which, was what she had wanted and so satisfied two honours when you thought about it.

But, no.

It still didn't feel right. He needed a way of screaming his brother's name physically through space and time so that — no matter what happened — it would echo out and out and still further out. Honouring his memory in eternity.

Avenging his death — somehow — once and for all.

Would one more kill really do that? Would it suffice? Could it?

He was running out of time.

The kill would certainly have to *mean* something in a way that none of the previous kills had done.

But who to choose? How? And why?

He had watched the man with the green eyes as he had secured his prisoner earlier; the knife-wielding amateur. There was something familiar about that one. Something half remembered; like a dream. And then there was his young officer, and the women ...

But it had to *mean* something.

This one *had* to.

It was the grand finale!

He growled. Impatient. Annoyed.

Your instinct has led you this far, brother.

Matty's voice. As before.

It was in his head, he knew, but it was so real that he swore he could have reached out and touched his elder brother's bristling face in the dark. That he could smell his heavy, distinctively male aftershave.

It'll come to you. If you let it.

'But, it can never bring you back.' he whispered, still hidden.

I'm always with you, you dick. Always here. Now, make them remember me. Fear me, as they used to.

He nodded, his eyes burning. 'They'll fear us both, brother. I swear it.'

Chapter Eight

Christine stretched out across the large, soft quilted bed; lengthening her spine as she twisted this way and that, curling and flexing her ankles and her feet.

Only as she yawned and turned over did she realise — to her own horror and immediate fury — that she had actually fallen asleep.

Feeling groggy and exhausted — and now also irritated with herself — she fought the urge to simply roll over and return to the seductive waters of the deep and all-consuming slumber that had apparently gripped her so forcefully.

Leaving Davies to continue the interview with Mike, she had returned to her own suite without detour. But she had felt drained and had made the decision to sit out on the balcony, hoping that the soft breeze and sea air would soon blast off the lethargy.

Outside, the warm afternoon sun had pushed through the few small, wispy strands of cloud, bathing the psychologist's tired body as she had struggled to wrap her thoughts around this case.

Case.

It was so easy to slip into old habits; old phrases and patterns of thought. But perhaps that simply meant that she wasn't quite ready to be put out to the post-career pasture just yet, after all.

And yet, she had honestly thought they had had him; she had truly believed that Mike Jones was their guy. That he was — at the very least — partly responsible for the mounting body count and the sabotage to the ship.

He seemed to have fit her rough and ever-evolving profile perfectly. And the more they had discovered about him, the more it had all seemed to link together.

But that was just it. That was the danger and the lure of patterns.

They weren't always real.

Christine knew that the human brain was notorious for wanting to rationalise and to organise; to box things off and make sense of the random.

But just because you saw a face, or a castle or even a dancing elephant in the vast formations of an expanding cloud, it didn't mean that they were actually there. Or that they had *ever* been there.

No. No pattern was ever a certainty in itself. No matter how much the 'evidence' seemed to suggest otherwise.

And yet, her instinct had never let her down before. It had been her gift, her talent; her unique selling point in this new, market-driven world of professionalism and crime.

It had been that same instinct and wit — her ability to see the patterns and appreciate them without jumping to any too-soon conclusions — that had led to the eventual apprehension of Thomas Butler.

Or *Tom the Butcher* as he had come to be known.

In her testimony, Christine had recommended that he be remanded into the custody of a psychiatric hospital rather than swelling the ranks of the traditional criminal justice system. She had also made herself crystal clear in her submissions to the court — both verbal and written — that Butler should be entered into the care system at the maximum level of security.

It was obvious to Christine that the man suffered with several acute personality disorders and in the time she had spent with him since the arrest, she had come to realise that he was also plagued with a number of other mental disturbances formed over a lifetime of neglect and abuse. It was — in her opinion — this systematic mistreatment of Butler as a child that had resulted in such a disturbing penchant for cruelty.

Speaking with him then, within the confines of a secure interview room, she had easily traced and connected his own youthful experiences to the mechanisms of violence and humiliation that he had later administered without remorse to the nineteen victims they knew of at the time.

In actual fact there had been twenty-two.

And that was before the names of both Janet and herself were added to that list. Though, Christine knew that — as victims went — she had been one of the lucky ones.

Both Ashworth and Rampton Secure Hospitals had the facilities to accommodate his needs, though Ashworth also had two specialist wards dedicated to patients with similar conditions.

She knew that in prison Butler would not have access to the full spectrum of medication and treatments he desperately needed to bring his conditions in line. And therefore to place him in a prison setting would be to place the staff who worked there — to say nothing of the other inmates — in very real danger.

So she had made her recommendation.

But, maximum security had always been Christine's gospel when it came to dealing with Thomas Butler.

Always.

She had sighed as she sat on the balcony, attempting to ward off the exhaustion and painful memories. She had thrown a longing glance over to the unopened bottle of Shiraz that seemed to tempt her with a siren's call from the dresser across the room. But she had resisted.

And she had done well to resist.

Though, she couldn't say the same for the lure of the soft, warm, inviting king-size bed on which she now lay.

What time was it anyway?

She checked the small travel clock on the bedside table next to her, which revealed that it was nearly ten past six.

'Jesus!' she cried, checking once more in the hopes that her tired eyes had somehow deceived her. But they hadn't. 'Christine, you dozy woman!'

She manoeuvred herself around the room as quickly as she could; reaching for the radio that Prior had given to her to keep in touch.

Not exactly certain of correct maritime radio etiquette, she picked up the two-way handset, turned it on and held down the call button.

'This is ... Dr Kane.' she said, groggily. 'If Security Chief Prior can hear me, please respond.'

No answer.

She worried for a moment before remembering the lack of signal down in the corridors surrounding the brig. It was possible, she thought, that he might still be down there.

Moving to take a seat at the vanity desk that had now become her office, Christine placed the radio down besides her and drew open her journal, running her finger over the soft material of the gold page-finder almost ritualistically.

She looked over the notes she had been making out on the balcony earlier, re-reading over her thoughts on the individual murders — the mechanism, the style, the display — and how they each seemed to indicate this personality type or that. She contemplated the profile that she had been building before they had apprehended Mike and found that, despite his obvious lack of involvement, it still seemed to point an extra-large, unwavering and guilty finger at the complex and aggressive male dancer who had the knife and the past and animal-torturing hobbies!

She blew out a long, exasperated breath, puffing her cheeks as she scrolled back a few pages.

KELLY LIVINGSTONE.

Those two words seemed to lift from the page and a soft smile danced across the psychologist's face as she read them; as she fell into re-reading the entire entry that she had inscribed following her first encounter with the artist who had, somehow — and without any real effort on her part — managed to captivate her completely.

She turned the pages, examining the notes she had made on some of Kelly's darker works; those which seemed to be desperately searching for something. Approval. Identity. Forgiveness.

The colourful and disturbing *Girl With Two Faces* still unnerved her, though she didn't quite know why. She shivered.

And all the while she read, she found herself lost in tactile imaginings. She gave herself over to the desire of wanting to hold Kelly, to embrace her as she had in the medical bay earlier that morning. Before she had been introduced to Shona.

But, even as she continued to read, her thoughts drifted slowly back towards their killer — or killers — and soon enough she began systematically rebuilding her original profile. Pulling it apart and relaying it, brick by brick.

What did they know for certain?

Twenty-three engineers had been trapped in a section of the ship that was then depleted of oxygen. All had died of anoxic asphyxiation. And Gary Blakely had been tortured for the information on how this might be achieved, as well as his knowledge and ability to temporarily disable the ship.

Once he had outlived his usefulness he too had then been killed.

Stacey Atkins and Fiona Jenkins were the only individual female victims. And there was certainly an undeniably sexual aspect to their murders or at least to the presentation of their bodies after death. From the stripping and the changing of the women to the oddly religious evocation and manner in which they had each been displayed.

There was clearly something about them physically that intrigued their killer, a physicality that he seemed to crave with them, which wasn't present in the murders of individual males including Blakely, Merko Solich and Dr Cunningham.

There was a clear pattern of necessity vs. enjoyment; of experimentation and exhibition vs. cold, meticulous killing as a means to an end.

It didn't make sense.

Unless there *were* two killers working together. But even Christine had to admit that she had her doubts.

Statistically, the likelihood of there being more than one killer present in such a contained and isolated situation was virtually none existent.

She knew that a pair of murderers working together would nearly always display a dominant/submissive relationship. But she was also certain that the nature of their confinement onboard a vessel like this would drive the submissive partner further and further from wanting to engage. The fear of being caught, of nowhere to run and nowhere to hide, would simply be too much for them.

That, in turn, would drive a wedge between the pair almost immediately and the partnership would have already broken down.

And yet there *were* two distinct methods — two distinct personalities — at work here.

Christine looked up from her journal, staring into the nothingness before her.

Then, as though a long, fluorescent tube-light had just been switched on inside her brain, her brown eyes sparkled. She began scribbling furiously, before the raw power of the realisation left her. Like a dream.

She needed to speak to Prior.

Not quite knowing where she should start in trying to locate the handsome Security Chief, but knowing — for certain — that she did not want to return to the many dark and winding corridors that made up the network of lower decks of the ship, Christine made her way towards the security office.

She was hoping to find the ever-cheerful Marc Davies lurking about somewhere nearby, or even Collins or one of the other junior officers; anyone who might then point her in the direction of Jonathan Prior.

It seemed, however, that luck was not on her side and she sucked in a breath, mentally preparing herself; resolving herself to the fact that she might yet have to face the dark and dismal depths of the lightless, winding passageways after all.

As she turned back onto the main corridor, Christine was almost bowled over by a short, fuzzy blur that she soon recognised as Adrian Kemp. Coming up just short of knocking her over, he held on to her for a moment, speaking in a hurried succession of breathless apologies.

'Are you alright?' she asked.

'Yes.' he said, nodding emphatically and finally releasing his grip on her arms. 'I'm on my way to the remembrance thing ... the ceremony.'

'What ceremony?'

He seemed unable to stand still, hopping from one foot to the other until Christine finally turned herself in the same direction as the man and they began making their way along the corridor. She struggled, but eventually fell in step with the hyperactive medic, huffing and puffing a little as they went.

'Captain Andrews has invited all free crew — and anyone else who wishes to attend — to remember all those we've lost on this hell trip.' he said, 'The total shutdown procedure took out all remaining power. Even the emergency power. Hence there being no-lighting in here now.'

Christine nodded.

'It's taken out the freezers where we were storing ... the bodies ...' He stopped. Physically and completely; staring into the ever-darkening corridor ahead of them. 'Captain Andrews was going to commit their bodies to the sea.'

Christine felt herself gasp, though Kemp didn't seem to notice.

'Prior was furious. And he told the Captain so.' Kemp said, absently rubbing his eye with the back of his hand in a very childlike fashion. Christine could just imagine the scene. 'Everyone was shouting and lots more of the crew objected ... but, Captain Andrews, he's just trying to do what he thinks is best ...'

'It can be difficult being the one in charge sometimes.'

Kemp nodded distantly.

Then they were on the move again.

'Someone suggested packing them with ice, you know, like those long-haul fishermen do. But those boats have massive machines churning out ice all the time and Andrews was worried that we wouldn't have enough to make a difference. But Prior said we should try and everyone agreed.'

'And is that what you've been doing? Fetching ice and packing the freezer?'

The wild-eyed hobbit nodded, solemnly.

'Why do you volunteer for these things?' Christine asked, a small grin on her lips.

For a brief moment Kemp looked hurt and confused; stopping, just as they emerged on the lower open deck and turning to face her.

'I just want to be helpful.' he said, 'I like to hear that I've done a good job; I like to see people smile when they see me. I like the way it feels to think that they know they can trust me and count on me. My father never trusted me to get anything done on my own. He was always checking up on me. Phoning to remind me of *my own* schedule! It was so annoying and used to drive me mad!' He looked up at Christine, 'But, now that he's gone ... I really miss it.'

Christine nodded, understanding completely.

Janet had had her own fair share of annoying habits and unfounded insecurities that would drive Christine round the bend at times. But now — she thought — she would give anything to mockingly scold her sister for arriving late — as she always did to every occasion — just one last time.

'Everyone's up here.' Kemp said, leading her over to the metal steps of the upper deck.

Quite a crowd had already gathered and as she scanned across them, searching for Prior, she began to pick out the faces of those crew members she had briefed so many hours earlier.

She sighed, still searching, before she felt a small, soft hand slip into her own.

It was Shona.

The dancer flashed a brief, sad smile at her, releasing her hand once more and nodding her head for her to follow. 'We're over here.' she whispered.

Christine followed Shona, glancing back to find that Adrian Kemp had already merged into the crowd; mingling silently with his friends and colleagues. She couldn't help but feel for the emotional young nurse, whose face was already slick with tears.

Poor lad.

As they approached the spot that Prior and Davies were currently holding, each of the men took a step to the side, allowing enough room for both Christine and Shona to stand snugly in between them; unconsciously protecting them and buffering them from the world.

In the distance someone began to sing.

It was a soft, sad song that Christine recognised as being from some musical or another. She looked up at Prior, who was staring — bleary-eyed — straight ahead, trying his best not to blink.

Trying desperately not to push out those tears already pooling in his bottle-green eyes.

Feeling, rather and thinking, Christine reached out, taking hold of his large, rough hand, much as Shona had taken hold of hers only minutes earlier. She squeezed it briefly then let go. But instead of releasing her as she had expected, Prior responded by holding on to her. Apparently comfortable with their new-found closeness.

Needing her to remain close to him.

And so they stood. Hand in hand, silently, amongst the crowd.

Listening.

Remembering.

Breathing in the salty sea air and drifting in the evening light under an already starring sky. Breathing. And living.

And bidding a final farewell to all of those — to every single person — they had each loved and lost in their own lives.

19:17

Sunday 15th May, 2011

Left alone in the dark, he had been contemplating the 'who' and the 'how' of his final kill for some time. He knew — instinctively — that this one *would* be the final kill on board this ship.

Perhaps even the last in his short-lived, but no less illustrious career.

There would, undoubtedly, be some small casualties along the last leg of this little journey. Those that would die simply for their being in the wrong place at the wrong time; and those that would die for foolishly trying to stop him.

He had contemplated the options available to him in the form of those he had been watching most recently and, though she was not connected to his brother in any way, he had come to the conclusion that it was the artist, Kelly Livingstone, who should feature in his final masterpiece.

She was, after all, the one who had inspired him in the first place.

It was she who had unknowingly set him on this strange and artistic path of self-discovery; she who had created such vibrant and haunting works that had reached out and connected with that subtle part of him that was hidden from Vince and Matty and all of those uncultured, crony meatheads in their service.

It was she that had come to mean the most to him. The only living person he now felt any kind of a connection to. Though, she was entirely unaware.

And so it was to be Kelly Livingstone who would be the ultimate sacrifice in memory of his brother. In honour of him. Dedicated to him.

And the bastard better fucking appreciate it!

He felt a pang of unknown terror and something like a great sadness settle on him as he made his final decision and prepared to leap from the shadows one last time.

19:17

Sunday 15th May, 2011

'Thank you.' Prior said, finally releasing his gentle grip on Christine's small hand.

She smiled at him, then watched as Shona intertwined her arm with Davies' and the pair moved through the crowd, looking like a Hollywood couple. Prior followed her gaze.

'She's so comfortable with herself.' Christine said, 'And she projects this massive confidence, even though she doesn't possess it.'

'What do you mean?'

'I had the opportunity of actually spending some time with Shona earlier. I got to speak to her properly for the first time.'

'She's an alright kid.'

'Aye. It'd have been so much easier to simply ... dislike her.'

'Well,' Prior said, with an amused smile, 'Unfortunately for you, that's one of Shona's best natural defences. She's good; she's kind and friendly and she'd do anything for anyone ...'

'I get it! I get it!' Christine said, holding up her hands in mock surrender, 'And, anyway, she's no kid. Though, I hadn't realised she was your step-sister.'

'Who told you?'

'Why? Is it a secret or something?'

'No.' he said simply.

'It was Marc. Though you could have said something yourself, you know.'

'You got the wrong end of the stick?'

'I don't even think I had hold of the *right* stick, never mind which end.'

Prior chuckled and she slapped him lightly on the arm. She shook her head and, with her eyes, made another quick sweep of the deck.

It had emptied considerably.

Shona and Davies would now — she knew, without the need for any kind of confirmation — be making their way by torchlight towards the medical bay. Towards Kelly.

Her heart seemed to skip briefly, then sink once more at thought of the azure-eyed artist with the raven black hair. At the mere soundless mention of her name.

She shook off the feeling and looked back up at Prior, who was now staring out across an ever-darkening ocean; the inky black water reflecting the handful of pinprick stars above.

'How about a coffee?' she said, feeling a shiver of cold despite the warmth of the evening.

'The power's off.' Prior said, without emotion, 'I think the last round of hot drinks would have been downed sometime ago.'

She nodded, feeling a little foolish. *Of course the power was off . . . That was the point of all this!*

'I wouldn't say no to a pint though.'

'In that case,' Christine beamed, 'the first round's on me.'

'We're having more than one round?' Prior asked with a cheeky, boyish grin.

'I bloody well hope so!'

19:36

Sunday 15th May, 2011

Agitated at having to now work by torchlight, Dr Matthews finished up her reports on last the two bodies to be stowed in the mortuary freezers. They were no longer powered, but — she deducted — should remain cool enough to keep the cadavers from degrading too badly before the power came back online. Before they could finally get back on track and pass out of the other side of this hellish nightmare for good.

She had taken the precaution of bagging each of the bodies, which would lessen the chances of any possible cross-contamination that might potentially occur during the forced defrosting of the chillers. Although, if her standards had been maintained correctly, there should have been absolutely no risk of contamination at all; as the inside of both freezer cabinets and their trays should have been immaculately clean and germ free.

But you could never be too cautious.

The autopsy and blood enzyme tests of Fiona Jenkins had been both interesting and informative in their revelations. An abnormal level of creatinine phosphokinase in the blood samples indicated that the woman had suffered a myocardial infarction that had led to a massive cardiac arrest only moments before death.

This, taken with the other physical evidence, including the lack of ATP in her muscles — along with what Dr Matthews had heard rumoured about the *accessories* littering that particular crime scene — had aided in the forming of her conclusion that the woman's final moments of life had been a rollercoaster ride between the sublime physical ecstasy of orgasmic delight and the mortal panic, pain and suffering of the heart attack that had then suddenly killed her.

But still, if this was the case, it meant that the cause of Mrs Jenkins' death had — despite the odd set-up of the scene and the placement of her cooling cadaver — in fact, been natural.

Yes, natural. She had suffered a heart attack.

Or rather, she had ridden the great wave of a heart attack during the final climatic moments of a gargantuan orgasm. Which, she had then paid for with her life.

Had Merko Solich not been so brutally murdered in such close proximity to her and, had she not also been discovered propped up in the manner in which she had been (which was hardly a 'natural' death-pose) Fiona Jenkins might never have even been connected to the other homicides.

Dr Matthews signed the bottom of the reports, slipped them into the relevant folders and tucked them under her arm, holding a small torch to guide her as she crossed the darkened room to file them in the tall, metal cabinet. It seemed to make an unnecessarily eerie noise in the lightless room and she found herself suddenly thankful that she was no longer alone.

She had relieved her staff earlier, sending them instead to the various medical posts dotted about the upper levels of the ship, but had soon come to feel the weight of lonesome regret in that decision. She had felt isolated and spooked no matter how many times she reprimanded herself for reacting so foolishly; so childishly.

But several minutes earlier, Shona Jacobs had strolled through the large, swinging doors, her arm snaking through that of security officer Marc Davies'. Dr Matthews had sighed audibly and with great exaggeration, though secretly she had been glad to welcome in the pair, who were at least living and conscious company for her.

They now sat at the bedside of the still-insentient Kelly Livingstone and Matthews watched them, irritated by their every movement.

Their every sound.

She had little time or patience for people like Shona. Or Davies.

But particularly Shona; being the bouncy, happy, chatty, pointlessly optimistic, boasting, bragging bundle of boundless energy that she was. It seemed that the girl suffered an incurable disease shared by those in the performing arts professions. Though, in Dr Matthews' opinion, the real acute form of this particularly annoying personality type definitely seemed to reside within those flighty creatures that were inevitably drawn to *dance* as a profession.

Oh, they were like lepers to her.

But, at least she was no longer alone in the dark with an ineffective freezer full of slightly chilled cadavers, furniture that had suddenly decided to mimic the sound-track to a horror movie featuring her as the disinclined victim and a freshly stitched and tended-to gothic-looking lesbian who seemed intent on carving a new career out of winding up bleeding and unconscious in her medical bay.

More than anything, Dr Matthews just wanted to get back to her room and relax. She desperately needed to rest and had already begun secretly planning a long vacation following the resolution of this whole manic and ridiculous debacle!

Passing by Shona and Davies, she rolled her eyes as Shona giggled yet again and squeezed Davies' arm. Oh, every tiny movement and sound that woman made grated on the last of her dwindling and weary nerves.

She pushed out another long and heavy sigh, hoping it would highlight her annoyance and her lack of patience with the pair. Hoping they might take the hint and shut the hell up.

But they didn't seem to notice.

Retaking her seat noisily and, folding her arms across the metal surface in front of her, Matthews lay her head down, listening as the security boy-wonder and Captain dance-pants continued to talk drivel in gratuitously cheery tones.

'Yeah ... so, I don't know but, I'm pretty sure she thought that you guys had been together at some point.' Davies chuckled, 'She certainly didn't have you down as being Prior's baby sister!'

Shona giggled. Again. 'Then again, me and Jon ... being related. If I was outside, looking in, I don't think I'd make that connection myself unless someone pointed it out.'

'But, at least you would have had the sense to ask, instead of just ... presuming stuff and getting all het up about it.'

'Yeah, but just coming straight out with it?' Shona said, shaking her head, 'Asking for the answer to a question like that is like asking for assistance to a woman like Christine. And I really don't think she's comfortable with asking for help at the best of times!'

'You're right there, kid.'

The pair laughed again and Dr Matthews found herself pressing her thumbs into her the lids of eyes as she began to drift in and out of sleepy consciousness, still aware of their ever-flowing and gossipy conversation.

It seemed to hop from one subject to the next without limit or closure as they speculated and commented on anything and everything. Nothing was safe or sacred or out of bounds for these two.

Didn't they ever tire? Would they ever shut up?

19:38

Sunday 15th May, 2011

Prior. Jon … Jonathan Prior.

DI Prior.

The man with the green eyes. Of course! That was his name.

How could he *not* have realised?

That's why he looked so familiar.

Oh, this was brilliant!

And to think he had come here in search of the artist; to take her life and give it to his brother. To create an everlasting image.

Though he knew it would pain him to take her life, he was more than prepared to do it. To do it, then shed a silent tear after. As he had with Nona.

And all for his brother.

To honour his brother with a meaningful sacrifice that would speak volumes; that would scream and fucking bellow their names in such an obvious way that people couldn't help but stop and stare. And remember.

And remember … forever and ever. Amen.

Kelly Livingstone was — after all — a celebrity of the art world. Talk about high-profile.

Despite himself, he had actually come to admire her.

In his own way.

He certainly admired her talent and her 'fuck-you' attitude to the world that was so clearly present in all her work. And he knew it would be a shame to put an end to that. To put a lid on that talent and nail it shut with such a shocking and brutal finality.

But, then again, had he not learned all that he could from her? What else did she have left to offer? To him and all the world.

He had grown so rapidly as an artiste, gone from a single-celled organism to a fucking Goliath of creativity in such a short space of time. He had generated works on board this ship that — quite simply — made the work of Kelly Livingstone seem dated, stifled and obsolete. He had quite simply eclipsed her; transcended the spectrum of her natural talent and ability.

She had been his unknowing master; he the careful padawan. If he didn't take the reins soon he would remain forever in the shadows.

Of Kelly Livingstone. And of Matty.

No.

What he had planned was sure to make waves, both in the whorish, media-driven *real* world and that of the creative looking-glass.

But, then again .... Kelly fucking Livingstone. He stopped. Considered. What was she to Matty?

Nothing.

And so it would mean nothing. It would be yet another empty sacrifice.

Another empty promise.

That simply would not do.

But the revelation of the green-eyed man's true identity; that juicy, little morsel of information was too sweet to be ignored. An absolute treat of a tit-bit that had been dropped into his lap. Dangled on a string and so easily within his grasp.

He could do so much more with this.

Jonathan Prior.

The memories flooded back in a vivid torrent of fresh and violent truth, as though Matty was standing there now, screaming at him; *Look, I've given you this on a plate . . . because you were too fucking dumb to work it out for yourself.*

For a moment he felt a tremor of shame and of anger. Nothing he did was ever quite good enough. And for those brief seconds he felt an absolute burning resentment towards the brother who still appeared to be organising his life, even from beyond the grave!

But then, Matty did seem to have a point.

This would be much more appropriate in the sense of an avenging sacrifice. And yet, he had planned everything so carefully now ...

Why not do both? Get creative. You were always good at that.

'Could I do both?' he whispered, questioning the voice that was his brother's.

Of course you could.

In the dark, he smiled, 'Thanks, Matty.'

20:39

Sunday 15th May, 2011

Christine pulled the soft cashmere cardigan over her arms as she stepped out through the double glass doors and made her way steadily back to the balcony.

Already sat at the patio table, Prior swirled a large glass of merlot in his right hand as he stared out across the sinister-looking unknown of the ocean.

'Penny for your thoughts.' Christine said as she returned to the chair next to him.

They had previously visited one of the largest of the upper level function rooms, along with several of the smaller ones, but had found each one to be ridiculously over-crowded and already struggling to accommodate the demands of the hundreds of card-bearing punters who now had nowhere better to go. And nothing to do, but drink.

Prior had shaken his head in irritation, 'This isn't going to end well.'

Christine had reminded him that it was no longer his problem.

At least not for this evening.

Catching up with the pair as they had made their way inside after the remembrance service, Captain Andrews had ordered Prior to take the night off and — as Christine had expected — the ex-DI had immediately objected.

But Andrews had been insistent.

At first Prior had been too annoyed to see what Christine had spied so easily; that Andrews was trying to make amends and to ease his own sense of guilt.

He was giving Prior the opportunity to mourn the loss of his friends and his lover.

Christine had finally been forced to reveal this notion to Prior, to spell it out for him as he had grumbled and complained his way through ship in frustration. Eventually, he had let the subject drop as they had entered the restaurant/bar and now general holding room-come-shelter that she remembered and recognised as the beautifully decorated *Grande Central Dining Hall*.

The tables had been cleared to provide more space, but the sheer volume of bodies — not to mention the noise that had also flooded the place — had been so overwhelming that it was not too long before Christine found herself suggesting her own suite as an alternative; listing its qualities in succession.

It was located — as they both well knew — within the upper levels of the ship and had a balcony. This meant that they would have access to plenty of fresh, unfiltered sea air and so wouldn't be going against Andrews' embargo preventing lower deck passengers and crew from returning to their rooms.

The fear of carbon monoxide poisoning had become suddenly very real to those who knew the true nature concerning the demise of the ill-fated engineering staff.

Prior had needed little convincing and on their way to Christine's suite he had called into one of the smaller function rooms, made his way behind the bar and lightened it of two deep-red coloured bottles of wine; bringing their personal stock to a now uneven three.

Under different circumstances this may have bothered Christine, but not tonight.

Odd. Even. It would all be drunk the same!

Prior had just opened the second bottle and had been refilling their glasses when Christine had left to find her cardigan.

He stared at her now as she sat opposite him.

She waited and lifted the glass to her lips.

'Sorry.' he said, 'Did you say something?'

She smiled, softly, 'I said penny for your thoughts.'

He nodded slowly and gave the only reply he could muster. 'Rachel.'

They sat in silence for several minutes, listening to the lap of the water as it batted against the sides of the ship, bobbing them about on this seemingly endless ocean.

Christine had all but forgotten that he was there besides her as she closed her eyes, allowing the soft motion to rock her and lure her into a relaxing state of being. She was drifting so far into her own thoughts that she was caught completely off-guard and jumped with surprise when she suddenly heard his soft, but gravelling voice intoning the words of a song she thought she knew:

> 'I've never been here before,
> Didn't know where to go,
> Never met you before ....'

'*The Stereophonics.*' he said, seeming to only just realise that he had, in fact, uttered the melodic words out loud, 'She loved them. They are a decent band, to be fair. I liked them myself, before ... though, I think I've heard more of Kelly Jones' voice in the past few months than I ever did when they were first out!'

'The things you do for love, eh?'

'I saw them play once, you know.' he said, nodding, his eyes clouded with memories, 'And it was quite an intimate, little gig too. I used to tease Rachel about it 'cause she'd never gotten round to seeing them play live. It was on her 'to do' list.' He brought the wine glass to his lips and drank a great gulp. He paused. And did the same again, replacing the near-empty glass — with a resonant *chink* — onto the table, 'I'd bought tickets for the O2 gig. December. We were both due some leave and ... I'd planned the whole weekend.'

'I'm sorry, Jon.'

'Me too.'

They sat in silence once more, listening to the waves. This time, Christine did not relax back into her chair. She did not close her eyes.

Instead she sat and watched him for a long time, wishing she could hear his thoughts, desperately wanting to draw him into speaking the words that weighed so heavy on his mind. Knowing that he would be silently blaming himself, retracing his steps; wishing he could change the awful way in which things had been played out. Wishing he could step back in time and pull Rachel free of harm's way.

'I know it doesn't help,' she said, 'Believe me, I do. But there truly is no way that you ever could have known. If you had had the slightest inkling of an idea that something like this was going to happen, you'd have never let her out of your sight. But you can't know. You couldn't know. You would never even imagine something like this happening. How could you?'

Prior nodded slowly, bringing his hands up to cover his face. Seeming to finally accept this as a kind of truth.

A harsh and unwanted truth; but, a truth none-the-less.

'I'm just so ... angry.' he whispered.

'I understand.'

'I'd give all I have and more to trade places with her.'

'I know.'

'I can't stand this ... this feeling of complete and utter ... helplessness. Of being unable to do anything.'

'But you can do something.' Christine said.

'But it's not going to bring her back, is it?'

Prior pushed out a long breath as he wiped his glistening face.

He shook his head absently, the tangle of self-blaming thoughts still clearly weaving their web around his weary mind. He took up the wine glass and downed the contents, returning it to the table before crossing the balcony to lean his arms against the rail, staring — as before — out across the vast and open ocean. He seemed to be avoiding Christine's eye.

He was ashamed.

'We can catch whoever's responsible. We can make sure they pay for what they've done.'

Prior shook his head, though not in answer to her statement. Christine could see that he was trapped, battling against himself; the personal vs. the professional; the grieving lover vs. the rational detective.

'I feel lost, Christine. It's got me questioning everything.'

'I know.' she said, manoeuvring herself to stand beside him. She reached out, placing her hand on his arm. 'And you won't feel any better until it's been put to bed once and for all. You know I'm right. And you know that we can bring this person to some sort of justice.'

He nodded. Slowly. But this time it was a sure nod of agreement.

'Then you can mourn her. Properly.'

He turned to face her, his emerald eyes still shining with the rawest of emotions. 'So, where do we begin?'

Christine let out a slow breath.

For a brief moment she had been convinced that he would refuse. That he would simply want to continue drinking until his brain was numb and the pain had stopped. Even for a little while. But he was suddenly quite focused.

Appearing sober, even.

Like he had been slapped in the face, dunked in cold water and left out in the snow kind of sober.

The change in him was physical and instantaneous.

Christine smiled, thinking, *You're so much stronger than I was.*

She coughed and collected her thoughts. 'When we were talking earlier, you mentioned some criminal family that had helped you — in your mind — to connect the Copina's to these murders somehow.'

'Yes,' Prior said, his voice low, his sorrow still clear, 'but, I don't think there's any real connection there. It just jogged my memory that's all. I mean, yeah, Mike Jones worked for the Copina's on and off, Stacey was marrying into the family, apparently her fidelity was going to be tested, but ...'

'Do you think it *was* tested in the end?'

'Someone else on board, also working for Michael Copina?'

Christine shrugged, 'It's possible.'

'But it's also highly unlikely. And the way in which she was killed and displayed was so brutal. No, I think that was definitely personal.'

'I agree.' Christine said, finishing the wine in her glass as she thought, 'You said it was the murders themselves that had jogged your memory concerning the name Copina. What did you mean by that?'

'The ligature marks around the neck. The violence ... the sexual aspects and the brutality, they reminded of the case I was working on in ninety-nine. Vincent Keating and the Simmons brothers had a hand in almost every case that landed on our desk back then.'

'Brothers?'

'Yeah. Jacob Matthew Simmons. He was the elder brother and in charge of running the *family estate*. With some help from Keating.'

'And the younger brother?'

'Isaac, I think. Isaac Simmons.'

'Biblical.'

'Indeed.' Prior said, his eyebrow arching.

'And was Mrs Simmons proud of the men her boys became? Was she even aware?'

'Oh, Jacob could do no wrong in her eyes. But, Isaac ... he was the one leading her *good boy* astray. How she came to that conclusion, I have no idea. It seems like the poor lad lived his life in the shadows of his elder brother and Keating. He wanted to be just like them. And they exploited the fact.'

'Sounds like you tried to help him.'

Prior nodded. 'I tried.'

Christine waited. She watched Prior shifting his weight from foot to foot, watched his grip tighten on the rail and relax once more. He sighed and shook his head.

'What happened, Jon?'

He said nothing for a very long time, but, eventually — quietly — he began. 'We'd planned to arrest Jacob Simmons and Vincent Keating. Thought that maybe young Isaac could be talked into testifying or something. We thought ... I thought — foolishly — that we could save him. He was only a lad, you know? Young, vulnerable; absent father ... so, naturally, he idolised Jacob and Keating.

'Oh, but, he might have had a chance ... then, that morning ... that day ... it was a set up. It had to be. They knew we were coming and they had men to spare. Must have called in every toe-rag and scumbag that could use a weapon. We were like fish in a barrel to them.

'I spotted Keating and Simmons on the upper level. They had this junior officer, barely a cadet, this kid ... and he was sobbing ... begging them to stop ...'

'What did you do?'

'He wouldn't have survived his injuries ... so, I made it quick for him.'

'You shot him.'

Prior nodded.

'And what happened to Simmons?'

'He tried to run. And I shot him too.' he said, 'That's when I was injured. Pipe burst behind me; steam under pressure. I was knocked unconscious. Pinned to the floor. I didn't see what happened next, but I guessed that Keating took his body.' he paused a moment, trying to find the right combination of words, 'That was the day I made Isaac Simmons heir to the family business. I killed his brother. And so, Keating took him completely under his wing. He became his new project ... his new protégée'

'You were just doing your job.'

'It was messed up, Christine. But, I couldn't just let him go, could I?' he asked, searching her eyes, 'But then, maybe if I had ... things could have been so different. Isaac might not have ...' he shook his head, 'but, under the tuition of Keating he didn't stand a chance. If I hadn't have killed Jacob ... he might not ... they might not have taken the lives of so many ...'

The words failed him.

His lips continued to move, though no further sound materialised.

Christine brushed her soft palm against his bristled face. 'That's a lot of *ifs*, Jon. And a great burden to be carrying around in your heart all these years. It's not your fault. You can try and give a person all the guidance you think they need; try as hard as you can to save them. But, sometimes, they just don't want to be saved. Sometimes nature topples nurture. And there's nothing you can do to change a person's nature.'

'He was there.' he whispered, 'I didn't know it at the time. But he was there, Christine.'

'Who was there?'

'Isaac. He opened the fire-door. Jacob ran towards it ... I couldn't let him go. I shot him twice. In front of that young, lost boy ... I killed his brother ... right before his eyes, Christine. I helped to create him.'

'No.' Christine said, firmly, 'You didn't teach that boy to hate the world. You didn't teach him to steal or to launder, to hurt and kill and destroy people's lives.'

'But I did destroy his life.'

'You can't always be the hero.'

'I never wanted to be a fucking hero!' he growled, pulling away from her, 'I just wanted to do some good.'

Christine nodded, understanding completely. Their past situations — their personal burdens — they weren't so different when it came down to it.

'So what happened to Isaac? And Keating?'

'They disappeared.' he said, plainly, 'They just disappeared. They'd leave a bit of a trail every now and then. Enough for me to bite onto; enough to taunt me ... let me know just who was behind it. But nothing that would ever stick. They were slippery as hell, surfacing for a month or so here and there, before evaporating again ... into thin air.

'When I discovered the truth about Isaac witnessing the shooting ... I was so scared. Not for myself, but for my family. I had plain-clothed officers following them, watching them; checking they were safe. I think everyone just thought I was overly-obsessed, that I was losing it. And I think after a while, even I started to believe that too. But they went on following my orders. For so long.

'Then, one day, my Super called me in to the office and we had a long chat about my conduct, my *obsession* ... and my future on the team.'

Christine stared at Prior for some time. She didn't quite know what to say.

The precautions he had taken sounded perfectly rational to her. Perfectly reasonable. But saying that, she supposed it would depend on the number of officers he had devoted to the task and for how long. She could imagine Prior's faceless Superintendent discussing *man-power* and *resources* and *budgets* with him in a stuffy, little office somewhere in Liverpool. Weighing the unseen cash-sacks against the lives of those most loved and cared for by the then-DI Jonathan Prior.

Berating him for presuming to use their limited means in such a *selfish* fashion.

She shook her head absently, marvelling — and not for the first time — at how the understanding, friendly faces of concerned colleagues could swiftly turn to the cold, harsh judgemental stares of those trying to avoid a public flogging themselves.

'Is that why you never mentioned that Shona was your sister?' she asked.

He shrugged, 'Force of habit, I suppose. I didn't do to hurt you. Or confuse you.'

'I know.' she said.

Prior leaned in, planting an honest kiss on Christine's cheek, 'Thank you.'

Feeling herself flush ever so slightly, she nodded and smiled.

'So, do you still think this has something to do with Michael Copina?' he asked, changing gear ever so slightly with the tone of his voice. It wasn't so marked a change as to be moving from intimate conversation to strictly business alone, but the deeply personal vulnerability he had revealed in the last ten minutes disappeared on the instant.

Christine stared at him, trying to read him.

But he was locked once more.

'Well, I had been re-thinking our killer's profile.' she began, 'And I'd been going over everything you'd said about it seeming familiar, which is why I'd asked about . . . everything. I needed to know the connection you'd thought you'd seen.'

'Right.' said Prior, clearly wanting to steer away from returning down that road.

'Because it seemed to me that the conflicting styles of violence — not to mention the obvious differences in the treatment of the individual male victims to that of the individual female victims — could be one of several things. Either, our killer is trying to emulate someone or something — particularly when it comes to the women — '

'Like,' Prior said, cautiously, 'copying, in reality, the work that Kelly Livingstone has done in paint.'

'Right. Exactly. Our killer does appear to have a passion and a flair for the artistic and dramatic. And, breaking into Kelly's room, creating new pieces that imitate her style and the thematic basis of her work while she is there ... I mean, that's him acting out a fantasy in itself. The very fact that those paintings reveal the final moments of real murders adds an entirely new dimension to that. It's like he's saying 'Look, this is what I really am. An artist. Just like you'. I think he wanted someone to understand him. I think he chose someone who he thought *could* understand him.'

'Kelly?'

Christine nodded.

'What makes you say that?'

'Well the fact that he could have just killed her, but chose not to, for one.'

'No, but she hardly escaped untouched. Did she?'

'You're right. But then, she doesn't remember much — if anything — about that particular evening. I know that she'd ended up feeling rotten on the Friday; migraine, vomiting, general nausea, which couldn't have helped. She might even have been given something to make her feel that way.'

Prior's eyebrows arched. 'Poisoning?'

'I don't know. Maybe. Maybe not. Hopefully, there'll be something in the blood samples that Dr Matthews took for toxicology to pick up on. That is, if we manage to reach land before they degrade,' she paused, waiting for Prior to nod; to indicate that he was back on board with wherever she might take this. 'But, I do think she might have fought with him. We don't know the exact time line and — so far — she hasn't been able to confirm anything, but ... maybe, she returned to her room to find him already at work; maybe, he was hiding at first. Maybe, he arrived after her, I don't just know, but, I do think she probably had a good scrap with him — possibly gave as good as she got — I think that *that's* how she suffered her injuries. And, more importantly, *why* she suffered them. I don't think he was planning on carving her up like he did Stacey Atkins. It's odd, but he seems to ... respect her in some way.'

Prior looked uncertain.

'We know he had a knife. Right?

He nodded.

'Mike's knife,' she continued, 'which Blakely had been carrying around all this time. The knife that was discovered in Fiona Jenkins room.'

'Right. And?'

'Well, Kelly was stabbed and slashed with a knife. Why don't we have Dr Matthews check and compare her wound with the knife we now have? The knife that we know was used in at least one of the other crime scenes. I know you thought it was one of her own knives that might have been used, but none of them are missing and they certainly don't appear to show any traces of blood on them. I don't even think she's had them out of their case since she's been on board.'

Prior nodded, slowly. 'I suppose it does make sense to compare them.'

'Thank you.' Christine said, a hint of sarcasm striking like iron under a hammer in her voice, 'Glad you approve.'

'So, what else?' Prior said, unable to keep the small curling smile from his lips.

'My other thoughts actually concerned approval. Particularly the seeking of approval from someone you idolise. Someone like a father. Or a brother.'

'Is that why you asked about the Simmons'?

Christine nodded.

'You think it could be Isaac? Tracking me down?'

'I didn't know your history with them then, or that one of them was now dead,' Christine said, shaking her head. 'But yes, I did wonder whether it could be the Simmons Brothers. It was the connection to the Copina family and the realisation that one personality seemed to be desperately trying to please the other that made me think along those lines. It was nothing personal.'

'But now you know that Jacob Simmons is dead. And there's no way Keating would have gotten on board — no matter what alias he might have booked in under — I'd have spotted him for sure.'

'What about the younger brother. Isaac?'

Prior shook his head. 'No one's seen or heard from him properly for years now. As I said before, he and Keating were slippery, but it seems Isaac was even more so. There was even a rumour — at one point — that Keating might actually have killed him.'

'Why would he do that?'

'It turned out that Jacob Simmons had been siphoning from their collective stock. Shifting certain assets; valuables, money and even bonds to somewhere out of Keating's reach. He could have been looking to retire ... who knows. I can't say whether he told Isaac about it. Still, that wouldn't have stopped Keating from *digging* around if he thought the lad knew something.'

'That's some twisted kind of family loyalty.'

'Keating was a bastard when it came down to money.' said Prior, his eyes apologising for the momentary lapse in his language even as he continued. 'And if he felt he'd been double crossed by the elder Simmons, I doubt he'd have had any qualms about taking it out on the young'n.'

'So, what if Isaac Simmons had come on board to evade Keating?'

Prior thought for a long time. 'This is all very interesting, *theoretically*, but ... I don't know. This stretches way back, Christine. I mean, the last time Isaac Simmons was seen for sure ... God, it must be nearly ten years ago now. Wow! That makes me feel old. I don't know. Maybe there was more to the rumours than I was willing to give credit to at the time. Maybe I *was* too close; too blinded.'

As they stood in silence on the balcony, each of their addled brains working furiously to construct the next logical stepping stone on which to gain some footing, to seek out and to dust off the next crooked piece of this bloody and — seemingly senseless — jigsaw puzzle, they felt something.

It was something that disturbed the great silence they had finally adjusted to. Become accustomed to. Devoid of the hum of the engines and the whirring of the other processes and systems on the vast ship, the initial pressing silence, the eerie silence that had befallen them at that time, had become merely *the silence*.

But now it had been broken.

The *something* they had felt was the faintest of slow, humming rotations. A distant generator beginning whir.

It was the airflow system.

Prior looked at Christine, who regarded him with an equal expression of hope. They stood still. Neither one of them wished to burst the bubble of that moment; each waiting expectantly for the next chord in the sequence of this return-to-form, mechanical hallelujah.

Waiting for the lights and the engines to resonate the triumphant perfect cadence.

But it did not come.

'Well, at least the air's back on.' said Prior. 'It's a start.'

Christine agreed and opened her mouth to speak. But, at that moment, Prior's radio — which had been resting on the table besides his empty glass — bleeped loudly, catching them both off-guard.

Christine jumped slightly, but recovered her composure as she listened to the crisp, clear tones of Captain Andrews bouncing over the statically disrupted airwaves as he called for his Chief of Security. She closed her mouth and watched as Prior picked up the radio, acknowledging Andrews.

'We've managed to get some of the back-up power online again. These kids really are good!' he said.

By 'kids', Prior assumed he meant the group of young engineers and mechanics he had had working on the problem of trying to restart the ship.

'We heard the air-flow system kicking in. What about the emergency lighting?'

'Not yet.' said Andrews, 'I've had them diverting all the power they can so that we can restart the surveillance system. They're downloading the images it captured prior to everything shutting off as we speak. I thought we could try and put a face on our killer before he realises we're back in business.'

Prior seemed impressed, his lower lip jutting out as he nodded his silent praise. Christine felt the corner of her mouth flicker to a cheeky grin. Prior caught her and almost laughed, in spite himself.

'Excellent plan, sir.' he said.

'Thank you. The emergency lighting and P.A. systems should be up and running in about an hour or so, which should give us more than enough time to scroll through the images in and around engineering and the other ... sites.' he paused, but kept transmitting. Christine could hear each torn and tested breath. 'That should also give the air-flow system enough time to start circulating properly. I'll make an announcement in — say — an hour and a half, informing the passengers and crew that it's safe to return to their rooms.'

Prior couldn't help but think that most of them would be unconscious through drink by that time, but that was beside the point. 'Very good, sir.' he said.

'I know I told you to take the rest of the evening off, but . . .' Andrews' voice trailed off and the transmission ended.

'Would you like me to come and take a look at the footage?'

There was a pause. Then a transmission of sheer static, just long enough — Christine realised — to account for Andrews holding down the call button and nodding his head. Then, in a somewhat relieved and only slightly flustered voice, he aired a second message. 'Yes. If you wouldn't mind.'

Prior also nodded, but accompanied this with a verbal confirmation, adding the freely volunteered information that he had been drinking.

Andrews gave a small laugh on the other end, which seemed to say *Well, if that's all you've done, you're better man than me!*

'Good.' he said, 'You needed it. I doubt it'll effect your judgement too much. You're still the best I have.'

Prior seemed touched by this last statement and didn't know quite how to react and so remained silent for a moment. 'Thank you. Sir.' he said. Eventually. 'I'll be up as soon as I can.'

'Right.' said Andrews, 'That's all.'

And he was gone.

'Well,' he said, turning to Christine. 'That wasn't at all what I expected.'

'And what *did* you expect?'

'I don't really know.' he said, frowning, 'He's usually adding further problems to the mix. Never offering solutions.'

'You need to give that poor lad a break.'

'That *poor lad* is the Captain of this ship. The commanding officer of us all; in charge of the health and well-being of every person sailing under him.'

'And don't you think he knows that? Don't you think he feels it?'

'If I'm honest, I don't think he'd grasped the full gravity of it until this voyage.' he said, 'I think he liked to *play* at being Captain. Liked to lord it over all 'the little people'.'

Christine raised her eyebrow. 'Do you know what I think?'

'I'm sure you're going to tell me.' Prior said, grinning boyishly.

'I think you want to like him. I think you've wanted for him to succeed and become the Captain *you* know he can be, for a long time. I've noticed the hold you seem to have on the young men and women of this ship. They look up to you, Jon. Especially Jason Andrews. And I think you know that.' Christine placed a gentle hand on his arm, 'You're a very positive paternal figure, you know. Incorruptible, logical, hard-working. And I think that you too might just have some paternal feelings towards those you count as being part of your flock.'

'My flock?!'

'Yes, your flock. This ship. You might not be the Captain, but you are certainly the steady course they all strive to follow.'

Prior took in a deep breath, releasing it slowly through pursed lips as he eyed Christine. 'So, no pressure then.'

She laughed, 'Aye. No pressure at all.'

21:08

Sunday 15th May, 2011

Shona blinked, but could see nothing.

She struggled to move her arms. But they were bound and tied behind her.

She was sat on a chair. Tied. To an uncomfortable, wooden chair.

She tried to scream, but the terrified noise building in her throat didn't make it past her lips and, with a sudden and absolute horror, she realised the reason for this. A length of gaffer tape had been less-than-lovingly slapped across her jaws, clapping shut within the confines of her mouth a well-worn rag that bore the faint, but unmistakable duel tastes of oil and alcohol.

Even as a second wave of panic broke on her, Shona found herself seeking out the awful material with the tip of her tongue. It seemed to snag and catch on every individual cell that stretched across the surface of that fleshy muscle, sending a horrid shiver down her spine. She gagged and struggled to suppress the urge to vomit as the cloth brushed against the backs of her teeth, squeaking like cotton wool.

She could smell wood and metal and paint and chemical cleaning fluid. And, though she could see nothing in the pressing darkness, she felt as though she were being held in a very tightly confined space.

She heard a noise beyond the wall behind her; objects being moved. The catch of a door. A handle being turned. Then the door was being pulled open, though little further light entered the tiny box of a room.

She was aware of a figure standing in the doorway behind her. She felt the presence and tried to make a noise. She struggled and squirmed to try and spy a friendly face; someone who would help her. Tell her what was happening. Explain why she was there and rescue her.

It was no use.

She couldn't turn her head or twist her body far enough around to make a difference. Her eyes could make out only shadows moving against the darkness. And for the moment, all was still.

Rolling her shoulder, she leaned into the chair and twisted in one last effort to try and see just who had struggled their way in here to find her. The presence that was now simply standing there. Watching her.

She felt suddenly, violently sick.

They weren't here to help.

In the next moment, a blinding torrent of blue-white light scorched her eyes and she turned away instinctively, blinking over and over. Trying to rid herself of the bright, burning orbs imprinted on her vision.

She turned back to see the wall before her.

Now lit by the harsh torchlight, she could see that the wall had been cleared of all that had been there previous. She could make out screw holes and bracket-shaped patches where the atrocious pale green paint that covered the wall was a shade darker, but no less awful.

But what really caught her attention — and was, no doubt, the true reason for the torch being switched on and aimed in that direction — was a lengthy message of capital letters scrawled in red marker pen across the puke-mint wall.

She read silently over each of the devastating words and could not help but acknowledge the hopelessness of the situation. She found herself staring at her silhouetted self, her shadow, projected onto that awful green wall; a background for the red-penned words that prophesied her death.

She felt a tear slide down her face as she read last six words:

Nod your head if you understand.

She did so and the light went out. Immediately.

She listened as the door was locked once more and the objects stacked back in place, barricading the entrance. She had no idea where she was.

She sobbed and sobbed and eventually tried to scream; to shout.

To make any kind of noise.

She tried twisting free her bound ankles and wrists.

When it became clear that this was fruitless, she began to press her tongue against the rag inside her mouth, to move it around; manoeuvring and manipulating it until she could reach the corner of her lips. Then, again with her tongue, she worked the sticky gaffer; despising the taste and the sensation.

If she could only force a gap . . . there might be a chance. She might be heard.

She had to try.

She didn't want to die this way.

She didn't want to die.

Chapter Nine

21:20

Sunday 15th May, 2011

Prior was pleasantly surprised at how quickly the surveillance imaging system had downloaded the video and image files it had captured in the hours before the ship had been sabotaged.

He sighed as he thought about everything that had happened since then.

It all seemed a lifetime ago. Not some mere twenty-eight hours.

He was sat staring at a monitor filled with black and white images when Commander Roberts passed him a small thermos cap full of coffee.

'I have no milk, but it's strong and there's sugar in it.' he said.

'That'll do nicely.' Prior replied, holding the cup under his nose for a moment, feeling the heat near his lips before he drank. 'Thanks.'

Most of the power on the bridge was still out. There were two monitors and a couple of processors whirring softly in the background.

He sipped at the coffee, his eyes locked on the somewhat fuzzy images that tracked the day's events outside the medical bay. He felt a sudden shiver as he saw the then-living form of Dr Cunningham approaching the camera in a stream of static poses. The camera recording one image every two seconds.

Prior held his breath and watched as Cunningham drew closer, reaching for the camera.

He shook his head and cursed.

They had already drawn a blank on several of the medical bay cameras from the Friday evening and — though no one wanted to speak ill of the dead — it was the general consensus that Dr Cunningham might have had more than a little to do with it.

Now he had the unfortunate proof. The damning evidence.

'What is it?' Roberts asked.

'It *was* Cunningham.' Prior said, annoyed, 'He turned off the main camera in the medical bay. I don't doubt he was responsible for turning the others off too.'

'Dozy bastard.'

'Damn it!' Prior said, angrily, mentally exploring his other options, 'I'll try the images from the camera in the corridor. I remember someone saying they'd had to reset it on the Saturday morning. I didn't really think anything of it then. Just thought it was a technical fault; a loose connection, low battery. Something like that.'

Roberts shook his head. 'It still doesn't seem right, does it? Sabotage. Murder.'

'It's just not something you expect.'

Roberts remained silent, returning his attention to the screen before him, which, like Prior's, was scrolling slowly through countless two second images.

It was laborious.

It was slow, boring and was beginning to make his eyes ache. But as a task with the potential for positively revealing the identity of their killer, it could not be overlooked.

Prior watched Roberts for a moment and saw that he was currently checking on images from all of the cameras surrounding room fifteen-thirty-four. Stacey Atkins' room.

He swallowed the last mouthful of coffee and sat the cup down on a spare bit of surface amongst the control panel. As he did so, he made the decision to start scrubbing through the images on his monitor at a higher speed.

He was just working his way through the day, when Roberts made an irritated noise in the back of his throat, distracting him. He paused the playback.

'You ok?' he asked.

'Just annoyed. There's a few times we should have caught him on the camera here.' he said and paused while Prior moved from his seat to stand next to him, before he scrolled back over the images, allowing the Security Chief to take a look, 'but, every time he's just out of shot. We get a shoulder or the back of his head or an extreme long-shot that's so fuzzy it's no use at all. It's like he knew where every camera on this ship was located. Like he could sense them.'

Prior could understand his commander's frustration. He remembered the first time he had had to go over grainy CCTV footage, searching for one person in a sea of other people. Not knowing what he was looking for and being told over and over that he would simply know it when he found it.

It was — he had to admit — incredibly irritating.

He sighed and lowered his eyes for a moment.

He was lost in contemplation, in the memory of scouring through hours — days — of video surveillance tapes when a particular video was suddenly ejected from his well-watered recall memory, planting itself firmly within the cinema of his mind.

He recognised it even before it began to play. Remembered it well.

It had been taken from a club in Matthews Street. Liverpool.

He had sat studying that tape for hours at a time. Over and over and over again in the weeks that had followed.

Prior allowed himself a brief smile, noting how strange it was the way that things could suddenly pop into your head like that. Things you hadn't thought about in years. Jogged by the slightest sight or scent, touch or sound.

The video had contained some of the last known footage anyone had managed to capture of Isaac Simmons. Isaac ... Leigh ... Simmons.

That was it. Jacob Matthew. And Isaac Leigh.

It was yet another piece of the never-ending jigsaw puzzle that had been driving him to distraction ever since Christine had asked about the Simmons' brothers earlier. She had stirred the waters and now the memories were slowly beginning to resurface.

Scum always rises to the top.

How could he have forgotten something as paramount as the lad's full name?

Then again, he *had* tried so very hard to forget so many aspects of those cases; certainly after the day that his life had slowly begun to crumble. The day that he had lost so many friends and colleagues. When he had shot Jacob Matthew Simmons.

The day that Isaac Leigh had watched his brother die.

He shook his head, thinking for a moment. Trying desperately to recall ... had there been something in the news recently? It was on the edge of his memory. Again, just beyond his reach. The outer ring of a fast-fading orbit.

What was it that Christine had suggested? That Isaac Leigh may have come on board?

He supposed it could be possible. But not without him noticing.

Surely.

'Do we have the footage from the security checks?' he asked, suddenly.

Roberts nodded. 'We should do. Are you thinking of comparing these images with the check-in video? Because you could be sat there for quite a while, if you are.'

'I know. But I was thinking . . .' he paused for a moment, considering his words, 'Whoever is doing this . . . if they're a passenger then they *had* to check in. They had to have come through security on Friday morning and so they would have to be on that video.'

Prior didn't fancy explaining the 'Simmons theory' to Roberts. He felt slightly foolish in even contemplating the idea himself, and yet . . . there was definitely something there.

He felt it.

It had all sounded so far-fetched to him earlier, but somehow Christine had managed to plant a seed in his mind that had matured into a great vine that now snaked through his active thoughts and long-shelved memories, connecting them in a way that shouldn't have been possible.

And then again, in a way that he couldn't quite explain — for reasons he didn't quite understand — it actually made a crazy sort of sense.

Still, he was probably better off not mentioning it to Roberts just yet.

'When will the satellite system and the servers be back online?'

Roberts shrugged, adding, 'Captain Andrews is with the team now, but, I really have no idea.'

Prior nodded.

If he could get online, he might be able to access a few files that he had attached to several personal inboxes via a series of emails he had sent to himself before he had left the force. He knew that the CCTV footage from the Matthews Street club was amongst them.

It had been a risk to copy the confidential files to his personal email, he knew that. He had known it at the time, but there were certain cases that a detective simply couldn't walk away from. Cases that stayed with him.

That stuck to him like a piece of gum on the underside of his shoe.

And the Simmons' case had certainly stuck to Prior. Like a ball of cheap, sticky, pink, penny bubble-gum. The shit you could never get rid of!

If he was lucky there might be a decent shot of Isaac Leigh's face that he could print out and ask Davies to compare with the check-in footage, while he continued to scour through the remaining images of the countless other cameras that may or may not have captured something.

As the thought struck him, Prior picked up his radio and called Davies.

There was no response.

He tried again.

Still, no response.

He was about to try and call a third time, when he paused.

He was still watching over Roberts' shoulder as he finished scrolling through the images on one camera and began loading those from another, when something caught his eye.

The figure was moving away from them, down the corridor. The image was terrible, but for a moment, there was a flare on the camera.

Roberts noticed it too. 'What was that?' he asked.

Prior reached for the controls, replaying the brief succession of images and pressing pause as the flare began.

'It's something in his trouser pocket.' Roberts continued.

'It's the chain he uses.' Prior said, astounded, 'Christine was right. He doesn't wear it around his neck. It's . . . what did she call it? A totem. Something he draws power from; that gives him a sense of purpose and strength that he feels he lacks.' Prior paused, tilting his head and thinking for a moment, then — pointing to the screen — he continued, 'When he goes up the steps out of shot, just round that corner,' he said, 'let's say he goes up two levels . . . that'd bring him out by medical, wouldn't it?'

Roberts nodded. 'Yeah, if he went up that far. He might even have gone further. Up onto the open deck and off across the ship.'

'What's the time index on that camera?' he asked, checking for himself before moving back to his own screen. He began hurriedly scrolling through the images as he continued, 'Even if he did go out onto the deck, I think he'd have retraced his steps rather than drifting too far. He couldn't have been too certain of his way at this point. I mean this ship does take some getting used to.' Roberts gave a nod. 'And we know that not too long after that image was captured he ended up in engineering, which — it seems — is where he wanted to be. Now that's either a massive fluke or — '

'He checked it out on a map.'

'Yes, and ... if he did go up on deck he will have passed that great big coloured schematic thing near medical. Ah ha!' Prior laughed with delight as the figure from Roberts' screen stepped into view on his. Prior pointed as the stills rolled slowly on; step, by step, by step. 'We still don't have his face, but that's definitely him. Look at the chain.'

Suddenly, the killer was on the floor and in another flurry of images he seemed to be picking up a multitude of pages spilled from files and handing them to another man who struggled to organise them back into a manageable pile.

'Who is he, do you think?' Roberts asked.

'I don't know.' Prior said, pointing to the newcomer on the screen, 'but, I know who that is. We really need to speak to Marc Davies.'

With a sudden crack of static, Prior's radio came to life.

Both Prior and Roberts jumped, though neither one acknowledged the fact. Each hoping the other hadn't noticed.

'Prior? Are you there?' the soft, Scottish tones of a female voice left little margin for error in guessing the owner was.

'Christine.' Prior acknowledged, holding down the button on the side of the radio. 'What's wrong? You sound breathless.'

'Thank you.' she laughed, 'You know how to cheer a lady up. I heard you calling Davies and I was on my way down to medical, thought I'd check in with Shona and Dr Matthews. See how Kelly is doing.'

'Are you on your own?' Prior asked, his voice full of concern for her.

'I'm fine.' came the cheery reply, 'I have a radio, I have the torch that Marc leant me earlier and a great big stick that I'm sure I could manage to beat any would-be assassin with quite well, should the need arise.'

Prior grinned, despite himself. 'Well, just keep the channel open will you? At least until you're through doors and I know you're in Davies' safe and capable hands.'

'Oh, he'd love that!' Christine giggled, and Prior listened as she opened one door after another. 'I might tell just him, the poor lad'll ...'

Christine stopped.

The channel was still open. She had simply stopped speaking.

'Christine?' Prior said, though he knew she would not be able to hear him. 'Christine?'

'Jon ...' she said, her voice suddenly trembling, 'You need to get down here. Quickly.'

He was already heading out of the bridge, taking the steps three at a time when she released her hold on the call button.

'Christine, I'm on my way. What's wrong?' he asked, breaking into a measured sprint.

'They're ... Jon ... Marc's injured and Dr Matthews' too. I think ... I think she might be dead.'

'What?'

The news stopped him in his tracks for the briefest of moments, before he started back at full speed once more, turning this way and that through the vast darkness of the ship.

'What about Kelly and Shona?' he asked.

'I don't know.' Christine said, the worry in her voice as clear and metallic as the ring of a great iron bell, 'They're not here.'

21:20

Sunday 15th May, 2011

Marc Davies opened his eyes. His head was pounding.

His nostrils were flooded with the scent of bleach and he could feel the smooth, chilled surface of a linoleum floor pressing against his cheek.

He tried to push himself up, but was overcome with dizziness. He rolled himself onto his back as a devastating coldness washed over his body. And suddenly he was shaking. Dithering.

'Marc? Marc, are you ok?'

The voice was distant, but he recognised it and felt an instant sense of relief wash over him.

'Chris ...' he struggled, trying to sit up.

She pressed him gently back down to the floor, placing something soft under the back of his neck.

'Don't move just yet.' she said, 'Take your time. You've got a nasty head injury there.'

He could well believe her.

After a moment he brought his hand up the back of his head, feeling gingerly with the tips of his fingers for signs of the wound he had already guessed was there.

His vibrant shock of golden locks were now a tangled and matted mess of blood. Dismayed, he blew out a lungful of air between his cut and swollen lips.

Though he couldn't remember much, it was obvious that he had been hit from behind. He had then fallen, bursting his lips and cracking his forehead on the hard, but clearly sterile floor.

Well, at least it was clean.

'What happened?' he asked, dazed.

'I was hoping you might be able to tell me.' Christine replied with a soft, but concerned smile.

'What do you mean?' With a terrible knowing — a nagging, gnawing suspicion of a feeling — he became suddenly aware of just how quiet it was inside the room. 'Where is everyone?'

At that moment Prior burst through the doors, torch in hand, expectant horror written all over his face. He had clearly been running, though was physically fit enough to not be overwhelmed by the fact.

'Davies.' he said, joining Christine at his side. 'Marc. Are you alright?'

Davies instinctively tried to sit up. Prior too pushed him back down.

He nodded. Agreeing to stay put.

'You just rest a moment.' Prior said, as he checked him over visually. Once relatively satisfied, he climbed to his feet and began exploring the room.

Davies looked up at Christine, who stroked his head affectionately. Soothingly. 'Where are they?' he asked.

Christine shook her head. Her eyes looked sad and tired.

'They're not here.' Prior said, trying — without success — to keep the agitated concern from his voice, 'Shona and Kelly are missing.' He paused for a moment, scanning the dark room with his torch. Then he stopped once more. 'Dr Matthews is over here.'

Davies watched as Prior moved to the spot and knelt down to look at her, though he himself couldn't see Matthews from where he lay, 'Looks like whoever knocked you out employed the same methods on her. Only with a much more brutal force.' he said, before pausing to swallow, 'The whole left side of her face is gone.'

Prior coughed and stood up.

This time Davies rolled himself onto his stomach and pushed straight up onto his knees. He breathed through the pain and the desire to simply drop back down to the floor and, after another moment, eventually climbed to his feet. He extended his hand to Christine, who had been knelt all this time at his side, and braced awkwardly to take her slight weight as his shoulder too began to twinge and complain.

'That hurting as well?' she asked, placing her gentle hand on the jarred joint.

He nodded and stared at her as she took up the thing that had been a soft pillow for him only minutes earlier. After a moment he realised that it had, in fact, been Christine's own light-coloured cashmere cardigan and that it was now irreparably stained with his blood.

'Sorry about that.' he whispered, his voice rasping; his throat dry and sore.

Christine smiled at him with her warm, chocolate eyes and he handed her the white and gold cane that she had managed to hook with a practised talent onto the back of the chair next to where he had lay.

It was only then that he noticed, as he turned around, the trail of blood that Dalmatianed its way across the room like a horrific dot-to-dot puzzle on the floor. There was a small pool near to him; a much larger pool near Prior.

'Oh my God.' he whispered as he and Christine Kane struggled to help one another across the, eight long and tiring feet of the room that separated them from Prior.

And the body of Dr Matthews.

Eventually reaching their destination, Davies released Christine, who then struggled once again to bend and examine the body.

Dr Matthews' usually perfectly-placed and scraped-back blonde hair had been ragged around this way and that as she had been dragged across the room. She had clearly struggled.

'Looks like she was first hit in the side the head. And with some force.' Christine said, pointing as she spoke, 'It seems to have been a fairly blunt object, but look at the damage it's done to her eye and the area near her temple.'

Davies leaned in to get a better view of the horrendous quarter-inch thick gash in the upper right-hand quadrant of Dr Matthews' face. The blood vessels in her right eye had ruptured on a massive scale and he wouldn't have been at all surprised to discover that the eye socket itself had been fractured; spider-web fractures that cracked the way *Polos* did when you dropped a packet on the floor.

And yet, the right-hand side of her face was a picture compared to what remained of the left. Her cheek, skull, jaw … all had caved in under the tremendous force of being repeatedly slammed into the bleached linoleum floor. All that remained now was a gooey, chunky mass of stringy muscles, tissue, bone and brain matter.

Davies gagged, coughed and tried to keep the bile from rising in his throat.

He swallowed it down once, but it was no good. It returned a second time with a renewed force, scorching its way up his throat and leaving him little time to turn his body from the remains of Dr Matthews before throwing up the contents of his stomach across the slim metal table that stood at least a foot to the left of him.

The largely liquid vomit splashed over the table and onto the floor as Davies wiped his mouth, apologising.

Prior looked at him, concern stamped clearly across his solid face.

Davies gave a small nod. He was ok.

He watched as his commander and friend pointed to a small metal instruments tray, the edge of which was covered in blood.

'I think this was the initial weapon used on the pair of you.' he said, 'It'd be about as sharp as a blunted axe, that would. But, it'd do the trick.'

'Clearly, it did.' Davies said, reaching up again to feel the open wound at the back of his head. It felt consistent with the look of the tray.

Prior nodded and turned his attention back to the body of Dr Matthews.

'Anything else?'

'It's another left-handed kill.' Christine said, 'Look at the way her hair is bunched. I'd say he was facing her when he killed her, when he drove her face into the ground. Just as he was when he drove Stacey's face into the side of the bath.'

Prior gnawed at his lip for a moment. He seemed to be considering whether or not he should air whatever it was that was troubling him. Finally, he relented, pushing out a long, slow breath. 'Isaac Leigh was left handed.'

Christine looked up at him, surprise and intrigue dancing plainly in her soft brown eyes.

Davies too seemed to understand the weight of this revelation.

'Isaac Leigh ... Simmons?' she asked slowly.

Prior nodded.

'Hold on, Guv'. Simmons? As in *Blood is the Pride of Red Merseyside* Simmons? The brothers?' Prior shuddered at the remembrance of Jacob Simmons' coined slogan. He — like Prior himself — had professed to being a red, but not for a love of the sport; only for the potential violence that might erupt after any given match.

That was sure to occur if he could only help it along.

The green-eyed Security Chief nodded his reply, running his hand absently over his stubbling, black hair, feeling the pencil-thin scar with the tips of his fingers and thinking — suddenly — about how Davies would now bare a similar scar.

The Simmons' Legacy.

St Helens born Marc Davies had reached the age of six before navigating his way a little closer to the centre of the city of Liverpool. He had also worked there the majority of his adult life. The city was in his blood, he knew both its older and more recent history; the good and the bad.

What he didn't know was that Prior had been the lead investigative officer in the botched warehouse sting that had been so widely publicised in the weeks that had followed. Or that he had been responsible for killing Jacob Matthew Simmons in front of his younger brother.

'But, they're dead aren't they?' Davies asked, as though reading Prior's last thought, 'Well, I know that at least one of them is. The other one was on the run wasn't he?'

'Christine thinks he may have run on board.'

'It's not just me who's beginning to think that way though, is it?' the psychologist said, without irritation or reproach.

Prior sighed, 'I think … that it's possible he might be on board.'

Davies regarded Prior, then Christine, and then Prior once more. 'So,' he said after a moment, 'are you thinking that the younger Simmons brother could be behind all this?'

'Perhaps.'

'I'm sorry, you know I'm always the first to get behind you and support you and …'

'And I've always appreciated that, Marc.'

'But I don't understand. Why here? Why now? Why all this? And, anyway, didn't he have some, like, massively crippling fear of water?'

Prior's eyebrow flicked up for a moment. 'He did, didn't he?' he said, contemplating 'But still, there's an incredible amount of similarities between the crimes that have been committed on board over the last two days and those that were committed during the time that the Simmons' brothers were most brutally active. Too many similarities to overlook.'

He was about to speak again when both his own and Christine's radios suddenly crackled to life; squawking under a deafening barrage of feedback as she stood at his side.

Prior stepped back and pulled the two-way free from his belt, putting some distance between himself and Christine; thus separating the angry-sounding equipment.

Davies frowned.

'Where's mine?' he said, looking around and listening.

The radios crackled once more, slightly out of time and echoing one another as though it were some sound-wave game of tag.

Davies glanced from Christine to Prior and back again. Both looked bemused and he could imagine a similarly perplexed expression plastered across his own face.

After another moment they heard a strange scuffle, like a plaster being torn from flesh. It was coupled with a gasp and a stifled cry. And then more silence.

Prior held in the button on his radio. 'Who is this?' he said before releasing it once more.

To their surprise and to their horror the voice that cracked across the static airwaves belonged to Shona.

She was trying to suppress the sobs that came as she attempted to speak, but it seemed that the harder she tried, the more desperately upset she became.

'Jon ...' she struggled, her voice small and distorted as it echoed with a millisecond delay across the two radios. 'Please, listen to me. There's a message I'm to ... pass on to you. I'm to read what's been written here and say nothing else.'

'We're listening.' Prior said, not knowing whether she had heard him or not.

Davies could see the very real fear in his commander's green eyes along with the beads of sweat that had suddenly broken across his furrowed brow.

'He says he knows what you did.' she said. Prior closed his eyes, his heart sinking; this couldn't be true. It couldn't be happening. 'He knows it was you and, in turn, invites you to come and witness the death of your . . .' she paused, weeping; unable to disguise or contain her terror and her grief.

There followed the sound of a swift and powerful slap, after which Shona cried out briefly, but then, pulling herself together, continued to recite the sickening message, '. . . to witness the death of you own sibling.' Her voice gave way to more sobs as she struggled with the final instalment of the grim communiqué, 'You'll be given further instructions once the stage is set . . . once the colours are properly mixed . . . then, you will watch and I will die . . . and honour will finally be satisfied. The debts paid in full.'

The transmission ended. Cut off without even a departing hiss of static.

In the next moment each of the two remaining radios bleeped furiously; each of the little red lights flashing before, following suit once more — one and then two — they switched themselves off.

'The batteries have gone.' Davies said.

'I'll kill him!' Prior shouted, spinning on his heel. 'I'll kill the little bastard! I'll tear off his head! I'll — '

Davies caught him by the arms, forcing him to stop. 'Hold on Guv'! Hold on. You have no idea what this fella looks like, who he is or where he's holding her. I think we need to — '

'It's Isaac Simmons, Marc. It's him. Ok? I don't know how, but it's him. I killed his brother. And he saw me do it. And now he wants revenge.'

'What?'

'Come on.' Prior said.

'You killed Jacob Simmons?' he asked, in disbelief.

Prior nodded and, leaving the radios behind, Christine and Davies followed him out of the medical bay. As they turned onto the corridor the entire ship seemed to judder forward.

This was instantly followed by a loud whirring noise, a hiss and then more juddering.

Both Christine and Davies were clinging to the wall, having thrown their weight against it in an effort to remain upright, while Prior lowered his centre of gravity, bending at the knee, his arms spread, not unlike a surfer atop a boisterous wave.

He scanned the darkness eagerly with his torch.

Then, as though a great switch had simply been flicked back to the *on* position, the overhead lighting panels began to blink and flicker in a steady progression along the length of the corridor. After an epileptic moment of electrical confusion the panels turned to solid blocks of light, which then became an unfaltering *string* of bright lights coursing a route through the ship as though they had never been out at all.

Davies blinked and shielded his eyes as they adjusted to the new level of brightness.

In the distant portions of the ship they could hear spontaneous cheers as the power returned; light and sound combusting all around them.

Switching off and pocketing his torch, Prior continued along the corridor, Davies and Christine following close behind. When they reached the set of stairs near the security office Christine caught hold of Prior's arm.

He turned and waited as she tried to catch her breath.

'Jon, I'm going to go back to Kelly's room.' she said, entirely out of the blue, 'There's a few things I want to check.'

'Like what?' he asked, a harsh edge to his voice that even he had not expected.

'Like whether Simmons has been back there, for one.' she answered, not liking his suddenly cold tone. She could understand that he was worried about Shona. Worried *for* Shona. She was too. But she was also concerned for Kelly and felt suddenly annoyed at the fact that she seemed to be having to justify these feelings to the green-eyed Security Chief she thought she had come to know so well. 'Kelly's missing too.' she said, 'And Shona made no mention of her in that message. She might not even know that Kelly is missing. I can't say for sure, but the one thing I do know is that we should be searching for her too.'

Prior swallowed hard, he seemed momentarily lost for words, but eventually nodded. 'Of course. You're right. I suppose it does make sense to go back there and check. After all, he felt secure enough in that environment to stand there and paint his boastful collection of confessions for however long it took him the last time. And he did leave Kelly behind once before. I mean, he beat her, but he let her live.'

'But it's more than that.' she said, 'I think he might even view her room as — I don't know — some sort of sacred ground. A shrine. Or something like that. He did all that work there and left it, almost like a dedication. There's no doubt in my mind that he's obsessed with Kelly.'

Prior nodded, slowly, fearing the awful sight that may already be waiting to greet the psychologist in Kelly's suite. But seeming to read his thoughts yet again, Christine reached out, taking his hand for a moment. 'We know that Shona is alive.' she said, an incredible strength and sadness behind her eyes, 'You need to concentrate on that. And find her.'

'You never know, Kelly might even be able to lead us to Shona.' Davies offered, raising his eyebrows hopefully. Though, Prior remained unconvinced.

'I'm not happy about you going on your own.' he said, turning back to Christine.

'I'll be fine. The lights are back on; the power seems steady.' she said, slipping her hand into the pocket of her chocolate, linen pants. She pulled out her Motorola flip phone, flicking it open with her thumb and holding in the button that powered it up. After waiting only several moments, she turned the face of the phone to Prior, 'Look, I even have three bars of signal, which means everything must be back online. Doesn't it?'

'I suppose.' Prior said, taking his own sturdy-looking and purely functional, no-frills Nokia from his right knee pocket.

Davies watched his commander follow Christine's lead in switching on the ancient-looking mobile and regarding it for several moments. Then Prior gave Christine his number and she in turn rang his brick of a phone, confirming that communication between not only the phones and their networks, but also between the ship and the outside world had once more been established.

Prior flushed a little and smiled, storing the number.

Davies felt that he had just been witness to some private moment that he should never have known. He felt the sudden awkwardness of the situation like it had burst into the air from some strange, emotional room diffuser.

The scent of teenage days.

And — as odd as it seemed — watching the pair, he couldn't help but be reminded of himself only a few years earlier; awkwardly fumbling to exchange numbers with cute girls and guys alike. He radiated confidence these days — even if he didn't always feel it — and managed to stifle a grin as he noticed that Christine's cheeks were also burning their own small, self-conscious blaze.

'Well . . . just, make sure you . . . stay in touch and . . .' Prior's voice seemed to dissipate along the corridor as he took out his master cardkey, handing it to Christine.

She smiled sweetly at him. 'Don't worry about me.' she said, 'Go. Find that bastard. And save Shona.'

That said, she turned and made her way down the corridor as fast as she could without breaking into a three-legged, hobbled run. Prior watched her all the way to the end.

Davies watched his chief.

'Fucking Kelly bastard Livingstone.' Prior exhaled, shaking his head.

Davies raised a curious eyebrow, convinced that he must have misheard. That his tired and perplexed senses were now in fact working against him to confuse and distract him even further. However amusing it might have sounded!

'D'you not like Kelly then, Guv'?'

Prior shrugged and expelled another short, sharp breath as he unlocked the security office. 'I really don't know that I feel anything for that woman other than an overwhelming amount of irritation.'

'That's a bit harsh, isn't it?' Davies said, following him into the room.

'It is, yes. And it's not like me. Well, you know me.' he said, as he switched on the lights and several of the computers before taking a seat. Davies nodded and sat opposite him, 'But, I don't know. She ... gets my back up, you know? She did from the moment she came on board and ... I don't know. It's just one of those things I suppose. It's not very fair of me to think that way, is it? I mean, she could be in real danger.'

'She could be dead.'

'She could be dead.' Prior echoed, 'I really don't know what's wrong with me.'

'Guv', may I offer my opinion?' Davies said as Prior entered a series of passwords into the computers. 'I think you see her as a threat.'

'What?'

'I think you feel threatened by her and that's why ... well, that's why you don't like her. You can't help it. Like you said, she just instantly got your back up. Look, you know I wouldn't normally bring anything like this up — especially with everything that's happened recently — but, I can see there's something — you know — between you and Christine — '

'There is nothing going on between me and Dr Kane.'

'I didn't say there was anything going on. But there's definitely something there. It's actually quite difficult *not* to pick up on it. D'you know what I mean? And, I don't want to over-step here, or anything, but I also know that she's kind of unresolved on some feelings that she's harbouring for Kelly. So I get that you — '

'Wait,' Prior said, raising his hand, 'did she tell you about that?'

'No. I picked up on some things . . . and she kind of spoke to Shona about it earlier . . . who then told me when we were in the medical bay.'

Prior couldn't help but laugh. 'You're such a pair of old gossips, you two.'

Davies shrugged, grinning. 'But, you see, I understand why you feel odd and threatened. Kelly's this random, out-of-the-blue, larger than life personality that's moved right on in with the two women you're closest to. You want to protect Shona — of course you do — and you also want the time to figure out exactly what it is you want with Christine. Exactly what it is that you feel for her. But, either way, Kelly's not allowing you to have that time. And it's not her fault. But *you* feel it like it's a direct attack.'

Prior sat considering Davies' words for a long time.

Eventually, he raised an eyebrow and smiled. 'Well, you're just full of surprises today, aren't you?' he said, standing and reaching into an overhead cupboard. He pulled down a medium sized first-aid kit and glanced at Davies, who instantly tensed. 'Come on then, Yoda, I think we should patch you up a bit before you pass out. Then, we need to find out all we can about Isaac Leigh Simmons, find out where he's holding my sister and go get her back.'

'It's nice to hear you say that, Guv'.'

'What?'

'Sister.'

'It's nice to say it.' Prior said, twisting Davies' chair around so as to tend to his injured head more easily.

'She tries really hard to prove herself to you, you know.'

'I know.' Prior said, 'She doesn't have to do that.'

'But she wants to.'

Silence.

'I try too, you know.'

'I know, mate.' Davies said, 'I know you do.'

22:15

Sunday 15th May, 2011

Sliding the cardkey through the reader, Christine pushed open the door to Kelly's suite.

She immediately found a series of light switches near to the door and flicked them all to the 'on' position, bathing the room in a not-too-bright blanket of artificial light. She drew in a sudden breath, seeing the room properly for the first time since finding Kelly on the floor on that awful Saturday night.

Even then the room had been in darkness.

And it had been the dead of night when Prior had summoned her to view those horrific paintings.

Seeing the remains now, she could only begin to imagine what Kelly must have suffered in here and felt suddenly quite thankful that the artist appeared to remember nothing of what had happened. Though that in itself was another worry.

There was blood and paint on the bed sheets; and on several items of clothing — Kelly's clothes — that had been discarded next to the bed. A torn shirt. A pair of pants.

What the hell had happened here? And why hadn't any of this been collected as evidence?

Christine felt herself flush with anger. The suite looked as though it had been hired out by some teenage rock band for the purpose of housing a post-gig party that had gotten terribly out of hand.

The floor was littered with the empty bottles of various alcoholic miniatures; the fumes of which had had at least twenty-four hours to really fill the room with that poignant and sickening stench of stale drink. Punching through the stink of 'old pub' was the bitter odour of day-old tobacco and the heavy laced, sickly sweet scent of marijuana. So, between the dirty, bloody laundry, the weed, and the alcohol, the general aroma that was now filling the air of Kelly's once-pristine and luxury suite was one that could only be described as ... vagrant.

Eau de Homeless.

Carefully, Christine navigated her way towards the French doors that led out onto the balcony, trying not to let her mind wander as her eyes fell on the bloodied bed once more. Trying desperately to keep her imagination from merging the tortured fates of both Fiona Jenkins and Stacey Atkins with that of Kelly.

'Oh Kelly.' she whispered, unlocking the doors and hurling them open.

As she turned back into the room she noted the empty-shelled remains of at least four different types of painkiller blister packs strewn about the tattered suite.

'Is that why you don't remember anything?' she said aloud, to no one, but herself, 'Did he drug you?'

Still scanning the room, Christine noticed an A4-sized sketchbook sat on the long desk-dresser. She took several steps towards it, reaching her hand out to take a hold of the book.

She paused. Something had moved.

The door.

The door moved and she realised, with an ice cold shudder, that she hadn't actually shut it behind her!

How could she have been so stupid!

Instinctively she snatched up the hard-backed sketchbook, holding it close to her chest.

Somehow, she managed to release her grip on her walking stick — which fell to the ground with an oddly slowed-down and surreal clatter — and spin around in an uncharacteristically fluid motion, throwing all her power and all her weight into the sketch book; raising her arms high, before bringing the hard face of the pad crashing down against the head of the creeping assailant.

Eyes closed, she felt the book connect with bone and hoped that she had caught his nose.

In the next moment she heard crashing and smashing as an unbalanced body slammed into the desk, knocking Kelly's neatly ordered perfumes all over.

She heard an annoyed growl of pain and opened her eyes, raising the book once more. Ready to strike.

She paused; unable to believe her eyes. Unable to accept that what they were telling her was — in fact — the truth.

'Agh! Christine! What the fuck?'

Resting against the dark, desk-dresser — gripping a red cheek and rubbing a thick ear, like a chastised child — stood one very confused, battered, bruised and now freshly beaten Kelly Livingstone.

22:15

Sunday 15th May, 2011

Shona stirred. She was now aware of a cold, hard surface pressing against her cheek. Her arms were twisted and her shoulder ached from lying on it.

She was no longer attached to the chair.

The bastard must have knocked her out following her ominous broadcast. She couldn't even be certain that Prior had heard the message. That anyone had heard it. But she knew one thing for sure. She had definitely been moved.

She had been dragged from the chair in the cupboard to a new, much larger space, where she had then been thrown down onto the floor like some unwanted Christmas toy.

Though she was no longer attached to the chair, her hands and feet remained tied together behind her.

And as well as the gag, she had now also been blindfolded.

She had never felt more vulnerable in her life.

22:34

Sunday 15th May, 2011

Christine had apologised profusely since attacking Kelly with her own sketchbook.

What the hell had the sassy psychologist been doing in her room anyway?

Not that Kelly wasn't glad to see her.

Despite the immense, throbbing pain she was now experiencing in her face!

'I am so, so sorry.' she had said again, handing over a cold, damp towel before taking a seat next to her on the edge of the dishevelled and bedraggled-looking bed.

Kelly pressed the towel against her cheek as she looked around, taking in the state of the place. She wasn't in any kind of mood to even begin thinking about tidying through all this mess and was becoming increasingly more agitated by its presence the longer she sat there. The suite looked like it had housed one hell of a party while she had been away. And — bizarrely — the thought that she had missed out on something that had taken place in *her own* suite pissed her off even more!

She tasted blood and felt herself swoon for a moment.

Christine's arm jutted out instantly to steady her.

'It's ok. Honestly, I'm fine. Now.'

'Oh my god, I really didn't mean to hurt you, Kelly. I thought you were — '

'What are you doing here, Christine?' Kelly bit, cutting her off. As she spoke the pain in her face and her head peaked, flooding her voice with an agitation and annoyance that was not directed at Christine. Still, it sounded cold, almost to the point of cruel.

And she really hadn't meant it to.

The tone of question had resonated as little more than a barking interrogation and she instantly regretted her decision to interrupt the strong, yet fragile conundrum of a woman sat before her.

This intriguing and insightful woman with years of practical experience in exploring the human mind, yet whose gentle, understanding eyes hid a great sadness; this enigma with her very formal style of dress and her wicked sense of humour. Her tightly pulled-back and controlled soft brown hair that exploded into a fountain of incredible curls; rigid, proper, understated control bursting into something creative and wild!

She truly was a wonder of natural juxtaposition and, silently, Kelly berated herself for the thoughtless outburst, knowing that she wouldn't have found Christine Kane wandering around her room and pawing through her possessions if she didn't feel that she had a very good reason to be doing so.

She lowered her eyes even as the warm psychologist turned away from her, gazing out towards the balcony.

When she spoke again, her voice was much quieter and quivered slightly in the relative silence. 'I was worried about you. In fact, I've spent most of this horrendous trip worrying about you.'

'I'm sorry,' Kelly said, placing her hand on Christine's good knee. 'I didn't mean to snap like that. I'm just ... I'm in pain.'

Christine's eyes followed the movement of Kelly's hand. Before she could stop it, a rogue tear from the relieved, but still, emotional faction building behind her eyes, rolled suddenly over her cheek and went splashing down onto Kelly's soft flesh as she tried to reassure her.

Instantly embarrassed and annoyed with herself, Christine wiped at her face angrily, turning from Kelly once more.

'Don't.' Kelly said, as she released her grip on the now not-so-cold, but certainly damp compression that she had been holding to her cheek. Bringing both hands to Christine's face and lightly wiping away the tears, she said, 'Please. Don't turn away from me. I've been wanting to speak to you again … but, I didn't really know what to say … didn't know *how* I was every going to speak to you again after you found … those …'

'The paintings.'

'Yeah … I was … I couldn't believe what I was seeing. And I didn't know whether you'd want to speak to me at all. Again. Ever. I felt like a kid that was being punished for something they hadn't done, but couldn't prove that they hadn't done it, you know? And I couldn't move past that look on your face; past the idea that you might think I could have had something to do with …'

'The murders.'

Kelly nodded. 'I felt … ashamed. I actually felt guilty. But, the thought of you looking at me the way that detective fella does …'

Christine sniffed and allowed Kelly to thumb away the latest pooling tears from under her eyes. 'Prior? How d'you mean? How does he look at you?'

'With revulsion and loathing. With open and unabashed, harsh, judgemental disgust!'

'Oh,' Christine chuckled, unable to help herself, 'that look.'

Kelly smiled a crooked, little half-smile and let her hand drop away from the previously sad, dark puddles that were now Christine's sparkling, puppy-dog brown eyes. Even as she did, the psychologist caught hold of her hand and Kelly felt her chest rise and fall again suddenly.

'There are certainly a fair few things I could see myself being with you, Kelly Livingstone, but disgusted is not one of them. Please, don't ever think that.'

'Oh … really?' Kelly said, her voice sounding a lot smaller than she had expected.

She had tried to respond in her old confident and cocky style; her own personal line of defence and patented avoidance strategy when faced with an all-too intense set of emotions like those that now swirled in the pit of her stomach. But — whether it was the surprise of seeing Christine reclaiming the moment with a sudden and self-assured control, or something else entirely — the sound had resonated as anything but the cool, calm confidence it was supposed to convey.

'Really.'

'Like what?' she said.

'Like being confused. I could quite easily see myself being and have — indeed — been very confused by you in the past few days. Perplexed, even.' Christine paused and Kelly gave a small accepting nod, suggesting that she understood completely. 'I've been annoyed with you. Really annoyed. Though, if I'm honest, that's not really your fault at all. I was annoyed with my own indecision; my absolute and crippling inability to make a decision. But,' she said, with a wry, delicious smile, 'I could also see myself being annoyed with you on quite a regular basis.'

'Oh, I do hope so.' Kelly said with a grin, as a licking flame of the old self-confidence returned to her voice.

'But then, I know that I could also find myself becoming quite enamoured with you. Falling dangerously head-over-heels in love with you, in fact.' Christine spoke the words quickly, not allowing herself the luxury of pausing this time, for fear — it seemed — that she might not otherwise speak them at all.

Silence.

And now, the silence seemed deafening. And it seemed to last an age.

Was she simply waiting for a reaction? Was she trying to find the right words to continue?

Would she ever speak again!

Kelly felt herself beginning to flush red; feeling that she was being subject to a vast and crushing scrutiny. Her mouth was suddenly very dry. She swallowed hard, trying to pull something together. Some suitable response.

She had nothing. No words.

'And that scares me.' Christine said, finally, 'Because it's so intense. That's an intense and all-consuming kind of emotion and it's not something I'm used to. Not in this way. I don't think I've ever known this or ever felt this way about anyone before.'

Kelly opened her mouth to speak once more. Then closed it again. She swallowed, and smiled at Christine. 'Now I understand.'

'Understand what?'

'I understand the real reason for you beating me over the head with that book.' she said, a wry smile spreading across her face, 'Caveman tactics, wasn't it? You suddenly went all dominant on my ass! And why use words when actions speak so much louder, eh?'

Christine laughed heartily.

'Yeah right, I can just see me now trying to drag you back to my modestly furnished cave. Can you imagine? I wouldn't even know what to do with you when I got you there!'

'Christine . . .'

'Kelly. It's ok.' she said, in that soft and juicy accent of hers, 'I don't even know why I told you. Why I felt I *had* to tell you. Though, I do feel a little better for doing so. I think.' She smiled sweetly and released her grip on Kelly's hand, 'I know about you and Shona. And I know I can't compete with that. I don't want to try and compete with that. She's beautiful and young and tight and supple . . . and annoyingly nice. And, d'you know, I didn't even realise that I looked at other women in those terms until I met you, but . . .'

Kelly couldn't help but laugh and — without a second thought — she leaned in, taking Christine's face in her hands once more, pressing her lips gently against those of the compliant — if not slightly terrified — psychologist.

The kiss was soft and uncertain and there was something remarkable about that. Something beautiful and tentative about it. About the simplicity of it. The innocence. It was cautious, but it was entirely giving; unassuming and without expectation.

Kelly felt Christine begin to relax further into the kiss, her lips parting and allowing her the opportunity to flick her tongue beyond the outer walls of those delicious fleshy battlements. To meet with Christine's tongue and to really explore her in a way that could only be achieved through such close, physical intimacy.

She tasted of spearmint and winter.

This discovery made Kelly smile as she gently rested her forehead against Christine's, planting a final kiss on her parted cherry-lips.

'You seriously need to re-examine the way you view yourself. Because that rock-bottom self-confidence of yours isn't exactly the charm that most women are looking for.'

'I don't know,' Christine said, moving in to land another kiss, meeting with Kelly's open mouth once more, 'it worked on you.'

'Well, I'm not most women.'

'Oh, I know that.'

Kelly laughed at the comment. It seemed too loud to have been genuine, though it was. And besides, Christine didn't seem to mind, she appeared completely blissful; content to sit there all day.

Then, like a sudden sharp, autumn breeze on a still day, she changed.

She stiffened and pulled away from Kelly, concern spreading across her face.

'Oh, my God. Oh . . . my God, I've been so selfish, I . . . Kelly . . . how did you get back here? Where did you come from? What can you remember from . . . earlier? Do you know where Shona — '

Before she could finish the sentence, Christine's phone rang out loudly.

After days without signal and especially after the intense silence that seemed to have swallowed them in the last few minutes, the sudden volume and shrill pitch of the phone made both Kelly and Christine jump, even as Christine cursed and scrambled to answer the call.

'Where Shona what? What's wrong with Shona?' Kelly asked, concerned.

Christine flipped open the phone and held it to her ear, trying to ignore Kelly. Instantly hating herself for it.

'Christine.' she confirmed, flustered.

Though Kelly could follow only one half of the conversation, she paid close attention to Christine's answers, watching as she stiffened; her professional, sensible other-self returning to take the reins once more.

'Yes, I'm fine. I just lost track of time ... I should have checked in ... No ... I'm in Kelly's room now. She's here with me ... yes ...' her eyes met with Kelly's for the first time since the phone had rung, '... she just arrived, now.'

Kelly couldn't help but smile to herself briefly.

Without realising or meaning to, Christine had just revealed the identity of the caller.

It was the Detective. The Security Officer; Prior. Checking up on her.

Like an old, married couple!

Or a jealous lover.

'Yes ... yes, I'll talk to her now ... Okay, I'll ask her.' she continued in frustration, 'Yeah ... okay. Okay, bye. Bye'

With that, she snapped the phone shut and sighed, rubbing her temples. Kelly waited patiently until she could wait no more.

'Ask me what, Christine?' she said, concerned, 'What's happened to Shona?'

22:58

Sunday 15th May, 2011

Prior hung up the call and sat back in his chair. His brow furrowed as he stared blindly at the monitor before him.

'Everything ok?' Davies asked, still busy sifting through all the useful and completely unhelpful pockets of web-based information that he could find on Isaac Leigh Simmons now that the satellite system was finally sending and receiving again.

'Yeah. Christine just sounded a bit ... flustered, that's all.'

'Kelly back then?'

'What do you mean by that?' Prior said, sharply.

Davies spun his chair round slowly to face him, 'I just meant is Kelly back, Guv'.'

'But, why? Why say it like that? And in response to my comment about Christine being flustered?'

'I didn't say it in response to anything ... I was ... it was just a question. Sorry. Anyway, I thought that's what we were hoping for. That Christine'd find her and that she wouldn't be some kind of bloody, horrific mural when she did.'

'It is.' Prior said. 'It was.' Then he returned his attention to the computer in front of him, bashing heavy-handedly on the keyboard.

Davies watched him in silence for several moments, before venturing to speak out again. 'So ... is she ok? Does she know what happened to Shona?'

'I don't know. Christine's going to speak to her about it now.'

'Guv' — '

'It's alright, Marc. Just leave it.' Prior said, as a new window opened revealing the slow progression of the several dozen selected files currently downloading. He had logged into a number of different previously-created email accounts with little trouble. These were the accounts in which he had successfully managed to store — undetected — the information that he had known he might one day need again.

Davies nodded, confirming that he had got the message.

Loud and fucking clear! He thought.

He decided to give Prior another few minutes before he would even attempt to speak to him again. When he eventually did, he made sure that he had altered his tone sufficiently enough for his commanding officer to easily recognise that he was — in no way, shape or form — foolish enough to even consider broaching the previous subject.

'So what, exactly, are we looking for here?' he said, as he typed a new batch of criteria into the colourful search engine.

'Anything.' Prior said, with a sigh, 'Anything that might tell us . . . something about what Isaac Simmons has been up to for the past eight or nine years. Any previous known whereabouts; particularly the most recent. And — if we can find one — we could do with printing out a decent and fairly up-to-date photo. That way we can see if anyone recognises him. See if the picture matches the guy you ran into.'

Davies nodded, only half listening as he began reading an article he had just pulled up from the *Chester Chronicle* website. 'Hey, I might just have found something here, Guv'.' he said, skimming the text, 'It's recent too. Something about Simmons and ... oh, my god, it's to do with that skeleton they just found in Delamere. Did you see that?' he asked, turning to face Prior. 'It was on the news just before we left.'

'I had heard something. So, do the police think he's involved with that?'

'Apparently so.'

'If he'd heard that an old skeleton of his had been discovered in the woods, that there might finally be something solid to connect him to a body . . . well, that might just have done it. That might have been

442

what drove him to come aboard, despite — as you, correctly said — his overwhelming fear of water.'

'D'you think he was planning to disembark in the Caribbean? With no intent of return?'

Prior nodded slowly, thinking.

Davies looked over at Prior's pc, distracted by the succession of small beeps indicating that several of the downloads had now completed. 'What are you doing?' he asked, bobbing his head in the direction of the monitor.

Prior returned to the workstation, manoeuvring his chair so that Davies still had a clear view of the screen. 'It's some stuff I put aside before I left the police. Documents, reports, CCTV video files. All specifically related to the Simmons' investigations. The Simmons' debacle.'

Prior stared at Davies for a long time; his piercing, bottle-green eyes hard and unwavering as he searched the blue counterparts of his colleague and his friend.

Davies felt as though his soul were being hand-washed and checked for impurities; for weaknesses and snags. 'I understand.' he said eventually.

Seeming to accept this, Prior summoned him over, wordlessly, and Davies scooted along on the three-wheeled office chair, coming to rest before the whirring pc.

He clicked on an icon and the computer began making even more noise, complaining as it reluctantly attempted to start up the media player software.

'Now, obviously he'll be older, but hopefully you'll be able to identify him and then we can — '

'Me identify him?'

'Yeah.'

Davies looked confused. 'Why me?'

'Because, you ran into him the other day. Literally. Outside medical.' Prior said, patiently, mistaking Davies' confusion for dumbfounded horror at the fact that he had unknowingly run into their killer and done nothing about it. Because, he hadn't then known. 'Roberts and I managed to track him on the CCTV following the murder of Stacey Atkins.' he continued, opening another file and double-clicking on a still image, 'He's only slight, but then he always was. The bastard seemed to know where all the cameras were, so we never got a decent shot of his face. But, we did find this.' he pointed to the screen as the image slowly revealed itself; moving from incredibly fuzzy and pixelated to slightly less fuzzy and pixelated over the course of a few seconds.

The younger man felt a sudden chill, followed by an immediate heat that seemed to radiate up from the inside out. The picture seemed to confirm Prior's story and revealed him, Marc Davies, picking up papers with a blurry figure outside the medical bay.

He remembered the day; remembered that moment clearly.

He felt suddenly sick to his stomach.

'Leigh.' he whispered.

'Isaac Leigh.' Prior said, nodding. 'His brother often operated using his middle name too; Matthew rather than Jacob. He idolised his brother, so I'm not surprised he's chosen to do the same thing — '

'No, Guv', Davies said, shaking, 'It's not that. It's not that at all . . .'

22:58

Sunday 15th May, 2011

'Is it that freak that burst into her room before? That Mike?' Kelly said, jumping to her feet furiously, 'Has he hurt her? What's he done, Christine? Tell me!'

'He hasn't done anything, Kelly. Sit down. Please.'

'What d'you mean he hasn't done anything? I was there! The guy was insane! Jealous, bitter, dangerous and insane.' she said, pacing around the room, 'I mean, for fucks sake, Christine, he left little to the imagination when he was explaining the reasons for his visit ... at knife point! I know exactly what he had in mind. And so do you. It wasn't your average fucking social call, believe me!'

'It's not Mike!' Christine said, raising her voice to a level that managed to stop Kelly in her tracks. 'We arrived just as he knocked you out. We took him in for questioning, but it's really not him. It's got nothing to do with him.'

Kelly stared at Christine for a long time; her eyes filling with wet despair and disbelief.

Eventually she returned to the appalling bed that — she felt ashamed to admit — reminded her of something by Tracey Emin. Only worse. And, for the briefest flicker of a moment she contemplated photographing the horrific, blood and paint-stained mess.

But as quick as the thought came, it was gone again and she sat across from Christine waiting — as patiently as she could — for her to divulge the rest of the tale.

'You were taken to the medical bay. Shona and Marc Davies followed ...'

Suddenly, Kelly lurched forward, doubled over as a violent, metallic pain sliced through her skull and twisted in her gut. Christine's voice became quiet and distant as she tried to focus on the psychologist's still moving lips.

She closed her eyes, her head spinning and pulsing with mixed and muddled memories.

She tried to stand. She was standing.

She was on her knees.

She was on the bed.

She looked back to that Emin bed and her stomach tilted and rolled again. Her head pounding as she started to recall . . .

'Kelly? Are you listening to me?' Christine said with obvious concern in her voice, 'Can you hear me?'

She watched as Kelly continued to stare in horror at the bloodied bed. She was beginning to shake now, and all the colour had drained from her face as a single, heavy, bell-bottomed tear fell from her terrified eyes.

'Kelly?' Christine said, again, touching her arm, gently.

The raven-haired artist jumped, instinctively raising her arms to protect herself. She seemed to see Christine and then lose her again, her eyes focusing and then glazing over. Again and again.

'Kelly, I'm not going to hurt you. It's only me. It's Christine.'

Kelly's eyes finally seemed to find her, to anchor onto her. She stifled a sob as Christine tried to take hold of her hands, rubbing the backs of them in a slow soothing motion.

'He . . . he tried to . . . with me. I went . . . and, then . . . and I did it . . . and . . . I . . .' Kelly continued to stutter, making little sense at all, but nodded determinedly as she spoke. 'Oh god, I . . . Christine . . . I did . . . I did it . . . He said he'd let me go. He lied. I had no choice.'

'It's ok.' Christine said, as Kelly shook even more violently, 'It's ok. Whatever you've done, it doesn't matter. We'll fix it — '

'You can't fix it!' Kelly shouted, pulling free from Christine and shaking her head, 'Even you can't fix this.'

'Is it Simmons? Is it Isaac Leigh Simmons? Is that who hurt you?'

For a moment Kelly appeared as helpless, as wounded and as confused as a child who has just shut their fingers in a closing car door. It was that same look of absolute wide-eyed terror; of cold, clammy realisation and the sudden understanding of exactly what that crunching sound just meant. That split second before the brain takes over and responds to the pain receptors as they scream out, hollering to inform you that something is really very wrong.

Suddenly, Kelly sprang to her feet, clawing at her eyes and her face, thrashing this way and that as though she were trying to escape some unseen demon.

Christine watched in silent horror. Dumbstruck and unable to react.

Not knowing — despite all her training and years of experience — what to do for the best.

She called Kelly's name over and over, but the tormented artist seemed unable to hear her.

She was lost once more to another world that Christine could neither see, nor taste, nor smell, nor hear. She was fast becoming hysterical, stumbling towards the dresser; struggling, searching and trying desperately to find her face in the mirror, only to laugh and sneer at it before howling in pain and falling to her knees, crying. It was the loneliest sound Christine had ever heard. And she recognised it instantly.

She had made such a sound in her sister's garage on that god-forsaken night.

Hobbling over to Kelly, she took her by the shoulders, struggling to pull her to her feet.

After a moment Kelly seemed to see her once more and instantly pressed herself into an embrace, burying her face in Christine's shoulder.

Sobbing as Christine wrapped her arms around her, stroking her shining, blue-black hair.

'I'm sorry Kelly, I'm so sorry.' she said, 'I don't know what you've been through. I can't imagine what you've suffered. And I promise I'll help you to get through it ... I'll help you through all of it. I swear. But, right now I need you here. I need your help. Okay? Shona needs your help. Do you know where she is?' she asked, her voice soft, but direct, 'Is she alive?'

Kelly nodded sadly.

'For now.' she said, sniffing as she looked up at Christine with her glassy, salt-water, cerulean eyes.

Christine relaxed her grip on Kelly, half expecting her to slump back to the floor like a sack of potatoes. But she did not.

'What do you mean 'for now'? Is that what he said? Does he really plan on killing her?'

'What would you do?' she asked, cocking her head to once side. 'I didn't want any of this. What if he comes back? I didn't want this, Christine. I don't want this!'

Without warning, Kelly pulled Christine's face towards her, kissing her hungrily, passionately; her hands instantly beginning to explore the shape of her body, to tug at Christine's clothes; searching for the tie of her chocolate linen trousers.

'Kelly, stop!' Christine shouted, pushing her away.

Her face was ashen.

In the very next moment she flushed red with anger, then embarrassment.

And then it seemed that all the energy had been sucked out of her as she sank to the bed, picking up the sketchbook beside her. 'I'm sorry.' she said, 'I'm really sorry about that.'

After that she didn't look at Christine again, but simply flicked to a clean page in the book and, slipping the 2B graphite pencil from the attached holder on the side, began working furiously.

Apparently now completely unaware that Christine even existed.

Christine rolled her lips and licked them without thinking, tasting Kelly's forceful kiss once more. Tasting Kelly.

It was a strangely familiar flavour; a strong, comforting tang that she couldn't quite place. Not that she spent too much time thinking about it. There were — after all — more important matters at hand.

She had just opened her mouth to address Kelly, to try and capture her attention once more — if only for a moment or two — when her phone burst into life again, startling her with its trilled melody as before.

Again, she jumped, though Kelly appeared not to notice. Instead, she seemed intrinsically focused on the shapes that were coming together thick and fast on the page before her; the shades of light and dark; the eyes. Lips.

A face.

Christine answered the call, stepping out onto the balcony as she did and closing the door behind her. It was Prior.

'Jon. You scared the crap out of me!' she panted, suddenly breathless, 'Kelly has — '

'Are you still with Kelly?' he asked.

'Yes, she's — '

'Has she said anything?'

'That's what I'm trying to tell you, man. Jesus, would you let me speak.' Christine didn't wait and give him the opportunity to interrupt her again, 'She's just suffered some kind of massive break down. Right in front of me! She's really not well, Jon. And I think she might have done something terrible.'

'I think you're definitely right with that one.'

'I mentioned the name Isaac Leigh Simmons and she totally flipped. I mean clawing at her eyes and everything. I'm really quite, quite worried.'

'I'm worried too.' he said, sounding suddenly more breathless than she did.

'Jon, are you running?' she asked, concerned.

'Yes. Are you still in the room with Kelly?'

'No, I'm out on the balcony. Why?' Christine asked, suddenly very aware of her heart beating in her chest. Thumping in her throat.

'It's her Christine.' Prior said, his voice shaking, but certain, 'She's the killer.'

Shocked at this bizarre revelation, Christine shook her head and spun around to peer through the glass door.

Her heart seemed to leap into her mouth as she found herself suddenly face to face with a horribly cold and staring creature; something that resembled Kelly, but that was not quite her. It leered at her from the other side of the thin glass pane; a mocking parody of the woman she had left in the suite only moments earlier.

She swallowed hard, trying not to shake; feeling the absolute terror palpitate inside her as she found herself staring into a pair of blue eyes that no longer seemed to belong to Kelly.

She proceeded to watch, in horror, as the thing that was no longer Kelly — the creature with the twisted predatory grin — reached for the door handle and began to pull it down. Slowly. Steadily. Teasing the terror from her.

Christine could hear Prior calling her name from the Motorola handset and screamed back, even as she dropped the phone, scrambling to hold onto the handle. To keep it pulled up. 'She's at the door!'

She used all her strength to keep the thing that wasn't Kelly from turning the handle, until the thought suddenly dawned on her that

— should it really want to get to her — it could simply break the glass. She looked back into the eyes of the Kelly creature and realised that it was simply toying with her.

It too seemed to notice the change in the psychologist and cocked Kelly's head in the same way it had before she had kissed Christine so forcefully.

Absently, Christine touched the tip of her forefinger to her lips.

Alcohol.

That was the taste she couldn't place. Because, she knew that Kelly didn't drink.

But, she was willing to bet that Isaac Leigh Simmons did. That he had been the one to empty the mini-bar so successfully, littering the room with his discarded bottles.

But that would mean that Isaac Leigh *was* Kelly.

Kelly Livingstone *was* Isaac Leigh Simmons.

She shook her head, unable to wrap her thoughts around the idea that this could — somehow — be the truth.

Seemingly bored of Christine for the moment the Kelly creature rotated, removed and then pocketed a medium-sized brass key; locking the glass doors.

Christine bent awkwardly to pick up the phone; her knee crying out painfully as she did.

Then, she put as much distance as she could between her and the room beyond; pressing back against the railings and judging the distance between the balcony of this suite and the next.

Mentally preparing herself for the jump.

'Jon. She's him. He's a part of her. I don't know how or why. I've seen people with multiple personalities before, but never like this. There was a real, physical change there, Jon.' she said, trying to stay calm, 'Jon?'

There was no answer.

Suddenly, the door handle begin shaking again. She heard it, though she daren't look back into the room.

She was terrified, without a doubt.

Struck to the core and unable to move. Unable, even to open her eyes.

She was right back there in Janet's garage sorting through the old Christmas decorations; discussing which ones she really ought to get rid of and which she should keep, when there had been a knocking, then a shaking and then a great thundering pounding on the metal drop-down door.

Christine slid down the wall, sinking into herself, dropping the phone once more.

There was a terrible crash as shards of glass splintered across the wooden balcony floor.

Christine screamed as a hand reached out and grabbed her arm.

'Christine.'

She opened her eyes.

It was Prior.

23:17

Sunday 15th May, 2011

Leigh spun around, laughing. Double-checking that Prior wasn't yet on his tail.

He had successfully terrified the shrink and locked her out on the balcony, before vaulting from the room, only narrowly missing the Ex-DI as he made his escape. He had been half-tempted to wait it out a little longer and confront the bastard there and then.

To spark the bugger out!

But, there were too many variables left unaccounted for when depending on such an emotionally-involved response. And besides, he had left a nice, big fat clue for the wonderfully dynamic duo to follow; if they had half a brain between them to figure it out.

It was better this way.

This way he was in control. They were playing his game by his rules.

Besides, Prior was in pretty good condition for a washed-up, old Mersey-beat dick, and — though he was loath to admit it — he hadn't exactly been on top form lately.

He didn't quite know what the cause was or why, but he had felt weaker recently than he had in a long time. It was a purely physical thing; but, it was annoying!

Everything just seemed to require so much more energy these days!

Like taking out Blakely.

He should have had no problem in flooring a skinny little rat like that, but the guy seemed to have some sort of hidden powers. Bags of energy. He just wouldn't give in!

Even Stacey Atkins had been a tough little nut to crack. Literally.

And — besides all this — was the slightly embarrassing problem that he seemed unable get it up at all recently!

What was *that* all about?

Maybe he was coming down with something.

He hoped it wasn't anything permanent.

23:17

Sunday 15th May, 2011

Christine took Prior's hand and followed him back into the abandoned suite, trying to make sense of what he was telling her, though most of it was still white noise.

'. . . It was the first time Davies had met her,' he said, 'and when she introduced herself as 'Leigh' he thought nothing of it. He said he questioned himself and Dr Matthews when she later referred to her as Kelly, but then he just dismissed it. Thought that 'Leigh' might be a nick-name or something.'

Christine was shaking. She felt cold.

Ice cold.

She sat on the edge of the bed and watched as Prior went into the bathroom. He ran some cold water into a plastic beaker and returned, handing it to her.

She sipped at the water noticing — as he stood before her — the small fire arm now strapped to his side.

'You have a gun.' she said, annoyed at how obvious a statement it was. How dumb she sounded.

'There are two on board. Locked up at all times; except in an absolute emergency. I have this one. Davies has the other.'

'Do you intend to use it?'

'I'm not wearing it for show.' he said, without emotion.

Christine nodded and took another sip of the water.

'Did she say where she'd taken Shona?'

Christine shook her head, 'That thing isn't Kelly. Kelly wouldn't harm Shona. I don't think she's even aware that he's around. But, it was definitely Isaac Leigh that locked me out there just now. And it was Isaac Leigh who killed those people. Not Kelly.'

'Which one of them is responsible for what isn't important right now,' Prior said, his voice raising a decibel with his growing impatience, 'What *is* important is the fact that Shona is in real danger of being hurt or killed. And I'm not about to just sit back and let that happen.'

'I understand that, Jon. But what you need to understand is that Kelly is innocent in this, she's not — '

'Kelly Livingstone killed Isaac Leigh Simmons.'

'What?'

Christine couldn't believe what he was saying; what her brain was translating from the sounds her ears were now receiving. It just wasn't possible.

She let the empty beaker fall on the bed besides her and, glancing down, noticed that the sketchbook had been left behind. She picked it up, cradling it as she continued to listen to Prior in disbelief.

'There's some old footage of Isaac Leigh circling round the inside of this club in Chester. He's like a shark; looking to pick up a girl or maybe two, but no one's responding. Eventually, he latches on to this young-looking girl in a blue dress. She doesn't even look old enough to be in the club.'

'And what does this have to do with Kelly?' Christine asked, leafing through the pages in an effort to discover the most recent edition to the sketchbook.

'A camera outside the club picked up the pair leaving together. The girl in the video is Kelly Livingstone.'

Christine laughed, 'I know that Kelly can look younger than she is . . . but, still. I mean, come on, can you honestly see her wearing a dress? Willingly? Slinking off with some dodgy guy? *Any* guy for that matter?'

As she turned to the next page Christine was struck with immediate horror by the image that waited to greet her. She gasped as she took in the perfect pencil drawing of Shona's disembodied head resting on a silver platter.

Her eyes were open and welcoming, greeting the onlooker in the same manner that Dr Cunningham had appeared to in the grotesque painting, *Dr Death*.

In a similar style to *Dr Death*, the centre of Shona's forehead had been split wide open, only, in this horrifically accurate illustration, the shredded strands of flesh and skull were being blasted outwards to reveal a perfectly bored hollow.

This was the image of an exit wound.

'The footage was recorded back in ninety-nine.' Prior continued, as though he hadn't seen — and still couldn't see — the dreadful and foreboding picture that rested in Christine's shaking hands, 'Kelly was sixteen then. She left with Simmons, who took her to a remote spot in Delamere forest with the intention of raping and killing her.'

'How do you know all this?' Christine asked; her voice now small.

'Because, I know the Simmons' Brothers. I studied them for years, I knew their ... habits, but I could never prove anything. Isaac Leigh picked up where his brother left off. He took his chain and used it in the same way that Jacob ... that Matthew ... had done. And, on that night he found a young and fragile Kelly Livingstone. And, he drove out to those woods with one thing in mind.'

'Oh, my God.'

'But it seems that she fought him off. Smashed him in the side of the head with a rock. And then she kept on smashing and smashing until she was sure he was dead.'

'Stacey Atkins,' Christine whispered, recalling the girl's cleanly polished, shattered cheekbone, as things — slowly — began to fall into place. 'and Doctor Matthews.' She put her hand to her mouth suddenly, closing her eyes, '*Not My Type*.'

Prior nodded. 'She buried him. Out in the woods.'

'No. No, Kelly couldn't do this.'

'She was young then. She was scared and in very real danger. We're all capable of it, Christine.

'How can you be so certain? How can you be sure that she . . .'

Prior took the sketchbook from Christine's still-shaking hands. Without looking at the image he closed it and threw it back onto the bed. 'There was a skeleton uncovered in Delamere forest. The same place, I'm willing to bet, that Simmons took Kelly all those years ago.' he paused for the shortest of moments, looking into Christine's eyes. 'It's just been identified. It is Isaac Leigh. It's been buried out there for a decade.'

'That's still not concrete — '

'Right now I don't care, Christine.' Prior said as he turned to pick up the psychologist's white and gold walking stick. He offered it to her, catching her eyes once more with his own sparkling emeralds, begging her silently to help him. 'Please. I just want to protect my sister.'

Taking the stick, Christine nodded, struggling up from the bed. 'I think I might have an idea where they could be.'

Chapter Ten

After what felt like an age of wriggling and squirming, Shona had finally managed to slip her wrists free from the tight, rope bonds that held her. Quickly, she flipped herself over, tearing the blindfold from her eyes before picking hurriedly at the further knots that bound her feet.

She had been correct in guessing her new whereabouts. She would have known that smell anywhere; it was so familiar to her that it was almost homely.

She was in a theatre.

And not just any theatre. She was now being held, she knew, in the *Dionysus Theatre*.

She knew it though the lights were down and the stage on which she sat was blanketed in darkness.

This was her stomping ground.

She smiled, relieved at the sudden realisation that she knew a hundred secret places to hide within the confines of the backstage area and fly tower alone.

She had spent so many hours up there.

Both alone and with company.

She tried to ease the gaffer from her lips with little success. Eventually, she pulled the skin of her face taut and, gripping the horribly sticky tape

459

tightly between her thumb and forefinger, tore it away in one swift, defiant motion.

The pain was incredible considering the mundane instrument responsible for its cause. It was like being waxed with a leech!

Her lips tingling, Shona swore, shaking her hand in an effort to rid herself of the sticky, silver gaffer. Then — delighted to finally be rid of it — she pushed the oily, metallic-tasting rag from her mouth with her tongue, coughing and spluttering as she did.

She sucked in several breaths of air — drank them in — before coughing violently once more and spitting the awful, dirty aftertaste back onto the rag at her feet.

Her lips were now burning and her tongue and throat complained, tormented by the remnant taste of the disgustingly caustic cloth that had been crammed into her mouth for so long. She raised her hand to her aching jaw, rubbing it.

Finding her bearings in the dark she turned to make her way off stage; into the wings. She planned to climb up the ladders and onto one of the high fly platforms; to sit up there and simply wait out whatever it was that was going on.

Up there she would have a chance of sensing movement — any movement — within the theatre, of spotting the bastard that had done this to her and of remaining out of his way.

After reading that message earlier she knew one thing for sure, she wasn't going to remain down here and simply wait to be killed.

Oh, no!

She was inches from the wings when she heard a sharp, clicking sound behind her.

She felt a cold, hollow, metal ring being pressed into the base of neck, below her left ear and she knew — instantly — that the sound had been that of gun, cocking.

That — she rationalised — meant that the metal hollow, now in point blank contact with the soft, depressed flesh of her neck, was — in fact — the barrel of the gun.

'Now, just where do you think you're going?'

Using the gun shaft to manoeuvre her around, Leigh led Shona back towards the centre of the stage. He pushed her this way and that for several moments until he was relatively happy with their position. Then he pressed her down onto her knees.

In his right hand he held a miniature, portable lighting control device that was — for all intents and purposes — an easy-to-use replica of the larger desk up in the lighting box. As he pressed the 'Go' button to call up the first lighting cue stacked in the show memory, he spread out his arms; a crooked smile on his face.

'And he said ... Let there be light.'

In an instant the stage was bathed in a cool glow of harsh winter colours that thrust the snow-covered forest set into almost animated life. For a moment he could do nothing, but stand there and admire the incredible — if not artificial — wintertide view and all the technical wizardry involved in creating such a scene.

'I'd have pissed myself if that didn't work!' he chortled, watching Shona as she stared intensely back at him, absolute horror painted across her pleasing, mocha face.

'Kelly?' she whispered, shaking her head.

'Oh, that's beautiful.' he said, misunderstanding her completely, 'That really is something. Here you are, all alone on this big, empty stage, confronted by some maniac with gun and ... a lighting gizmo ... ready to pop that pretty little head of yours right off the top of those deliciously slender shoulders. And your first thoughts are not concerned with your own preservation, but with the preservation of someone you care for.

Someone other than yourself. It's . . . commendable. Really. That you should be thinking of your lovely lady lover at a time like this. Ah, I tell you, there's not a dry seat in the house!'

He laughed out loud, enjoying the sound of his own voice and the way it echoed all around the auditorium.

'Hey, it's good in here, isn't it?' he said, looking around, the gun always on her, wherever he moved, 'Mind you, them lights get hot quick, don't they?' He paused and Shona nodded, still unable to tear her eyes from him. 'Do you enjoy being on the stage?'

Shona didn't answer. He took a step towards her and she shuddered, pulling back.

'Oh, come on, don't be like that.' he said, crouching in front of her.

'Why are you — '

'Why am I doing this?' he said, interrupting her, 'Well that's easy. I am doing this because your murdering bastard of a brother took mine from me. And now . . . well, I want revenge. That's why. Plain and simple. I thought you got that from the message on the wall. It was clear, wasn't it? I thought it was fairly obvious.'

Without warning, Shona leaned forward, reaching her arm out towards him. He jumped back just beyond her reach, pulling the gun on her as he moved.

'That's a pretty stupid fucking thing to be doing, if you want to be keeping your brains on the inside a little while longer.' he said, smiling as he calmed himself back down. He needed to relax if everything was to happen as he had hoped it would.

As he had planned.

'I really don't want to have to cause you any undue pain or suffering, my dear . . . it would be a shame to put an unnecessary blot on perfection such as yours.' he said, easing himself forward once again and stroking her face; lifting it towards his. He looked into her deep brown, watering eyes as he brushed the gun barrel against her soft cheeks, 'It really doesn't have to hurt. But he *has* to pay. Do you understand that? He has to.'

Shona nodded slowly.

'Good.'

'Who are you?' she asked, hesitantly.

'My name is Leigh. Don't you remember me?'

Shona opened her mouth, her face now wet with tears.

No words managed to escape and, after a short moment, she pressed her lips back together, pushing out a long breath as she shook her head. 'Should I?' she whispered eventually, her voice cracking as she spoke.

'You gave me some pain killers the other day. Up on the open deck.' he said, briefly lost in the memory. 'You were incredibly ... friendly up there. Are you usually that forward with people you've never met before?'

Shona closed her eyes for a long time and Leigh watched as yet another wave of tears coursed their way over her delicate, olive cheeks. She swallowed and looked back up at him. 'I thought you were someone I knew.' she said, eventually.

'You know, if it hadn't been for you winding me up like that ...' he paused, shaking his head and gnawing on his lower lip, 'Oh ... But then, who can say for sure?'

'What do you mean?'

'Well, you'd already wound me up good and proper, you had. And then I ran into Stacey and ... well ...'

'The bride?' she said, shaking her head in disbelief. 'You didn't do that. Tell me, please, tell me you're not responsible for that. That wasn't you ... it can't have been ...'

'Of course it was me! That was one of my greatest works, that one.'

'Kelly — '

'Inspired me certainly, but even little miss push-the-boundaries herself — the unassailable Kelly Livingstone — couldn't have conceived of the kind of work that I've created here on this ship. I mean, I like her work a lot, but I'm beginning to find her representations of sex and violence and human existence all just a little bit nineties. Don't you agree?' he said in his best 'art critic' voice, laughing raucously as he played to an invisible crowd.

'Where . . . where is she?'

'Don't worry, she's around somewhere. I let her live, Shona. I could have killed her, but I didn't. And that, my dear, is my gift to you. Because I like you. Yes, it's true. You've got spunk. And I like that.' he said, grinning carnivorously at her, 'You see, I'm not the bad guy that everyone paints me out to be. I just want what's mine.'

'And what's that?'

'Justice.'

Shona closed her eyes, trying her best to stop the tears.

She revisited her memories of the meeting that 'Leigh' had just described, seeing only Kelly on the open deck; reliving the moment that she had flirtatiously slipped the packet of ibuprofen into the pocket of her slim, figure-hugging jeans.

Seeing only Kelly in her memories. And seeing only Kelly before her now.

Spying a sudden flicker of movement up in the lighting box, Shona dared herself to look briefly over Kelly's shoulder.

Over Leigh's shoulder.

Because, though her eyes saw the shape and form of Kelly — that amazingly talented woman who she had come to adore; someone she had laughed and cried and made love with — every cell in her body, every fibre of her being, told her that this was not *her* Kelly.

Whoever — whatever — this was, it moved differently to Kelly. It sounded different; spoke with a completely different tone and pattern.

But the eyes, that was the real give away. They were cold and cruel and in no way resembled those of her lover.

And yet she couldn't help but think of Kelly — couldn't help but see *this* Kelly — standing over each of those mutilated bodies. See her flicking the switch that had condemned the engineering crew to their awful and unnecessary deaths.

She closed her eyes for the briefest of moments.

When she opened them again, she saw the movement. Again. In the lighting box, as before. Someone was in there.

She didn't want to draw attention to the fact and so, covertly — whenever Leigh's gaze was averted — she would flick her eyes back towards the distant rectangle.

Whoever it was inside the lighting box appeared to be signalling to her.

At least, she hoped they were.

Silently in her heart, she prayed they were.

She had been so busy looking up at the lighting box as Leigh continued to used Kelly's body to strut around the stage, that she had lost the thread of the conversation a little.

She began to panic, knowing that he wouldn't take too kindly to her not lending him her full and undivided attention.

'... I just want what's mine.' he said.

'And what's that?' she asked, looking up into the blue eyes that were no longer Kelly's.

'Justice.'

She glanced up to the lighting box once more in time to realise that the figure was gesturing for her to move to her left. This time Leigh followed the movement of her eyes and swung Kelly's body round to see what Shona was staring at.

At that moment, all the lights in the theatre — even the working lights — cut out and, seizing her opportunity, Shona tucked herself in and rolled left as fast as she could into the wings.

She heard the gun fire twice and had no doubt that either one would have succeeded in killing her had she still been there.

Suddenly a voice boomed across the PA system; 'And now for my next trick!'

It was Prior.

'You fucking bastard!' Leigh shouted, enraged beyond measure.

Shona grinned, even as she heard Leigh struggling with the portable control box, trying to bring the lights back up. After a moment he gave up on the task, slinging the box and clattering across stage after her.

For the moment she had the advantage. She could find her way around here with her eyes closed, which was — in its present state — an incredibly useful skill to have.

By the time Leigh had used Kelly's body to stagger and stumble across the stage, heading towards the wings and searching in the absolute pitch black for the smallest sign of movement, Shona had already rolled underneath the vast and lengthy props table.

Slowly and quietly, she crawled along beneath the table towards the far end where she knew there was a small gap between the wall and the stack of leaning flats that were always rested there.

If she could make it to the gap, she could inch her way through it and head for the wrought iron pegs that led up onto the fly tower and the gallery platforms above.

She stretched out her hand to feel for the wall and found it just ahead of her. She twisted her body, so as to slip between the flats and the wall without fuss.

She was almost there when she felt a sudden and crippling pain that turned her right knee to jelly. She knew the culprit immediately; a rogue screw.

Dropped onto the floor at some other time and never picked up.

She pulled her hand to mouth, biting down on the skin between her thumb and forefinger to keep herself from calling out as she shifted her weight off that knee. She reached down and pulled the screw from the softer flesh beneath the joint, feeling the hot stream of blood begin to pour like a red wine that had suddenly been uncorked.

As she placed her hand back on the floor to begin moving once again she realised, quite suddenly, that all around her it had become incredibly quiet. This realisation did more than simply unnerve her; it terrified her to her core and she found herself momentarily unable to move at all.

She could feel eyes searching in the dark; could sense him nearby as she had when Mike had startled her the day before.

It was sink or swim; she couldn't stay down here forever!

Closing her eyes, she threw herself forward through the gap and wriggled, pulling herself through on her elbows.

In the next moment she felt something clamp onto her ankle and drag her back.

Not about to give up and knowing that Leigh still had a gun, Shona twisted around and kicked out wildly, landing a good solid boot to the ribs, one to the face and, finally, one more that sent the gun flying across the floor.

Shona's moment of glory was short-lived as Leigh grunted in pain and annoyance.

With the gun removed, Leigh now had two hands with which to grab the lithe dancer. In the same instant that she realised this, Shona was dragged out from under the props table and flung back onto the stage.

She yelped as every millimetre of exposed flesh seemed to scorch with the heat of friction and her arms and legs were instantly covered in hundreds of tiny scratches and slices; scuffed by the rough edges of the winter set.

She tried to scuttle away once more, but felt an iron grip twist her tousled hair; holding her in place.

'Oh, I don't think so.' the voice that wasn't quite Kelly's hissed in her ear, dragging her forward.

She cried out, but it did no good. She tried to scratch at the hand that held her hair so tightly and received only a sharp slap across the face for her trouble.

'Please, Kelly ...' She whimpered as they came to a halt near the front of the stage. Leigh was searching for something.

Something on the ground.

Still holding the feisty little latte by her hair, Leigh finally spied the portable control box he had dropped minutes earlier and — throwing his weight behind it — pressed his knee onto the 'Go' button.

Time appeared to move just that tiny bit slower and, holding Shona, he scanned the room even as the scene began to light once more. He spotted Prior waiting beyond the stage; a gun in his hand, raised and aimed squarely at him.

In the next moment the stage lights reached their full power, blinding him to Prior and anything else that lay beyond the edge of the stage.

But he wasn't done yet.

With a speed that surprised even himself, he managed to heave Shona up in front of him as they knelt on the flooded stage and, twisting her hair tightly in his right hand, he tugged back her head exposing the full length of her throat.

With his left hand free, he now produced — from his back pocket — one of artist knives that he had taken from Kelly's room just half an hour earlier.

Keeping Shona in front of him all the time, he pressed the blade to her throat and called out beyond the light.

He called out to Prior.

'Come on now, Detective. I can see you out there.'

Prior swore, cursing that he hadn't been quick enough or confident enough to just take the shot. Now, he had placed Shona in an even worse position than she had been in before.

'This wasn't how this was supposed to play out Mr Officer Man, but now you've gone and got this pretty little Prior in a right old mess.'

It was Kelly's voice taunting him. No matter how much Christine had tried to convince him that it wasn't; hers was the only voice that he heard.

'She's not a Prior.' he said gruffly, taking several steps towards the stage and stepping into the light. His gun was still raised.

Still locked on Kelly, though he had no clear shot.

'Now, don't try and lie to me, *Guv*,' Kelly said, taking off Marc Davies quite well, 'I heard your pretty boy wonder and this one here discussing it in that hospital area.'

'And why do you think that is?' Prior said, edging still closer. 'Do you know why you where in the medical bay?'

'I was planning on taking the artist. Matty wanted a sacrifice. But then I heard them talking and I realised who you really were — why I recognised you — and realised too that you had a sibling of your own, ready for the slaughter and available without delay on this very ship ...' Prior watched as Kelly smiled capriciously, 'Well, Matty changed his mind, didn't he? He said that if I do this well, I can have his tags — actually wear them — and the keys to his new car. He's never driven it, you know. You saw to that.'

'You do know that your brother is dead, don't you?'

'Of course I know it! That's the reason that we're here now dickhead! And we all know who is responsible for his murder.' Kelly spat, vehemently, 'I watched you take the life of my brother, now you can watch as I take the life of your sister.'

'She's really not a Prior, you know.'

'Then, I suppose a step-sibling will have to do.' Kelly said, pressing the knife into Shona's throat until a line of dark red blood dribbled over her skin.

'This is important.' he said forcefully, stopping Kelly for the time being, 'She's not a Prior. Just as you are not a Simmons.'

Kelly laughed a loud and brutal laugh.

It was a cruel laugh that sounded so much like that laughter which had haunted his dreams for so many years; Like that of Jacob Matthew Simmons.

For the first time he began to question what he believed. To question whether all that Christine had said might just be possible.

'That's a good one,' Kelly said, pointing the knife at him, 'So, what? Was I adopted? Is that it? Is that the big reveal? He was still my fucking brother, you bastard!'

'No,' Prior said, calmly, 'No, you weren't adopted. You were killed.' Kelly stopped laughing. 'You were killed on September twenty-fourth, nineteen-ninety-nine. You were murdered in the woods by the sixteen-year-old girl you'd planned on raping and killing yourself.'

Kelly tightened her grip on Shona, shifting her weight from knee to knee.

'Don't be fucking stupid.' she said, 'That makes no fucking sense! You cunning bastard, you're just try to confuse me.'

'He's not, Kelly. Please, you have to listen to him.' Shona whispered, trying her best not to move for fear of her life.

'Shut the fuck up.' Kelly said and Shona became rigid once more. 'Shut the fuck up! Now!'

Christine made her way onto the stage from the prompt corner, downstage left.

She noticed, absently, that she was leaning on her stick a lot less then she had been during the day, which was good as she had noticed that the handle was beginning to work its way loose.

In her right hand she held the gun that the Kelly creature had handled in her left only minutes earlier. And she seemed prepared to use it.

'You should listen to them, Kelly.' she said, making a steady approach, 'I know you're still in there somewhere. I know you can fight him. You've done it before.'

Leigh turned Shona, placing himself behind her so that neither Christine, nor Prior could take a decent shot at him without risking the dancer.

'No. This is bollocks.' he said, 'All bollocks and trickery.'

These were Leigh's words, but when their eyes met, Christine could see that — for an instant — Kelly was home.

Christine decided to keep the pressure on. 'Do you remember the first night we met? We sat up on the balcony and talked about . . .'

There was silence for a long time.

Then, slowly, Kelly begin to make her answer. 'We talked shit.' she said, loosening her grip on Shona's hair, 'We flirted a lot. Discussed labels and social divide and I had a headache. I was going to see the show . . .'

Without warning, Kelly began to shake, her eyes rolling back in her head. Shona cried out as knife nicked her over and over adding to her rapidly mounting flesh wounds.

'Don't, don't think about that, Kelly,' Christine said, struggling to keep her accented tones as soft and soothing and light as possible, 'Listen to my voice. Just listen. Stay with me. You bought me a drink that night. What was it?'

'A *Mojito.*' she said with a grin.

Her eyes were half-closed and as she continued to speak the shaking subsided and she seemed to relax again. 'Shona mixed it. I didn't know what to order for you.' she laughed, relaxing, still further. Shona was almost free. 'She suggested a *Sloe Comfortable Screw*, but I didn't know if that was a bit too forward as we'd only just met!'

Christine kept the gun on Kelly as Shona wriggled slowly, inch by inch, from her grasp. Just as she seemed to break free, Kelly's grip on her hair tightened once more, reining her back in.

'Christine, shoot me!' she screamed, pleading. 'Please, I can't hold him. I can't control him. Please, don't let me hurt anyone else. Kill me. Please. SHOOT ME!'

Even as Kelly protested, Leigh brought the knife towards Shona's throat.

Prior took the shot.

But the trigger mechanism caught.

As his eyes dropped to inspect the weapon he heard a bloodcurdling scream and his heart sank.

He looked back up just time to see Shona drive a screw through Kelly's knife-hand.

Everything that followed seemed to happen at a quarter of the speed as he slung the pointless weapon and ran towards the stage.

Kelly released both Shona and the knife, staring at her hand in horror and disbelief as Shona dived to the floor. She twisted onto her back, grabbing for one of the small, rounded rocks that Prior had thought to be simple paper mache set dressings. But, as Kelly — Leigh — dove towards her with murder in her — his — eyes, Shona brought the rock up, smashing it into the thing-that-wasn't-quite-Kelly's face.

It slumped to the ground, blood pouring from the upper left-hand side of its face.

Prior was now on the stage and dragging Shona from underneath the unconscious body.

He wrapped his arms around her, kissing her forehead over and over.

'Is she dead?' she whispered, 'Did I ... Did I kill her?'

Prior shook his head. Hoping he was right only for Shona's sake.

'Can you stand?' he asked. She nodded. 'And walk, can you walk okay?' Again she nodded. 'How about climb?'

'Yes.'

'Then I want you head for the gallery level emergency exit,' he said, pointing, 'It'll bring you out near the closest medical point. Go and get help. And wait for me there. Don't come back.'

Shona nodded, understanding his reasons for choosing her.

She doubted that Christine would make the climb up the slick metal wall ladders and there was no way that Prior was about to leave either of them alone with Leigh. Or Kelly.

Shona kissed him on the cheek and mouthed 'Thank you' as a trail of blood still trickled from her throat, adding a much more sombre colour to the spectrum that already littered her now-somewhat wrecked and ragged, slim-fit t-shirt.

He watched until she reached the ladders and then turned to face Christine. 'Are you ok?' he asked, seeing her hands shaking, seeing that the colour had drained from her face.

She gave a single nod and continued to stare at Kelly's unconscious body.

'I don't believe you.' he said and extended his arm towards her as he climbed up onto his knees, resting there for a moment.

She smiled sadly as she made her way towards him, slowly.

'What do you think happened to Marc?' she asked, following Shona with her eyes as she emerged on the gallery platform.

'I don't know. I'll go look for him once we're — '

At that moment Kelly sprung back into life; as though she had simply been suspended, mid-animation all this time. Somehow she managed to sweep Prior's legs from under him before he could stand, butting him in the face so that he toppled backwards.

Then, whipping the gun from Christine's hand, she shoved the psychologist backwards and turned to the gallery platform, taking a steady aim.

Christine didn't know what had happened until she felt her back slam painfully against the floor. Her head too went back and she cracked it hard, blinking through the pain as she tried to scramble back to her feet.

Leigh now held the gun. And he had Shona in his sights.

Just as Shona reached the emergency exit, the heavy door was flung open. The light cascaded in around a very dazed and confused Marc Davies, who stumbled this way and that, holding on to his head.

She heard Leigh laugh as he had before. Cold and cruel and calculated.

'Perfect.' he purred, as though it were one lengthy syllable, 'Time to play.'

Christine became aware that Prior too was struggling to find his feet; that he was trying to reach Leigh; to stop him.

She knew that he simply wouldn't make it in time.

She lowered her eyes, feeling her cane in her hands. The handle had now twisted completely free of the shaft and she examined it, pulling it apart; though she had no real clue as to why she had decided to do such a thing.

But as she sat in the fake snow of the winter scene — time halting all around her — Christine's dark, chocolate eyes widened with the realisation of what she was holding; it was dagger.

An incredibly sharp and very real, gold dagger that sparkled under the theatrical lighting.

She couldn't believe it.

For a moment she imagined that she heard her sister's voice, saying; *Well, you never can tell . . .*

Then, as Leigh prepared to squeeze the trigger and Prior tried to stop him, she — forgotten amongst the chaos — the poor, pointless, crippled Christine drew herself up. She raised the dagger high above her head, flinging herself forwards to drive the blade deep into Kelly's shoulder.

Leigh fired the shot. But it went high.

Marc Davies pulled a frightened Shona to safety.

Prior pounced, retrieving the gun with ease and pinning the creature that wasn't Kelly under the weapon's close sight. Holding her there.

As Christine slumped back into the delightfully warm and open arms of unconscious exhaustion she saw the chain that bore the tags of Jacob Matthew Simmons — the chain that had been a key weapon in so many of the murders and that had meant so much to Isaac Leigh — slip from Kelly's pocket, landing just beyond reach of both the Kelly creature and Leigh himself.

12:19
Wednesday 18th May, 2011

Heathrow Airport

Christine escorted the cuffed and stitched Kelly Livingstone through the sea of reporters, trying her best to protect her. In every sense that she could.

They had just touched down following their thirteen-hour flight from Miami.

Kelly had been no trouble, really. No trouble at all.

In fact, during the whole of the return trip, she had barely spoken a sentence. But then again, Christine had stabbed and disabled her only three days earlier.

She had even been prepared to kill her in those final, testing moments. She knew that she had. And realised that Prior had been right all along.

Anyone was capable of murder.

It was the conditions which drove them that made the difference.

She didn't know how comfortable she felt with this knowledge. With knowing that she could have — and would have — taken the life of this woman, through whom her world had been turned upside down.

'It's okay. You'll be fine.' Prior had said, seeing her and Kelly — and their quartet of armed guards — to the waiting, blacked-out SUV, 'These are the kind of things that either make us or break us.'

He had meant to cheer her up, though, just how that statement was meant to make her feel any better about herself and her actions, she had no idea.

She did, indeed, feel broken.

Still, she had put on that same brave face that she always carried around with her and had embraced — in sequence — the trio of bandaged brigadiers that were Marc Davies, Shona Jacobs and finally Jonathan Prior.

Shona appeared not to know quite how — and even whether — she should really say goodbye to Kelly and had hung back to the last, with tears in her eyes.

Sensing her watching, Kelly had looked up and raised her hand to cover her own throat, staring sadly at the bandage around Shona's in a silent apology. The dancer had nodded, but no more had passed between them.

Then Kelly had been secured into the back of the SUV with a guard on each side as Christine had finalised plans with Prior. He had agreed to take control over the organising of having both Kelly's and her own belongings packed up and sent on to her address.

He had smiled, though his stunningly beautiful eyes were tinged with sadness as he had handed her the white and gold walking stick for the final time.

'And who would have thought,' he had said, 'there was a time when you were afraid that this might break.'

She had held his gaze, feeling the heat of tears building behind her eyes, 'Perhaps it's not as fragile as I once thought.'

He had nodded, understanding.

Then he had planted a farewell kiss on her cheek; his rough, stubbled face feeling like a welcome friend. And they had parted.

Now, back in England, she had anticipated the media circus that would greet them and was prepared for it.

She had anticipated yet another, long, escorted drive in yet another blacked-out SUV.

What she hadn't expected was the stirring mixture of emotions she apparently felt for the artist who was now world-famous for all the wrong reasons; Kelly Livingstone.

Receiving their returned passports and replacing them in her bag, Christine spun around to speak to Kelly only to find that she had wandered off and — though still cuffed — appeared to be hassling an elderly gentleman, who was growing more agitated with her every word.

Calling to the pointless guards that were supposed to be minding her, Christine arrived in time to hear the silver-haired fox spitting a torrent of abuse at Kelly before turning his back on her.

'She's fucking crazy!' he had shouted and Christine had bit her tongue as she struggled to calm Kelly and usher her — under guard — out through the crowded foyer and into the waiting car.

'What was that all about?' she said, turning around in the front passenger seat to touch Kelly's hand, rubbing it as she had done back in her suite.

Kelly met her eyes. But said nothing.

Epilogue

From: _C.Kane@KaneConsultancy.com_
To: _JonPrior13@gmail.com_
Date: 17.12.2011 10:34

Dear Jon

I hope this email finds you well.

I enjoyed speaking to you on Friday, even if it was for only a couple of minutes. Speaking of which, I now finally have a mobile that works as it's supposed to (and does much more besides!). I treated myself to a Galaxy SII, though everyone is constantly raving about Iphone. Personally, I think that's what puts me off. But, you know me!

Work is good; the business is slowly developing a positive name for itself. Though, I think the (somewhat expected) media coverage of what happened on the Ianus back in May might have had more than just a little to do with that. But, I'm learning to cope with the media much better these days. Learning to harness them and use them to my advantage.

My knee is much better too. I hardly ever need to use a stick these days. Besides, I had to have the one Janet bought for me encased in a glass display box. It was either that or hand it over to the local police knife amnesty!

How is Shona doing?

I had a three hour session with Kelly today. She was quite lucid, not like when we first arrived. Did I tell you about that? She was cuffed the entire flight and under supervision, but somehow managed to approach and fluster some old

479

codger when we landed. He was a feisty old bugger and was shouting all kinds at us ... particularly at Kelly.

Still, it was her that the papers had a field day with!

But, anyway ... she was asking after both you and Shona today. And Marc too.

It's very rare that she suffers with her 'Leigh' episodes anymore. At times you'd hardly believe that he'd been there at all, but, then it's also strange to think that there was a time when she was more 'Leigh' than 'Kelly' And then I remember ... surviving it. And I know that it was real.

And a remember those who weren't so lucky.

I don't think she'll ever be released.

I know it's a lot to ask, but if you could convince Shona to come and visit her I think it would do them both the world of good. I know it's difficult. Emotionally as well as physically (with her being away now). But, I'd really appreciate if you would ask her again.

Have you decided what it is that you want to do yet?

Right, I'm off to do some Christmas shopping.

Last Saturday before the holidays and all that!

Keep in touch.

With love

Christine.

From: JonPrior13@gmail.com
To: C.Kane@KaneConsultancy.com
Date: 17.12.2011 18:22

Hi Christine

What do you mean, the 'last Saturday'? You've got Christmas Eve to shop!

I'm good, thanks.

No, I've still not decided what I want to do now that I've thrown off the shackles of Golden Star. Although they did offer me some consultant position within security, overseeing a standard across the fleet, but ... it sounds like too much paperwork to me.

Part of me would like to go back to the force, but, after everything that's happened ... the way I left, the things I've seen since then ... I don't know. Never say never, eh?

With regards to Kelly; I'll ask Shona. I can't say fairer than that.

Take care of yourself.

Jon

From: C.Kane@KaneConsultancy.com
To: JonPrior13@gmail.com
Date: 19.12.2011 15:12

Hi Jon

I take it you're one of these crazy, last-minute shopper types then, are you?

I can't stand that, myself.

This is just a quick email; I'm supposed to be working, but then again, I suppose that's the beauty of being your own boss!

I managed to dig up some information on Fiona Jenkins the other day. I know you'd said to leave it alone, to leave it to police now, but it was bugging me still … her connection to all of this. It turns out that she had a few galleries both here and in the States.

Apparently she purchased and displayed some of Kelly's work a couple of years back. It didn't go down too well and she was up to her eyeballs in lawsuits … lost nearly everything. She was divorced and ditched. The Copinas completely cut her off.

But she still had a few pockets of money and her possessions. She was diagnosed with a nerve and muscle wasting disease back in February. Though, I don't know how long she had been suffering.

Anyway, what I really wanted to ask was what you were doing for Christmas?

See you soon.

Christine

From: JonPrior13@gmail.com
To: C.Kane@KaneConsultancy.com
Date: 20.12.2011 16:19

Hi Christine

Yeah, I am pretty last minute when it comes down to stuff like this!

Shona is home for Christmas. She said she's enjoying being at uni and the course is great. She seems a lot happier.

She said that just the fact that her letter of recommendation came from you scored her some instant and major bonus points with the psychology faculty!

Thanks again for all your help with that.

Well . . . for Christmas we were just going to do something quiet, but when I mentioned about your asking her to visit (and to visit Kelly) she started looking for hotels near to you. I think she's going to call you. I gave her your number. Is that ok?

I'm glad you found some answers, but you need to put this to bed now. You're doing what you can to help Kelly and that's enough. Let it go.

I read in the paper that the hospital had a security scare last week. Is that true? Are your alright?

Look after yourself.

Love

Jon.

From: C.Kane@KaneConsultancy.com
To: JonPrior13@gmail.com
Date: 20.12.2011 20:45

Hi Jon

No need for hotel. There's plenty of room at mine. Seriously, I was thinking of renting out a couple of the rooms, it's just depressing!

I did speak to Shona; we've got it all planned. You just need to pick her up tomorrow and get yourselves over to mine. It was nice to hear her voice again. I didn't realise just how much I've missed the pair of you.

Yeah, there was a break-in on Kelly's ward. The police think it was just some yobs or something looking to see what they could get away with.

It's minimum security down there and the day room is pretty well fitted out. Most likely, they were after some new electrical goods. It's always a bit dodgy around Christmas.

You still trying to protect me, eh?

I'm really looking forward to seeing you and Shona!

Christine.

xx

From: Dr.Kimbatu@ApplebyWard.cwcp.gov.uk
To: C.Kane@KaneConsultancy.com
Date: 22.12.2011 13:32

Dear Dr Kane

I have left several messages with your office now and have had no response. I know you will be on Christmas leave now, but I think you should consider looking for some new admin staff in January.

I am only writing as you wished to be contacted in the event of any changes to the usual behaviour of the patient, Kelly Livingstone.

It is nothing drastic, but you stated that you wished to be informed and so I am informing you.

This last week Miss Livingstone has taken to ordering a bacon sandwich for her breakfast, rather than her usual cereal or porridge. She has also cancelled her order for Christmas dinner as she will now be spending the day, under supervision, with her father.

I would have liked to have consulted with you on this matter prior to its organisation and would have done had I been able to reach you, but a decision was necessary and time was short.

Yours

Dr O Kimbatu

From: D.Stone@cwccpf.gov.uk
To: C.Kane@KaneConsultancy.com
Date: 26.12.2011 09:12

∞**Attachment**∞ *Chronicle Article:*   **PATIENT   SPRUNG   ON CHRISTMAS DAY**

∞**Attachment**∞   **VKeating.jpeg**

Dear Dr Kane

Apologies for the delay in my response. I believe you spoke to DS Coleridge on the phone.

At this moment we are unable to rule out the possibility that Miss Livingstone was forcefully taken from Appleby Ward on 25th December 2011. Though, evidence suggests that she may have gone along of her own volition.

We have confirmed with staff on duty that she was present for checks at 13:00 and that she was then escorted off the premises, but continued to be supervised by the two members of the security staff who followed her along to the house of the man then claiming to be her father.

We can now confirm the identity of that man as being Vincent Keating, and we believe that Miss Livingstone may have approached him once before. The address given as his home address was later found to be abandoned. It is at this address that the bodies of the two ward security staff were discovered.

If you have any information regarding the whereabouts of Miss Livingstone, please contact me immediately.

I know that you have worked with Miss Livingstone since before her incarceration and have a greater understanding of her than anyone else. I would really appreciate hearing anything you have to say on the matter.

Thank you for your time.

Yours

DI Diane Stone.

Cheshire West and Chester County Police Force

From: C.Kane@KaneConsultancy.com
To: C.Kane@KaneConsultancy.com
Date: 26.12.2011 18:00

Dear Christine.

I had a good friend of mine hack into your email so that I might write to you just this once.

I want to tell you that Kelly is safe. She's here with me and I promise I'll take excellent care of her.

She wanted to thank you for your patience and for your trust, and for that kiss that she will never forget. She liked how you tasted.

Spearmint and winter.

Take care now, Christine. And don't come looking for me.

I'm off out.

... It's time to play.

Lightning Source UK Ltd.
Milton Keynes UK
UKOW050350260612

195036UK00001B/7/P